About the Author

Jacqui Wood is a British archaeologist and writer, specializing in the daily life of prehistoric Europeans.

She is director of Saveock Water Archaeology, her own excavation which had a National Geographic TV documentary made of it and has been written about in the world media.

She was a member of the National Education Committee of the Council for British Archaeology (CBA) for three years, and is archaeological consultant to the Eden Project in Cornwall.

As a prehistorian she has lectured throughout Europe at archaeological conferences and published many academic papers. One of which is a full international academic paper on 'Food and Drink in European Prehistory' which makes her a world authority on the subject. As a consequence of this she has appeared over the last 20 years on numerous television programmes.

Last year she was featured on BBC Coast demonstrating log boat fishing in Denmark and demonstrated Bronze Age Technology on Channel 4's Sunday Brunch and was consultant for a celebrity reality programme 'Time Crashers'.

She has reconstructed many high status artifacts for museums around Europe, one being the Grass Cloak and shoes for the Otzi the Iceman museum in Northern Italy and the Orkney Hood for the Orkney council.

Dedication

I would like to dedicate this book to everyone that believes that there is a parallel Universe out there where Magic exists.

JACQUI WOOD

Cliff Dreamers
The Goddess Returns

Contents

Preface from the Archaeology

Our story starts about 6,000 years ago, in Northern Europe. This Europe was a very different place to the one we know today. The farther north you travelled, the closer you got to the ice sheets of Scandinavia, and the sparser the settlements. During those times it is well known from the archaeology that huge log boats carved out of massive tree trunks were used to trade various goods, and at the same time link the isolated settlements.

Those traders would have had very high status in Stone Age society, for they brought news and knowledge from strange and faraway lands, where there were already great civilisations. Many settlers, however, would probably have thought that the traders made up their stories of great cities, and lands that were always dry. For their world was always shrinking as the ice sheets melted, and water constantly covered the shorelines where they lived.

There was an island about that time called Dogger: found halfway between Britain and Scandinavia, it used be the mountain region of a great plain that stretched across what is now the North Sea. This island, with its deep lagoons and rising peaks, remained above the water for more than four hundred years, before finally being engulfed by the North Sea.

Jacqui Wood
Author and Archaeologist

Introduction

As I sit on the sand cliffs and look across the wide desert landscape before me, I suddenly think of the events that brought me here, all that time ago in the far north. I have had a good life, and now I near my place with the earth Goddess in the heavens.

I can see Dala, my young servant, starting the long climb from the temples to where I sit. I can see a lot of myself in Dala, for she is a wilful child, but the Goddess is always close to her. I have often told her that I would tell her my story, one day, before I leave this earth. Over the last few moons I have felt somehow distant from the world around me, so I know my time to sit in the palm of the Goddess is almost upon me. It is as if my soul has already left, and is waiting for my body to follow. I long to be there now, with Kemit and the crew, and dear Borg. I can almost feel them waiting for me with their paddles, ready to take me on to another adventure.

I can see she is climbing the last dune, and will be with me in a little while. Lately, I have not been able to stop my thoughts from constantly drifting to those last days I spent on Dogger Island, in my childhood. Dala sits by my side now and waits for me to speak. Then, from my distant past, in another world from here, I hear my grandmother calling me down from the sand cliffs...

1 DOGGER ISLAND

My grandmother was calling me from the beach. She hated me sitting on the sand cliffs, dreaming of far off lands beyond the water. She was constantly telling me that I was too much like my mother, Finlea. She would remind me of the terrible fate that befell her, because she was a dreamer too. My mother died giving birth to me, which was a common thing in our tribe when a maid took a man in her first woman's summer. Strong maids waited till the next summer, or even the one after that, as my grandmother did before having a child to care for.

It was apparently the dreaminess of my mother that led her to believe the first boy that promised to take her off the island. She never did leave the island, because the young man decided to travel home to Brit Land later that summer. He did not know that she carried his child, or he would not have left her... or so I like to think. Some old woman told me once that my mother just pined away while she carried me, and when I was born a very strong and healthy girl, she died a sun later of the fever. Maybe she loved the boy so much she did not want to live with the reminder of what she had lost.

So that is why my grandmother, Lene, came to be looking after me. Any sign that I was dreamy she felt it her duty to stamp out, in order to protect me from myself. I knew Lene loved me, but did she have to make my life so hard?

'Coming,' I shouted back to her, then I ran down from the sand cliffs to her hut, avoiding the clutter of drying skins and the fish smoking racks on the way.

Lene was waiting for me with her hands on her hips outside our hut, and shouted for all to hear, 'What have I told you about sitting on those cliffs, staring out to sea?'

I held my head low and replied meekly, 'That I will end up like my mother if I do?'

She shook her head in exasperation and replied, 'Yes you will! I asked you to shell the small nuts yesterday, and here I find a whole basket of them under the roof at the back of the hut. Did you really think I wouldn't notice?'

I did not look up, I just replied in a whisper, 'Sorry. I was just coming, but the boats were going out to catch eels, and the fires in the boats looked so pretty as the sun was colouring, and I love to see the bits of flaming bark drop onto the water and float away. I will do the nuts straight away.'

Lene glared at me, and through clenched teeth said, 'You will have to do them after you have ground the grass seeds for the pot tonight. Then you can do the nuts. After the grass seeds mind! I will have another job for you to do at first light, so do not think you can leave it again. You know how busy this time of year can be. Do not make me shout at you every day, Mia.' She turned and walked away with a shrug of her shoulders.

'Sorry, I will get the grinding stones and start right away.' I shouted after her, but I knew she did not hear me. She never heard me, she just shouted at me. Whatever I did, no matter how hard I tried to please her, she always shouted at me. I turned and looked at the huge basket of small nuts and said to myself, Nuts! Nuts! Nuts! It is the end of the near winter time, and the small nuts must be done. I have only eleven winters, but I have seen enough nuts to last at least three lifetimes! I do not even like them, but a maid my age gets all the boring jobs. I always hated crushing the small nuts, but as my grandmother would say time and time again, maybe those nuts would save our lives in a bad winter. All the nice big nuts were dried on racks and stored in baskets for the winter. It was the nuts that were too small to store that had to be taken out of their shells when they were picked, as they would shrivel to nothing if just left to dry. I knew that even if I spent hours on the beach, looking for rocks with little cracks in them to hold the nuts while I crushed them, they would always fly away from me if I hit them at the wrong angle. That was why small nut crushing had to be done outside or in a storage hut away from everyone else.

I remembered the time when I was crushing some nuts (the near winter before) in the middle of the moot hall during a meeting of the tribe. One nut flew with incredible accuracy into the mead of the sharing bowl! It was that night that this rule was made. I thought our chief almost smiled at me when I did it, but the stern looks of the elders made him order me from the moot in front of the whole tribe. I remember crying myself to sleep that night, I was so upset, and even grandmother was kinder to me the next day.

So there I was, crushing nuts and cutting my cold hands on the shells, after spending an hour grinding grass seeds. It was worth it though, I thought, to see the eel fishers going out with their flares, and their little fires glowing warm and friendly at the end of their boats.

One day, I thought, I would go out on one of those boats, and maybe paddle to Brit Land or Scan Land! I would go on from there to the Great Plains, where you could travel all the winters of your life and never see the rising sea again. I used to love the stories told by traders of the always dry lands, where people never had to move their huts from the rising waters every spring. They told us too, that somewhere there was a land where strange fruits grew, and it was always warm. How could there be a land where it is always warm? I thought to myself. How would they know when the winter was? How could they say that he or she has had eleven winters when there were no winters? One day I would find out if such a place really exists, I thought... But then suddenly all I could think about was going to sleep in my place near the fire, before the moon rose too much. It would be another long day when I woke, and I was sure my grandmother would fill it with boring chores for me to do again.

After making sure I had collected every last nut in my basket, I pulled my fur over my shoulders and walked towards my grandmother's hut. It was not a big hut, but it was well furnished with baskets and furs. My grandfather had been one of the elders, before he died in the hunt, so some of the best furs in the settlement were ours to sleep on and under.

I entered the hut and crept past my grandmother, who always fell asleep in front of the fire in the middle of the evening. By last food, maybe the small nut baskets in the store might have run out, but somehow I didn't think so. Little did I know then that I had seen the last small nut to shell in my lifetime...

I woke to the sound of my grandmother stoking the fire, and mumbling about something. She was always mumbling about something. I used to think it must have something to do with her having white hair. All the people in the tribe with white hair seemed to be annoyed about something most of the time.

My grandmother had noticed I was awake and said, 'Ah Mia, it's about time you woke up. Here is some dried fish. Eat it quickly, and don't forget to fill the water bag after you have had a drink. We have a lot to do today. Danz and Volk are making tar, so there is more work for all of us.'

I was surprised at what she said, and stated, 'Tar today? But it sounds windy!'

She gave me a weary look, as she always did when I questioned what she said, and replied sternly, 'Windy or not, we have to do it. There is a hunt next week, and the men need to make some more arrows. So they need tar. Please do not annoy me today. After you have eaten, get to the woodpile and start stripping bark.'

I nodded, and asked, 'Can I ask Karn to help me?'

She shrugged, not turning around as she replied, 'If he wants to, and he is not busy with his chores, you can ask him.'

I quickly chewed the fish, re-filled the water bag from the stream, and set out to find Karn. I knew I would have to find him early, or he would be off with Simi, his friend, on some adventure or other. Their days seemed to be filled with fun and adventures, as opposed to mine, which were filled with my grandmother and tedious jobs that apparently no one in the whole tribe could do but me.

Tar making was a very important task though, and without birch bark tar we could not stick the flint arrowheads onto the arrows. It was also a job that the whole settlement had to be involved with, even the Shaman. Important magic was needed to make the tar in the first place, to help aim the arrows into the beasts. Apparently, the magic to aim straight and true was in the tar, and not in the bowman. I always thought it was the bowman myself, as he had to practise firing his bow.

I would never mention those thoughts to anyone else though, not even Karn, as the Shaman was a very frightening person. You wouldn't want him to even notice you in a crowd, let alone know that you had questioned the use of his magic. All the hunters feared him, because he could ill-wish their hunt. If a hunter failed too many times, the elders had to decide if he could stay or not –

they thought that his bad luck might affect the other hunters. If the Shaman said so, the hunter and all his close family were then banished from the tribe. So, no hunter would ever challenge the Shaman's words, on anything.

I purposefully strode through the settlement till I reached the net store. Karn and Simi were often there those days, hanging around between the stretched nets, chatting about hunting, and more often than not about maids! I fortunately didn't fall into that category as I was still just a friend to them. If they ever looked upon me as a maid, our adventure days together would be over. Lusa and Mayni, who had fourteen winters, were always trying to catch Karn and Simi's eyes, asking them to carry baskets for them, when they were perfectly capable of carrying their own baskets! Karn and Simi didn't seem to mind though. In fact, I had noticed that they seemed to be hanging around Lusa's and Mayni's huts most evenings lately. What was it that seemed to affect everybody when they reach a certain age? I thought to myself. They didn't look any different. It was like some strange fever took over only their brains. Or maybe the Shaman had something to do with it, I thought. I shuddered then, thinking it best not think about it too much, or I might be infected too!

I rounded the end of the pile of boat rollers and there they were, giggling and whispering to each other about something.

'Hey Karn! Can you and Simi help me today with the bark stripping?'

They just looked at me blankly, burst into hysterical giggles, and started rolling about on the floor. Then I heard Karn mutter something about Lusa, and stripping, and they were off again.

I stood, hands on my hips before them like my grandmother, and asked indignantly, 'I don't see what's so funny. Are you going to help or not?' I was starting to get very annoyed by then at being left out of some obviously hilarious private joke.

Karn, then pulling a very serious face, replied, 'Sorry Mia, of course we will help you to strip.'

At which Simi broke out into hysterics again. What was the matter with them? I thought.

The job of bark stripping was not that difficult, or unpleasant, but it was tedious, and if you had some friends to help pass the time it was not so bad a job at all.

'It must be an important hunt for them to be making tar on such a windy day, don't you think, Simi?' Karn stated.

'I heard that a family of elk have been seen not far from the north shore forest. It will be good hunting for ten or more days, they say. Maybe as so many hunters are away in Scan Land, we might be able to go with them,' Simi said hopefully. Simi could not wait for his first hunt, and his becoming a man in the tribe. But he had to wait until he had fifteen winters before he could go, and he knew it.

'In your dreams Simi,' Karn replied. 'We will just have to wait till next summer. If we wish for a good tar burn today, maybe we will be given some for our practice arrows.'

Karn and Simi spent most of their days, when not giggling in corners about maids, hunting small animals to prepare for their first hunt and manhood.

'Keep peeling you two,' I urged, 'I want to get two baskets filled before midday food, then maybe we can watch the Shaman do the ceremony later. I have seen the stone pit that Grandmother is preparing for the tar making, and it is not too big, so two baskets should be enough.'

We stripped the bark until we had enough, and wandered up the hill to deliver it to the Shaman. Even though the Shaman had been in our settlement all my lifetime, I had only looked at him directly five or six times. Simi suddenly stated, as we walked, that he had seen him looking at me lately, and said it was probably because of my red hair. Nobody in our settlement had my colour hair; most people had fair hair, or almost black, curly hair. My hair was the colour of the near winter leaves in the forest, and it was also very wavy and thick. It must be Brit Land hair like my father had, everyone said to me. Yet when we saw Brit Land traders visiting the island, their hair was a lighter red and curlier than mine. Maybe it was the mixture of the two tribes' hair that had made mine so unusual, I had often thought. I just ignored what Simi had said, as he was probably just teasing me.

Everyone was gathering at the stone pit for the tar ceremony when we arrived. Grandmother was already there, tapping her foot impatiently when she saw me coming, saying, 'Mia, just how long does it take to strip two baskets of bark? And you had lots of help by the looks of it. Karn, put the baskets to the side. It is very good of you boys to help Mia – she gets away with far too much in this settlement as it is.'

'Don't shout at Mia,' Karn replied, 'it was our fault it took so long. We spent a lot of time choosing good bark before we stripped it.'

Lene just smiled at Karn, and scowled at me, replying, 'Well, now you are all here, you can knead the clay for the stone pit.'

Lene put a pile of wet river clay in front of us, and we started pressing it in between the cracks in the stone lined pit. Getting the tar out of the birch bark might seem a simple thing, but you could never tell if it was going to work or not. A pit was always dug in the ground, and was lined with fire stones. After the stones were sealed with the wet river clay, which is what we were doing, a small fire was lit in the pit to dry it out before the tar making. My birch bark was then placed in the centre of the pit, and a frame of more stones was put over it, to make a kind of hut for the bark. This had then to be sealed with more clay, until not even a tiny crack could be seen. A very special fire was then made over and around the birch bark hut, which the chief had to light. Lastly, the Shaman's 'Pure One' had to dance around it as part of the ceremony. The fire then had to be watched, and kept burning: not too fierce, or the bark would turn to ash, and not too weak, or the bark would not have changed at all. If the fire was just right, and lasted for at least six hours, when the hut was broken apart there would be a pool of tar in the bottom. The tar had a wonderful smell, and most people would walk around the tar to get the scent of it into their clothes, to bring them luck.

We eventually finished the pit, and after my grandmother had lit the test fire and put it out, the ceremony could begin. We moved our buckets, and cleaned the ground around the pit with sticks, before moving to the back of the gathering crowd. Then the pure white fur that covered the entrance to the Shaman's hut was pulled back, and Sula stepped out in her ceremonial white dress. In her fair hair there was a crown of red leaves, and a necklace of red berries was draped about her neck. She was very beautiful, and Karn and Simi, who were sitting next to me, looked at her with their mouths wide open and their eyes gazing.

Sula was the Pure One of the Shaman. He always had a young maid in his hut, about fourteen winters old, to wait on him and to help with the ceremonies. After the Shaman felt she was no longer pure enough to help him, he would allow one of the young hunters to take her for a bound woman. It was thought to be a great honour to have the Shaman's maid for a woman.

Sula carried a rug of white fox fur, and laid it on the ground before sitting on it next to the Shaman's chair. The Shaman's chair was made of water reeds, and was always decorated with a cloak made from eagle feathers. He walked out of his hut and sat in his chair, laying down his staff in front of him. There were so many tiny bones dangling about the top of his staff, that when he moved about the settlement you could hear the bones long before you could see him. On top of the staff was the clearest, most beautiful piece of amber. I and most of the tribe wondered where it came from, but the Shaman had it when he first came to our island, and no one would dare ask him about it.

Sula got up then, and started dancing, with a basket covered with shells under her arms. With smooth and delicate movements she strewed the contents, a fine white sand, onto the ground around the edge of the fire pit, until it was completely covered. Then she kneeled before the Shaman, and with outstretched arms, waited for him to place a small bark container in her hands. She arose, and her dancing became more elaborate as she wove and twisted about the fire. With her bare foot she traced wavy patterns in the white sand. As she did that, she sprinkled red earth in the grooves that her foot had made, until the white sand had a network of red earth patterns within it.

It was then time for the Shaman to weave his magic. Sula lay prostrate at his feet, and he got up and stepped over her. She could not then move until the ceremony was finished, or the magic would be broken. The Shaman stamped his staff suddenly, the bones tinkled, and he ordered the chief to light the fire. It was very important that a new fire was made for this ceremony, and not a fire from another pit that may have been contaminated, perhaps by cooking.

Barl, our chief, kneeled in front of the pit, and with the red stone and flint, started to spark the bowl of seed heads in front of him. He must make the fire using no more than nine strikes of the flint, or the tar pit would fail. This was never a problem, as if the chief couldn't light a fire in nine strikes, then we were all doomed anyway!

The fire was lit, and the leaves and berries of the juniper bush were sprinkled on top of it to give off a lovely aroma, and make the flames flare. The Shaman chanted some magic words, and that was basically that. The crowd went home then, except for the team of hunters chosen to keep the fire burning.

Sula was allowed to get up and follow the Shaman back into his hut, and we went off to get some food. I was so hungry! I had been so keen to find Karn earlier, that I had only eaten one dried fish for first food. Karn said I could go home with him to eat, as he had caught a puffin the day before which was already stewing in the bag over the fire. Karn's mother was always pleased to see me, and was always so very kind to me too. I am sure she would have had me living with her, but her man would not be responsible for another man's child. Still, he was not around today, as he was hunting bull in Scan Land. I could smell that puffin stew four huts away too! I loved puffin, but we very rarely ate it at home. Grandmother said that eating it gave her a pain in her stomach. I think she just did not like having to ask Karn's father for anything. They did not get on, as she thought her other daughter should have been bound to a prime hunter, and not just one of the followers, which is what Karn's father was.

I sat down outside the hut, and was given a wooden bowl of the delicious smelling stew by Sedle. From where Karn and I were sitting we could see the tar pit fire, and we both wondered if it was going to be a successful one. So much of our lives revolved around good or bad luck… will the tar flow from the bark? Will the hunt be successful? Will the sea rise more this year than last? Or will it be a good year – cold, but no sea rising?

It was not surprising the Shaman had such power, as whole settlements can have some sort of bad luck from time to time. Like last winter, when the mountain people became ill. It was days before the valley people noticed they had not seen them out hunting. The Shaman ordered flaming torches to be shot into their settlement, to kill the bad spirits and stop them from walking down to the valley. The bowmen said they had heard the sounds of people screaming as the fires took hold, but the Shaman said it was just the bad spirits trying to fool them. I was not so sure. What if there were people still alive in there? I had thought. Perhaps it was not bad spirits, just simply bad meat…

I always wondered why nobody challenged the Shaman, or at least asked some questions? Maybe it was just me, a half Dogger maid. Maybe it was the Brit Land blood in my veins that made me question things. I knew one thing though – when I grew into a woman, I would question. I would probably be banished from the settlement because of it. But maybe that would not be such a bad thing; I could go on my adventures then. But, eating a good bowl of puffin stew, and sitting by the doorway looking at the tar fire, was about as good as life could get for me at that moment.

My peace was suddenly shattered, and I shuddered as I heard Lene calling angrily, 'Mia! Mia, where are you?'

Sedle called her mother over, and replied, 'She's just having some stew, Mother. Can't you leave her to be a child just once in a while?'

'Maybe,' Lene stated, with her hands on her hips, staring down at me, 'but she stripped the bark, and must at least take an interest in the tar making. The Shaman has asked why she was not by the fire this night. He had asked that she, and no one else, get the bark for the pit, for some strange reason. Karn, you and Simi had better come too, as you helped Mia. We will pick Simi up on the way.'

We reluctantly followed Lene up the hill, and I was glad we had finished our stew at least, or we would have been made to leave it behind. It was a very important rule that no one could eat or drink next to a tar fire, so as not to spoil the magic. Simi's hut was halfway between Karn's hut and the tar pits, and was very small. His father had been killed in the hunt three or four winters ago. He and his mother had to live on the kindness of others, and by doing the jobs no one else wanted to do. That was why Simi was so keen to hunt, so that he could raise their family status again, up to the level of others in the tribe.

As we walked through the settlement I wondered why the Shaman had asked that I should strip the bark. I felt very uneasy with the obvious attention I was getting from him. He was very old and ugly, and he smelled so bad. I didn't know how Sula could live with him. I also thought it couldn't be very long before he found she was not pure enough for the ceremonies. But I was not going to think about what that might mean for me, when I was old enough to be a Pure One. I visibly shuddered at the thought, and Karn, who had his arm around me as we walked, looked at me quizzically and held me closer.

As we approached the tar fire, the hunters had their heads together, and were talking intensely in low voices. They looked up and saw Simi, and immediately stopped talking. The three of us then sat down together around the fire, feeling a little out of place. The hunters were like members of some sort of exclusive club in the settlement; they did not mix with other people if they could help it. They spent a lot of time visiting the Shaman, to ask for hunt magic. Their lives were dominated by the last hunt, and their plans for the next. I thought that was incredibly boring, but Simi and Karn were obsessed with it all. There was an awkward silence as we sat down, and one of the hunters said, 'Look, Simi is old enough to know the truth. Why do we not we tell him?'

Simi's face went very pale, when he realised that the conversation they were having before we arrived had something to do with him. Maybe they were not going to allow him to hunt next year? I thought. Young boys could only join the hunt after a unanimous vote from the hunters. The life of each hunter was held in the hands of the weakest member of the hunt. A rejected boy would have to approach the fishermen, who were also very superstitious people. Such a boy could spend many winters, net making and fish gutting, before he would be allowed to go out in the boats. Some boys were rejected by the hunters, and the fishermen, because someone or other did not like them. All they could then do was to make a basket boat, and go out fishing alone around the island. No one could make a log boat on their own, but a basket boat was within most boys' ability, or maids, for that matter. If they were allowed to make one, I thought.

Borg last year found himself in that situation. He had been pestering the youngest daughter of one of the hunters, and so he was rejected from joining. While he was always very strong, he seemed to find it difficult to get on with people in our tribe. He just did not seem to have any respect for rules, or even the Shaman, though I did notice he went out of his way not to offend him. Anyway, he decided to build a basket boat, and in order to get the skin for it, he supplied cut wood for the homes of two hunters, for a whole winter! He seemed to think it was worth it, and you could often see him skirting the lagoon in his boat, catching fish and sea spiders. I liked him, and sometimes he would take me out in his boat, when we were well out of view of the settlement.

It is forbidden for women or maids to get into boats. I think it goes back to some ancient law, brought about when the island was new, and a lot of women did not wish to be trapped on it. They just got into boats, legend has it, and paddled themselves to Brit Land, or Scan Land, and were never seen again. The island started to become short of women for the hunters and fishermen, so the law was made that no woman could ever get into a boat. In other words, no woman born on Dogger Island could ever leave. That was probably all right when Dogger Island had a vast plain, stretching out into what is now water. A trader told us one day that Brit Land, Dogger Island, and Scan Land were actually joined up once. He said Dogger Island was the mountainous part, in the middle of this great plain. I thought the story was a bit farfetched. If that was so, where did all the water come from? And why did it come? Although the stories of traders are great to listen to, they are just stories, made up by people wanting a free dinner and bed for the night, for the most part.

While I had been pondering the rules of hunting and traders stories, there had been a lot of intense mutterings going on within the group of hunters. The Shaman, who had just been sitting in his chair stroking Sula's hair, picked up his staff, which was leaning against his chair, and stamped it on the ground, twice, until the bones jingled. Instantly everyone stopped talking, and almost held their breath: it was as if the fireside scene about us had been frozen in time.

'Tell him tomorrow! It is time he knew his father's death tale,' the Shaman stated indifferently.

The whole group turned and looked at Simi, who nearly squeaked with fright. Even though it was a really serious moment, I couldn't help wanting to giggle at the sheer intensity of it all. It must have something to do with Simi's father's death in the hunt, I thought. No one ever talked about the fact that he did not come back. Although there was some sort of air of disgrace and sadness about it, no-one knew why.

'Simi, as you will be joining the hunt next summer, you are old enough to learn what happened to your father,' Danz the hunt leader said.

Then the Shaman said, 'Let us plan your route for the hunt, next half moon, and where you should place the charms I will give you.'

One of the hunters stood up then and said, while pointing his finger at me, 'What about the maid?'

Another said, 'She must go! This is only for the ears of hunters.'

I was about to get up and leave, reluctantly, as I thought it was just getting interesting, when the Shaman shouted, 'No! She stays.'

They all looked at him in amazement, and then at me. I was suddenly becoming scared and replied, 'I really don't mind going.'

The Shaman shook his head, and said in almost a whisper, but that all could hear, 'She will know the ways of the Shaman before the heat of next summer's sun. So she stays.'

There was an audible a gasp around the fire pit. They all knew what knowing the ways of the Shaman meant. Only the Pure One can know them. But I was only eleven winters old, even though I was bigger than most maids my age. I still had only eleven winters. The Shaman's Pure One had to be fourteen winters old before she would be given to him by her family. I watched Karn and Simi look at each other in horror... but when I looked at them they turned away. I could not believe what was happening. Surely my grandmother would not allow him to take me, not for another three winters?

But I knew in my heart, that if the Shaman wanted me, whenever he wanted me, he could take me. Unless I could somehow get off the island. Maybe he would change his mind? I thought to myself. Maybe he did not really mean what we all thought he meant?

Danz stood up then, and asked Simi to sit down between the hunters. Simi got up, and with visibly shaking knees, walked around the fire to the hunters' side. I did not really listen to the Shaman's instructions as to where to place his charms for a good hunt. All I could think of was taking Sula's place in the Shaman's hut, washing his clothes and smelling his horrid breath all day long. Also, no one knew what a Pure One had to do to help make the magic for the ceremonies. I had heard tales once from an old woman, who had been a Pure One when she was young. She said that you had to chew raw beetles and spit them into a pot for potions. Then there were the snakes he always had in that basket... I had always been terrified of snakes, as I was nearly bitten by one as a child. I had been sitting on the beach alone, playing with some shells, when I looked around and saw a strange piece of seaweed next to me. I sat for a while wondering what kind of seaweed it was, as I had not seen one like it before. I looked away, and when I looked back, I could see it had been a snake all along. It had made me think it was seaweed! The fact that a snake took over my mind disturbed me so much, it was almost two summers before I would sit on that beach again.

I do not know how long I sat there, gazing at the tar fire, but I suddenly became aware that people were standing, and it was time to go. The fire was going out, and we would not know if the tar had flowed until first light the next day.

We all walked back to our homes, and Karn walked with me. It was a very different walk home for Karn and me, we were totally silent. He stood apart from me, not walking as he usually did on a cold night, with his arm around my shoulders. Our thoughts were on one thing only, the Shaman and his announcement.

He said nothing when we reached my grandmother's hut. He just patted me on the back and walked quickly away. I stood at the pelt door and watched him disappear from view around the huts. How could everything change so quickly? Karn, my best friend in the whole world, was suddenly keeping his distance from me. Maybe he had to, if he wanted to be a hunter next season. It would be unwise for him to pay any attention to me from then on, even as a friend, because I had been announced as the next Pure One after Sula. My training would begin before the next full moon, which was only half a moon from then! Did my grandmother know? I wondered. Was that why she had been so hard on me, to make sure I did my share of work before I entered the Shaman's hut? A Pure One has to provide for the needs of the Shaman, for as long as he wants it. I could be in his hut until I was twenty winters old; it had been known before. I would never be allowed to speak to anyone else apart from him too. My life would be over! I would certainly not be allowed to sit on my beloved sand cliffs and dream of far off lands. I felt warm tears run down my cheeks at the thought of being close to that horrible old man, and went inside. My grandmother was not there, which was unusual at that time of night, so I covered myself in my furs and drifted off into a fitful sleep.

The next morning I woke and thought I must have had some kind of nightmare. I looked across to the smoking fire to see grandmother stoking it and cooking fish. Cooking fish! It was not festival time; we only cooked fish in our own homes at festival time. Fish was usually smoked on great racks and eaten cold at first food. Today she was hot smoking fish in our hut for first food. Maybe it was not a dream after all. Oh please let it be a dream, I thought!

Lene had noticed me stirring and came over to me, saying gently, 'Mia, you must get up and have some food. You have a big day ahead of you.'

Her tone of voice was almost respectful. It was then that I knew it had not been a dream. The Shaman wanted me to be his next Pure One.

'Grandmother, at the tar fire…'

But she cut me off before I could say anything more. 'I know, Mia. The Shaman sent for me at first light, and told me his wishes. It is a great honour for our family. He said I was to cook you hot fish for first food, and bring you to him when you had finished.' She handed me a bowl of delicious smelling smoked fish.

'No! No! Never! He is ugly, and he smells. I will not spend a night in his hut, let alone many winters.' At the word winters, my voice became no more than a whisper.

'You really do not have a choice, Mia, his will must be obeyed.'

There was a strange softness in her voice that I had never heard before that moment. I ate my fish, and wished it were not a delicious treat that came to my bowl via the Shaman. My grandmother gave me my best soft leather dress, the one I would wear only at festival time. It had been my mother's, and Lene had decorated it with hundreds of blue shells, so it made a pretty noise when I moved. She washed my hair in water heated with fire stones and scented with herbs. When I was ready to her satisfaction, she walked me up to the Shaman's hut.

All the people we passed knew where I was going, and why. The news of the announcement was all over the settlement, before first food I imagined. They wondered why their more eligible daughters, of the right age, had not been chosen. Most of them surmised, understandably, that it was because of my hair colour.

But they also wondered why he could not wait another three winters for me, when it would be right and proper. Others had apparently noticed his lingering looks at me during moots, and knew he would not wait long for me. The Shaman makes the rules, and he knows he can always have his way, saying it is in the name of good magic for the settlement.

Sula was sitting outside the hut waiting for me when we arrived. She did not look happy at all at the thought of being handed over to some young hunter next summer, to live an ordinary life like the rest of the settlement women.

She spoke in a very formal tone. 'Greetings, Mia. He is waiting for you inside.'

My first inclination was to turn and run, run anywhere but into that hut. Sensing that, my grandmother blocked my retreat and just pushed me inside.

It was dark inside the hut, and there was a strong smell of herbs from the fire, the sort of herbs that sometimes were given to hunters to invoke the hunting trances. As my eyes adjusted to the light, I could see the Shaman sitting quietly in the corner, watching me, like a leopard about to pounce.

'Come and sit next to me, Mia. I won't hurt you. We have much to talk about before you become my Pure One.' His voice was quiet, and as friendly as he could make it.

'Mia, have you nothing to say about this honour I have done you?' His voice was becoming a little irritated now, I thought, so I said in the calmest and most natural voice I could muster,

'I am just surprised, my lord. I did not think I was old enough to become the Pure One.'

'I could see the readiness of you, which others could not. That is the way of the Shaman. Your hair is the colour of the near winter leaves in the forest. It is the colour of the Earth Goddess. You will not just be my Pure One, you will

27

stay with me all of your life, and become my own priestess. We will work magic together that has never before been seen in the northern waters.'

His voice was taking on an almost frenzied tone as he spoke, as if he had forgotten I was there, and he was speaking to someone else.

What on earth was I supposed to say to that? I thought. Oh yes, lord, I can see myself not just being your Pure One for a few winters, but I will be your priestess for the rest of my life…! Just keep calm, I thought to myself. I knew I mustn't let him think for a second that I was not absolutely overjoyed at the prospect. I whispered in reply, as demurely as I could, 'I am not worthy, lord Shaman.'

After I spoke, he produced a flint blade, and looked at me and smiled. What is he going to do now? I thought. Kill me? I wanted to run then, but my legs would not move. I was so frightened. He crawled, or more or less slithered, over to me, with his blade in his hand, and I involuntarily let out a very small squeak. He started to smile at me then. At least I hoped it was a smile, and not a sneer, but I just could not tell in that light.

'Why you are trembling? Is it the thought of our great and wondrous union that makes you tremble? Do not worry, it will be soon enough that we will work our magic together, but we must keep to the rituals for a union as great as ours. I am going to cut a little piece of your hair now, to start weaving the bond that we will make together. I will keep it close to me, until you are with me forever.'

At that, he reached out and held a piece of my hair, fondling it in some sort of daze for at least a minute, until he came to himself again, and cut it with the blade.

'Can I go home now?' I asked, as meekly as I could.

'No, not yet. Sit here, on my knee, and I will hold you for a while, so that we can feel each other's energy, and let the earth magic flow through us.'

I suddenly became aware of the crystal I had worn around my neck since I was a baby. It had been my mother's, or so Lene had told me. I always wore it under my clothes, in case one of the settlement maids saw it and took it off me. Then, although I could not see it, I felt it was all of a sudden warm, and that warmth made me feel that I would somehow be all right. Then he threw some herbs on the fire, and I must have fallen asleep. I awoke, still sitting on his knee, sometime later. All I could see were Sula's eyes, glaring at me from the darkness of the hut. The Shaman had gone to sleep too – I think it must have been the herbs he put on the fire. I gently got up, so as not to wake him, and crept out of the hut. Sula followed me.

'You cannot come to this hut again until you start your training, in half a moon's time. Go home now,' she whispered, with as much hatred as I imagine anyone can put into a whisper.

She thought I wanted to come back? My legs were weak from the fumes of the herbs, but not weak enough for me not to run like I have never run before. Straight through the settlement and out onto the sand cliffs, to my favourite place amongst the dunes. How could one day change my life so totally? I thought desperately. My best friend in the entire world shuns me. My grandmother, who suddenly looked like a pretty soft option, was giving me away to an ugly old man so that he could keep me prisoner for the rest of my life! The day before, I was moaning to myself about my dreary life, doing chores for my grandmother. Since the Shaman's announcement, I would never have to do a chore again, but at what price? I thought that it could not be. It would not happen. I had to get off the island, and I only had half a moon to do it, or I felt I would be lost forever.

I thought again about my crystal, and took it out from under my clothes and looked into it. I had done that so many times as a child, to escape unhappiness. The cracks and flaws in the clear crystal made valleys and mountains inside when you looked at it, and sometimes, if the light was right, you could even see rivers made of rainbows there. But that time it was different. There was a sort of glow coming from deep in the heart of the crystal that I had never seen before. As I looked at it, I felt somehow calm again, and in a strange way very, very old.

I don't know how long I sat on the cliff, looking out to sea, but I was brought back to my new reality by the calls of my grandmother. A sound which I usually found annoying, as it meant that I had to leave my cliff and do some tedious job or other. Now it was at least the sound of normality, and maybe I thought I could lose myself in some work for the rest of that horrible day. My grandmother was actually climbing the dune cliffs, and coming towards me. I don't think I could ever remember her doing that before. She usually stood, hands on hips, screaming at me from the beach.

'Mia, Mia, you must be hungry for midday food. You must look after yourself now, come down with me,' she said in a quiet voice.

'You are not calling me to do some work?' I asked incredulously.

'Of course not. Your days of doing my chores are over. You are to be the Pure One, and you must not do work like the rest of us anymore. You are special now. Come down, you might get cold sitting on the damp grass, and if you become ill, I will have the Shaman to answer to!' She took hold of my hand and led me down to the settlement.

I walked with her as if in a daze. Nothing seemed real. It was as if my life had become some sort of distorted dream. I must not do her chores, she had said! I had been doing her chores for as long as I could remember. She had constantly told me that that was my sole purpose in life, and that I should be grateful to her for caring for me at all. How could one day make such a difference? She was treating me as a guest in her hut suddenly, not a tedious inconvenience.

We were walking past the skin drying racks, where a few hunters were giving the women some new pelts to scrape. As we walked past they looked at my grandmother, and then at me, and politely nodded. I automatically smiled and nodded back, and they looked away. As we walked almost out of earshot, they all started talking avidly, and I caught the words, '... eleven winters' and, '... conniving maid' before we were too far away to hear anything more. What did they mean? I thought. They thought I wanted to be picked as the next Pure One? To most maids in the settlement, being the Pure One was like being made into a chief's daughter. They would talk with envy about the carefree life they thought the Pure One's had. I could understand the part about never having to work again at home. But not living alone with an aged old man, and never being able to walk alone on the island again. Never to talk to anyone other than the Shaman. I supposed to those women and their families, I had stolen some sort of prize from the hands of their daughters. If they only knew the horror I felt about it, they certainly would not accuse me of deviously tempting the Shaman to take me to his hut so young.

'Here we are, sit down and I will get you some food. I had Sedle bring you some puffin stew specially, I know how much you like it.' Lene placed a steaming wooden bowl in front of me, and waited for me to pick it up and start eating.

Then I just lost control, and screamed at her, 'I ate this puffin stew at Sedle's yesterday, with Karn, before the tar fire. Last time I ate this puffin stew, I was just Mia. I don't want to be the Shaman's Pure One. Please grandmother. Stop this... please! Can't we just go back to you shouting at me? Give me some small nuts to crush! I will do baskets of them. Don't give me to the Shaman...'

I collapsed then in a heap on the floor, and sobbed uncontrollably. Muttering the words over and over again, 'Please help me, please, please don't let him take me. I am not like the other maids. I don't want it. I never wanted it, Grandmother.'

I do not know exactly what happened next. I just saw a flash of white light, and felt a sharp pain on my cheek. My grandmother had slapped me across the face, so hard I stopped crying instantly. She grabbed my hair, and pulled me away from the fire, pushing me onto a pile of furs in the corner.

Her eyes were dark, and with a look of absolute rage on her face, she said, 'You will go to his hut and you will like it! You will do all he bids you to do and you will make him think you are blissfully happy. How dare you suggest that you don't want this honour to befall our family? How dare you? I have had to look after you and care for you when your stupid mother died, and it has not been easy. If you want to blame someone for your fate, then blame your father for the colour of his hair. If the Shaman wants you, he can have you. He is the Shaman. He holds the balance of life and death for the whole tribe in his hands, and if he needs you to make his magic, then so be it. How ungrateful can you be? I have been told to give you all you wish before you begin your training, and you like Sedle's puffin stew, so you will eat it! Get up! Dry up your eyes and do not speak to me of such thoughts again.'

She pulled me up, wiped my face with a moss net, and placed the bowl in my hands. I began to eat. My grandmother was my only hope that my family would help. Karn showed his feelings the night before. His destiny was with the hunt, and he would not lift a finger to help me. That would be the same for Simi. I was truly alone.

The taste of the stew did make me feel a little better. It helped wipe out the last traces of the Shaman's herbs from my body. I had to be strong, I thought, if I was to get out of that situation. But get out of it I would. I didn't care that all the people I knew in the whole world were against me. I was my own person, and I would not obey them. It must have been my Brit Land blood that made me so independent and strong, even though it was my hair colour that had caused the trouble in the first place. I had just half a moon to get off the island. Once I began my training, I would never be left alone. I finished the stew, and my grandmother looked pleased. She thought she had curbed my rebelliousness. I knew she must continue to think that, if I was to have any chance of escape.

I looked up at her, smiled weakly, and said, 'I am sorry, Grandmother. I do not know what came over me. Maybe it was the Shaman's herbs I breathed in at his hut that made me panic. Of course I am honoured. When I am the Pure One, I will ask the Shaman to have a new hut built for you, near to his if you wish?'

Maybe I had gone too far with that suggestion, I thought. Surely she did not believe me? Did she?

'We will not speak of it again. It probably was the herbs, as you said. I have heard they are very potent, and you are not used to them yet. I don't need a new hut, Mia, I have always lived at this end of the settlement. Thank you though for the thought. I am sure you will be very happy as the Pure One. What a life you will have before you. Can I get you anything else?'

She stood before me like a servant then. How incredible it was that she had changed so much. I had always thought she was strong and independent, like me, but I could see that it was just a front. She was weak, like everyone else in this tribe. Like a herd of antelope moving and twisting as one behind their leader. I don't know why, but I suddenly felt very grown up and strong at that moment. Circumstances were making me grow up before my time. I actually felt sorry for my grandmother, but at the same time the last bond with any family I had on that island had finally gone.

'I will go for a walk now. I feel the need to be alone, Grandmother, and think about my new future.' Standing, I just walked out, grabbing my fur by the door, before my grandmother could reply.

I walked purposefully down to the beach, past the skin drying racks and the smell of animal fat, not even looking at the women that time. I was just about to walk up to the sand cliffs when I suddenly decided to go the other way, towards the north island lagoon. I did not usually go that way in the winter, the cliff path was sometimes slippery and it was a good morning's walk. But I made my way up the path anyway, and instead of skirting the shore I decided to take the path through the forest, over the peninsular to the lagoon. I loved the forest at that time of year. When I was younger, Karn, Simi and I often came to play the "Disappear" game. One of us would have to go and hide, and the others had to find us, not going too far from the forest clearing. I used to find a pile of fallen leaves and lie under them, spreading my hair over the leaves to match their colour, making it easier for me to hide. I could peek out from under the pile, and not be seen by the other two. Unfortunately, after doing that a few times, they worked out that I was always hiding in the brown leaves, but they still pretended not to see me until the last minute.

As I walked through the clearing, I decided to lie down in the dry leaves and think for a while. That was always such a happy place for me. I spread my hair over the leaves and watched as a small red leaf gently drifted though the still air, from the trees above onto the forest floor. Maybe the Shaman could see that I have some bond with the Earth Goddess. I lay there, looking at my hair disappearing under the leaves, and fell into a deep sleep.

I dreamed I was sitting on my sand cliffs, and holding my arms up to the sky. I was looking for something. A white snowy owl flew at me from behind a cloud, and sat at my feet. I was then riding on the back of the owl, flying high, high above the island, and looking at the settlement from above. I flew over the north island lagoon, and swooped low over the marshlands. I awoke with a start.

'By the tree devils! I nearly stepped on you!'

Borg was standing next to me, with a look of total astonishment on his face. I replied in a dazed way, 'Oh… I… I must have fallen asleep.'

I sat up, and found that a thick carpet of golden brown leaves had completely covered me while I lay sleeping. Borg had nearly trodden on me, as he carried his basket boat on his head through the clearing.

'You look like the Earth Goddess herself, melting into the forest floor like that! My, your hair really is beautiful, just the same colour as the leaves that you sit on.'

Maybe Borg had just come to that conclusion, but it was not what I wanted to hear right then! And I exploded at him, 'Yes, yes, Borg, and I am so lucky to be the next Pure One, am I not? I am so well suited to be an Earth Priestess! You had better get on your way you know. You do not want the Shaman to see you looking at me, and noticing my wonderful hair, do you?'

I tried to leap out of the leaves and stride away, but my knees went weak under me. I half got up, and fell down again; the effect of those herbs was obviously still in my body. I felt sapped of energy, and so just sat there looking at Borg's startled face, and I began to sob my heart out.

'Hey, what is the matter with you? You are always such a tough little maid. This is not like you. Are you all right? Do not stand up just yet, you are obviously not well.'

He sat next to me and put his arm around me, and held me tight. His strong arms were warm and comforting, and I realised that it was the first kindness anyone had shown me since the announcement.

'You must not hold me. The Shaman will punish you if anyone sees us.' I suddenly came to my senses then. I liked Borg, and I did not want any harm to come to him because of me.

'What do you mean? Why does the Shaman care about what happens to you?' he asked.

'You do not know?' I asked.

'Know what? I have been camping on the north island lagoon for the past three suns, catching the best eels I have caught this summer. I had to stay and smoke them before I came back, or they would have spoiled. What could have happened in three days to turn the toughest young maid in the settlement into a snivelling heap?' He looked at me with real concern in his eyes.

'I was sitting by the tar pit last night. The hunters were about to talk about the placing of charms for the hunt, after deciding to tell Simi his father's death tale, and they said I had to go. I was just getting up to leave, when the Shaman said I could stay, as I would be his Pure One before next summer,' I said in almost one breath. Then the tears were welling up in my eyes again as I told him, and he knew that I was telling him the truth.

'But you only have eleven winters, do you not?'

'Yes, but the Shaman said I was ready anyway. My grandmother took me to his hut after first food, and he told me that I was not just to become his Pure One before next summer. I would also become his priestess, and live with him for the rest of my life! He sat me on his knee and threw some herbs on the fire, and I fell asleep. When I woke up he was still sleeping, so I left his hut. Sula was furious. She told me I was not to go back until my training begins, in half a moon's time.'

I poured out the facts without pausing for breath, it was so good to tell someone how I really felt.

'The Shaman is evil. What does your grandmother say about it? Surely she won't let him take you until you have had fourteen winters?'

'She thinks the whole idea is wonderful, and a great honour for the family. I thought she loved me, and that she was hard on me because she cared about me, but she was hard on me because she resented my mother dying and leaving her to look after me.'

I realised as I spoke that what I said to him was true. I had misinterpreted her hardness as her love for me. I suddenly felt very alone, especially after Karn's reaction the night before.

Borg had a very serious look on his face as he sat next to me. He did not say anything for a long time, and the sun was slowly taking on colour in the sky over the tree tops. He suddenly got up, and pulled me up too. He bent down because he was so tall, and held my shoulders and gazed into my eyes for what seemed like an age.

Then he said, keenly, 'You have only two choices that I can see. Stay and become his maid, or leave, and remain your own person! I can help you if you want to leave the island, but it must be your decision, and I cannot guarantee it will have a good ending if you do leave. It is up to you.' He then let go of my shoulders, and watched my face for a reaction.

'I have to leave! I would sooner fall on a flint dagger than stay! How is it you are not afraid of the Shaman, like everyone else? Karn would not even look me in the face after the announcement. Simi too, and they were my best friends.'

'I am not surprised at Karn. His heart has always been with the hunt, and even leading it one day. Simi is weak. He dreams of being accepted by the hunt and moving his mother into the main settlement. By the way, I must ask Simi to tell me his father's death tale when I see him, I have always wondered what happened... But not now! It is getting late, and you will be missed. Even though you have not started your training yet, people will still want to know where you are most of the time. No one must see us together if I am to get us off Dogger. Go home now. I will stay here a while, so that no one sees us talking to each other. Meet me in the crack of the big pine on the promontory to the lagoon, tomorrow after midday food. Now go!'

2 THE TRADING FLEET

I did not need any encouragement from Borg. I smiled back at him and ran out of the clearing, down to the fork in the paths at the cliff edge. My mind was racing at the same speed as my young legs through the forest. I had hope at least! Borg became the most important person in the world to me that day.

As I rounded the corner and the settlement came into view, I could see that something was happening on the beach. Small groups of people were huddled together looking out to sea, and lots of other people were running about and shouting to each other. My view of the bay from where I stood was obstructed by high bushes that lined the cliff side of the path. So I quickened my pace to the sand cliffs, when I would be able to see what was going on. I hoped that nobody had missed me, because it was already getting dark and there was a chill wind blowing. I reached the end of the path and looked at the scene on the beach below me.

A trading fleet was arriving! Twelve or more log boats were negotiating the surf, and beaching themselves on the sand. Teams of island fishermen were collecting the boat rollers and lining them up on the beach. The tide was out, and it was going to be a long haul to get the boats to the safety of dry land and the settlement. They must have been waiting for the tide all afternoon, I thought, as they would never intentionally land so near to darkness.

Our bay had some very dangerous cross currents in it, and it was fine to launch small, lighter fishing boats at high tide, but not big sea going traders' boats. They needed the tide to be right out, or they would be turned on their approach and lose their cargos in the surf. Everyone was so busy that they did not notice me slip into the back of the crowd to watch the spectacle. The trading fleet only came once or twice a year from Scan Land, and some years it did not come at all. Because of this, when they arrived everyone did nothing but talk, eat, drink, and trade until they were gone again. I knew that by that time the elders' women would be supervising a feast for last food in the moot hall that night, and they would be getting out their best fruit mead to impress the traders.

I could just make out Karn in the thick of the hauling teams, pulling the ropes for all he was worth. They had seven or eight boats already on the rollers, but they wouldn't pull them right in until they were all safely through the surf. I watched all the activity, gratefully glad for something to take my mind off my own problems.

35

Two of the women in front of me turned round and noticed me behind them, and immediately took a step away from me. It was like the antelope herd again – in an unspoken wave the crowd seemed to simultaneously move away from me, until I stood alone on my own stretch of sand. Two maids ran off, then came back within minutes with my grandmother striding behind them. Her face was like stone, but her voice was soft and courteous.

'Mia, we were wondering where you had gone. The Shaman woke and asked for you again. He did not give you leave to go this morning. Sula said you just sneaked out of his hut when he was asleep. She said she tried to stop you, but you just ran away. What were you thinking?'

'I... I thought I was supposed to go then. Anyway, you remember the herbs that made me sleep, they must have addled my mind too. In fact, I went for a walk in the forest, and when I sat down for a while I just fell asleep. I must have still had the herbs in me. I just woke up a little while ago, and came straight here. I did not think you would mind me watching the trading fleet land.'

I tried to keep my voice as normal as I could. There was no use challenging Sula's word, she was obviously trying to discredit me. I just wished she could. She was welcome to remain the Pure One for ever, as far as I was concerned. My grandmother just took my hand, and started leading me back to our hut.

'Let me see the first boat roll up to the bank please!' I pleaded.

'Oh, very well, if you wish. You cannot stay too long though because you have a special place at the moot tonight, next to the Shaman, and you must be prepared.'

'But I am not a trainee yet! I don't have to drink the seeing potion yet, do I? I am really not ready. I will not know what to do! This is an important trading fleet, you would not want me to embarrass the settlement by not behaving correctly, would you?'

I thought that was a good argument, but she just looked at me and smiled, saying, 'You will not do anything wrong, you silly child, you just have to sit on the red fox fur rug and wear the ochre dress, and say nothing. I doubt he will give you the seeing potion until you are much older. I know it is not usual to wear the red dress until you begin your training, but the traders are here and will not return until next winter. The Shaman wants to show you off to them. Watch one or two boats, then you must come with me to Sula's hut, and she will prepare you.'

Grandmother strode off then, after saying something to the two maids that had gone to fetch her. They just looked at me with arms folded, and waited. Their glares were really off-putting, so I thought I would see if I had any real power yet, and ordered them to stand behind me so as not to obstruct my view. They instantly obeyed me, which brought a smile to my face, because I knew how much those two maids would have hated doing what I told them to.

The fleet was through the surf soon, and they were all positioned on rollers. Teams of settlers pulled on the ropes, and young boys like Karn and Simi took the last rollers and ran to the front with them, placing them in position. It was an important and sometimes dangerous job to do that, and there had been many crushed fingers in the past for the roller boys. Before long, the boats glided over the rollers on the sand like they were still in the water. It was a wonderful site to see. By that time it was quite dark, and there were dozens of flares held by the settlers along the shoreline to guide them onto the dry banks at the edge of the beach. I would have been so happy to have seen that sight two days before, but all I could feel by then was dread at being displayed in the trainee's dress, in front of all those strange men.

I supposed there was no point in putting it off any longer, as I had no idea what preparations were needed before I could wear the red dress of the trainee. So I clicked my finger at the maids, and they visibly scowled at me. I looked at them with a questioning glance in reply, and they smiled sweetly back and led the way to Sula's hut.

I had to admit, I particularly liked ordering those two maids about. They had always been so cruel to me in the past, thinking themselves so superior to the little orphan child with her grandmother. They used to say that my hair was ugly, and the colour of mud. I thought as we walked, they probably wished that they had my colour hair now, as those maids would love to take Sula's place as the Pure One. Before long we reached the hut, and they stood outside and gestured for me to go in. This was because no one but the Shaman and the Pure One were allowed inside. Sula silently came out and took my hand, and led me to a table behind a fur screen in the corner. She looked me up and down, then and said in a very abrupt way,

'You must take all your clothes off and sit on the table.'

I did not speak immediately, then I asked, 'I don't want to take all my clothes off. Can't I just take off my dress?'

'No,' she replied impatiently.

I could see I was not going to have any say, so I undressed. I had never taken my clothes off before, other than in my own hut with my grandmother. I sat on the table, and looked down at pots of red ochre and animal fat laid out on another table next to me. Sula began to rub my skin with a moss net, dripping with juniper and pine leaf water. It smelled really nice, but it was very, very cold. I was sure she was supposed to make the water warm with a firestone, but that was probably her way of getting back at me, as I was going to take her place. She dried me with a cloth, and told me to sit very still while she painted wavy lines of warm fat down my shoulders and legs. She took great care with the painting, and even painted tiny patterns on my feet and hands. When she had finished, she sprinkled the red ochre onto the fat, and suddenly my body looked like a decorated log boat. Then I put on the soft red leather dress of the trainee. It had the same wavy patterns all over it, just like the ones on my arms and legs, but they were painted onto the leather with black soot.

She then combed my hair till it flowed in waves down my back; she reached into a basket for a crown of red berries that she must have made for me to wear that day.

The dress had a very short skirt that stopped almost at the top of my legs. The black lines on the dress joined up exactly to the red lines on my legs and arms, so skilfully had Sula painted them. I looked down at my legs, and the dress, and it was as if I had become one big wavy line pattern! It was not a dress for a maid of eleven winters though, it was a dress for a much older maid, ready to look for a partner. The thought of Karn and Simi looking at me like that would be so embarrassing, it filled me with horror. They treated me as a friend, as a sister even, not a painted maid with berries in her hair!

Sula prepared herself then. She did not have any body paint on her, apart from the white chalk outline on her eyes and shoulders. She was the Pure One. I looked like the wicked one! I asked her if there were any herbs I could take to stop my legs from trembling. By then, my body was going into uncontrollable shivering fits, as my nerves got the better of me. She nodded, and with a look of almost pity, brought a stone bowl with a dark liquid in it. A thought crossed my mind at that moment, that if I died, right then of poisoning at Sula's hands, it might not be such a bad thing. I drank the liquid, which was very nice and sweet with honey. I felt the liquid warming my whole body as I swallowed it. I felt so good after a few minutes, that I began to wonder what I was worrying about.

I heard a drum beat start in the distance, at the moot hall, and Sula wrapped my red fox fur around my shoulders and led me down the hill to the moot. I could hear the crowds roar in the great hall two huts before we got there. There were flaming torches at the entrance, and the drum began beating faster and faster as we approached. When we reached the door, Sula stood behind me with her hands on my shoulders, and waited. Then the drum beat changed to the familiar entrance rhythm, and she pushed me forward.

The chatter and laughter stopped immediately, and there was an audible gasp as they saw me walking to the high table, where the Shaman sat. My fox fur cloak only covered my shoulders, so my dress and painted arms and legs were there for all to see.

By that time, the mead had really taken effect, and I really did not care at all about the eyes of the men and women on me. The Shaman stood up and gestured for me to sit on my rug, and Sula on hers on the other side of him. I did not see anyone in the crowd that I knew, they all seemed to be traders at the front. Then I saw him. Karn was sitting in the midst of the traders, as he had shown himself to be so helpful during the boat rolling. His eyes met mine instantly, and I am sure I saw the glint of a tear in his eye, before he looked away. Maybe he did care for me after all, I thought. But not enough to risk the hunt for me.

I don't really remember much more about that night, apart from the looks the Shaman gave me, and the leering smiles one of the chief traders kept giving me. However, I do remember a fight breaking out after a trader tried to touch my shoulder. The rest of the night passed in a dreamlike haze. I woke before first light, still in the red dress, on my furs in the moot hall, with Sula tugging at me. She told me that it was nearly first light, and we had to go.

The settlement was deserted, as everyone had drunk large quantities of the traders' myrtle mead, or Masha, as they called it, and they were all sleeping it off. I rushed up the hill after Sula, anxious to get that horrid dress and the body paint off me before anyone saw me. The mead had worn off, and apart from a pain in my head, I was wide awake and aware of nothing but my very short skirt and painted legs! How could I have sat in front of the whole tribe wearing it? I thought. Please let no one I know see me before I get changed. I prayed, as we rushed up the hill.

The gods were friendly, however, as we reached Sula's hut without seeing anyone at all. She took some stones from the fire with two sticks, and put them in a bowl of water. Into that she poured a little wood ash from the fire, and mixed the foaming water well. After she took the stones out, she started to wash me with the moss net and the hot water. I must admit that it felt good, although I would have preferred to wash myself rather than have Sula do it. But what did it matter, I thought. I would still get clean. I put on my loincloth and my mother's shell dress and left the hut. I had no words to say to Sula, and she had no words for me.

People in the settlement were beginning to wake up by the time I entered my grandmother's hut. She was wide awake, and looked at me long and hard when I walked in.

'It looked like you had always sat on the high table last night, Mia. I would never have believed how you looked, if I had not seen it myself. You were every bit the priestess of the Earth Goddess the Shaman said you would become. I hope you do not forget your family when you are in such a position of power. You had every man in the settlement, and half the traders, in awe of your looks last night. Yes, you are destined for greatness indeed. Can I get you some hot fish for first food?' she asked meekly.

I realised then that as the effect of the mead had worn off, I was suddenly incredibly hungry. I hadn't eaten anything at the feast, I was just too drugged to notice the food. So I said loudly, 'Yes, I would like hot fish, and a sweet hot drink too!'

My grandmother was a little taken aback by my tone, and the request for a hot sweet drink. Such drinks were only given if someone was ill, but she did not say anything. She just busied herself getting it for me.

I finished my food, and was about to change into my normal clothes when my grandmother insisted that I must only wear my best dress now, to show my new status to the tribe. I picked up my fur and just walked out of the hut without turning back, and went down to the beach. There was a real chill in the air that morning, as there was a mist still hanging over the lower parts of the settlement. Thin streaks of smoke could be seen weaving their threads from the roof tops into the pale winter sky. I was glad of the fur around my shoulders and held it tightly about me as I walked. I was beginning to become accustomed to the courteous nods from people that I had known all my life. People that had usually either ignored me, or treated me with contempt until then.

The traders could not have come at a better time for me, as the influx of goods and more than ninety strangers in the settlement took everyone's mind off my new position in our small community. It was also the only time during the year that someone was not scraping skins near the drying racks.

As I reached the beach, I stood and watched the spectacle before me. Our shoreline was being transformed into a glorious market. People were rushing here and there with intense urgency, hoping to strike the best deal for the goods in the boats when the trading began. The twelve log boats, each the length of five men, were evenly lined up along the beach. They always spaced themselves apart like that, so that each boat could accommodate large crowds around it. The traders were setting up their stalls. Each of them had three or four roof sections, which they brought with them. They were made of worked wooden stakes that were pegged together, but not tightly, so when you pulled them out, a lattice frame of wood was formed. The frames were then staked into the sand outside the boat, bent over the boat, and staked in the sand on the other side. Onto these frames large skins were draped to form a sort of roof. The traders were putting up three or four of these frames over different parts of the boat that contained different produce. That way, twelve boats had been made into forty-eight or more stalls for trading. Mats made of rushes were then placed on the sand at each of the roof ends, to give the appearance to the islander of entering a hut in order to bargain.

The goods were being put on display, and it was a rule that none of the islanders must go too close, or begin to trade, until all the boats were ready. One time the traders, when ready, looked up at the eager shoreline crowds, and sat down and drank some mead before beginning to trade. That, I think, was a very clever thing to do: by the time the traders had drunk their fill, the crowd was at near fever pitch, ready to exchange goods with them.

I had always admired the traders. They were an exotic looking bunch of people, and they all seemed to have different coloured hair, although more had fair hair than any other colour. Some even had different coloured skins, and their clothes were wonderfully bright. I often wondered where they came from, and where their wives and children were. I didn't think they all lived in Scan Land, even though most of their produce came from there.

I decided to go up to my sand cliff to watch them, as I kept seeing glances and looks from the people standing around me. If I went up to the sand cliff, they could all have a good talk about seeing me last night at the moot. The very thought of the night before made me shudder. Yet as I sat down on the grass in my usual spot, I felt a strange kind of mood coming over me. Somehow, I felt that I had begun an adventure, and the traders, and the last few days, were just the beginning of it. The same adventure I would dream about, as I sat on the cliffs, whenever my life became either too hard or too boring to contemplate. I would sit there, dreaming of distant lands, and peoples I knew I had never met, yet at the same time somehow seemed to know.

I was just about feeling my old self again, when I noticed a movement in the distant crowd on the beach. It was Sula, and the Shaman! I could just hear the faint jingling of his staff bones on the wind from where I sat. He was making sure the tribe knew that, exciting though the traders were, they were not to trade until he had been given his tribute, and that it was satisfactory to him.

The traders were very careful not to offend a Shaman, even more than the chief of a tribe. In our world of changing seas and hard winters, the magic of the Shaman is all that holds some tribes together, and they knew that. Personally, I had always thought that too much was credited to the Shaman's magic, and not enough to the skills of the people.

There he was, standing with his staff on the open beach between the settlers and the traders, and Sula was weaving some dance in front of him. She seemed to have a special dance for every situation; the one she was doing then involved her feather cape. I had always quite liked that dance, and she wove about as if she was a bird, swooping and diving across the sands. I thought it had something to do with travelling away, as the birds do each year... it made me think about the dream I had in the forest. I felt at that moment that I was somehow not alone, that there was someone, or something, with me. I had often had that feeling, while sitting on the sand cliffs in the past, but the feeling this time was so much more real. Did the Shaman see something in me that I could not see in myself, after all? I thought. Was I really close to the Earth Goddess, as he said?

The rhythm of the drums was getting faster, which usually meant it was about to stop. The Shaman held his outstretched arms to the chief trader, who walked across the sand to him and handed him a little bag. The Shaman looked inside, and must have been content, because he then lifted his arms to the sky. Poor Sula had to lie at his feet with her face in the sand, while all that was going on. He shook his staff, and the stampede began. Like a herd of antelope with a lynx after them, the tribe ran to the boats.

The Shaman started looking round about him, and I realised he was probably looking for me. I ducked quickly beneath the dune grasses, and lay very still. I could feel a darkness about me suddenly, as if a cloud has crossed the sun, but when I looked up the sky was clear. I looked down at my chest as I crouched beneath the grasses, and caught sight of my crystal, glowing slightly beneath my dress. I took it out and held it tightly, and suddenly it was as if the sun had come out again, and the darkness had gone. My heart started to beat fast, and it was some minutes before I lifted my head up to see if the Shaman was still there. I could see him walking off the beach and going back into the settlement, with Sula following a few paces behind him. I lay back on the soft grass and waited until my heartbeats began to slow, as I looked up into the pale winter sky. I became aware of a flock of tiny white birds flying past me, and they seemed to circle the beach directly above me for some minutes before flying on. Slowly, I began to feel myself again, and after a while, I thought I would go down and join in the fun.

I decided it would be best if I went back to my grandmother's hut first, and collect my leather cape to put over my fur, as the air was still and it was very exposed on the beach. As I approached my home, I heard someone talking inside. It was my grandmother talking to Sedle, her daughter.

'Surely there is something to be done! Mia is too young for such a fate. I could not look at her last night. I felt so sad for her, she will never be able to go out without him, once she is the Pure One, and she so loves sitting on the sand cliffs when the sun colours. I know, I know it is such a great honour for our family, but do you have no feelings for the poor child?' Sedle urged.

'Of course I have feelings for the child! What sort of life will she have without this? It is a blessing from the gods themselves, you will see that I am right. She is made for this life. I have not that many winters left, and what will become of her then? She is too old to enter the women's huts. Your man will not protect her, and young Karn knows well enough not to get involved with such matters. It is best. I know she is young, but she is strong in body and mind, and she will make the best of her new life. It will not be all bad, her position in the tribe will be one of honour and respect. She will have a good life.'

There was a long silence after my grandmother had spoken, and I decided against getting the cloak, in case she would not allow me out again. I picked up a piece of soft leather that was hanging with the baskets behind the hut, and went back to the dunes. If the traders recognised me, they would not speak to me, as they would not want to offend the Shaman. So I thought, as there were such big crowds around the boats, that if I covered up my hair with the piece of leather they would probably not notice me. Oh, how I wished then that I had dark hair like everyone else. I used to think it was nice to be different. How wrong I was!

On the beach the first boat I came across was filled with furs, as soft and as thick as it was possible to imagine. What kind of beasts wore those coats in their lives? I wondered. There was much haggling going on, and heated arguments in a light-hearted way; that was our way of trading. The settlers pulled sledges of their wares up to and around the boats in the soft sand.

There was really only one trading commodity from Dogger Island, and that was decorated wood and bone wares. They were very much sought after in Scan Land, particularly the decorated wooden paddles for boats.

The creation of those goods was only due to the law that forbids women from leaving the island. Long ago, there were too many maids born on the island; far too many to ever have enough men to go around. Those maids grew into womanhood, and finding no men, chose to live together in huts of their own. With so much time on their hands, as they had no man or children to look after, they began to gain skills in decorating bone and wood. During the first years of the women's huts it was very hard for them, as they were not allowed to hunt or fish with the men. They lived on the shells that clung to the rocks, and the seaweeds around them. They became skilled at finding wild bee honey in the forests, and started making meads. They then had something to trade for their food, which meant they could spend more time developing their craft. At first, their decorations on wood were simple. But as time went on, they developed methods for colouring and inlaying the wood with tar, ochre, and resins from the pine trees. They would bake the ochre, to give colours from bright yellow to blood red. They mixed these with wax from the wild hives, and polished the wood, so that it shone like the sun on a still pool.

That was many generations ago, and their craft became famous throughout Scan Land. Each generation in our tribe there were surplus maids, so their families would send them to spend their lives in the women's huts. Some of the produce they made belonged to their family to trade with, and so this island, in the northern waters, had a product worth trading for.

Before that time there was little else that was tradeable, apart from the women's mead. The animals on Dogger were less varied than in Scan Land, and the flint on the Island was not special. The skills of the settlement wives were not very good, and the fish we ate and dried was nothing different. We didn't even have much amber on our shores, and what we did have was small and dull. That is why the law forbidding women from leaving the island became so strict, as the whole prosperity of the island depended on having surplus women to work in women's huts.

The women began to keep apart from the rest of the island people, except at festival times, when they would deliver their work to their families for trading. Eventually, they lived in their own settlement, on the edge of the mid-island cliff face. I did hear once that there were deep caves behind their huts, where they held strange rituals and such, but they were only rumours told around a camp fire. No maid goes into the caves unless she is going to stay there. Men are forbidden to enter their settlement too, which had only one entrance on a very steep path that clung to the side of the cliffs. It was said that the first women picked that place and chipped the path into the cliffs themselves, to protect themselves from men who might steal their mead, and virtue!

I often thought that I might end up there. My grandmother would have profited from my work for the rest of my life, and would not even have to feed me. But being the Shaman's Pure One would have been far better from her point of view. She would become an important woman again in the tribe, as the grandmother of a future priestess. The traders would give her goods, just to be allowed onto the island to trade. I wondered then if it had been her plan all along, that I should be given to the Shaman.

I decided to wander about the boats, and as I did the traders smiled and talked to me, just as they did to everyone else. I was just looking into the last boat, at some beautiful honey and green amber, when I saw Borg on the other side, looking at the same display. He looked straight past me, and I knew well enough not to let anyone see me looking at him. It was nearly midday food, and

I was to meet him in the crack in the old pine on the promontory. He walked away then, and the trader touched my shoulder. He was a tall man, with dark curly hair and a kind smile.

'Here, take a piece. You should have a pretty thing like this, sweetness,' he said gently.

He put a piece of amber into my hand, and I looked at him straight in the eyes. As our eyes met, I saw his eyes widen slightly, and I knew that he had recognised me from the night before.

'Go on, keep it, and think of Kemit when you look at it,' he whispered.

My eyes filled with tears then at his kindness, and I ran away, not looking back. I realised in doing so that I might attract attention to myself, so I slowed my pace and walked up to the fish fire at the other end of the beach.

At trading times, and festival times, the fishermen would hot smoke fish for the tribe and traders alike, to show their hospitality and prosperity. Little nut and honey sweets, bound with ground grass seeds, were cooked on hot stones and eaten with the fish. I was so hungry that I hoped I would be given a big bowl. I sat on a log by the fire, and took off my leather head wrap. Suddenly I was the object of everyone's attention again. The cook came over to me with a huge bowl of the best fish and big nut sweets. Someone else gave me a shell with some mead in it to drink too. Maybe that sort of life did have its advantages, I thought then, until I saw Karn and Lusa sitting very closely to each other on the log next to me. She looked over at me, and said something to Karn and giggled. He just smiled at her and gave me an embarrassed look, and turned away.

They say that it is only when you are in trouble that you find out who your real friends are. Who would have thought Borg would help me, and not Karn? I ate my food, and leaving the bowl on the log, wandered through the settlement to the cliff path to the north island lagoon, hoping nobody had noticed me.

The sounds of the settlers trading on the beach became fainter, as I walked along the cliff path towards the promontory between the settlement and the lagoon. With each step my heart sank, as I was walking away from the distraction of the traders to thoughts of my own immediate fate. The air was still, and although it was after midday food, it was still misty and very cold.

The crack in the pine tree was a place of fond memories, of my childhood games with Karn and Simi. We would pretend it was our home on some distant island, and it would be the base for most of our childhood adventures.

As I approached the tree, I started to wonder why Borg was helping me. It would mean immediate banishment, or worse, if he were caught helping me evade the Shaman. Did he want me for himself? I thought. Had I suddenly found myself exchanging one fate for another? If Borg wanted me for his maid, so be it, I decided. Even though I did not know the ways of a woman and a man, I knew if I was going to find out at my age, I would prefer it to be with Borg, as I had always liked him, in a way more than I would a friend. I decided that I must find out where I stood with him, before we made any plans. If nothing else, I had learned in all that had happened to me that I had to know what was expected of me.

I climbed the crag on the top of the cliff and crawled into the back entrance of the root room, under the great pine. I had not been there since the summer, but the pile of soft summer grass Karn and I had collected from the marsh was still there in the middle of the floor. There was no sign that Borg had been there before me. I sat there, with only the sound of the waves on the rocks far beneath the cliffs to break the all-embracing silence, and I started to cry. One tear rolled down my cheeks, then another. I made no sound. I did not sob, or wail. I just sat there in silence, allowing the warm tears to flow down my cheeks, thinking about the futility of my position. How could Borg help? He was almost an outcast in our settlement already. His little basket boat would break up if it entered the surf around the island. Even if he could get us over it and out to sea, he could not know the way through the currents.

I did not know how long it was before he came, but it must have been a while because I realised how cold I had become. I heard him climbing the crag at first, as he must have dislodged some stones, which cascaded over the cliffs down to the rocks below.

He whispered, 'Mia, are you there?'

'Yes,' I replied quietly.

'I had a job getting away, I can tell you. People kept coming up to me, and showing me what good bargains they had got for their paddles. As little else ever happens on this godforsaken island, it would have looked very odd if I were not to show an interest. Then Karn and Lusa tagged along with me. All they wanted to talk about was you. Well, at least Lusa did. Karn was, I think, reluctantly agreeing with her, just to make her happy. She was saying that you must have been working very hard to tempt the Shaman away from Sula. She even said you were some sort of devil, and that she had always thought there was something very odd about you! That, coming from one so self-centred, is a cheek, I must say. Karn has certainly gone down in my opinion though, to let her speak about you in that way. Then I had to speak to the traders, to plan your escape...'

He sat next to me and put his arm around me, as he could obviously see I had been crying.

'Hey, you are freezing! Come under my fur and get warm. You must not get ill with the journey you have ahead of you!' he said, and enclosed me in his cloak and held me tight, rubbing my hands and feet until they began to take on colour again.

Borg's body felt warm and strong, and I nestled my head up against his chest, like a child might do to her father. Except he was not my father, or my brother. Not even a strong friend, like Karn and Simi had been. Was he pretending to help me so he could take me away for himself? I thought again. Suddenly, I felt afraid again. My body stiffened, and I sat up. I had to know why he was helping me, so I stood up.

'Borg,' I said, in the most mature and steady voice that I could muster. 'Borg, why are you helping me? Do you want me to be your maid? I must know what you intend, so that I know what you expect of me.'

Borg looked up at me, with a startled expression on his face. He stared at me for some moments before he broke out into seemingly uncontrollable laughter. I felt very stupid then, standing there, trying to talk as I thought a woman would talk to a man, and all he could do was roll about the floor laughing! I started to get annoyed at his obvious rejection of me as his maid. I just did not understand! He suddenly sat up, and looked at me with such kindness, that if he had wanted to he could have kissed me then and there.

'Mia, Mia. What has happened to you in the last few days? You were such a strong maid. Now you talk to me as someone of many more winters might do. How could you think I was trying to take you from the Shaman, just to have you for myself? I want to help you get away from that evil devil, because your heart is too sweet and true to be crushed by his putrid flesh.'

He stood up and held my hands, and looked down into my bewildered eyes, saying, 'I will save you, have no doubt about that. He will not touch you, but you will have to risk great danger if you are to escape. I cannot promise we will make it. In fact, I cannot promise anything. But know this. I will die in the attempt, if need be.'

Then he put his arms around me and held me tight, and I felt safe, really safe, for the first time. He said, with a twinkle in his eye, 'Anyway, you really are not my type! I like a maid with a bit of meat on her, and you are as skinny as a rake!'

At that comment I pushed him away, and tried to look cross, but we both burst into laughter.

'Now to business!' he said. We sat down together again, and he began to tell me his plan.

'You know the trader, Kemit? The one that gave you the amber?'

'Yes, he had a kind face.'

'He is kindness itself! He is a good friend of mine, and he took a shine to you when he met you today. I told him about the Shaman's plans for you. He has no love of Shaman's himself, and would not like to see you become his slave. He is going to talk to his crew and let us know what they say. Even though it is his boat, he is a fair man, and would not put his crew at risk without asking them first.'

'How do you come to know him?' I asked. 'I don't remember him coming to the island with the last traders.'

'I have been going on trips on his boat for a few summers now! You know when I would say I was going to the forests, to collect wood for the skins? I was collecting wood at first, then Kemit started to pick me up at the north island lagoon, and took me on trips to Scan Land with him.'

Borg looked at my puzzled face, and realised that he had to tell me the whole story, or I would not understand. He had been trying to fish off the inlet to the lagoon, on a collection of logs he had cut down and tied together with bark string. Kemit was passing the island on his way from Brit Land to Scan Land, and noticed his craft and told his crew to stop, so that they could watch him. Apparently, the traders passed our island many times a year on route to Brit Land, but only stopped now and then to trade, to keep the prices of the decorated wares up.

Kemit thought Borg was either very stupid, or very brave, to take such a craft so close to the surf that surrounded the island. But after talking to him he decided he was brave, and at the same time good company. Kemit offered to take him to Scan Land with him, if he wanted. So Borg went with them, and after that they became good friends. Borg would be put ashore on the north island lagoon a moon later, and no one would know that he had been anywhere. He would then carry on collecting wood, as usual.

I thought for a moment, but could not help asking him, 'What I cannot understand is why you came back? There is nothing for you here. You were banned from the hunt, so why did you come back at all?'

A shadow then fell on his face, and he looked away from me and replied, 'One word will answer that question. Sula.'

I looked at him in astonishment, and asked, 'Sula? What have you got to do with Sula? I heard you were banned for pestering the youngest daughter of one of the hunters, not Sula!'

He did not answer at first, but looked out to sea between the roots of the pine for some time. He must have realised I was still waiting for an answer, so he told me his tale. Sula and he had grown up together, and as she approached the end of her fourteenth winter, they planned to announce their bond as man and woman to the tribe. One day Borg visited her home, and her mother said she had gone away. He knew that Sula would have told him if she had had any plans, so he asked all the people he thought that might know where she had gone. Most of them would not talk about her, but he came across Danz, who had always been kind to him as a boy. Danz took him to one side, and told him he must forget about Sula. She would never be his, as the Shaman had taken her as his Pure One trainee. Danz could see the shocked look on his face, took him home, and tried to distract him from anything reckless he might have been planning to do to get her back. Borg knew that once a maid became a trainee, she was never left alone until the ceremony of the Pure One, when she is given to the Shaman.

During the rest of that winter Borg tried to get word to her through her family, mostly through her younger sister, Gaddy. Gaddy did not want Sula to be with the Shaman any more that he did, and they had many secret meetings to talk about her. Gaddy would also pass messages on to her sister from him. When one of the elders found them together, he thought Borg was pestering the little maid, and so had him banned from the hunt.

'So now you see why I will not let that evil man ruin another young maid's life, simply to feed his useless magic.'

As he said that, he stood up and brushed the grasses from him, as if he was brushing away the painful memories of Sula from his mind.

'You must go now, or you will be missed. There is much to plan before the traders leave in two days' time. I will meet you here again tomorrow after midday food.'

'No, we had better not meet here,' I said. 'If Karn is walking openly with Lusa, he will probably start to bring her here. Meet me in the forest clearing where I met you yesterday. We can walk into the deep forest after we meet, and no one will see us.'

I stood up and brushed the grass from my cloak too, and Borg replied,

'Very well, until tomorrow then. Do not worry, Mia, we have a powerful friend in Kemit,' he said, and he watched me climb down the crag and onto the cliff path beneath the old tree trunk.

3. THE TRADERS' ANCESTOR DAY FESTIVAL

It took me some time to walk back to the settlement, as the leaves on the path were making it slippery and my soft leather shoes kept sliding. I could have taken my shoes off and walked down bare footed, but it was just too cold to do that. I thought as I walked, that we might see the first heavy frost of the near winter that night. Eventually I walked past the fish fire on the beach and Sedle called over to me, 'Mia, where have you been? Your grandmother has been very worried about you. You must not keep disappearing like this, now that you are to be a trainee soon. Do not look like that. I am not scolding you. Come, we will walk to your grandmother's hut together.'

She stretched out her hand to me and smiled, and we walked to my home in silence. It was an awkward silence too. Sedle and I had always had so much to say to each other, but not any more. Even the bond with my mother's sister seemed to have gone. Either that or she was afraid to tell me how she felt, as it might give me false hopes. My grandmother was sitting by a fierce fire when we entered the hut.

'Mia, where were you? You cannot behave as you have always done, not anymore. You belong to the Shaman, and if anything happens to you before he takes you, I will be banished,' she whispered, more to herself than to me. 'Look at the fire we can have now. He sent some men to bring a huge pile of wood over today, so you would not be cold. Sit down and I will make you a sweet drink again.'

She busied herself with the herbs and honey, and Sedle, without another word, just turned and left us.

I had to think of a reason why I kept disappearing, if I was going to have any hope of escape. I had also not thought of what would happen to my grandmother until then if I did escape. Yes, she would be surely banished immediately, and with the winter approaching she would not survive the first snows. So be it! I thought. I was amazed at my disregard for my grandmother's life, but then I had changed in the last few days. I had seen my grandmother's so called love for what it was. If she had any love for me she would not have been so overjoyed at her new settlement status at my expense! She had had her life, and I was not going to sacrifice mine to make hers more comfortable.

'Grandmother,' I said in a sombre voice.

She turned curiously and looked at me. 'Yes Mia, do you wish me to get you something?'

'No. I must explain to you the strange feelings I have been having during the last few days.'

I said this in a soft and hopefully mysterious voice. She came straight over to me then and looked at me like a child waiting for a story. I really could not believe how differently she was behaving towards me. From me being her hut slave, she was now my servant, and all in two days – incredible! I continued, after a pause for effect. 'It is ever since I breathed in the herbs with the Shaman yesterday that I have noticed the changes.'

Her eyes widened and she sat before me, completely transfixed. I continued, 'I feel the calling of the Earth Goddess already. The Shaman said I would one day be his priestess, after my time as the Pure One, but I feel the Earth Goddess calling me already. She speaks to me now, and tells me I must walk alone in the forest to be close to her. You remember yesterday, when I fell asleep in the leaves of the forest? It was then that she entered my body.'

My grandmother's face became white and she moved back away from me a little, as if she had suddenly become afraid of me,

'I see. Should I go and tell the Shaman this wonderful news?'

'No. The Goddess wants to tell him through me at the giving ceremony. You must not speak of this to anyone or the Goddess will be angry with you. I must spend as much time with her as I can, before I enter my training time, she has told me. So I will spend more time in the forest in the next full moon. I will come back each night before the sun takes colour though. Maybe you could make some food for me to take during the day?'

'Of course, of course. I will ask Sedle to make you some carrying food,' she said, keen to do her bit to help the Goddess.

'She must not be told though!' I said, with as much sternness as I could muster.

'Do not worry Mia, the Goddess's secrets are ours. Oh, what a glorious future you have ahead of you. Who would have thought it? The Shaman has very strong magic to see this in you. Mind you, when I saw you at the moot I did not recognise you, you looked so distant, and your eyes seemed to look far away from us all.'

If only she had known it was just the strong mead that had provided that distant faraway look! She had taken the bait totally, I thought. I should have no problem with her alerting everyone to my disappearances from now on. She really was despicable, yet somehow I began to feel sorry for her. I could see how feeble minded she really was. Fancy the goddess speaking to me. But as I thought that, I had a strange feeling, as though I had thought the same thing long ago, when I wasn't Mia. I cast those silly thoughts away, and sat down.

My grandmother's sweet drink seemed to become sweeter each time she made it. It was as if she thought that by adding more honey she would sweeten my mood. I drank it, and settled myself down in my furs to go to sleep. I do not remember actually going to sleep, but I had such dreams! Over and over again, I saw myself on my sand cliffs, running and running, not daring to glance over my shoulders at those that pursued me. The dream always ended with me finally looking back to see the whole tribe chasing me. All the familiar faces I had grown up with merging into one face. The face of the Shaman. As I recognised him, I would stumble and fall. I always seemed to fall for a long time, then suddenly I would be picked up by the great claws of a bird, and gently put down on high ground. Then I would wake.

I heard the crackle of the fire, and saw my grandmother staring into it. I do not know what part of the night it was, but it must have been very late. That time in the middle of the night, which as a child I dreaded. I don't know why, but it was a time of devils and fears. It was usually long after I had gone to sleep, but also long before first light. It was the darkest hour, and one I did not want to be awake in. I was so very tired, but after having the same nightmare twice I was reluctant to fall asleep at all. What would become of me? Then those thoughts suddenly changed to a feeling of peace, as I thought of Borg and his trader friend, and I knew I would be all right. I must have drifted off to sleep again.

When I awoke it must have been quite late, as the sounds from outside the hut were loud and filled with much activity. I could hear people running and shouting, and wondered what was going on. As I stirred, my grandmother noticed and said, 'You must have been very tired, my dear, to sleep so late. I will prepare some food for you.'

'No thank you, Grandmother, just water please. What is all the noise about?' I asked.

'Just water? Is that enough for you?'

At which I just stared at her intently, then she replied meekly, 'Of course, if you wish just water that is fine. There is much excitement, as the traders have said they will entertain the whole tribe in the sand dunes tonight! Lord knows why, they have never offered to do such a thing before. It is apparently some sort of religious day for them, and they are to celebrate it here with us. Everybody is off to trade today as they say they will leave tomorrow, after their festival.'

As she told me the news I looked away, to hide my shock that they were leaving a day early. How was I going to wait until after midday food before I could meet Borg again? I dressed, and after collecting my fur at the door, walked out of the hut without a backward glance. I could not believe my grandmother had fallen for my Earth Goddess story so easily. I decided to look at the traders' stalls again, to pass the time away till I could meet with Borg. As I passed the boats full of furs, fine plant cloth and stone axes, I noticed a stall that I had missed at the end of a fur boat. There was quite a crowd looking into the end of the boat, so I pushed my way past to see what they were bartering. As the settlers noticed it was me that was pushing past them, their looks changed from annoyance to fear, as no one would want to offend the next Pure

One. Before I knew it, I was the only person at the stall, as the crowd had quickly dispersed.

The trader looked at me and said, 'You certainly have had some effect on my trade, sweetness. Who are you? Some elder's daughter, or maybe the chief's?'

I looked back at him and wondered how he did not recognise me, as I had not covered my hair, and he must have seen me at the moot the night before.

'You do not know me?' I asked.

'Sorry, should I? I apologise if I have offended you,' he said politely.

'No, it is fine that you do not know me. It is, in fact, very fine. My name is Mia,' I said.

'I am proud to meet you, Mia of the beautiful hair. My name is Sern, and I come from a settlement in Scan Land called Tybrind Vig.'

He stood tall and straight when he said the name of his home, so I knew it must be a very important place. 'Did you not go to the moot the last night?' I asked.

'No sweetness, I had to guard the boats with my crew, but I heard it was a wild night that they all had. Your Shaman has some very beautiful women, I heard too. Especially one dressed in red, my friends told me.'

As soon as he uttered those words he looked at my face, and I could see he had worked out who I was. His face then became stern, but still somehow kind. He asked in a quiet voice, 'That was you, was it not? Just how many winters do you have? No, I am sorry, I offend you. Please forgive my stupid bundling behaviour.'

I felt I should have become fearful, but I knew I was safe with that man. I somehow instinctively knew I could trust him.

'No, you have not offended me. I am glad you are at least speaking to me. I have eleven winters now.'

At hearing that his face became so red that I thought he had become suddenly ill, until I realised he was trying to control his anger.

'Eleven winters? I have a daughter back home at Tybrind Vig of eleven winters. How is it that you can be given to the Shaman so young? In my settlement a maid goes of her own free will, but not until she has at least fourteen winters or more. What does your family say about this life you have chosen?'

His voice showed genuine interest and concern, and I told him briefly what had happened, and how pleased my grandmother was, but how devastated I was about it all.

'I do not want to offend you again, sweetness, but I do not like this grandmother of yours already!'

A small group of people were moving down the boat again towards us. Then I said quickly, as I picked up one of his tooth pendants, trying to look as if I was bartering for it, 'Please do not speak of this in front of these people, or the Shaman will find out and I will be punished.'

He looked at me keenly and nodded.

'Yes, a fine fox tooth you have there!' he bellowed, for the benefit of the crowd. 'Please take it as a gift for the trainee of the Pure One.'

At those words, a murmur of approval travelled through the crowd. To give a gift to the Shaman's maids was a symbolic gift to the settlement as a whole.

I moved away and began to walk across to the next boat. As I looked back, the trader was handing out his wares for inspection; but as he talked to a settler he looked back at me, and in that split second I knew I had made a friend in Sern.

I had no interest in the other boats, so fingering the fox tooth pendant in my hand I walked towards the fish fire, to sit down and warm myself. There were not many sitting on the logs around the fire, as most people were trading desperately now that news of the traders' departure tomorrow was known. I was immediately given sweet nut cakes and left to myself. Various people wandered to the fire for food and warmth and left again.

After glancing at me, most stayed on the other side of the fire though. I had begun to get used to that kind of behaviour from my tribe, and in a way I preferred it to them sitting near me and muttering. I was looking at the fox tooth, and thinking that if I made some fine bark twine I could hang it around my neck with the amber pendant Kemit had given me the day before, and my mother's crystal that I always wore.

The crystal was in fact the only thing I had of hers. When I was small and my grandmother had been particularly cruel to me, holding it had always somehow given me strength. I would hold it tight and close my eyes, and feel a warmth travel through my body, and whatever I was upset about suddenly did not seem so important. I had held it tight a lot during those days, and doubt I would have slept at all if I had not had it. I wished my mother was with me then more than I ever had done. I wished I had known her just a little, too. I stopped myself thinking those thoughts as I was suddenly feeling very lonely, and I knew I needed to be strong.

So I took my damp shoes off and warmed them by the fire, nibbled my sweet nut cakes and was at peace again for a while. That peace was almost immediately shattered at the sight of Sula walking towards me across the sand. She looked so beautiful, wrapped in her white fox fur cloak, and it was not surprising that Borg had fallen in love with her. I did not resent her as much as I had after he had told me their story, even though the years she had spent with the Shaman had turned her into his woman. Still, I did not hate her quite so much anymore either.

'Mia, have you heard of the festival tonight?' she asked as she approached. Without waiting for a reply from me she continued, 'You will be needed again to sit next to the Shaman on the high table. You know now what is expected of you, the same as for the moot the other night.'

She looked into my eyes, and saw the horror in them at the thought of being paraded in front of the tribe again, and said impatiently, 'It is no use Mia, it has to be. You will get used to it, until it means nothing to you. You will soon find that all you wish in life is to please the Shaman. It is a life of great honour and fulfilment, and I will leave it with great sadness next spring. I have grown to love to please him, and you will too. Do not worry, I will prepare the sweet mead again for you, and you will not care about the glances of the crowd.'

I realised that it was no use objecting. I knew I must not let Sula think I wanted to escape my fate, or I would be imprisoned until the giving ceremony in the spring. At the same time I must not suddenly seem too keen either.

'Do I have to be prepared now? I wanted to watch the women from the cliff settlement trade this afternoon,' I said.

'No, you do not need to come to me until the sun is starting to colour. You know what I have to do to prepare you. If you are still, it will not take too long to paint and dress you. I will come for you here when the sun colours. You must be here though, Mia. I am going to trust you. We are going to have to live together soon, to start your training, so we must try to get along.'

I smiled at her and replied meekly, 'I will be here, Sula, I promise.'

At that she turned and walked away, without looking back.

The trading of the cliff women was a wonderful spectacle to watch. The traders always kept their best and most expensive wares for the cliff women, as the cliff women kept their best wares back from their families too. That was the work that they did for themselves, to trade for their own furs and cloth and amber. Plant cloth was the most expensive item the traders usually had, as it took such a long process, getting the thread from the stinging plants before it could be woven into the finest softest pure white cloth. It was a statement of their wealth that all the cliff women wore this cloth dyed in many shades of gold with the marsh herbs they collected. It was this same cloth, kept pure white, which Sula wore at all times. Each woman gave some of her decorated bone and wood to her family in exchange for meat and fish. Their leader always kept the best of everyone's work that year, to trade directly with the boat traders for their finest goods. The traders would stop dealing with the rest of the tribe then, and prepare their best goods to display to the leader of the cliff women.

I decide to walk down to the beach and sit on the promontory side of the sand cliffs, from where I could get a good view of the women when they arrived. It would also be a good place to leave the dunes and meet Borg in the forest, as I would be sitting on the edge of the forest path and no would see me go from there. I had not seen Borg that morning, but I was sure he would keep to our arrangement.

I could just hear the swan bone whistles in the distance, so I knew the women must be entering the edge of the settlement. I loved the sound of their whistles, as they played such haunting tunes on them. The whistles became louder, and all other settlement noise immediately stopped. The settlers had to stand on the spot where they first heard the whistle, and wait in silence for the women to pass. This was a very old tradition within our tribe. In stories, as a child, I was told that if anyone moved or made a noise as the women passed, they would not live to see another winter. Those kind of stories were still believed by the settlers, so just in case it was true, people stood still until all the women had passed.

The cliff women reached the beach, and looked beautiful in their long dresses of gold and pale green cloth. They also always tied bands of different coloured cloths about their hair, and almost looked as bright and exotic as the traders, yet in a more mystical sort of way. Reed bundles were laid down in straight lines for the seven head women and their leader to sit on. The other women with the whistles stood at each end of the rows and stopped playing. Maids started to bring out the trade goods, and after rolling out golden cloths to cover the sand just in front of the head women, they started to arrange and display their work. Paddles and bone tools for the main part, but also strings and strings of the most beautiful beads inlaid with resins, ochre and tar. I could not of course see them clearly, but I had seen them before and always wondered how they made them.

The traders were sitting on a row of logs in front of the women, and in front of them their crews displayed their finest thickest furs, axes, and amber goods. They also had some very, very bright cloth decorated with coloured threads that rippled in the wind as they were carried. I thought as I watched that it could not have been plant cloth, because it moved like cobwebs. It had not come from Scan Land, I was sure.

I watched for another few minutes and then turned and headed up the path to the forest clearing. That time Borg was waiting for me. As soon as he saw me he gestured for me to follow him into the thicket. He was obviously taking care that we were not noticed by anyone passing by. Once we were out of sight of the clearing he held me at arm's length, and looking me keenly in the eyes said,

'Are you sure you were not followed?'

I told him about the story of the Earth Goddess that I had told my grandmother, and he broke out into a broad grin, saying, 'We may be needing the help of the Earth Goddess before we are finished. It was very clever of you though, she would not dare ask about your movements any more, as she thinks she is privy to some magical secret. Well now, unfortunately, or fortunately for us, the traders are leaving tomorrow as you know, so we are to leave tonight!'

I could not believe my ears! Had he arranged for us to be taken away by the traders? Surely not, I thought. They desire their trade with the cliff women's goods too much to risk annoying the islanders, did they not? Then I asked, incredulously, 'How can that be? They would never offend the Shaman, or they would lose the island trade.'

'Mainly, because most of them know nothing about it! You have made two very good friends in Kemit and Sern. Especially Sern, for he is the leader of the trader guards, and without his help we would have little hope of escape. What did you say to him today, for he is ready to take up arms to defend you to the death?'

'I do not know, but I think it was because he has a daughter at home my age.'

'Ahh, that accounts for it. No man of honour would give their daughter up to a man like the Shaman at your age. Anyway, whatever you did, it was brilliant! He will help us to leave after the festival tonight!'

Borg's voice was excited at the prospect of a daring adventure ahead, I could see. Then I realised something, and asked, 'What do you mean we will escape? Are you coming too? What of your love for Sula?'

'Sula is lost forever. She is now the Shaman's, and soon to be handed over to some young hunter as a prize. I could not bear to see her walk about the settlement with the other women every day. At least when she was with the Shaman she was kept away from the tribe, except for ceremonies. No, the plan is set. We will escape together.'

In his voice I could detect a great sadness too, as though he had come to himself in some way, in deciding to leave. Then I realised I was to be at the festival that night, in full view of everyone. How could I leave with Sula watching me so carefully?

'Sula told me that I am required on the high table again tonight, next to the Shaman. How am I going to get away from Sula after the festival? She watches me all the time when I am near the Shaman, and she will want to take me back to her hut after, to clean the paint off me.'

'I will think of something to distract Sula, and anyway, most people will be drunk and will fall asleep till morning where they sit. Sern will not be at the festival, as it is his job to guard the boats with his men, and Kemit and his men will not drink, so as to be able to help you to his boat.'

Then I remembered the drink that Sula was going to give me, and I said, 'Drink! The drink! How can I take the mead Sula will give me, if I am to escape while everyone sleeps? I will be asleep too.'

'Well, just do not drink it. Say you do not want it. Sula will only give it to you if you ask her,' he said, not realising what taking that drink meant to me.

'I must drink it. I could not sit there letting everyone look at my painted legs and short skirt without taking that drink. Please Borg, there must be another way…'

His face was suddenly grave and sad, when he saw the look of dismay in my eyes. I knew he must be remembering the dress the first time Sula wore it, at the ceremony when the Shaman first nominated her. He knew it was the dress a woman would wear, not a young maid like me.

'Mia, I know what you must wear. Sula wore it once, and I know drinking the mead will make it bearable, but you must not drink it.' His voice was kind yet urgent. 'There is no way we could get you away in the boat if you were drugged. You will need all your wits about you when the boat hits the surf. You will have to hold on tight, and you will have to lean if the boatman tells you to. If you are drugged or asleep you could be washed overboard, and you would not survive if you did. You must be strong and brave, and tell Sula you do not need it. It is just for one night, and if we are successful, you need never see any of those people again!'

He held my hand tight as he spoke, and I knew he was right. I would just have to keep that thought in mind, and hope I did not tremble too much. Then Borg untied something from around his neck and handed it to me.

'Here, take this,' he said. 'It is my most precious possession. Hold it tight in your hand tonight with your mother's crystal, and think of freedom, and good friends, and distant lands.'

I looked down at my hand, and saw the most beautiful piece of stone I had ever seen. It was the colour of the richest blue of the night sky, and it was flecked with tiny pieces of sunshine all over it. It was like a piece of sky covered with stars.

'It is beautiful. What is it, and where did you get it?' I asked gently.

'I bought it when I visited Scan Land with Kemit. They call it Lapis, and it comes from the distant dry lands. Take it and keep it safe. It will give you strength as it has to me, over the long winters without Sula.'

'Thank you, Borg. What did I do to have such a good friend? I will not have the drink. This will help me, I know it. But it is getting late and I must meet Sula at the fish fire. Tell me what is going to happen, and what I have to do.'

'No. It is better that you do not know, do not worry. I will come and get you when it is time. Now go quickly, Sula must suspect nothing. Till tonight, my brave little one.'

He got up, walked in the other direction from the clearing and was gone. I walked quickly to the clearing and down the path, taking care not to fall on the slippery ground.

I arrived at the fire just as Sula was walking onto the beach towards me. She saw me looking at her, and gestured for me to come. I followed her without a word, up the hill to her hut at the end of the settlement.

Once inside her hut, she said, 'Sit down while I prepare the herbs to bathe you with. I have some of the mead ready for you to drink before we go, too. So there is nothing for you to fear.'

Sula was talking to me then as if we had been friends all our lives. What a difference a day can make, I thought. She had obviously come to terms with me taking her place.

'I... I think I will not be needing the mead tonight, Sula.'

I tried to make my voice sound natural, but my stomach was turning at the thought of going through the crowds, all painted again. Sula stopped what she was doing and came over to me. She had a look of real concern on her face, and said, 'Mia, you will need the mead, believe me. Tonight is the traders' festival, and who knows what favours they might ask for. The Shaman will not interfere with the religious traditions of other peoples. They might want to parade you before them, and maybe even touch you.'

The last few words she said with almost a whisper. My stomach was really turning over then. What did she mean, touch me? It was no use though, I would have to take the chance, and if it came to it, endure what I had to endure. I could understand what Borg had said about the surf. I could drown if I was drugged.

I clasped my piece of night sky in my hand hard, and replied, in as mystical a sounding voice as I could, looking her straight in the eyes, 'I have the Earth Goddess with me now. She will give me her strength for the festival. I belong to her now, as well as the Shaman. It is her will that I have all my senses clear tonight.'

Her eyes widened and her mouth opened, and she suddenly looked like just a simple maid instead of the Pure One.

'You have spoken to the Earth Goddess?' she whispered.

'Yes, in the forest. It is she that gave me hair the colour of near winter leaves, and it is she that speaks to me now I am to be trained in the ceremonies,' I stated, in as haughty a voice as I could.

'I have never talked to the Goddess. The Shaman always told me what she wanted me to do for him. You are truly blessed. It is an honour to train an Earth Goddess priestess in her first ceremonies. Do you think you might need an initiate? Maybe I could stay with you when you become the Pure One, and serve you?'

Sula was obviously seeing a way out of being given to a hunter, I thought. Her desire to please me might be useful tonight though. Sula busied herself with the herb water to wash me with, and began to cleanse me for the body paint. My mind was so full of the night ahead that in no time at all she had painted me and sprinkled on the ochre. I just had to wait for Sula to dress, and we were on our way to the dunes. I did not seem to care about the looks of the people as we passed. I just held my piece of night sky hard and walked slowly behind Sula till we reached the edge of the dunes. The Shaman was waiting for us when we got there. His eyes lingered on my painted legs, and he looked up into my eyes and smiled. I felt that I must have cut my hand on the rock, I was clenching it so tightly.

'Mia, you are very beautiful. Come, let me lead you to the festival.'

He held out his hand and clasped mine in his, leading me into the dunes. He was not supposed to touch me in public yet, my mind screamed to itself! One night. It was only one more night, I thought. I could endure anything, anything, for one night. I said those words to myself over and over again as we walked. He held me tight with his rough fingers, and he kept glancing at my legs as I walked beside him.

We entered a clearing the traders had made for their festival, and went to the seats of honour halfway up one of the dunes. In the middle of the clearing was a strange wooden statue, shaped like a headless body, with arms stretching up to the sky. The body of the statue was draped in the most beautiful cloth I had ever seen. It shone in the last rays of the sun like a rainbow of colours. It had no colour, yet it was all colours. It was so fine that the light breeze in the clearing made it ripple and dance about the feet of the figure. The traders were all sitting opposite us in their finest clothes, and our tribe filled the space on the left. The crew of the boats were opposite them, on the right.

They had all been waiting for the Shaman to arrive before they could begin. I thought everyone was there, until I heard the swan bone whistles in the distance. The cliff women were coming! That was unheard of, I knew. They never joined in the ceremonies of the settlement any more, for they had their own rites in the cliff caves. But it was not one of our ceremonies, it was the traders' ceremony. Maybe they had arranged to come during the trading. The Shaman got up and walked across to them, as they sat next to the traders.

'Great Lady Vrana, I would be honoured if you would sit with me for this festival.' He addressed the head lady in a very stiff and formal way.

'Thank you, but no. I wish to sit with these good people, and share in their festival of celebration. We find this festival has many similarities with one of our own, and we plan to join with them in their worship.'

The Shaman took a step back, and looked visibly amazed. He knew the cliff women had their own special religion, but how it could have similarities to the traders' he could not fathom. He did not like it at all, as the women were openly challenging his power as the island shaman. He walked back to Sula and me with a face full of anger. The women had settled themselves down with the traders, and the drums began to beat.

A trader that I had not noticed at the edge of the clearing was walking to the head trader, Tashk, with something in his hands. Tashk took it, and walked with the drum beat to the statue in the centre of the clearing. He took the cloth from the object, and our tribe gasped when they saw a human skull in his hands. He held the skull high, chanting some words in a strange tongue, and placed the skull on the headless body. At that moment the drum beat stopped. We all looked on, in awe and silence, as the statue, with its skull head, was illuminated by the dozens of flares around the clearing. The eye sockets had been filled in with clay, and two shells had been pushed into them to form eyes like slits.

Suddenly the drumbeat began again. The cliff women formed a circle with some of the traders and danced around the figure to the beat. I could see the Shaman was becoming more and more angry at this scene. He did not mind the traders performing their rites, but he was not going to stand by while islanders joined in with them without his permission. He had to do something to show his power, but it was clear the situation was so unexpected that he had not thought of what to do. The dancing became more and more frenzied, until the traders and cliff women broke into couples and ran to their seats, to eat some food and drink some mead.

The mead was flowing freely by then, and so our tribe, the traders and cliff women were becoming less inhibited. The Shaman stood up and shook his staff and gestured to Sula, who immediately got up and slowly walked out into the centre of the clearing. She began to dance the fertility dance of the Earth Goddess, and within a few moments everyone became transfixed with her flowing movements as she swept around the edge of the crowd. Even Tashk had stopped talking and was watching her, mesmerised. The Shaman had gained control again, and he was going to take full advantage of it. Sula by that time was moving along the row of trader chiefs, until she was almost up to Tashk. She suddenly stopped in front of him, fell to the floor, and writhed about like a snake in the sand. The trader was spellbound by the moves of the pure yet beguiling beauty of Sula. He made a move to touch her, but immediately the Shaman stamped his staff.

At the sound of the bones, Sula instantly ran to the Shaman and lay prostrate at his feet. Tashk shot an angry glance at the Shaman for seemingly offering Sula to him, and then taking her away. The Shaman turned and looked at me, and smiled to himself. He could not give Sula to the trader because she was the Pure One and was to be touched by no one but him. I, however was not yet a Pure One. In fact, I was not yet a trainee. Therefore he would break no laws in using me to gain favour. The drums had stopped and a tense silence cut the air of the gathering like a blade. The traders were starting to mumble in anger at the insult to their chief by the Shaman.

The Shaman walked over to me, leaving Sula on the floor, and took my hand tightly, pulling me to my feet. He jerked me so quickly that my red fur cloak fell from my shoulder, and I stood there trembling as I realised what was about to happen. Without the fur for some protection, my short skirt and painted legs and arms were then gazed upon by hundreds of eyes.

'Come Mia, you can entertain this good man with your sweetness and Goddess magic. Come walk with me, so I can give you to him,' he whispered.

Goddess magic? What was he talking about? What was I supposed to do? What magic did he think I had? I thought desperately. As we walked across the clearing, I was aware of the looks the cliff women were giving me. I glanced up at Vrana, the head woman, and saw compassion in her eyes as she became aware of just how young I was. I tried to move in a calm and strong way, but due to the trembling of my knees I kept half stumbling. The Shaman's grip was so tight, I am sure if I had not kept pace with him, he would have just dragged me over the sand as he walked. We reached Tashk eventually, who was now standing with his hands on his hips, and the Shaman pushed me forward until I fell on my knees at his feet.

The crowd began to roar in approval, and the music started up again. The women and men began dancing around the statue in the clearing. The Shaman turned around and walked back to his seat, just leaving me there. It seemed like an eternity that I sat there with my head bowed, and could see nothing but the huge feet before me. Tashk then put his hand on my shoulder and I tried very hard not to flinch, but I jumped so much he took his hand off my shoulder again.

Vrana then said quietly, 'Look at her, she is like a frightened deer! How could he hand you this child, and expect her to entertain you with magic? The

Shaman has lost his mind if he thinks this little creature has anything to do with the Earth Goddess.'

I did not move as she said those words, but somewhere within my very being I knew she was wrong about me. I did have the Earth Goddess within me, and she was beginning to awaken.

Vrana continued, 'The Shaman does not know the kind of man you are, as I do, Tashk! He thinks you will believe anything he says.'

'I know he does! I hate these shamans. Every settlement and island has them, and I have yet to find an honourable man in them. We must keep them happy or we will lose the trade, but this an affront to my intelligence. This poor creature is no more an earth goddess than my first crewman. Eh, Graff?' He shouted to a rough looking man to his right. With a toothless grin Graff nodded, and drank from his mead bag till it dribbled down his face.

I could not believe it, but I was getting annoyed at what they were saying. I stood up suddenly, put my hands on my hips and said confidently,

'The Goddess is always with me and always will be!'

Tashk turned to me with a look of shock, as if an antelope had just turned and faced the leopard. After a few moments he burst out laughing, and replied courteously, 'Well said, my little Goddess, well said! What do we simple traders know about such things anyway?'

I started to get irritated, sensing he was being sarcastic. When he saw that, he continued, 'No, really, forgive me. Come sit next to me and Lady Vrana, and have some food.'

I hesitated, and then sat down between them. I felt very uncomfortable until Vrana whispered to me, 'You are Mia, are you not? Your father was a Brit Lander, and your mother died at your birth. I often wondered why your grandmother did not bring you to us when you were born. Maybe she just wanted to keep you for herself. Yet I heard she is happy enough to give you to the Shaman. He is cleverer than I thought, to have acquired a real maid of the Earth Goddess. For there are many that say they are, but few really walk with her. I sense the light in you now, and know that she is with you. You are truly blessed. You are safe here from the Shaman, for tonight at least. Unfortunately, you must go back to him tomorrow, because he has announced your fate, and nothing can change that. What truly wonderful hair you have. It is no wonder you are so prized by him. Here, have some mead. It will help to calm your nerves.'

'Thank you, but no. I would like some water and fish though,' I whispered.

'Very well. You are obviously stronger than you look. Take my cloak and cover yourself. Your ordeal is over for tonight, at least. Tashk will make no demands on you. I cannot say what will happen to you tomorrow though, when the traders have gone. I wish I could take you with me, back to our home, but I have only a limited amount of power here.'

Vrana gestured to one of her maidens to bring me food and water, and I spent a pleasant few hours, listening to them talking and watching the settlers become more and more intoxicated. One moment couples were dancing with each other, the next thing they would disappear over the dunes into the darkness and not return. Many were eating and drinking in the centre of the clearing, which was by then filled with people. Vrana got up and walked over to one of her women, and I was left alone for the first time with Tashk. I became nervous again as he turned and looked at me, then he spoke. His voice was soft and kind, like Sern's and Kemit's. I knew I had nothing to fear from him, but I felt I had to say something, to break the silence.

'Whose was the skull that you placed on the statue?'

He looked at me and my serious face, trying to talk to him in such a grown up way, and replied, 'It is the head of one of our ancestors from our homeland. We honour him for his knowledge of the sea that enables us to trade with distant lands like these.'

I thought for a moment, then replied, 'Distant lands like these? It is strange to think Dogger Island is a distant land to anyone.'

At that he roared with laughter, so much that the people on both sides of us started to laugh too. I really did not think it was that funny. As they laughed I looked over the dune tops and could see the sea in full tide, and remembered that my night was just beginning. It was a calm night, and many of the people were asleep already in the dunes. How was I to leave Tashk and Vrana without arousing suspicion?

My opportunity soon arose, when I was least expecting it. Tashk and Vrana wanted to be alone together, they said, but that would not be permitted by Vrana's laws. They decided that if I left the festival with them and entered the dunes, it would look as though Tashk had decided to go for a walk with Vrana and me. They asked if I would mind helping keep up the pretence, and I willingly agreed. It could not have worked out better for me. I could go over the dunes in darkness with Tashk and Vrana, and no one would dare follow us in case they offended them. After a few words to her servant, Vrana led Tashk and me over the dunes, into darkness, and out of sight. When we were some distance from the feasting, they asked if I would sit and wait for their return. I said I would probably sleep. Tashk gave me his fur to cover me, and they left me alone. I waited for as long as I could make myself, then I ran onto the beach, where I found Kemit, Sern, and Borg, talking avidly. They did not know it was me at first, as I was wrapped in Tashk's fur. Then I said, 'Here I am. Is everything all right?'

They all spun round and smiled, and Kemit said, 'It is now! How did you get away? Don't answer me. We must go, we have only another half hour of the tide and then it would have been too late!'

I walked over to Kemit's boat and climbed in. It was deeper than I thought. Huge, in fact. I sat down where Borg told me to, and waited.

Kemit put his hand on Sern's shoulders and asked, 'Are you sure about this, Sern?'

A broad smile filled Sern's face, and he replied, 'Sure as I have ever been about any venture in my entire life. You must get that poor child away. I can take Tashk's anger, we have had many years and adventures together. He will have to show his anger for the benefit of the Shaman, but I think she is worth it. I could not look into my daughter's eyes again, if I did not help! Be gone Kemit! Your men are with you. Be Gone!'

At that the two men hugged each other, and within seconds the crew were in the boat with us and we were floating out to sea. The crew began to paddle and I suddenly began to be fearful, as I heard the roar of the surf as the tide pulled the sea over the reef that surrounded the island. A member of the crew came over to me and said, 'Tie this around your waist, and I will tie you onto the goods' hooks. Do not fear. We have done this more times than we can remember, and Kemit's boat is the best in the trading fleet!'

At those words the two men that were paddling in front of me smiled, and turned back to their job. They were such good people, and they were risking their lives, taking the boat out at high tide for me. The sheer humanity of it made me cry suddenly, but my tears fell unnoticed as the sea spray splashed in my face. Borg was up ahead in the boat, paddling fiercely. They all were. The noise of the surf then became deafening, and the boat rolled as Kemit shouted some orders to his men. I began to think that wet and deafening hell was going to be the last few minutes of my life, when suddenly the boat became still, and the sea was calm. We were though the surf! We were leaving the island!

The men paddled even faster then, until the boat was out of sight of the beach and around the promontory by the north island lagoon. I looked back at the shore, and I could just see the twinkling lights of the flares around the feast in the dunes. I imagined Tashk and Vrana, showing their love for each other, as so many of my tribe were doing. In my mind's eye I could see Sula, sitting on her white fur rug next to the Shaman, waiting for another night of ceremonies to end. Somewhere my grandmother would be drinking mead with her friends, and dreaming of the bright privileged future she was going to have, in exchange for my freedom.

Karn and Simi were probably sitting with Lusa and Mayni, and thinking of their first adult festivals next winter, when they would become men and women and go into the darkness of the dunes together. Lastly, I thought of my sand cliffs and the dreams I used to have of one day leaving the island, just as my mother had done before me. But my mother never succeeded, and she gave her life in the trying.

As the rhythmic sound of the paddles, cutting through the calm sea, filled my ears, I drifted off to sleep. I drifted into a long, peaceful sleep, with the knowledge that whether the voyage reached land or not, I had left the island. I felt I was in that distant speck of sea that I used to gaze at from the sand cliffs as the sun went down. Whether or not I was in reality, I felt truly free for the first time in my short life.

4. ESCAPE FROM DOGGER ISLAND

I woke to the sound of water gently lapping the sides of the log boat. As I slowly became aware of my surroundings, I realised that I had entered a whole new world. I had left Dogger Island! I was at sea in a log boat! I looked over the sides of the boat and I could see nothing but thick mist. The mist was white and cold, so I knew it must have been well past first light. As I moved I found that my body was stiff with the cold. Then as I stirred, a hand was placed tightly over my mouth. I tried to pull it away and struggle, until I saw Borg looking straight into my eyes. His look was enough to make me realise that we were in some sort of danger. He put his finger to his mouth, to tell me to be still and silent. As I looked down the boat at the crew, I could see they were all just sitting there in silence too, looking out into the thick mist that surrounded us.

It was an eerie scene to herald in my first day in a new world. What was happening? Why were we all afraid to move, or speak? My questions were answered a few minutes later, when I heard a voice calling from the mist itself.

'Kemit! It is no use. Tashk has vowed to take her back! This is so stupid! How did you think you would get away with it? Kemit! Kemit! I know you are not far.'

The voice sounded as though it was only feet away. In the space of a few moments I had rejoiced at my new freedom, just to have my hopes of escape stolen from me. My eyes met Borg's, and his look made me realise we were all in great danger. As the water lapped against the sides of the boat I could hear the movement of paddles all around. We were surrounded. How could they have caught up with us so quickly? Just at that moment, I saw Kemit signal to one of the crew to begin to paddle slowly. We began to move, very, very slowly. Only four men were paddling, the rest were just sitting in silence, like Borg and I. I could hear voices in the mist, very clearly then.

'This is a fine state of affairs, to end Ancestor Day. Who would have thought it of Kemit?' the first voice said.

'I know, I know. He always seemed a straight and fair man to me. How did he think he was going to get away with it? He must have known Tashk would have followed him, to make an example of him and his poor crew,' the other voice then said.

'Maybe that little red haired vixen was just too much for him to resist!'

'Hmm, maybe. The old devil!' the second voice replied.

They both laughed and laughed, and in the mist, the sound of their laughter seemed to echo around our boat, so that it appeared as if they were all about us. Borg came over to me silently, and put his arm around me. I suddenly felt then that I didn't care anymore. Borg would not let them take me. I realised that Borg was just a young man, but he had such a presence about him. I somehow knew he was going to become a part of some great destiny, and as long as I stayed close to him, I would be all right. Our boat was moving more quickly by then, as Kemit had signalled for another two men to start paddling. How did he know where we were going in the mist? Then I noticed what he was doing at the head of the boat; he had a long piece of twine in his hand, and he kept pulling it up and down in the water ahead of us.

Borg whispered to me when he saw my puzzled look, 'He is testing the depth of the water. If the rock touches the seabed, he can feel it in the string. We are paddling through some very dangerous waters in order to escape. Usually the traders avoid this area when they journey from Dogger to Scan Land, but Kemit knows these waters better than most. If I had a choice of who I would be afloat with, it would always be Kemit.'

Borg suddenly stopped whispering at a signal from Kemit. Then a loud voice boomed out from the blanket of mist, 'Kemit, you idiot, show yourself!'

It was Tashk himself, I thought, as I would remember his deep voice anywhere.

'You have done some stupid things over the seasons, but this is idiotic! Where do you think you are going to take her? Not to Estergard. You must know you will never be welcome there again. The council will not forgive you for risking the Dogger trade, just for some child you took pity on!'

I looked then at Kemit and his crew, and their faces all had the same determined look on them. I did not realise what they would have to give up in order to help me. They didn't even know me, yet they were all in great danger, and it was all my fault. I started to stand up to tell Kemit I would go back. I could not let them give up their homes and families just for me. Borg pushed me gently down and shook his head, holding his finger to his lips again, signalling for me to be silent. Kemit saw what happened, and with a broad smile on his face that lit up his eyes, he put his finger to his lips too. I did not understand it. It was as if I had fallen into some sort of game that men play with each other.

'Kemit. Do not make me hunt you. Damn you! I know you are near. We jeopardise the whole Dogger trade if we do not get her back. The Shaman has invoked all the island in this. Even Vrana will not help. The maid's fate was sealed as soon as he announced that he wanted her. Just give her up, and we will let you go at least. Do not make me kill you, old friend.'

Tashk's voice was beginning to fade as the crew continued to paddle. It was unmistakable, though, to hear the deep sadness held in his voice.

After that, the crew paddled for what seemed like hours, through the thick mist, until we could hear nothing but our own paddles again. Kemit then signalled for the crew to stop. We all sat in silence for a few minutes, until Kemit finally said, 'They are all in the north straits now, so we have some distance from them at last. They will not guess we have doubled back to the south. Good work, men. Let us get a fire going and have some food. We do not want our precious cargo to starve!'

At this they all laughed, and the mood of the boat changed as they busied themselves storing the paddles. A man at the end of the boat started kindling the fire, while others set lines over the side to fish. Kemit came over to Borg and I, and sitting down, asked, 'How are you, sweetness? I am sorry if things seemed a little tense after you woke, but we were surrounded not just by mist, but the whole trading fleet! They are in different waters now, so we are clear for a while at least. Hey, what are these tears? I very much hope they are tears of joy?' he asked.

'How could you give up your friends, just for me? You do not even know me. I am so sorry...' I said, with tears streaming down my face.

'We do not know you, but we do know Borg, and his friends are our friends. How could we not help you, sweetness? We are traders, but we are still men of honour. Tashk thinks too much of profit and his position these days, to think of what is right and wrong. He was a noble man in his youth, but now he has too much love for his wealth to let deeds of honour get in the way. He is also angry at himself for his stupidity in taking Vrana into the dunes and making your escape possible. If we cannot live with honour, we would rather not live. Hey men!'

At this, he raised his voice, and the crew smiled and shook their fists in the air in agreement. Then, within minutes, fish were being hauled over the sides of the boat and onto the hot stones next to the fire. The smell of that fish was the best smell I think I could ever remember, and it tasted so sweet too. I ate at least two before I even looked up. Then I realised, whilst licking my fingers, that three of the crew had been watching me wolf down my food. One of them said, 'I think if she eats like that every day, we will have to put in an extra hour of fishing, just to keep up!'

I looked up at them, and we simultaneously burst into laughter. Laughter born of relief from the stress we had all been under that day. After we had all eaten our fill, the fire was dampened down, and we continued our journey. It soon became dark, and due to the still present mist, there were no stars or moon to relieve the total blackness that enveloped the boat.

'Here, you might need some more furs tonight. It will get colder before first light.' Borg said.

In no time at all he and I lay huddled together under the furs, and I must have been very tired, as I do not remember going to sleep that night.

It was very cold when I woke, and still very dark. Borg was still sleeping with his arms around me, and I lay very quietly, so as not to disturb him. Then I became aware of a voice close by.

'So, Kemit, it looks like our days of adventure are not yet over. Just when I thought we were getting old and fat, we seem to have leapt back into the days of our boyhood.'

Kemit's voice replied, 'Aye, it is not for us to know ahead what seas the gods wish us to travel. I feel it in my bones that we are following a powerful current here. This maid and Borg have some great path ahead of them, I know, and I am glad that at the end of our journeys, we can help them a little.'

The other voice then replied, 'Two of the men said much the same thing last night, when we broke through the surf on Dogger. We all feel it Kemit. Do not worry, we are with you, to the man.'

After a moment, Kemit continued, 'It does my heart good to hear you say that, Uin, for we are not out of trouble yet. When we break through to the south sea, we will have to decide our route from there. I was going to take us to Tybrind Vig, to Sern's home, but we do not know if Sern's story will have held up. It depends on how determined Tashk is to get the maid back. I think it is best we keep away from Tybrind for a while, until we find out what has happened to Sern. The way I see it, there is only one place to go, and that is west to Brit Land.'

After hearing that I must have drifted off to sleep, with thoughts of Brit Land filling my head. The next time I opened my eyes I was in another world again. It was a world of wind and sea spray, and violent rolling of the boat.

I felt Borg shaking me, then saying, 'Mia, wake up. We are entering the south straits, and you will need to hold on to the boat hooks again. Here, let me tie your waist to the hook. These are very dangerous waters, as the tide races between two great rivers here, and the currents are fierce. Fear not though, if anyone can get us through the straits, it is Kemit!'

Borg shouted those last words to me as he moved to his position at the end of the boat in order to paddle, and after tying myself to the hooks, I looked on helplessly while the crew battled with the currents. The men were constantly lifting their paddles at Kemit's direction, to one side or the other, and then paddling fiercely again. I just sat wrapped in my furs, not even daring to lean up and look at the wild sea that surrounded us. From the glimpses that I got of the sea when the boat rolled, it was just like the surf around Dogger Island, but we were flowing with it rather than crossing it.

As the spray constantly splashed over the sides, it began to fill the bottom of the boat. One of the men left his paddle and handed me a wooden bowl, saying that I was to start scooping out the water when it reached a particular mark. I was so glad to have something to do, rather than just sitting there, holding tightly onto the hook in horror. I was not afraid of hard work, so I piled the furs to the side of me and started to scoop out the water. It was only then that I suddenly became aware of my appearance. I still had the red dress on with its short skirt, and my arms and legs were still smeared with the ochre paint of the Shaman. The memory of Sula painting me for the Shaman filled my mind, as I scooped water out of the boat. It was a monotonous job, so my thoughts kept drifting back to Dogger, and I wondered what had happened to my grandmother. I felt strangely distant from her then though, not just because I was a long way from the island, but emotionally too. It was as if she was just someone who I used to know, instead of the person who had filled my life from my birth. I was brought back from those thoughts by a tap on my shoulder.

'Here, sweetness, put this on. There are no places for fancy red dresses on our boat. You are a crew member now.'

It was Uin, the man who had been talking to Kemit in the night. He handed me a leather tunic, which I gratefully put on, and continued to scoop out the water.

My arms were tired, but they could not have been as tired as the crew's, for they had been paddling vigorously for hours.

'Paddles in!' Kemit then shouted suddenly. 'We are through, my friends! It should be calm waters ahead now to the Brit coast tomorrow.'

As he said that, I could sense an air of relief sweep through the men.

'Hey, I saw you with the bowl. You make a good boatman, Mia!' Borg said when he came over and sat next to me. 'You know your father came from Brit Land…' he stated then.

'Yes, but I do not know which part, or even his name. My grandmother forbade me to even ask about him.' I replied.

Borg sheepishly looked away.

We ate hot fish again for midday food, and after the break the men went back to their seats and paddled steadily westward. After a few hours, I noticed a rock on the horizon with a great pine tree on it. As we neared it, I realised that that was just what it was – a rock with a giant tree on it! It was a strange sight, as the lonely yet majestic tree was surrounded by a vast open sea. The base of the tree stood only a man's height from the water, but the tree must have been very old, as it was so tall, and its trunk was huge. The crew were heading straight for it, and I thought that the boat might be damaged on the rocks, until I realised that the island was surrounded by deep golden sand. The men skilfully beached the boat on the sand, and tied the rope at the end to the trunk of the great tree.

Kemit then shouted, 'We will rest here tonight, friends. The old pine will watch over us if the wind gets up.' Kemit then jumped ashore, and helped his men secure the ropes.

'This is a strange place,' I said to Borg, 'the tree looks so very lost. It's so tall, standing on its little rock in the middle of the open sea. It should be in a great forest. Have you been here before Borg?' I asked.

'No, I have only gone to the edges of Scan Land, with Kemit, before. This is a strange place, though, as you say.'

We jumped ashore, and stood on the tiny patch of grass at the base of the tree trunk.

'Still, it is good to stand on dry land again, even though it is a very tiny bit of land,' I said.

At that we both laughed, and all the tension of the night before left us. We watched then, as the men were busy tidying the boat after its stormy journey. The goods were all in a clutter at the bottom, and there was still quite a lot of water to scoop out. Kemit saw us watching, and turned to us and said,

'I see you have met my old friend, The Lonely Pine. Many a stormy night I have been grateful for its deep roots. It stands about halfway to Brit Land from the edge of the southern straits. Many a log boat has gone down to its depths, looking to it for protection, when caught out by a storm on this route.'

'It seems a very lonely sight to see, this great tree standing on such a tiny rock,' I replied.

Kemit nodded, and said, almost to himself, 'In my grandfather's day it was surrounded by a lot of land, and when he was a child, he said, there were even a few homes here once. So it is in this land of widening seas. Maybe one day there will be no land left above the water. Maybe even Dogger Island will be swam over by fish,' he said, smiling.

We laughed at such a ridiculous thought! Dogger Island, with its mountains and forests, would never be covered completely, we knew. Kemit looked at us and smiled, stating, 'We will tie the boat up here tonight, and tomorrow paddle north. We will not be able to travel in sight of land until we are very far north, in case word gets back to Tashk where we are heading. Do not worry though, it will only be another four, maybe five, days at sea.'

After saying that he turned and tended to his men. We just looked at each other, and we knew we were thinking the same thing. Another four or five days at sea! We certainly were travelling far from Dogger Island! I did not know the coast of Brit Land was that long, I thought to myself. After a while, we walked back to the boat, and after eating went straight to sleep under the boughs of our protector, The Lonely Pine.

I dreamed that night of a vast plain, in which the pine tree was one of many such trees in a great forest. I saw settlement after settlement being abandoned by the ever rising waters, just like our own settlements on Dogger, which had to keep moving inland each season. Then I dreamed that all the land was gone, after a huge wave hit Dogger. I felt I was drowning in the sea, going down, down, and gasping for breath. I woke with a start to find it was first light, and I was amidst a bustle of activity again as the crew of the log boat prepared to take to the water.

Borg saw the look on my face and came over to me, asking, 'Are you all right? Your face is white. Did you have a bad dream?'

I smiled weakly, and replied, 'I dreamed that all the land was gone, as if the world was covered with water, and I was drowning.' I reached out and clung to Borg, who just held me in his arms and whispered, 'There will never be such a time, and you are not going to drown, for the gods would not let you. Here, take this fish. After you have eaten you will feel better. Kemit says we should have a good day today, as the wind is going to blow us where we want to go. It was probably seeing the old pine that made you dream about the water rising. I have to say though, it makes you think, seeing such a tall tree in the middle of the open sea like that.'

He smiled at me, and went to his seat to wait for Kemit's orders. I sat up and began to eat my fish as I watched two men on the shore untying the ropes from the tree. When it was untied, another two jumped out and helped to push the boat into deeper water, off the sandbank that surrounded that strange little island. Within minutes they had pushed it enough, and jumped in and joined the others at their paddles.

'We have a good wind behind us today, my friends, so we will make good time if we put our backs into it too,' Kemit shouted above the howling wind.

He was certainly right about the good time, I thought after a while. We were skimming across the water at real speed that day. The rest of the morning was uneventful, which was a refreshing change compared to the other days of that week. Was it just five days ago, that the only problem I had in life was avoiding crushing small nuts for my grandmother? Now I was racing across the sea in a log boat, with a crew of traders, all risking their lives and livelihoods to help me. People that did not know I existed a few days ago, were turning their lives upside down just for me, I thought incredulously!

An hour or so went by, when the crew lifted their paddles at Kemit's signal, and the boat just kept on gliding along until it eventually slowed and stopped.

'Food men!' Kemit shouted, and they set about their now familiar routine, lighting the fire and fishing. Borg came over to me, with his eyes bright and full of excitement.

'Did you see the speed we were going? It was fantastic! My arms just seemed to paddle by themselves... in out, in out... like they were working with the boat as one. One day I will crew a boat like this, and race the seas like a bird. I do not even feel tired!'

At that statement, he just flopped down beside me, and I laughed, saying, 'You certainly look tired to me!' and we both laughed together.

While we were eating a particularly delicious fish that I had not tasted before, Kemit came over and sat with us. 'We are making good time today. We have the wind at our backs, and it is pushing us along a pace. We will still have to keep out to sea though for another few days – Tashk will look for us at our regular Brit Land ports, when he does not find us on the Scan Land coast,' he explained.

'Where are we going then?' I asked, in a voice with a note of concern.

'Do not look so worried, you will come to no harm on my boat. We are heading to a settlement I used to know, in the far north of Brit Land. I stayed there when I was a boy. My grandfather was a trader, and in those days there were not many that would travel those waters, due to the dangers of floating ice and the cold. It was my grandfather who used to stay in the huts on Lonely Pine rock, before the waters took them. It is still very cold where we are going, and with winter setting in, there will not be many choosing to head north to follow us.'

'What if the people you knew have gone, or the land has gone? What will we do then?' I asked. I could not disguise the fear in my voice. I had heard tales of the far north, the land of ice and snow all year round, where terrible wild beasts roamed.

Kemit smiled, and put his arm around me, replying, 'What will we do then? We will find somewhere else and make camp until the spring. Do not worry sweetness, we will be fine. These men are not just paddlers, they are the best crew of hunters and warriors in all the known seas. That is why they are my crew, heh Borg?'

At that he slapped Borg across the shoulders, and Borg looked up at him, smiling, and nodded as if Kemit had done him some very great honour. He left us to finish our food, and before we knew it we were on the move again.

I must have drifted off to sleep not long after, because of the smooth movement of the boat, and the comfort and warmth of my fur bed. I drifted in and out of dreams, about flying through the sky over an endless sea below me. When I awoke the sun was starting to take colour. The men paddled on for another hour until it was starting to get dark, and Kemit ordered them to stow their paddles and rest for the night. We did not have the Lone Pine to tie up to that night, and I was fearful that we would drift onto rocks, or an unfriendly shore. I told Borg my fears, and he said we were fine to drift out there, because the wind was still gently blowing us in the direction we wanted to go, and that we were in the centre of the vast northern sea, a long way from any rocks or shore. He spoke with such confidence that I snuggled up to him and fell fast asleep again.

The following days were very much the same, except the wind was not so strong, so the boat did not go so fast. By the time the sun was taking colour again at the end of the fourth day, the men started talking excitedly, and I looked up over the bow and saw a faint line on the horizon. It must be land! I thought to myself. The men began to paddle hard, as they obviously wanted the boat to be grounded that night if they could. Slowly the black line became wider, until it was possible to see a line of mountains, and then trees. The last land we had seen apart from the Lonely Pine was Dogger Island. Having spent all my life there, and much as I wanted to see new lands, I was, at the same time, suddenly frightened by what we might find.

Kemit was totally absorbed with the boat, and went to the front and started to hang the string over the edge again. I should imagine it was a fearful thing for the traders too, to land in a strange place, because they did not know what rocks or dangers were lying under the water. There were only four men paddling then, and even though it was starting to get dark, they paddled very slowly. I could by then see a beach surrounded by dense forest, with high snow-capped mountain in the distance behind. Borg came over and sat next to me, whispering excitedly, 'Is this not great! The men say that most of them have not been this far north before, and they are amazed to see the trees and mountains. Some of them were telling me when we were paddling, that they had been told there was nothing up here at all but snow and ice!'

Suddenly the boat jerked, then there was a terrible grinding noise, and we thought the boat must have hit a submerged rock or something. Kemit started shouting orders, and a man jumped into the water to look at what we had hit. He dived under the boat, and then leaned over the side, speaking to Kemit quickly.

'We must move everything in this part of the boat to the other end. We are too heavy, and if we are not quick the outgoing tide could break our back,' Kemit then shouted.

We all got up and started carrying everything that was heavy to the other end of the boat. But it was not until Uin moved the huge leather water bags that the loud grinding noises started again, and we could feel the boat moving a little.

'Jump! Jump for all you are worth!' Kemit ordered.

We all started to jump, at first slowly, then more quickly. Suddenly the boat moved, and we were free, as we were afloat again.

We then had to move everything back to where we had taken it from; when we had done so four men started to paddle, and we gradually made our way to the shore. There was no surf between the shore and the open sea, as there was on Dogger Island, so it was almost an anti-climax when the boat gently glided onto the sandy beach.

Immediately Kemit and four men jumped ashore with spears in their hands, to check that there were no unfriendly inhabitants in the area. We watched them keenly as they disappeared into the forest that lined the beach. They would not pull the boat right up onto the beach until they knew it was safe, so it was a tense time for those of us left waiting for their return. After a while Kemit came back smiling, and one of the men was carrying a young deer over his shoulders.

Before reaching the boat, Kemit shouted, 'It is fine here, there do not seem to be any settlements near, as we found no paths in the forest. And look at what we have for last food! No fish tonight men! We eat well. It is a good omen!'

After that we all helped to pull the boat onto the sand, and a camp was made. Almost within minutes a huge fire was lit, and the beast was skinned and starting to roast. The fish had been good, but this was wonderful. I was sitting on the sandy beach of another land, a distant land from my home island, and I was eating deer meat! We never ate deer at home, only the hunters and their immediate family would eat it. Sometimes Sedle, my mother's sister, would bring us some of the poorer cuts when her man was not at home, but we never ate the best parts, as we were going to then! A bowl of fruit mead was handed around after the food. I drank some, and felt a warm glow in my stomach.

As I sat looking into the flames, the crew and Borg talked about their hunting triumphs of the past. My mind drifted back to the circumstances that had brought me to that distant shore, not more than seven days before. I tried to remember just when my adventure started, and somehow thought it must have been the night that my grandmother shouted at me for not crushing the small nuts. I suppose it was the fact that that was the last night of my childhood, as I had known it...

5. A NEW HOME AND A NEW FAMILY

I woke up to find it was already past first light, and the men were busy cutting down tree branches and starting to erect a hut, next to the cliff at the side of the beach. I looked around for Borg, and saw him with the crew, busily doing some job or other at the edge of the forest. I realised then that I had fallen asleep by the fire on the beach, and someone must have put me in the boat. I was completely covered in thick warm furs, and smiled that someone had taken such care of me. I was really not used to anyone caring for me like that. It was enough for my grandmother to let me stay in her hut, let alone cover me in furs to keep me warm while I slept. I wrapped one of the furs around my shoulders and walked over to the fire to keep warm. Uin, Kemit's first crew man, was there, cutting a piece of freshly cooked meat off the roasting stick, when he saw me.

'Mia, come and have some food. Deer tastes good after days of eating nothing but fish! Here, this is a good piece.'

He handed me a huge piece of the meat, and I sat down next to him to eat it. After I had relished the delicious meat, I asked, 'What are they doing? Are we going to stay here for long?'

He smiled at me and handed me another piece of meat, and said, 'Maybe, sweetness. We will have to see. This would be a good beach to spend the winter. The cliffs shelter part of it, and the forest is close for wood and beasts to eat. Kemit has decided to make a camp here, before the winter snows come, and then we can search the coast for the settlement he's looking for when we have a base. We have done this many times in stranger lands than this, so do not worry. You are with the best group of men in six trading fleets!'

I nodded, saying that I was not worried, and he left me by the fire to finish my food.

Every so often Borg came over to me, with news of the wonderful hut that they were making under the cliff overhang. He was obviously so happy to be with those men. For him, it was a relief to finally leave Dogger Island and his lost love Sula, and not be an outcast any more.

After a while I felt useless sitting there by the fire, when everyone was so busy. I was not used to it, so I thought the best thing I could do was to make sure the fire was kept going. The men obviously thought that was a good idea too, as every so often they would put a pile of wood next to me, until we had a pile that was huge. It was in fact so big, it would have lasted my grandmother and me a month or so! By the end of that day, the main part of a huge long hut was tucked underneath the overhang in the cliff.

The men worked tirelessly, and within a few days the hut was bigger and stronger than the moot hall at home! It was very long too. I had not seen a long hut before, with a central passage and lots of wooden walls alongside it, making separate rooms within the hut. It was like lots of little huts within a hut. We never had separate parts to our huts on Dogger; they were always just one room with perhaps a screen of fur at one end. I wondered if all the huts in the traders' homeland were like this. If they were, their settlements must have been vast.

One day, just as the sun was starting to colour, two crew men walked out of the forest with another beast on their shoulders. This time it was a boar! We were going to eat boar, I thought to myself! I had only ever smelt if before, as it was chief's food on my island. It had always smelt so very good too. I could not believe I was finally going to try it! Later that night, when I sunk my teeth into my first piece of boar meat, I could not believe anything could taste that good! It tasted better than it smelled too. My enthusiasm must have been noticed, as the men roared with laughter at my delight in eating something that they thought of as normal fare. They did not realise what restrictions island people had to live under. They just went out, hunted what they wanted, and ate it! What a life those men had! I had always thought the traders were blessed with their life of travel and adventure, but I had not imagined just how good their lives were until that moment. The crew were delighted at my overwhelming pleasure at eating boar for the first time, and they promised me that we would eat it often.

I asked them then about the hut they were building, and they enthusiastically told me all about their Scan Land traditions and building techniques. They told me that the whole roof would be covered with tree length strips of Birch bark, and not skins as they were on Dogger Island. On top of the bark they would put a thick layer of turf, cut from the clearing just to the right of the beach. I thought that it seemed to be a lot of work to do, when all they could do was hunt, and get skins for the roof instead. But then when I looked at the size of the roof, I could see it would take them a long time to hunt and prepare that many skins. Also, there was a definite chill in the air that day and it looked like winter was much closer there than it was at home on Dogger, as we were a lot farther north. Later that night I crept back into the boat to get some sleep, and left them around the huge fire in the shell of their hut, laughing and talking together. As I watched them in the firelight from the dark beach, I looked at Borg's happy face as he joined in the conversations. He and the crew certainly did not seem to be put out by their adventure; they behaved as if travelling to the far north to an unknown land was just part of normal life to them.

Just before getting into the boat, something caught my attention at the water's edge. It was sparkling in the sand, and each time a wave washed over it, it seemed to radiate a blue light. I thought at first it might just be a shell that was glowing in the moonlight, but I had to take a closer look. I cautiously walked towards it. As I did I heard the crew around the fire burst into laughter, and turned just in time to see Uin pat Borg on the back for saying something very funny. I smiled to myself, at his delight at being in the company of the crew. When I looked back towards where the glowing object had been, it was gone. I suddenly felt a great sense of loss, as if I had lost something precious.

After walking up and down the beach hoping to see it again, Ras, one of the old crew men that was tending the small boat fire, leaned over the boat side and called to me, 'I would not walk along the beach alone, deary. You never know what might be out there in the dark.'

I smiled and nodded at him, and climbed into the boat. The kind face of Ras smiled back at me, and the lines on his face seemed to radiate his smile as he asked, 'What were you looking for? Have you lost something in the sand?'

I sat down next to him and replied, 'I thought I saw something sparkling in the sand, but when I turned away from it, it was gone.'

The old man smiled again and said, 'It was probably a shell, deary, catching the moonlight. I reckon you should get some sleep, as it will get mighty cold before first light and we have a lot to do if we are to finish our hut before the first snows come.'

I nodded to him and went to my furs, snuggling down into them and thinking that he was probably right in saying I had just seen a shell. Then, as I shut my eyes to go to sleep, I suddenly saw lots of sparkling lights. I opened my eyes and looked down the boat to where Rasa was stoking the fire, but everything seemed normal. So I slowly shut my eyes, and there they were again, but this time they had form; they were lots of faces. Beautiful, smiling faces. I watched, fascinated, and did not feel afraid, just very content. Then a voice came into my head, saying,

'Beware, Mia, all is not as it seems, and all new friends are not your friends. A cold hand is something to be wary of...'

Suddenly the faces were gone, and I opened my eyes and looked up at the stars, wondering just what else was going to happen to me. Over and over again, I thought about the words I had heard, that all new friends were not my friends. I found it hard to imagine that any of the crew, or Borg, could not be my friend. I eventually drifted off into a troubled sleep, wondering just what had happened to me, and if the faces would come back to me again.

The next day was another matter entirely; a wind was getting up and there was snow in it, and it was bitterly cold. Borg gave me some more furs to wrap around my legs, and a pair of fur lined shoes that were too big, but very warm. I hurried to the fire and started helping the men to cook some of the meat left over from the night before. After eating, six or seven men left the camp with a collection of axes and flint blades, to cut the bark off tall birch trees for the hut roof. Before they left, I asked them if they had to cut the trees down, and wouldn't that take a long time to do? They told me that they did not need to cut the tree down to get the bark, they just slit it along its length and it peeled off. Not long after they had gone, Borg and two men made a rough sledge with some of the logs that had not been burnt in the fire, and went off to the grassy clearing to collect some turf to hold the bark down on the roof.

I decided to go with them and help, as I would have felt guilty just sitting by the fire all day, as I had the day before. They said that if I wanted to help, I should get a blade from the flint bag and follow them. When I joined them at the clearing I could see that there must have been a lot of animals grazing on the grass, as it was short and very thick. Borg and I took one side, and the men started on the other. I was not quite sure how we were going to get the turf off the ground, until Borg showed me that it had to be cut into squares with a good long blade first. Then, with another blade, an edge had to be lifted and the roots cut, and the turf rolled up, ready to be put onto the sledge.

I quite enjoyed the root-cutting, until my hands became so cold that I could not even feel them anymore. Borg gave me some bits of leather that he had wrapped around his hands, and we swapped jobs. I then realised that his job was much harder on the hands than cutting the squares out, as peeling the turf back and laying it on the sledge made my hands even more painfully cold. However, we worked away all morning, and took turns dragging the piles of turf with the sledge, until it was time for midday food. We were just about to eat some more of the delicious boar from the night before when the other men came back from the forest. They had huge rolls of bark over their shoulders, and after piling them against the hut frame, came over to get some food.

'These forests are full of good bark, and the game is just running into you! I have never seen such good hunting in Scan Land. There cannot be many settlements near here, or the game would be at least a little frightened by us!' Uin said.

'It is a good sign. I could ask for nothing better than to have found virgin forest for our winter in the north. We must get on though, as the weather is closing in and we will need some good shelter soon,' Kemit replied, and after eating the men got back to work.

I watched as the men unrolled the long strips of bark and laid them on the wooden frame. A man, who I found out later was called Valdas, started to put little pegs through the bark with the side of his axe, to secure it as he moved along the roof. Another two men started layering the turf on top of the bark, and within a matter of hours our new home had a roof! Which was good, as the flecks of snow that fell in the morning had become big and fluffy, and the ground was turning white around us.

'Borg, we need to move the fire into the hut. Could you and Mia get some stones to lay it on?' Kemit asked.

'Right away. Come on Mia, we have a job to do,' Borg said.

We took the sledge and filled it with fire stones, being careful which we chose, as the stones there were slightly different to the ones on our island, and we did not want to make a mistake and put a dangerous stone under the fire. It took us the best part of an hour to collect them, and as we were dragging the sledge to the hut we saw that the walls were already up! With more sheets of bark and a woven band of sticks at the bottom, the walls were finished too! The hut looked so strong. I had never seen anything quite like it before. We dragged the sledge to the edge of the hut, and asked Kemit where we should put the stones.

'You see that area in the middle, where there is a flap of bark held up with that stick on the roof?'

We followed his gaze, and Borg answered, 'Yes, shall we put it under the stick? But will the rain and snow not fall onto the fire there?'

'No lad, the stick holds the bark up just enough to let the smoke out, but not enough to let the rain in. This is how we build our homes in Scan Land. Do not worry. It will be a good hut, you will see.'

Kemit walked away, and we took our stones and made a round hearth where he had told us to.

Suddenly Uin shouted, 'Get the fire, men! The snow is falling thicker, and there is much to do before it is dark!'

The men all stopped what they were doing, and shovelled the fire from the beach in long pieces of curved tree bark, putting it onto the stones we had just laid. Within minutes a warm fire was roaring inside the hut, and for the first time since leaving Dogger Island I felt at home. The traders had told me that they looked upon the boat as their home for most of their year, but it had felt so open and exposed to me, as I was used to a hut built on solid ground.

'Everybody to the boat!' Kemit then shouted.

We all ran out and started carrying everything from the boat into the hut. It was not until we started to move the contents of the boat that I realised just how much there had been in it! Endless piles of furs, bags, and bark boxes of all shapes and sizes. It was very dark by the time we had finished, and we all just ate some meat and found a corner to sleep in.

The next day there was a thick layer of snow on top of the turf roof, and after first food Kemit ordered all the men to go and get some dead wood to be stored behind the hut, under the cliff overhang. Kemit came over to me and asked, 'So, how do you like our little home, sweetness? I have a very important job for you to do today.'

I looked at him, and wondered what I could do that was in the least bit important. 'What do you want me to do?' I asked. 'I do not have many skills, but I will try, and I can learn very quickly.'

He patted me on the shoulder and smiled, saying, 'You are a young woman, and that is the skill I need. A woman's skill. I want you to do what the women of our tribe do, when we build a hut. You must make it into a beautiful home. Here, look.' He took me to the end of the hut, where the stretchy partitions they had used to make the stalls over the boats were piled. 'Get Borg to help you stretch these frames out to separate parts of the hut. Then with the cloths and furs in that pile over there, use them to cover the partitions. I want you to decorate our new hut. We men can build it, but it is up to the women to make it a home!'

I looked at him with sheer delight. I was really going to enjoy that job, I thought!

Borg and I spent the rest of the morning putting up the partitions. We kept a large area around the fire for a moot room, and separated four sleeping areas, one for stores, and a small one at the side of the store for Borg and me. After midday food we covered the partitions with the brightly coloured cloths. I had never seen or touched such cloth; it was fine and soft, and coloured red, green and yellow. The walls of the hut really started to look like a home, when I covered them with baskets and bags, and the usual homely things like bark buckets, and wooden spoons. Kemit and the rest of the men spent the whole day collecting dead wood from the surrounding forest, until we had a wood store that would last for months. They were obviously expecting a hard winter, and due to their work that day, we were at least going to be kept very warm. I finished the furnishing of the hut with the furs, which I put in the sleeping areas and around the central fire.

Kemit came in just as I had just finished, and smiled at me, saying, 'I knew if we had a woman to do this job, we would have a home to be proud of! Well done, sweetness. Come with me, Borg, we have one more thing to get, to make our home complete.'

I watched Borg and Kemit go out again, wondering what it was he was talking about. I could not think what else was needed, but I sat down by the fire and waited patiently till they returned. It was not long before they came back, with some long split pieces of birch wood and some bark string.

Kemit smiled at my curious looks and said, 'When we sit around our fires in Scan Land, we like to lean back. So if you lash these strips of wood around those six central posts, then drape some furs over them, we will sit like Kings of the East around our fire!'

I had never seen such a thing before. We always either sat cross-legged on the floor, or lay down when we slept. We never sat up and leaned on anything in that way. But we also did not have a great aisle of double posts to hold up the roof in our huts, either, I thought.

When we had finished lashing the poles and covering them with furs, Kemit gestured for me to sit down, saying, 'Here, sit on the furs, and lean on the fur back rest and see how it feels.'

I sat down, and leaned carefully back on the furs draped over the poles. It was wonderful, so much more comfortable than just sitting cross-legged. But who were the Kings of the East? I wondered. I was just about to ask him when a man came running in, calling for him. He whispered something in his ear, and immediately Kemit's face became serious. We quickly followed him out of the hut. Once outside, Borg and I followed the gaze of the men to the edge of the clearing, where a group of strangers stood watching us.

'We have company, I see. So this forest is not uninhabited after all,' Kemit said casually.

He gestured to us all to stay where we were. He and Uin walked purposefully towards the clearing and the motionless group that stood there. As he got closer Kemit slowed his pace, so as not to appear in any way threatening to them. Then he sat down a few feet away from them and waited. It was a tense moment for us, waiting by the hut; Kemit and Uin were very vulnerable, just sitting down like that in front of the strangers. If they had been intent on harm, they could have easily taken advantage of them and attacked them. I looked at Borg, who saw my worried face.

He put his arm around me, and holding me close, whispered, 'Do not be frightened Mía, Kemit knows what he is doing. He has met many strange peoples on his travels, and he seems to have a way of making friends easily.'

He had just finished telling me that when we could see movement from within the strangers' group. They all took a pace forward, sat down in front of Kemit and Uin, and began talking to them. We all visibly relaxed then. Even though Borg's words made sense, I noticed the crew were fingering their spears as we waited. They were indeed an experienced group of men, as they seemed to know what to do without being told. I suppose that came from having a lifetime of adventures together. We stood for an hour at least, not moving, just looking at the distant groups sitting and talking excitedly. Suddenly, Kemit and Uin stood up and walked back towards us. As Kemit approached I could see he had a broad grin on his face, and I knew we would be all right. Then he shouted to us when he was halfway across the beach,

'We have found a good place to make our home this winter. I know these people! Or I should say I have met them before, in my childhood! Come, I must find a gift for them to take back to their settlement.'

He entered the hut, and I followed him to the new store area, watching him methodically move the bundles of trade goods until he found one with strange marks on it. He cut it open with his blade, and it was as if a rainbow had burst into the storeroom. I saw colours I had only seen on flowers before, bright reds, yellows, blues and purples. Purples! I did not think it was possible to have any cloth in such a colour! It was not just the colour of the cloth though, it was the cloth itself that was strange. It flowed down the sides of the box, as if it were made of water, as it slipped onto the floor. Kemit looked at me and smiled.

'One day, sweetness, we should visit the far eastern lands where they make this cloth, for it is another world from here. I must hurry though with my gift. Which one do you think is the best?'

I looked at the cloth, and Kemit gestured for me to pick it up. As I touched it, it was like touching the softest fur, yet it was as smooth as the petals of a flower. I just wanted to run my hands over it again and again, but I realised Kemit was waiting, so chose the bright purple one. He smiled at me then, and said, 'A fine choice, sweetness! That is the colour of the Kings of the East. You must have noble blood in you, to recognise that it was the best! I must go. Stay here with Borg and the men until I return.'

He left the hut and walked with Uin over to the sitting group at the far edge of the beach. I could just make out the purple cloth, rippling in the breeze, as he showed it to the strangers. I am sure I saw them almost take a step back too, at its beauty. When they took it they made some sort of gesture of salute to us, and disappeared back into the forest with Kemit and Uin.

Kemit had told the men not to expect them back that night, but to keep a guard up all night at the door of the hut, just in case of trouble. That night around the hearth, the men talked enthusiastically about the strangers. They did not look too worried either, as they knew Kemit would not have gone with the group at night if he had any doubts about them. Valdas came over to Borg and me, and as we sat by the fire said, 'You have made a fine home for us Mia. Eh, men?'

At those words they all mumbled and nodded at me in agreement.

'Do not worry about Kemit,' Valdas continued, 'he has seen those people before, in his grandfather's day, and he said they are a friendly people. He would also not have given his best silk to a stranger he had any doubts about.'

'Silk?' I asked.

'Yes. The fine cloth he took over to them is called silk, and it comes from the Far East. It is Kemit's most precious trade good, and not given away lightly. Come, let us eat, for we have boar again tonight, Mia!'

The crew started to laugh when they saw my face light up at the thought. Rasa commented, 'What it is to give such joy to such a lovely face as yours, simply for the price of a chunk of boar meat!'

The mood had suddenly changed, and we spent a pleasant evening listening to tales of the crew's travels, and eating the crispy boar meat. The hut was warm and comfortable, and I must have fallen asleep by the fire. I woke the next morning covered with a huge pile of furs that someone must have put on me while I slept. When Borg noticed I was awake, he came over with a bowl of meat and sat down next to me, saying, 'We have to be ready for Kemit and Uin's return, so put your shoes on and come outside.'

I followed him quickly and opened the door to a world of pure white light. It had snowed heavily in the night, and the beach and forest were bright with snow.

'Oh how beautiful! I love the snow, but it never falls that thickly on the Island. I can see now why the men were so keen to get the wood in yesterday, for it would have been impossible to find any dry wood under snow that deep.'

'These men know what they are doing. I wish Kemit would return though, and tell us about the strangers,' Borg whispered.

I looked at his face with concern, as I had realised that he had spoken his thoughts out loud, and replied, 'I am not worried about him, just curious as to who those people were.'

He looked deeply into my face, to see if I really meant that I was not worried. We decided to go for a walk on the beach, and were just passing the log boat when a voice from within said, 'I think it best you stay in the hut for now, me dearies.'

It was Rasa again. We both visibly jumped, because we had not realised anyone was in the boat. The voice laughed, and said, 'Hey, do not jump! It is just I, Rasa. Kemit wants us all to keep close to camp until he returns.'

I thought of the other night when I had last seen Rasa in the boat, but pushed the memory to the back of my mind. He was quite an old man, compared to the rest of the crew. His skin was darker than most and very wrinkled. He had a kind look in his eyes though, and I had taken a liking to him immediately.

'Can we stay in the boat with you? We will not make any noise, or get in your way,' I asked.

'I do not see why not. I am not doing anything but waiting and watching the boat, and I would be glad of the company.'

Borg and I climbed into the boat and sat around the boat fire, waiting for signs of Kemit's return. After about an hour of silence, Rasa said suddenly, 'If these are the peoples I think they might be, we have paddled into very good luck this journey. I was a young man working in Kemit's grandfather's boat when I last journeyed this far north. We had been caught up in a great storm, and the boat was damaged. We beached it somewhere along this coast for repairs. It was a summer storm, so we set about the forest, getting bark and wood to fix it. Kemit was a very young lad then; he can't have had more than five or six winters. I used to have the job of watching that he did not get into trouble, as trouble used to follow that boy. He was so curious, and the questions! He would never stop asking questions!'

We all laughed, and Borg and I were trying to imagine the great Kemit as a little boy, asking lots of questions.

'Go on, tell us what happened,' Borg urged.

'I do not see why not, it is not a secret. One day, not long after we had arrived, I was supposed to be watching him, when he gave me the slip and just disappeared. His grandfather was beside himself with worry! He had promised his daughter that he would take good care of Kemit too, because she thought he was too young to travel so far from home. We searched and called out to him, but there was no sign of him and it was beginning to get dark! I felt such guilt, I don't mind telling you, because I was supposed to be the one looking after him. So I just left the beach and made my way through the forest, determined to find him or die in the attempt.

'I walked and walked until I came to the edge of a lake. I was just about to turn back and look in another direction, when I heard Kemit's voice call out my name. I could hear the fear in the tone of his voice, and held my spear tight, ready for trouble. I moved carefully through the reeds on the edge of the lake, in the direction of Kemit's voice, until I saw him. He was perched on a tussock of grass on the edge of the lake, with a young maid. He had a big stick in his hand, which he was pointing at a dark shadow in the grasses in front of him.'

Borg could not help blurting out, 'What was it?'

'It was a leopard, lad, and it was ready to pounce on the pair of them. I aimed my spear, and with all my strength I threw it at the beast, and got it! It thrashed about a bit, but it was a good clean shot and its fate was sealed. Then the brave but inwardly terrified little Kemit jumped from the tussock and ran into my arms. I told him to help his friend, who was still sitting on the tussock at the edge of the water. He ran back and introduced her to me as Inja, who came from a settlement on the other side of the lake. He told me that he had been walking around the lake and saw the leopard stalking something. But instead of running in the opposite direction, as most boys his age would, he found a big stick and circled the lake edge to find out what its prey was. He discovered the young maid, playing alone with a little grass boat on the water's edge, oblivious of the danger. But as he tried to warn her, the leopard crawled another pace towards her on its stomach. He could do nothing but leap up and run towards her, waving his stick at the beast!'

When Rasa said that, Borg and I gasped. It was a very brave, or very stupid, thing to do. We all knew people that had been killed by leopards.

'Yes! Unbelievable, eh? He did just that! He shocked the leopard instantly, which gave him precious minutes in which to grab the maid and get her up onto the tussock at the water's edge. He knew that leopards avoid getting wet at all costs, and he had thought that if the worst came to the worst, he could jump into the lake with her. They might drown, but at least the beast would not get them. They had been standing on that tussock for at least an hour before I came across them. Every so often, the leopard would creep closer, so he told me, and then at the wild waving of his stick, it would move back a little. As he recounted his tale, the maid confirmed it all, with wide eyes and enthusiastic nodding. I thought it best to get the maid home, so I walked them around the lake carrying the leopard on my back, until we came to her settlement.

'It was built on the edge of the lakeside, and at the sight of the little maid the settlers came running. It turned out that she was the chief's daughter, Inja, and was known for wandering off alone along the lakeshore. When they heard the tale, and saw the leopard, they were overwhelmed with gratitude. They asked us to stay and have some food, but I told them that the boy's grandfather would be beside himself with worry at his grandson's disappearance. They understood, and asked for the whole crew to come back that night and feast with them, to celebrate Inja's narrow escape thanks to young Kemit's bravery.

'I gladly accepted for the crew, as I knew stores were low and in that part of the world, you did not refuse hospitality when it was offered. Within an hour I had told Kemit's grandfather about his bravery, and the offer of a feast that night. It was a joy to see the pride in his grandfather's eyes!'

'That evening, we sat down to a wonderful feast of wild duck, and strange but delicious fruits and good sweet mead. After that, Kemit's grandfather and the chief became good friends, as Kemit and Inja did too. We spent a happy summer at their settlement. They even built us a new boat, as a way of thanking us for saving their precious Inja's life. That was a gift indeed, because a boat, as you both know, needs a large group of skilled men to work for a month to make. So it was in a magnificent new boat that we journeyed home to Scan Land before the end of the summer. They asked us to stay the winter, and I must say a lot of the men were sorely tempted. But Kemit's grandfather had promised his mother they would be home before near winter, and he had to keep his promise.

'It was later that winter that Kemit's grandfather was wounded in the hunt, so his crew disbanded for two seasons, and went on to other boats. All except me, that was. I stayed with him till he was walking again, and here I am today crewing for young Kemit himself. Kemit often asked his grandfather if they could go back to the lake settlement as he grew up, but for some reason or other his grandfather always refused, saying there was no trade to be had that far north, and so there was no point.

'So, do not worry, Mia, about Kemit leaving everything he held dear to come north and help you. He has been hankering for an excuse to find that settlement again all his working life. Helping you get away from that evil Shaman was a bonus to him, in a way.'

We sat there in silence, thinking about Kemit as a brave little boy, challenging the leopard. We continued listening to more tales of Kemit's youth, and the time just flew.

6. INJA AND THE SWAN TRIBE

I was looking at the edge of the beach a little later, when I noticed a group of people come from the clearing and start walking towards the hut. It was Kemit, and he looked so happy his face was hardly recognizable. He was walking with his arm around a beautiful woman, who was wearing a cloak of what looked like white feathers from a distance. We jumped out of the boat with Rasa and walked quickly towards them.

'Ahh, here is the little beauty that brought us to your shores. Come, sweetness, meet my old friend, Inja, queen of these good people,' Kemit said proudly.

I hesitated at being presented in that way, but I controlled my sudden nerves, and walked as steadily as I could up to Kemit. That was Inja, I thought! The child we had just heard about from Rasa. What were the chances of meeting her after all those years? Maybe it was the will of the gods that they should meet again. If my desperate plight had brought them together, then maybe my troubles with the Shaman were some sort of plan of the gods! As I neared them, Inja held out her hand to me, which I took, bowing my head as I did. She was a queen, and I must not look at her straight in the eyes, as my grandmother had constantly told me.

'Do not bow your head, child. What is your name? For I am sure it is not sweetness!' She looked at Kemit, and he smiled at her.

'My name is Mia,' I whispered.

'What a beautiful name, for a beautiful young woman! Come hold my hand, we women should stick together!'

The instant she touched my hand I felt coldness spread up my arm. Her hand was fine and delicate and she held mine gently, but it felt as if I had put my hand into an ice pool in a winter lake. I immediately tried to think of the warning that the faces had given me that night in the boat. What was it, I thought…? Then I heard the words again in my mind. *'Beware Mia, all is not as it seems, and all new friends are not your friends. A cold hand is something to be wary of…'*

I shuddered inwardly, as I knew instinctively that Inja was the one the faces had warned me about, so I tried not to let it show to anyone how uncomfortable holding her hand made me feel. I was glad when we reached the hut and she released me. She stood in front of our hut, and said admiringly,

'You have built a fine home on my southern beach, Kemit, and so quickly too! You have only been here a few days. Oh yes, my men knew the moment you landed on the beach. We chose to watch at a distance until we could gauge what kind of people you were. It is best to be careful of strangers in such a land as ours.'

Kemit looked at her with complete admiration, for she was truly a good queen, he thought. Kemit and Inja went inside alone, and we waited outside. I said to Borg, to make conversation and try and forget about the coldness I still felt in my arm.

'Did you see that cloak? It was made of hundreds of swan feathers, I am sure, and when we walked together, it rustled with the noise of a flock of birds flying low.'

Borg looked at me curiously, and did not seem in the least bit interested in a swan feather cloak. He looked so intently at the door to the hut waiting for Kemit to come out, that I wondered to myself if he had felt some sort of warning about Inja too. After a while Kemit came out and beckoned for us to come in out of the cold. I was glad too, for as much as the snow was beautiful, my feet did not think so after standing in it for too long.

'Mia, come and sit with us. Borg, you too,' Kemit said.

Borg visibly stiffened, before he formally strode over and sat by the roaring fire that Inja was feeding with wood. Kemit went on to say, 'This is the brave young lad that has given up so much to help his young friend.' Borg looked very proud to receive the respect Kemit gave him, as he did not think he really deserved it, and he went quite red in the face.

Even though it was not time for midday food, some of the men were starting to cook meat, and we all drank some mead to celebrate the coming together of two old friends. It was a warm and friendly scene, in our new hut by the fire. Every so often a few snowflakes would drift over the flames as they blew in through the flaps in the roof, reminding us that it was very cold outside. Inja's men were getting on very well with the crew too, and I really felt we were going to have a good winter there. After a few hours Inja said she must go home before it became too dark, but before she left us she invited us all to visit her settlement the next day.

After she left, we all looked at Kemit in silence, waiting for him to say something. He looked back at us all with a blank look on his face, then burst out laughing and we all joined in. After we had gained control of ourselves, Rasa asked, 'So, you have found your old friend Inja, after all these years, Kemit. I know you have thought of her many times as we have journeyed through the known world, and I always wondered why you did not try to find her again.'

Kemit smiled at Rasa, who was more like his uncle than a member of his crew, and replied, 'You are right, my friend. I have thought of her many times during my life, and I nearly came this far north countless times to look for her. But somehow, something always stopped me. If I am true to myself, I did not want to find her with a man and half a dozen children. My image of our summer together when I was just a boy was so good, I did not really want to spoil it.'

All the men nodded, and Uin asked, 'That is understandable. So, does she have a man and half a dozen children then?'

We all looked intently at Kemit's face. He looked back at us blankly, then slowly began to smile at us watching him and said, 'Look at you men! You sound like a crew of old women. No offence, Mia. No, if you must know, she does not have a man, or children. In fact, she is just like me, a person who lives alone.'

There was a faint 'ahh' sound from the room, and we all knew that we were thinking the same thing. Kemit must have had at least forty winters, yet he had never taken a partner, and neither had she. So the gods had a hand in the meeting, and no mistake, they all thought. Kemit had had many women since they had known him, they told me later, but never anyone that made him go back to the same hut after each season.

Most of the crew had women at home, and even though they might journey for the best part of the season, sometimes many seasons, they always returned to the same woman and their children. I was, for the first time, seeing a new side to Kemit as they spoke. Of a brave little boy who could not get the memory of a maid in a distant land out of his mind, and always one day determined to find her again.

Kemit saw me smiling to myself at that thought, and said, 'Sweetness, I can see that dreamy look in your eyes. The look all women have when they see a man about to be trapped by a woman! She is just a good and very old friend that is all. She is also a queen.'

I looked back at him and smiled. As he smiled in return, I replied, 'Oh of course. I could see that!'

The next morning the hut was full of activity. Some of the men were cooking first food and re-filling the wood pile inside the hut. Others were busy doing something with Kemit at the storeroom. I got dressed quickly, and went over to see what they were doing. Kemit had all the trade bags in a line, and was cutting them open, looking for something. I walked over to him and asked, 'Have you lost something?'

Kemit turned round and replied, 'Yes, sweetness. I am looking for the bag of decorated beads we traded with the cliff women. They should be in this pile.'

'Oh, I know where they are. The bag was very wet from the journey and I thought it best to put them in one of the bark containers. I hope that was all right. I am sorry I did not tell you,' I apologised.

'You did right, do not worry. I am happy to know my goods are in such caring hands. Ah yes, here they are. You did well, a wet bag could have damaged the paints on the beads if they had been left in them too long. Here, take this necklace as a gift from me for your quick thinking!'

Kemit handed me then the most beautiful necklace of decorated bone beads. The beads were inscribed with criss-cross patterns, and those lines had been filled with alternate resin and tar. In between the lines were dots of resin mixed with yellow ochre. They were simple patterns, yet stunning. I was so pleased; I put it on straight away and ran back to the fire to show them to Borg and the crew, who all laughed at my delight.

After we had all eaten enough, and the fire was made safe, we set off to visit Inja's settlement. Borg told me that he was very impressed with the necklace I had been given, and hastened to tell me just how many of the best quality furs it would have cost if I wanted to buy one from a trader. He also said it looked very nice around my neck, too. Which was all I really wanted him to say!

We were all in a good mood, and after walking for a while through the snow covered forest, we could hear the distant honking of swans on a lake. Kemit came to us then and said, 'Wait till you see this!' He pointed to the reed beds ahead of us. Borg was about to run over to see what it was, and Kemit called to him urgently, 'Borg! Wait! Do not go near the water's edge just yet, wait until the settlers come. We will wait here by this fallen tree. They will be here soon.'

Borg looked at him curiously, wondering why he could not go near the water. I walked over to Kemit and asked, 'What is the matter? Are we in danger?'

Kemit smiled and answered, 'Well, we might be if we had come across this settlement and did not know the inhabitants. But do not worry, Inja's people will be here soon and we will be sitting by a warm fire in no time.'

We all waited by the logs, and I could not help noticing that most of the crew looked puzzled too. Then we heard the sound of honking birds again and the crunch of feet in the snow. Suddenly a group of men appeared from the reeds in front of us.

'Greetings, Kemit the Brave!' the first man shouted, and we all turned round and looked at Kemit. He instantly looked embarrassed, which made us all laugh. Then he replied,

'Greetings, Grunet! It is good to see you!'

They patted each other's back as we all stood and watched. Then Grunet said, 'It is important that you keep together in a tight group, until we are nearer the settlement, just until the swans get used to you.'

After he said that, we all looked even more puzzled. Kemit thought we needed an explanation, as some of the men were beginning to look uneasy.

'These good people have discovered a wonderful way to protect their settlement and their children. They have tamed and bred a huge flock of swans, in much the same way as the Lower Brit Landers have trained dogs. I must say, I would rather take on a dog any day than a flock of swans! Do not worry, Mia, if we keep close together they will not attack us.'

The men looked amazed at the thought of it, and Borg and I decided we would walk right next to Kemit till we got to the settlement. As we moved through the reeds the lake came into view, and suddenly we were confronted by a sight that took my breath away; by the looks of the men's faces, it shocked them too. At the water's edge, just in front of us, there must have been hundreds of swans! I had seen swans in the past in twos or threes, but never in such numbers together. They were beautiful, so pure and white, like the snow of the landscape surrounding the lake. Then they saw us, and the noise was deafening. They screeched in unison, flapping their wings. A few that were closest put their necks down and hissed at us. I had not seen the crew look quite so nervous before. The dangers of the sea and the hunt were tame, it seemed, compared to hundreds of aggressive swans just feet away.

Grunet walked steadily over to the swan in front and stroked it, and immediately the others turned and did not seem that interested in us anymore. We walked on along the lakeside till we rounded a promontory, and saw the settlement on the lake before us. It was huge; dozens of huts seemed to be perched over the lake itself, on some sort of wooden platforms. I had never seen huts over the water before on Dogger Island; we moved our homes farther inland when the water got close. The homes before us were actually perched over the water, yet they were surrounded by dry land! As we neared the settlement a small group of people were waiting to greet us, with Inja at its head.

'Greetings, my friends. I hope the swans were good to you. Come inside, it is a cold day,' she said.

She walked onto a sort of path that went out over the edge of the lake. It was made of wood, and seemed to be almost a man's height from the cold and freezing water below. We followed her, and as we started to walk along the path, it moved gently beneath our feet. The end of the path separated, with branches leading to different huts, just like the paths around a normal hut, but all floating on the water! Children were playing outside of the huts too, and I noticed one very small child sitting by a hut door, with a rope tied to its leg.

Inja saw me looking at the child with some concern, and she came over to me and whispered, 'Do not worry Mia, we are not cruel to babies! This is what we do with very small children, so that they cannot crawl too far away from their homes and fall into the lake. When they are old enough, we teach them how to float on the water.'

Kemit, who had been listening with interest, butted in, saying, 'You float on the water? This far north?'

She looked at him, and suddenly realised that what was perfectly normal to her people was perhaps not so to others.

'We all learn as children to move and float freely through the water like the swans. When the spring comes, and it is not so cold, we cover our bodies with swan fat first, and jump in. I will teach you!'

Kemit shook his head vigorously, replying, 'Thank you, but no. I do not think even in the summer the northern waters are warm enough for me!'

I had to ask then, 'You mean you go into water that is higher than your body, and you move through it? How can that be? You do not have a tail like a fish, or feathers like a swan. How do you float?'

Inja just laughed, and walking ahead shouted back, 'You will have to wait until the spring, my dearest, and I will show you!'

I walked then behind her in silence, trying to understand how people could do what only fish and birds could usually do. Inja's hut was the biggest at the end of the pathway, and over the deepest water, almost in the centre of the lake. I must admit I did feel a little uneasy being so far away from solid ground, and not in a boat. When we entered the hall though, I was so amazed by our surroundings that I forgot we were over deep water. All the walls of the hall were covered in swan feathers that glowed as bright as a winter's day. It looked as if we had entered a nest, or that we were sheltering under a giant swan's wings!

As I thought about giant swans, something seemed to stir in my memory. But I knew it was no memory I had of my life on Dogger. It was somehow the memory of another me, another Mia that knew a giant swan. I pulled myself back from those thoughts, thinking that I was simply becoming fanciful. Just like the maids in my settlement that dreamed they lived in the stories they were told, before they went to sleep. I knew very well there were no such thing as giant swans.

Kemit noticed our faces, and said enthusiastically, 'Is it not amazing?'

We all muttered in stunned agreement, then sat down on some seats made of reed bundles. In the centre of the room was a good fire, set on a sunken hearth that seemed to be made of clay, decorated with patterns all around the edge.

'Come, take some bullace mead,' said Inja, as she passed a wooden bowl around with a most delicious drink in it. It was a sort of light mead, not so strong that it burned your throat, but tasted of sweet fruit and honey. A maid came in that looked about my age, and handed round some sort of dried fruit. We all took a piece, so as not to offend, but hesitated as we put it in our mouths, because we did not recognise it.

'Here, taste it. It is good,' the maid said.

I could see the crew out of the corner of my eyes, watching me as I took a bite. It was tough on the outside, but soft and sweet inside, very chewy and delicious. At my reaction they all tried theirs. From the mumbles they made to each other, I could see that they thought the same as I did.

'What is it?' I asked the maid after we had all taken another one.

'They are called Bullace, and they grow on trees in the forests. My name is Lazdona, by the way, after the goddess of nut trees.'

I must have looked at her curiously when she said that, as she asked me, 'Are you all right? You looked a little strange when I told you my name.'

She had a worried look on her face, so I replied quickly, 'No, no. There is nothing wrong. You have a lovely name. My name is Mia. It is just that you reminded me of some nuts I was crushing not more than half a moon ago. My life has changed so much since then, and I had forgotten just how boring my life used to be.'

I looked over to Kemit and Inja as I said that, and saw them both looking back at me. I felt that we must have been transported to heaven, to some sort of magic land, where people lived on water and slept under swans' wings and ate delicious fruits.

We spent a pleasant few hours, eating the dried Bullace and talking about their wonderful homes. After the midday food had arrived, which was a bowl of roasted duck and wild berries, Kemit asked Inja to explain to us all about the swans, and the huts over the water.

She looked at Kemit for some time, then said, 'The reason we live in such homes, and have tamed the swans so, is solely as a result of Kemit's bravery as a boy!'

We all looked at Kemit, who held his hands up, as if to say he had no idea what she meant.

'You will probably have heard the tale of how he saved me from the leopard, with the help of good Rasa.'

Rasa stood up and took a bow, and we all clapped.

'My father, the chief, was so concerned at how close I came to being eaten by the leopard so near to home, that he had the idea of taming the swans on the lake, to make them stay close to the settlement. Perhaps we could then train them in some way, to make a noise and warn us if any predator was near our children. For many summers we collected the young that had just hatched from their mothers, and reared them in pens until they looked on us as their family. It took generations of swans to make the flock you see today. A fearsome force if any of our people are threatened, by beast or man.

'The swans saved our people just a few winters after my father died. Some people from a settlement farther south, decided that their chief's son should take me for his woman, to merge the two tribes.'

Kemit visibly stiffened.

Inja saw, and said, 'Do not worry. I did not like this idea, and the elders were also not happy about it. The tribe to the south were an aggressive people, and we knew they would not just take our refusal without a fight. So we decided to build our homes on these platforms over the lake. We had always had platforms going out onto the lake to fish, so it was just a case of making the platforms bigger, to hold our huts. It took us the rest of that summer to make the first few huts, so that we could run to some sort of shelter if we were attacked. And attacked we were!

'One night as we were eating, the swans alerted us, to something wrong. We quickly and quietly gathered in the two huts we had made on the platforms, and waited. Before long, a group of men with spears entered the settlement. We always kept most of the swans in pens at the shore end of the platforms at night, so we could easily feed them in the morning before setting them free each day. That guaranteed they would stay tame, when they became adult swans. As we quickly walked onto the platform, we opened the gates to the pens, and let the swans out! They immediately saw the strangers moving through the settlement, and attacked them. It was so funny, those fierce and battle hardened warriors were terrified! They did not know what had hit them, when thirty or forty swans flew at them from the darkness of the night!'

She had to stop talking then as tears of laughter filled her eyes.

'They did not come back,' she eventually continued, 'and we have had no contact with them ever since! But just in case, we decided over the following few summers to build the rest of our huts on the lake too, and keep the swan pens along the shoreline. Even though those people have not returned, there have been bears and leopards that have tried to attack us. So we just set the swans on them too! I don't think there is a man or beast that will take on a flock of thirty swans and win. Our whole culture is now based on our protection by the swans, and when one of our people die, we bury them in the ground on top of a swan's wing, for protection in the other world.'

I could see by the reaction of the crew that they thought what she had told them was very clever indeed. They all knew it was always best, when threatened, to have a deterrent rather than to actually fight. Because whether one side wins or loses in a fight, it always costs lives. It is very dangerous to have any kind of deep wound, and it can always go bad, even if moss is pushed into the wound straight away.

The look of pride and admiration on Kemit's face was evident to us all, and after a pleasant afternoon we said our goodbyes and walked happily with an escort to the edge of the lake. As we passed the swans, we wondered why no one else had thought of such a good idea, and we made our way back to the beach. Everyone's mood was good that day, and we spent a light hearted evening around the fire in our new home.

The next day, as I was eating first food, Kemit came and sat down next to me, and said, 'Sweetness, now we have prepared ourselves for the coming winter. Inja suggested something to me yesterday. She thought you might be happier spending your winter in the settlement, rather than on the beach with us old men. You would have Lazdona for a friend, and there are lots of women there to keep you company. What do you think?'

I could not help giving him a startled look, and replied, 'I did not think that you would want me to leave you all. Am I not doing enough work? I can do more, when I know what is needed to be done.'

He patted me on the shoulder then and replied, 'Hey, hey, do not be alarmed. I am not telling you to go! You can go if you wish to. If you wish to stay with my men and me, we would all be delighted. I just thought you might prefer to stay in the settlement, with the other maids and women.'

I looked back at him, and said hesitantly, 'I am sure Inja and Lazdona are really nice people, but...'

'Go on,' Kemit urged.

'But I have never been one who enjoys the company of women and maids.' I tried to look very grow up then, but he burst into laughter. In fact, he laughed so much I thought he would choke. I sat motionless, and looked at him eventually, saying, 'Just why is it that you always laugh so much at what I say, when I am trying to be serious.' I was glaring at him by then.

Kemit recovered his voice, and replied with such kindness, 'You are so very precious, Mia, you seem to always say the exact opposite of what I expect you to. Tell me, what do you mean when you say you do not like the company of maids and women? Tell me, really, I want to know.'

After a moment, I replied cautiously, 'Well, if you are not going to laugh again, I will tell you.'

'Promise!'

So I explained, 'I have been brought up on my own, you see, just with my grandmother. As a child I found it difficult at first to get on with the maids in my settlement. I just found them boring. They either wanted to copy the chores of their mother, and pretend they were in charge of their own homes, or they seemed to be constantly talking about each other behind each other's backs. They would change their very best friends, at least twice a moon, and the whole thing seemed to me to be a complete waste of time. They would soon enough have to be looking after their own homes, and working from waking to sleeping, So why did they want to play at it, when they had the chance not to?'

Kemit was looking at me seriously then, and said, 'Go on.'

'So I would find myself playing with the boys instead. They would play good straight games, like hunting, or having stone throwing contests. They would build camps in the woods, and make fires and knap flint. Their games and friendships seemed to be honest and true, and I spent most of my childhood playing as an equal with my cousin Karn, and his friend Simi. Borg too, used to like my company, and he would take me out on his boat and teach me to fish and throw a spear. I can, you know! They said I was quite good too, and I don't think they would have said that, if it were not true. I do not know if it is because I am a half Brit Lander or not, but I do not sit happily in women and maids places.'

After pouring my heart out to Kemit, I sat with my head held low looking into the fire, and waited stiffly for him to start laughing at me. If he had that time, it would have really hurt me, I thought to myself. After a few moments I looked up, as I had heard no sound coming from him. Then he looked into my eyes, and I could see genuine admiration in them.

He said quietly, 'I am truly blessed to have rescued such a free spirit. I have had some experience of women and maids in my youth, but none of them have ever felt the way you do. You speak with such strength of character too. You will not be moulded into the role a maid would usually be happy with. You also seem to have gained the admiration and friendship of young lads, which is no mean feat, as boys that age find most maids your age totally intolerable. Maybe it is your Brit Land blood. I have known many a Brit Lander over the years, and yes, they do seem to have more respect for individual characters. But their women do tend to be the same as women all over the known world. Except...'

He stopped then in mid-sentence. I looked up at him and asked, 'Except?'

But he shook his head, and replied, 'Let me say this to you, noble Mia. You are more than welcome to stay with us, and when we have time, I would like to see you shoot an arrow myself. Now, we still have much work to do to prepare for the winter. I would like you to go through the stores and put all the dried food we have together, so we can keep an eye on how our supplies are lasting. This is not, by the way, women's work. All crew men have to do store work.'

He looked at me sternly, and I laughed. He walked outside, and I sat for a moment thinking about what he had said, but mainly I wondered what exactly he meant by the word, 'Except'... But, there was work to be done, so I started looking at the bags and bark buckets in the store room as he had told me to. There were some very strange things in that store too, I thought. Mainly lots of bags of shrivelled up brown fruits that I did not recognise. I opened bags of very strong smelling sticks too, of some sort of red bark, I really liked the smell of them. So I continued to tidy up and discover things for the best part of that morning, and when midday food was ready, I had it all sorted. All the trade goods and cloths were on one side and all food stuffs were on the other, dryer side of the store.

We spent a very pleasant half-moon after that day, preparing for winter. The wood pile was huge by then! There were strips of bull meat drying over the fire day after day, too. Bulls were not small beasts, and the one that the men brought back one day had the same amount of meat on it as eight boar. So we ate well, and fell asleep each night with full stomachs. But even we could not eat it all, so we dried a lot of it. Dried meat was very good to just keep in your pocket, when you were out in the cold, as it could be chewed at any time, and it helped to keep you warm. A full belly did seem to keep you warm longer than an empty one, everyone knew.

One day, Kemit got some of the red, sweet smelling sticks from the store, and we cooked them with some meat in a leather bag of seawater over the fire. It tasted so good, and the next day it could even be eaten cold for first food. I actually thought it tasted better the next day too! We were well prepared by the end of that time for any harsh winter; it could have snowed for many moons, and we would have not minded at all, in our cosy home under the cliff.

7. THE FESTIVAL OF ZVERYNE

One day, during next full moon, Borg and I were scraping a deer skin and preparing it for smoking, when we saw Inja and a group of her people walking over to us from the clearing.

'I see you are all very busy. That is a fine skin you are scraping, Mia,' Inja said.

I jumped up and ran over to her, taking care not to touch her, partly because of my greasy hands and partly because I avoided touching her skin whenever I could. It was not just the coldness of her hands, it was something I could not put into words, but I just did not like touching her. It made me feel very guilty, thinking that way about her, because Kemit was so very fond of her. But the warning from the strange faces that night on the beach, when we first arrived on that shore, was always in the back of my mind; perhaps she was not the friend she appeared to be. But I thought that I should tell her how I felt about her invitation to spend the winter in her settlement.

'I hope you do not mind me not coming to stay in your settlement.'

She smiled back at me, although I was sure I saw a shadow pass over her expression, and she replied, 'Of course not! Kemit told me what you said, and there are a lot of things that you feel that I have felt myself, too. I am sure you have a great destiny ahead of you Mia, and I am glad to know you as a maid.'

I wondered how I should reply to that, when Kemit came over, saying, 'How does this day find you, my dear?'

The affection in his voice was unmistakable, and then he kissed her on the cheek.

Hmm, I thought to myself. He did not kiss her on the cheek the last time we saw them together, and Kemit had been away from camp more than one night over the last moon.

'We are on the eve of the festival of Zveryne, the goddess of the evening star, and the hunt and all wild animals. We invite you and your crew, and of course, Mia, to join us in our celebrations. We also have a gift of dried plums for your stores. They taste very good when eaten with boar meat in a stew, you know.'

She handed over a basket of fruit to Kemit, who asked if she would come inside and warm herself for a while, but she replied, 'No, thank you, Kemit dear. We have much preparation to do for the festival this night. We must leave straight away. I wanted to bring the invitation to you personally. Our men will come and escort you past the lake, as the sun is just colouring. Until tonight!'

She turned and walked away, and we all stood there looking at the huge basket of dried plums that Kemit held in his hands. When he had stopped staring at the speck that was Inja and her group in the distance, he became aware of our eyes on the basket he held. Then, laughing delightedly, he said, 'Go on then, you can all have a few!'

We all jostled and took handfuls of the delicious fruit, then happily went back to our jobs, chewing away. Kemit walked back to the hut with what was left of the gift and put it in the food store. After a busy afternoon finishing up our jobs, we put on our warm furs and waited by the fire until it was time to go to the festival. I knew that it was a completely different situation, and they were different people, but I could not help thinking about the last festival I attended on Dogger.

It was a clear night, and the moonlight was brilliant as it reflected on the snow, lighting our way to the lakeside. As we approached, we saw a small group of Inja's men holding bright torches, waiting for us. I had asked Borg that afternoon if he knew what kind of ceremony it was going to be. But he said he did not know, as each shore seemed to have different ways of celebrating the beginning of winter, so Kemit had told him. He looked at me kindly, and told me that whatever the ceremony was, it would not have anything to do with me, of that he was sure. We were going to be guests, not settlers, and anyway, he assured me that Kemit would not allow me to be upset in any way. He was quite right, I knew in my heart, because he and his crew would not have given up so much to save the last years of my childhood, in order to have it taken away by other people so soon again. So I was feeling a little more confident, as we approached the group at the reed beds.

Once we got close to them though, we could see what they were wearing. They had the skins of animals draped over their shoulders; the heads of the beasts, mainly deer and boar, were skinned too. These were worn like a cape, over their heads and faces, and their eyes looked out through the sockets where the beasts' once had. I had to admit they were a little scary to look at, but their manner was kind and friendly. I still held on tight to Borg's hand though, and he looked down at me, and smiled reassuringly. There were no women in the group, so all the way to the settlement, I was trying to imagine what they would be wearing! As we neared the edge of the settlement we took a path to the right, towards a small round pond that I had noticed when we visited before. There was a fence around the pond made of hazel and willow fronds, and there was an archway at the end of the path, covered with thousands of bright red and yellow berries.

As we neared the arch, the torch men told us to stop and wait. Then we saw her. Inja was coming through the arch like a swan that had taken on human form. She wore a long tunic completely covered with swan feathers. The skirt was made up of strands of some sort of string, with swan feathers attached to them, so that as she walked you could see her bare legs underneath. Even her shoes were shaped like little swans, with beautiful swans' necks made of tiny feathers. At the top of her foot was a tiny bent swan's head, and the tail feathers clung to the back of her heels. Borg nudged me; I was so transfixed by her shoes, I had not noticed that she was holding her hand out to me, to go with her. I looked at Borg and Kemit, and they gestured for me to go. I supposed it must have been all right, but I was really feeling uneasy at leaving the protection of Kemit and the crew.

Inja took my hand and smiled at me. I tried not to let her see me wince slightly at her icy grip, as she led me under the arch and into the gathering within. There was so much light-hearted chatter amongst the people there that my mood seemed to lighten with it. That was until she handed me over to a woman, who was standing next to the door of a hut made of hazel branches, and covered with red berries.

'Mia, this kind lady will give you some special clothes to wear, we must all look our best for the ceremony, must we not?'

I must have looked back in horror, as she asked, 'Whatever is the matter, Mia? It is a very beautiful dress that you are to wear.'

Yes, I thought to myself, and I was sure that the men of Dogger Island thought the red dress was beautiful too. I knew I had no choice though, as it would have been a great insult to such hospitable people if I refused. I thought that it really could not be as bad as the red dress and the painted legs, so I walked into the hut with the old woman. I was greeted by six smiling faces, who immediately started to take my clothes off. I stood by the fire for a few moments, naked, apart from my loin cloth and belt. Then I saw it! The old woman and two of her assistants very carefully lifted my dress from a platform at the edge of the room. It was the most beautiful thing I think I had ever seen! It was a garment made of pale grey heron feathers, sewn onto a white plant cloth dress. As they put it on me, it fell softly over my shoulders and hips, to the tops of my knees. The neckline was high, and edged with wispy black heron chest feathers, so that it looked as though I was wearing a black feather necklace. The skirt was not split to reveal my legs, but flared so that I could move freely in it.

I was so taken aback by the beauty of it, and the relief that I was not going into a crowd with a short skirt on, that I did not see the old woman come over with the shoes! They were made of hundreds of black and grey feathers, sewn over a plaited grass shoe. As I put them on, and adjusted the strings around my ankles to make them fit, I was speechless. The women then started to comb my hair till it flowed like a mantle down my back, and after turning me around two or three times, they pushed me out of the door.

While I had been in the hut, the crowd around the small round frozen pool were seated, and all were quiet. The hazel fence was lit with dozens of torches, and the scene within was as bright as daylight. I saw the crew, and Borg and Kemit, sitting on the opposite side of the pond, on some sort of raised platform. Inja came over to me, smiling then, and asked, 'Mia, you look beautiful! Do you like the dress I had made especially for you?'

I tried to think of words that would describe how I felt, but all I could do was look her straight in the eyes, and nod.

'I can see you do. Come, we must take our seats before the start of the ceremony.'

She took my hand again, and we seemed to glide to the other side of the lake with a rustling noise, as the feathers on our dresses caught the breeze of our movements. I then realised what the raised platform was, when we got up to it. It was a line of huge swans nests made out of rushes from around the lake, and filled with the down from hundreds of ducks and geese. We climbed the steps into the main nest, where Kemit and Borg were waiting. They looked as amazed as I was at my outfit, and when they saw my expression they grinned.

Kemit broke the silence, saying, 'Sweetness, you look really beautiful! Come, sit next to Borg, we must not hold up the celebrations.' Borg was sitting at the edge of the nest, with Kemit on the other. Inja and I sat between them.

'We must wait a little while for the men to shut the gates to the arch, and let the swans out,' Inja said.

We all looked at her quizzically, wondering if she was expecting trouble. Then she said, laughing,

'Do not worry, it is just a habit we have got into when we are busy with our festivals, and we are not watching the lake. We let the swans roam the shoreline to guard us against any unwelcome visitors we might not notice.'

Inja stood up after a while, and raised her hand. A drum started to beat. On the frozen pond in front of us, a group of maids walked out with baskets filled with some sort of white powder. They were wearing normal skin dresses decorated with red berries, and they had red berry crowns on their heads. They placed their baskets, nine in all, evenly around the edges of the pond. The drum beats became faster, and the maids danced and wove about each other, making patterns in the ice with their grass shoes. I could not imagine how grass shoes could make such marks, and Inja, noticing my puzzled look, said, 'The shoes the maids wear have the teeth of boar sewn in lines underneath them. So when they move their feet in a certain way, they make those patterns in the ice. Watch now, and see if you can guess what they are doing.'

The maids started to make tight little ring patterns in the ice around their baskets. The dancing got a lot more frenzied, then suddenly the women ran to their baskets and stood still, as if they were waiting for something. A group of young men came in, wearing ordinary clothes apart from headdresses made of strips of fur. Each man went over to one of the maids, and kissed her on the cheek, at which the maids all slapped the men across the face. Then the men immediately turned and formed a circle in the centre of the pond, each looking directly at their chosen maid. The maids left their baskets and started to dance behind their circles.

The drum beats suddenly stopped, and each maid poured the whole of the contents of their basket into the circles they had made in the ice. I saw pools of water start to form, in the ice within the circles, and I realised that the white powder must have been salt! Each maid then stood behind their circle, and with outstretched arms gestured for the men to come to them. The drum beats started again, and one by one the men walked over to the edge of each circle, and stopped. They then all looked at Inja. She stood up, held her arms up to the full moon, and then suddenly dropped them again. The instant she dropped her arms the men took one step, and stood in the centre of each circle of melting ice. The maids then did their best to try to make the men move. They did that by reaching out to them, and gesturing that they would like to kiss them. Some of them even held long sticks with feathers on, and tried to tickle the men so they might jump about. The crowd were all laughing and shouting by then, telling the men to stay still and not to move. I looked at Inja, who explained to us all what was going on.

'You see, each of these men want to take one of these maids for their partners, and this is a test to see how strong they are at resisting the temptation of other maids. In a moment, the maids will change partners, and they will try to tempt the next man to move from where he is standing too. The ice is melting quickly now; any movement on the part of the men could make it break, and the men would then fall to their knees in the icy water below. The first man to fall through the ice gets the last choice of one of these women for a partner. The last to fall gets to choose from them all. So, if the men have a desire for a particular maid, they must stay above the water the longest, so as to have the most choice. However, they will soon be falling through, and the women must work fast to make sure the men they don't like fall in first. Of course, Vehn over there on the right is the one they all want so, if you notice, they are very careful not to make him fall first!'

She laughed as she told us about the ceremony, which was wonderful entertainment for us all. Just when I thought none of them would fall, there was a crack, and one of the men fell through. He leapt immediately out of the water and ran over to a row of seats just in front of us. The maids were really trying to tempt all the men now, apart from Vehn, and the crowd roared with laughter. As they moved they dropped through the ice, one by one, until only Vehn and Saun only left standing. They were both fine looking young men, and I think the women would not mind if they were picked by either, but eventually Saun fell, and Vehn leapt from his circle the victor. He then did a fine dance around the pond, as the maids formed a circle in the centre, looking outwards at the crowd. Vehn came over to Inja, bent down on one knee, and asked if he could choose one of the maids. Inja placed a crown of white swan feathers on his head, and gave him another crown to put on the head of the maid of his choice.

There was intense silence as Vehn walked with the maiden's crown in his hands, to the circle of maids in the middle of the frozen pond. He slowly walked around them, until he stopped at one maid. He looked deeply into her eyes, placed the crown on her head, and kissed her. She then took his hand, and they walked together, over to a line of nests at the other end of the pond. They climbed into one, and disappeared from view. Their bonding ceremony was now complete, and from that moment on they would be bound together for the rest of their lives.

One by one the men, in order of their falling through the ice, would place a crown of different coloured birds' feathers on the maiden of their choice. They too would then disappear into one of the nests at the other end of the pond. When there were just two young women left, the second man to fall was taking a very long time to choose. The maid of his choice had probably gone by then, we thought, and he was enjoying making those two maids wait, to see which one he chose. One of them looked very sad, as her choice must have gone too. Either that, or she did not want to be the last choice of all the men. He put the crown on the other maid's head, and after kissing her, took her to one of the remaining nests. The last young maid then stood alone, and I felt very sorry for her, as the crowd looked on in silence.

The last man came over to Inja, who said loudly, 'Up to now your friends made the choice, but your match was made by the gods, so it is truly blessed. Take this crown of jay feathers for your mate, and may you be blessed with a child by summer.'

The crowd cheered, and the man took the crown and placed it gently on the maid's head, and kissed her with such tenderness. The crowd looked on in silence as he took her hand and led her to the last nest. Then the feasting could begin.

The gates opened in the archway suddenly, and within minutes wooden bowls and strips of birch bark were filled to brimming with the most delicious looking foods. As the women piled our bark platters with the food, we realised just how hungry we were. The rest of the evening involved eating and drinking, while the hunters performed their hunt dances. These entailed a boy wearing a deer or boar skin, and the hunters pretending to hunt him across the frozen pond. It was great fun to see them slip about on the ice.

That was just how I felt a festival should be; a little ritual for good luck, and the rest of it feasting and dancing under bright starry skies. I kept looking down at my beautiful dress and shoes too, and felt like I was the daughter of a chief that night.

Inja asked me at the end of the evening, 'Well, Mia, how did you like our festival? It was good fun, was it not? I am glad you liked your dress and shoes. I have been watching you looking at them during the evening.'

I replied enthusiastically, 'It is so very beautiful. I have taken great care not to get any food on it for you. Yes, I have really enjoyed this evening. All festivals should be like this one!'

She touched my hand then and said, 'I am glad you have taken care of the dress, but it is no longer mine. I had the women make it for you, as a gift. I hope it gives you much pleasure. Wear it when you feel sad, and the feathers around your neck will tickle you and make you laugh.'

I looked at her, and spontaneously, and without a word, leapt over the seat and hugged her tightly. As I did that she visibly stiffened, and I suddenly felt very short of breath. I then thought that it might not be appropriate to do that to a queen, and stood back suddenly. Inja momentarily looked shocked, then looked at me curiously and said, 'Do not worry, Mia, I am glad you wanted to hug me so. I know we are going to become good friends over this winter. I think it is time for you to go now though, as my people relax more when guests are no longer watching them.'

Kemit stood up and signalled to his men, and we happily walked through the arch with our arms laden with gifts of dried fruits and meat for our first food the next day. As we left the lakeside and walked into the snowy forest, we could hear squeals of delight from the frozen pond, as the settlers celebrated the making of life while the Earth Goddess slept. As I walked back to the beach, I shuddered inside every time I re-lived the sensation that I felt, when I took Inja off her guard and hugged her. How could hugging someone make me short of breath? I wondered, and thought there was something very secret about Inja, something that she was trying very hard to hide.

I snuggled up in the furs on my bed when we got to our home, and looked at the feather dress that I hung on the wall. I suddenly felt very guilty regarding my suspicions about Inja, and drifted into a fitful sleep, dreaming that something was chasing me. I could not see what it was, but I kept hearing the flapping of wings...

The next day first food was like a feast, and I forgot my bad dreams as I savoured the delicious flavours! The men had laid down their platters from the feast by the fire for us all to share. My favourite was the cold duck and bullace stew, which we brought back in the leather bags that it was cooked in. After we had eaten, most of the men went to sleep, due to the amount of mead they had drunk the previous evening. Borg and I spent a happy work-free morning, eating, and talking about the festival of the night before.

8. RASA'S RECIPE

Those days, living in our home under the cliff on the beach, were happy and contented, when I look back on them. The main excitement each day was what beast the men brought back from the hunt, or what fish they caught on the few fishing trips they took in the boat. They would only take the boat out when the weather was very still and calm in the morning, and they always made sure they were back well before the sun coloured. Apparently, Kemit had told me, storms could brew up very quickly in the winter in the north, and a boat of that size would not be seaworthy in a winter's storm. Yet every so often, they went out and we had fish for a change from meat. I never thought I would ever feel tired of boar meat, but I had been eating so much of it by then!

One day, after a very successful hunt with some of the settlers, they brought back three boar! Kemit asked Borg and I to go to the lake and ask Inja for some baskets of salt to cure it with. Rasa decided to come with us, so we took the bull horn Inja had given us, to signal to the settlers and let them know we were approaching, so that they could walk us through the swans. Although, by that time, I had noticed that the swans were starting to get used to us, and did not hiss as much when we passed them. It was a fine, bright day when we set off for the lake, but by the time we reached the reed beds and blew the horn for the settlers, that beautiful sunny day had become dull and very dark. The sky continued to look menacing as we walked along the lakeside to the settlement.

As we neared the first hut Lazdona ran over to us, and led us to where Inja was having a meeting with a group of men.

'Welcome, my friends, it is good to see you. Are you all well? Come, sit down, we have finished our meeting. Have something to eat.' Inja gestured to one of her women to bring refreshments for us.

Rasa said formally, 'Thank you, my lady. We have a wish to cure some boar meat, and would ask you for some salt, if it is possible.'

Rasa was so formal and stiff when he talked to Inja. He was an old man, and used to addressing nobility in a certain way. Inja was not like normal nobility, but he did not seem to appreciate that, and felt it disrespectful to be too familiar with her. Inja must have been thinking the same, for she said, 'Come now Rasa, why so formal? Are you never going to relax in my presence? Of course you can have some salt, as much as you wish. I would be interested to know how you are going to cure the boar meat though. We only cure fish here, because with the lake frozen, it is a food hard to catch in the winter, unless we keep cutting holes in the ice.'

Rasa was glad of the opportunity to tell Inja his special recipe for cured boar, so we sat down and he enthusiastically started to explain the process, completely forgetting he was sitting next to a queen.

He went on, 'We first saw it done in that way, when we travelled up one of the great rivers of Scan Land that flows towards the distant dry lands of the East. It was the people we passed in that region that taught us this recipe. We decided, after that, to trade with them, for the special type of spicy berry they used in the recipe. It is called juniper, and it tastes very good in boar stew. It also helps to preserve and flavour the meat, if the meat is soaked in a salt brine containing the berries. After about three moons the meat is ready to eat, and tastes very good indeed. You can either eat it as it is, raw like dried meat, or cook it on hot stones by the fire. It is this last way of eating it that is, I think, the best of all.'

'I would dearly like to taste this wondrous meat! Do you have any of the berries in your store?' Inja asked.

'Yes, my lady, we have a few bags left. I would dearly like to get more though.'

Inja sat up then and asked, 'What do these berries look like, Rasa? Maybe in the forest, inland of here, there are such berries. We do not usually travel far from our lake as there is nothing we wish from other lands, but maybe this is a good reason to explore!'

Inja got up and went out of the hut. I could hear her calling to someone in the next hut. After a few minutes she returned with Vehn, the winner of the maiden's choice ritual at the festival. I could see why the women liked him; he was tall and strong, and had such wonderful dark straight hair. He sat down between Rasa and Borg, and waited keenly for Inja to speak.

'You remember Vehn, do you not? He was the champion at the feast!' Inja smiled with delight then, causing him to look embarrassed. She asked him, 'And how is your beautiful young woman?'

Vehn sat up proudly, and replied, 'She is very well, and if the gods bless us, we will have a child before the summer. I grow weary of the lake though, and would be glad of a journey, if that is what you have in mind. You say you are looking for a certain type of berry. What type of woodland does it grow in? For I know most forests between the sea and the Mountains of the Heavens.'

Rasa took out a small bag from his belt, and showing him the berries, explained, 'They are shrivelled and dried now, but they grow on the bushes for two years. The first winter they form they are green, and it is not until the next winter that the green berries turn black, and are then ready for picking. The type of forest in the land that we got them from was mainly tall pine forest, where the elk roam.'

Vehn stood up excitedly and said, 'I know these bushes! Are the leaves like the feathers of a bird, soft and a pale grey in colour?'

Rasa's eyes lit up, and he replied, 'Yes lad, you know the bushes then? There is only one type of bush in the forest that looks like it. Where is it? Is it far? If you have that berry in your lands you have a good trading product here, and no mistake!'

Inja also looked very excited, as having something valuable to trade with was what every tribe wanted. 'Will the berries be still on the trees now?' she asked.

'Oh yes. They stick to the trees like glue in the winter, and only drop in the spring with the warm weather. Or they may be eaten by elk. I will go with them, if you wish, to make sure they find the right ones.'

Inja nodded, and turning to Vehn, asked, 'How far is this forest, Vehn?'

'Not more than three days from here, on the slopes of the Mountains of the Heavens. We will go and find them with a small group of men, my lady, if you will allow it. It is a safe journey, as there are no other settlements in that area, and only one major river to cross, which is easy to cross farther up on the mountain slopes.'

Borg and I looked on at all this excitement over a few berries, and thought it a little strange. Yet I was sure that Borg started to take more of an interest in the conversation, when the word journey was mentioned. Borg stood up then, and said suddenly to the group, 'I would be honoured if I could join your men, my lady, as I long to visit more of your land, and have always had a great love of mountains.'

Inja looked up at him and replied, 'If Kemit allows it, I do not see why you could not go with them. Do you mind Borg joining you, Vehn?'

Vehn patted Borg on the back, smiling at his enthusiasm, and replied, 'We would be glad of Borg's company!'

'Well, that is all there is to say about it for now. As a storm is coming, no one will be going anywhere for a few days, I should imagine.'

Borg and I looked at each other, and suddenly realised she meant that we would not be going back to our beach that night, either. She noticed our glances, and confirmed our thoughts, saying, 'I am afraid so. You will not get back to the beach before the storm hits, and it is treacherous to enter the forest when it blows. You will have to stay here as our guests for a few days, until it blows itself out. Then we will start to make preparations for your journey to the mountains, Borg.'

I knew there was no point in my saying I would like to see the Mountains of the Heavens too, as I was too young, and just a maid. When I was a woman, I thought, there would be no reason for me not to go on any adventure I wanted. I would certainly see to that! My next thought was about the coming evening, and where we were going to stay. I hoped I would not be put in a hut full of women. I had only spent a few days with the local maids, but after a few hours, I couldn't think of anything to say to them. So I usually ended up sitting in a corner, listening to them talk about nothing. I needn't have worried though, because Inja gave Rasa, Borg and myself a small hut next to hers to use, until the storm had passed. We used to get storms on Dogger Island in the winter, but none that blew so fiercely as the one that came. I had never heard the wind make such frightening noises before! It was as if the air outside the hut was filled with devils, trying to get in to us.

After we had eaten, one of Inja's women showed us to our hut, and I had to grip very tightly onto Rasa and Borg, to stop myself from being blown into the water, spraying all about us on the walkways. The lake was whipped up into a raging sea, and it was certainly good testimony to the people who had built the platforms, that they were not just blown away.

As we tried to get to sleep that first night, my thoughts were only of the deep dark waters that lay beneath our hut, and the sound of the wind. I was sure that Borg's thoughts were only on journeys into strange mountains to look for berries, with the best hunters in the settlement. Because of this, I don't think I slept much at all that night, and when a woman came in at first light with food, I could not believe the wind was still blowing.

It was maybe because of the generous gifts of the furs that I wore, or the fact that I spent most of my days sitting by a hot fire, but I kept forgetting how much farther north we were than Dogger Island. I had never experienced winds so fierce, or that lasted for so long. We stayed in the settlement for another two suns, when the wind dropped as quickly as it had started. We were suddenly living in a sparkly white, snowy land again, with blue skies and bright sunshine.

Just as we were preparing to walk back to the beach, we heard the horn blow from the reed beds, and a group of Inja's men ran over to meet the visitors. It was Kemit and Uin, and a few of the crew that strode towards the lake a few minutes later. I ran over to greet them with Borg. I had not realised how much I had missed Kemit and the men until I saw their smiling faces before me.

'How is it with Mia today, then?' Kermit asked. 'What a storm that was, eh sweetness? I am glad we set our hut back from the beach under the cliff. We would have been in danger of losing it if it had been nearer that sea when she blew. We have lost the boat though. There was no way we could get her up from the beach in time. She was swept out to sea, and is probably halfway back to Scan Land by now, if the tide has taken her.'

Inja walked over to him, took his hand, and looked at him with such sorrow, for she knew how much that boat had meant to him. It was the first boat his father had given him, when he became a man, in which to go trading. Inja had heard from Kemit, on their long nights together in the settlement, of the wonderful lands he had travelled in it. He had told her, too, about the wonderful goods he had brought back to his father within it.

'Oh Kemit, I am so sorry,' she said, as he held her in his arms. 'We will have another boat made for you, as my father did for your grandfather before. No. Do not look at me in that proud way, Kemit. I will have a boat made, and that is the end of it!'

He looked at her for a few moments, and it was hard to imagine what he was thinking, apart from the love that he had in his eyes for her.

'Thank you. As it seems to be a tradition now for your family to make my family boats, I gratefully accept!'

We all smiled, and went into the hall to make plans for the boat building. During midday food, we told him about the expedition to the mountains to find the juniper berries. He said that just as he thought the winter was becoming tedious, suddenly it was filled with plans of adventures and boat building.

It was a light-hearted group that walked back to the beach that afternoon, all except for me, of course. Everyone else had a job to do, apart from me. Kemit and the crew were planning a new, more splendid boat than the one before. And Borg was going on and on about his journey to the mountains.

Kemit must have noticed my mood, and he came over to me as we walked, saying, 'Sweetness, do not be so sad, Borg will not be long. He has to go to prove his manhood, you know. He is not a boy any more, and this sort of adventure is what boys have to do to become a man. I have asked Inja if you can stay in the settlement for a few days, while my men and I hunt the forest for a suitable tree for the boat. We will be gone for a while, as when we find the tree, we have to cut it down, and then get it back to the beach to work on it.'

I stuttered, almost unable to speak, 'But… but… can I not…'

He stopped me before I finished, saying gently, 'No sweetness, you cannot come with us. It is dangerous in the forest, and we do not know if we might meet any of the men from the other settlement to the south. If we do, we might have to fight them. That is no place for a young maid, even a young maid such as yourself. Inja will look after you, and it will only be for a few days, maybe half a moon at most.'

I smiled back at him, hoping he did not see my tears, and we walked on to the beach in silence. When we got there, it was strange to see the beach without our boat on the sand bank. The boat had always meant we could leave whenever we wanted to, but then I realised we were stranded on that distant shore, until we had a new one. I could see Borg was thinking the same thing. That night, however, he talked about nothing else but the Mountains of the Heavens, and his coming adventure with Vehn and his men.

I slept uneasily again that night, and that time dreamed of Borg being in great danger. There was also something in my dream about Inja, too, but I could not quite remember it, as it was all mixed up with my concerns for Borg. Then I started to worry about Kemit and his men, as well as Borg. What if they were all killed, and never came back? Nice though Inja was, apart from the creepy cold hands, I did not wish to spend the next few winters living at the settlement, eventually ending up as one of those maidens being chosen at the festival on the pond. Echoes of all my fears before I left Dogger suddenly came back to haunt me, and I shuddered to myself.

Borg saw me shivering and, thinking that I was cold, put some more furs on me and held me tightly. It felt good to be held in Borg's strong arms, for he was like the brother I had never had, rather than a young man.

9. SETTLEMENT LIFE AGAIN

The next day, we waved goodbye to four men that were left to look after the goods in our hut, and walked towards the lake. The time to get to the settlement seemed to get quicker every time we went, I thought. Maybe it was because I was so used to the journey now, or maybe because I did not want this particular journey to end. The most precious people in my life were just about to disappear into dense unknown forest, and I was really frightened about it. Inja must have guessed how I would be feeling, so did not leave my side for a minute. She constantly fired questions at me, to keep thoughts of their imminent departure from my mind.

Almost at once Borg, Rasa, Vehn and his men waved us goodbye and headed off to the west of the lake. Borg gave me a hug and told me not to worry, and without a backward glance was gone from view within minutes. Kemit was also ready with a large group of the lake men with long bark ropes hung around their shoulders, and bags of axes and flint and food supplies.

Kemit came over to me and said, 'Sweetness, you and Inja are the most precious people in my life right now. Do not worry, I will be back soon. We have braved fiercer lands than these, and remember, my men are good warriors as well as traders.'

Then looking at Inja, he said, 'I know you will take good care of her, my dear.'

He kissed Inja on the lips, in front of the whole settlement, and picked me up and kissed both my cheeks. Then he, too, was gone within minutes of entering the forest. Even though Inja did her best to make me feel welcome, I could not stop thinking about my whole world walking into possible danger in the dense forests that surrounded us.

Lazdona came over to me not long after they had gone, and invited me to share midday food with her and some of her friends, in a hut at the other end of the settlement. I did not want to offend her, so I followed her meekly through the network of passageways between the huts. I really could not get used to the huts being over the waters of the lake. Every so often we would walk over a stretch where the wooden walkway was spaced a little wider. On those stretches you could even see the dark, cold water beneath as you walked. To make matters worse, Lazdona skipped along ahead of me, making the wooden planks visibly bounce, which absolutely terrified me. We eventually reached the hut of her friends, and I was glad to be indoors again and forget about the lake surrounding us.

Inside there were three maids sitting by the hearth, cooking some strips of deer meat over the hot stones at the edge of the fire. They looked like they had a few more winters than me, but we should still have a lot in common, I thought to myself. Apart from my recent adventures with Kemit and the crew, that was. They talked about the endless chores their mothers gave them, and in that I found could relate to them completely, thinking of the never ending jobs my grandmother had always had for me. The main topic of conversation though was Vehn and Saun, and the festival.

'Did you see that maid kiss Vehn, Rae?' one of them asked the maid sitting next to me, and they all burst into fits of giggles.

'Yes, I did. How could she do that, in front of the whole settlement, do you think?' Rae replied, in a very disgusted tone of voice.

'It worked though, did it not? Vehn then picked her to be his mate!'

Rae turned and looked at the chubby maid opposite me, and said sarcastically, 'I suppose you would have to do that to get a man, Brigit, would you not?'

At that comment they all laughed. Brigit looked really uncomfortable, and I took a sudden dislike to Rae.

'No, of course not!' Brigit replied, almost in tears. 'How could you imagine I would kiss a man I was not bonded to like that?'

'Well, we thought that someone with your looks would have to put herself forward like that, at such an event, so as not to be left until the last.'

When Rae said that to Brigit, the atmosphere in the hut changed to something that felt very familiar. They were treating Brigit just as Lusa and Mayni used to treat me at home. I hated that type of maid. They were always so pretty, and so popular with maids and boys alike. I had often thought in the past that the gods, in giving them beauty, seemed to have missed out their kindness and compassion.

Then Lazdona said in a stern voice, 'What kind of impression are you giving Mia, Rae? Do not be cruel to Brigit, she has been a good friend to you.'

I was glad Lazdona had said that, but I decided that some young maids were the same no matter how far north you travelled. Rae then turned her attention to me, asking, 'So Mia, you must have loved the dress our Queen Inja gave you. I thought the colour went very well with that lovely hair of yours. Did you know, it took three women days to make it for you? It is the sort of dress that only nobility can wear in our tribe. Are you of noble blood then, Mia?'

I found myself a little taken aback by that question, as I was not expecting it. Was I of noble blood? I hardly thought so, if they only knew about my background on Dogger Island. Then I found myself saying it! I don't know what came over me, but I replied instantly, 'Yes, I am.'

I just did not want those shallow maids looking down at me! And as I was so far away from home, they were never going to go to Dogger Island to find out the truth. So I thought I could get away with a little stretching of the truth.

'Really,' she replied, suddenly smiling at me, 'I thought you must be, or our queen would not treat you the way that she does. What position do you hold with your own people?' she asked.

I knew Rae was a maid that lived by the rules and status of others, and before I knew what I was thinking, I said, 'My mother was the chief's daughter, and my father was a prince from Lower Brit Land.'

What was I doing? I thought. The truth was bound to come out somehow. But I soon overcame my disgust at myself, and started to enjoy the new status that this lie had given me.

The days passed quickly in the settlement from then on, as the complicated web of lies that I poured out to the maids on a daily basis took all of my concentration. I was starting to feel really ill at the thought that they would find out, and I would be branded as a liar and a nobody again.

They were all talking one midday food about crushing small nuts, and how they all hated that job. I was just about to reply that it was my most hated chore of all, when I stopped myself. A maid of noble blood would never crush small nuts! How ironic. I had finally found something in their lives that I could really relate to, and I could not share it!

The next day, I decided to ask Inja if I could go to the beach and visit the men there, to get away from it all for a while. She said it was fine and she would arrange for some men to accompany me. I was just about to set off with the men, when I saw Brigit standing alone at the edge of the lake. I walked over to her and asked,

'Brigit, what are you doing over here on your own? Where are the others?'

As she turned I could see that she had been crying, as her eyes were red and swollen. 'What is the matter?' I asked.

'Oh nothing, really. Rae and the others were going to visit the net makers and they did not want the boys to think I was a close friend of theirs. It's understandable, they do not mean any harm by it, it's just that the boys will make jokes about me, and they will be embarrassed.'

Yes, I thought. Those maids are just the same as Lusa and Mayni. I suddenly decided that I had had enough pretending to be something I was not, just to keep them as friends. They would never be true friends anyway, so I said, 'They are cruel, and I do not think I will eat with any of them again!'

Brigit looked at me in shock, and replied, 'Oh, you must not do that, or they will never speak to me again!' and she started sobbing again.

I could see the men on the path were waiting for me to follow them, and I asked her, 'Will you come to my home on the beach today? I could show you where I live, and maybe we could look at some of the trade goods in the store too.'

She looked at me as if I had gone mad. 'You want me to come with you? I would love to! I would first have to ask my mother's permission though,' she said.

'No need,' I replied. I walked up to one of the waiting men, and told him that Brigit was coming with us. They said that Inja would want me to have company, and they were sure it would be fine.

'There, it is the will of your queen, so you have to come now!'

She got up and we laughed, and skipped ahead of the men towards the path through the reed beds. Brigit told me they were never allowed out of the settlement usually, apart from one week in mid-summer, when they had a festival on the beach. Then they would spend days boiling seawater in leather bags, to get the salt they needed for the winter. I could not imagine spending my life so close to a beach, and yet never going to it.

As we walked ahead of the men, I decided to confess to Brigit about my non-existent noble blood. She stopped in her tracks when I told her, and looked at me with a face that was so very shocked, that I had to laugh out loud. So much so that the men came over to me and asked if I was all right! When we all started walking again I told her about my life on Dogger Island, and how Lusa and Mayni used to treat me the same way that Rae treated her. I told her of our journey from there, and Kemit and Borg and the crew. I missed out the bits about the Shaman and the Goddess, and the red dress. Maybe one day, when I was older, I would be able to talk about that with someone else. As it was, I just said that I had been unhappy, and my grandmother was cruel to me. The traders took pity on me, and helped me to get away.

As we approached the clearing I started to run over to our hut under the cliff, and Brigit ran after me. We burst into the hut so quickly that the crew, who were eating their midday food round the hearth, jumped back and grabbed their weapons.

'Hold it! It's only me!' I exclaimed.

Brigit was terrified by the crew, as they certainly did look rather fierce. But when they saw it was me, their faces beamed with happiness.

'Mia, you gave us a start! You must have grown swans' feet, living by the lake. We did not hear you approach at all! Come, sit down and get some food for you and your friend.'

I gestured for Brigit to sit down, and she was given some food immediately. Then I said, 'There are some lake men with me too, so we will need another four bowls.'

The men had approached by then, and the crew made them feel at home and gave them some stew. After we had eaten, I signalled for Brigit to follow me into the store.

'Come and look at the goods,' I said, and I opened one of the bags with the silks inside. After I made Brigit touch it, she just sat there stroking her face with a piece, and smiled. Because her eyes were alive and bright, she looked really very pretty, I thought. She was just a little more rounded than most, that was all.

'That is called silk, and it comes from the dry lands of the Far East! Isn't it wonderful? One day, I plan to go there and see them make it! Here, look at some of the things they make on my island.'

I reached over to the bark bucket and showed her the necklaces made by the cliff women. Then she sat down, and I poured the bucket full of the brightly patterned necklaces onto her lap. We had such a good time, looking at cloths, and hanging dozens of necklaces around our necks. I really took a liking to Brigit that day. After a while we placed everything neatly back in the bags and I showed her the rest of the hut, then took her outside. The men had finished telling each other tales of their youth, and said it was time to go back to the lake. After saying my goodbyes to the crew we started walking back.

'It is really wonderful at your hut on the beach,' Brigit said, just as we were about to lose sight of it on entering the forest. She continued wistfully, 'I wish I were you, and lived in a hut on the beach with the traders.'

I did not say anything for a while, then asked her, 'Surely not. You have your family at the lake, do you not?'

'Not really. My brothers are all men with women of their own, and my mother and father do not speak to me much. I think they are disappointed that I am not as beautiful as Rae, or the others. My brothers, you see, are all so handsome.'

'You are not bad to look at, not at all. You are a little more rounded than most, but I knew a maid on my island who was much bigger than you at your age, and when she turned fifteen winters she became as thin as everyone else,' I said

'Really? It would be good if I was the same as her then!' she replied.

On our way back Brigit and I talked about Rae and her friends, and I decided to not spend so much time with them anymore. I liked Brigit, she was the closest I had ever been to another maid, and I knew we would become good friends before the spring thaw came.

When we entered the settlement I went to look for Inja, to ask her if Brigit could spend her time with me instead of with her family doing her chores. Inja said she was delighted that I had found a friend, and gladly agreed to my request, saying that she would like to meet her. She suggested Brigit might like to stay with me in my hut, next to her hall, while I was there, as she thought I was a little lonely on my own. I had not thought of that! So I thanked Inja, and went in search of Brigit with the good news. I found her outside her hut, grinding grass seeds.

She did not see me approach, and just as I was about to speak to her I heard a harsh voice from inside the hut call out to her, 'Brigit! Finish that and come in here and stir this bag of stew. We cannot all go off on little trips to the beach, without a by your leave. Get on with it. I have plenty more jobs for you to do after that.'

Brigit sighed, and looked up. She saw me standing there, and the look on her face told me all I needed to know about her home life. It was a look that I am sure I had worn for most of my life, living with my grandmother.

'I am sorry you had to hear my mother shout. It means nothing really, it is just her way,' Brigit apologised.

I sat down quietly beside her, and whispered what Inja had suggested in her ear. She looked at me with a mixture of shock and delight at the same time.

'My mother would never allow it!' she said.

'She would have to if Inja told her to! Come, let us give your mother the good news!'

I was just about to walk into the hut when Brigit pleaded desperately, 'No, you cannot. She will be very angry.'

I leaned down and looked her straight in the eyes, then said, 'Do you want to come and stay with me in my hut, and spend the half-moon wandering about doing nothing, or not?'

'Of course I do. We had a wonderful time today. I do not know when I enjoyed myself so much,' she replied.

'Well, that's enough for me,' I said, and went into the hut.

When my eyes became accustomed to the darkness, I realised it was very, very untidy, and had a damp, musty smell that comes from wet leather and grasses. There was a woman dropping a hot stone into a leather bag full of stew next to the fire, and she spoke to me without turning, saying, 'You ugly creature, it's about time you finished grinding those seeds. Get over here and stir this stew.'

Her voice was bitter and hard, and I took an instant dislike to her. I replied in the noblest voice I could muster, 'If you want me to stir that stew, I do not think you should call me ugly!'

The woman jumped back and looked at me, with an expression on her face as near to abject panic as I could imagine!

'I... I... thought you were somebody else! Do forgive me, my lady. Please, please forgive me. To what do I owe the honour of this visit to my very humble home?'

Her voice was suddenly soft and gentle compared to moments before. At least my grandmother used to be harsh to everyone; she did not pretend to be something she was not, as Brigit's mother obviously did.

'I have come at the request of your queen, to take Brigit to my hut to stay with me for a while, as my companion.'

She just stared at me, and said in a bewildered voice, 'Of course, of course. I will get her sleeping furs to take with her.'

She went over to a pile of stinking, moth-eaten furs, and started picking them up. I shouted to her, 'That will not be necessary,' not wanting those horrible smelly things in my hut. 'We have furs enough in my hut for Brigit to sleep on. I think we will be going now.'

I turned and noticed Brigit, who had been standing at the doorway all the time, with her mouth wide open. I grabbed her hand and pulled her out after me; we walked quickly until we were a few huts away. Then I stopped and turned to look at Brigit. She still looked shocked, but there was also a sparkle in her eyes as she said, 'Mia, what have you done? My mother will beat me well when you go back to the beach. Not that I mind. It would be a beating I would not mind taking this time. How you just stood there, ordering my mother about! And when you refused the furs... I had to stop myself from laughing. She was mortified that you did not want them!'

I laughed with her, and replied, 'Yes! Sorry, Brigit, if I went a bit too far, but the way she spoke to you really annoyed me. And you could not possibly sleep in those furs, they were horrible!'

'Horrible. You do not have to tell me. They are the furs I have slept on for as long as I can remember. I used to go and pick marsh mints in the summer and spread them over the furs to make them smell better, but the scent would only last so long, and after a while you do not seem to notice the smell. Did Inja really say she wanted me to stay with you in your hut? Or was that just one of your tales?'

I tried to look a little affronted by that suggestion, but could not stop myself from laughing, saying, 'Yes, of course she said it! I would have told tales, mind you, just to get you away from that place if I had to. You are my friend now, and you must be treated with respect.'

Brigit looked at me as if I had gone completely mad. She could not imagine anyone in her settlement treating her with respect. So we walked happily past Rae's hut, just as she was about to go in. When she saw us she called over, 'Mia! Are you coming over for midday food with us?'

I replied as we walked past, saying, 'No, not today. Brigit and I have a meeting with your queen. We must go.'

We walked quickly away before she could reply, and were soon standing at Inja's door. One of her women was sitting outside. I asked her if Inja was busy, and she said she would go and see.

'What are you doing?' Brigit whispered urgently. 'You did not really mean it when you said we were going to a meeting with the queen? I thought you were just saying that to upset Rae!'

'Of course we are going to see Inja. She is happy I have found a friend. She said that when I brought you here, she wanted to meet you.'

Brigit's face went white, and she looked like she was suddenly stricken ill. 'Are you all right? Come, sit down here, while we wait.'

I had not realised, until Brigit told me later, that she had never been close to Inja in her life before. Even though her settlement was not that big, she lived in the poorer area, and only ever saw the queen at festivals, from the back of a crowd. Inja's woman came out and told us that she was able to see us. I had to hold Brigit's hand tight, and physically pull her into the hut behind me. She immediately dropped to the floor as Inja came over to us.

Inja looked at her for some time, which I thought was odd, eventually saying, 'Stand up, my dear; if you are Mia's friend, then you are part of my special family.'

Brigit stood up and looked at her in utter disbelief, at the queen speaking to her directly. Inja laughed at her, but it was a kindly laugh. She held out her hand to Brigit, and led her to her seat by the fire. We sat down on the deep soft furs and warmed ourselves for a few minutes. I thought perhaps I should tell Inja what I had seen at Brigit's hut. Inja looked at me sternly, and then every so often at Brigit. After I had finished telling her about the hut, and Brigit's mother, and the disgusting furs she had to sleep on, we all sat there in silence. I knew it might have been embarrassing for Brigit, but if she was going to have any life in the future, she had to get away from her family home.

Inja gestured to her woman to bring us some food, and after we had eaten, said, 'Brigit, it gives me great sorrow to think that someone in my settlement is being treated so badly. Mia was right to tell me about it, so do not worry, you need never go back and live there again, if you do not want to. You have found a good friend in Mia. I know she will be good company for you. Maybe later, if you wish, you could become one of my hut women?'

Brigit had by then composed herself, after eating the meal and adjusting to the magnificent surroundings of Inja's hut. She replied quietly and politely, 'I would dearly love to stay with Mia for a while, and I have no wish to ever sleep at home again. I do not know how to thank you.'

'No thanks are needed. As I said before, if you are a friend to Mia, you are part of my special family. I think you should show her your hut now, Mia, for I have a meeting with the elders soon.'

We got up to leave, and Inja whispered in my ear, 'Fear not for Kemit. I had news today that they have found a good tree, and will be back with it within seven suns.'

I smiled at the good news, and led Brigit out of Inja's hut and across the walkway to my own. When we went inside, I realised it was actually quite a big room, with a central hearth and huge piles of furs around the walls. In fact it was the enormity of the fur piles that made the hut look a little small. We flopped down on the furs and I said, 'Well, what do you think of my home then?'

Brigit replied excitedly, 'It is wonderful! I have never seen such a pile of furs, and they are soft, and newly cured. Oh Mia, you are so good to me. I really do not know why you prefer my company to that of Rae and the others. I am a nobody.'

I looked at her sadly, as she had such little opinion of herself, then replied, 'Well, here is one nobody, to another. We are going to be good friends, I know it. You are a good person, not sly and shallow like the others, thinking of nothing but boys and how they look. Do not talk any more about me doing favours for you, or I will start to get cross. We are equals, so let us see if there are any of those dried fruits left in the bowl. I feel the need for something sweet to nibble on.'

When I said that we both burst into fits of giggles, and laughed and talked about the other maids, and how they would hate Brigit's new status in the settlement. That night, we finally went to sleep after eating huge bowls of nuts and dried plums.

That night though, I had a troubled sleep again, dreaming of some sort of dark place, and having a feeling of loss of hope and desperation. When I woke I was in a sombre mood, thinking of my dreams the night before. Then I saw it. A very large black feather was lying on my pillow. I picked it up and looked at it, wondering where such a huge feather had come from. I thought perhaps Brigit had put it there as a gift, but when I looked over to the furs where she lay, I could see she was still fast asleep. I sat up by the fire, fingering the feather, when one of Inja's women came in and caught sight of it. The look on her face was one of absolute terror! I asked her, 'Do you know where this feather might have come from? Here, look at it, it must be from a very big bird.'

I stretched over to hand it to her, and she took a step back, nearly knocking over the bowl of nuts. She stumbled out, saying, 'I really don't know, my lady. I…' And she was gone. Curiouser and curiouser, I thought. I looked over to Brigit, just in time to see her wake, and said, 'That was odd. I have never seen anyone quite so terrified of a feather before.'

'Where did you get it from?' Brigit asked.

I shook my head and replied, 'It was just lying on my pillow when I awoke.'

Brigit immediately looked up into the roof space, presumably looking for the bird that had dropped the feather. Just then, a very flustered Inja came in and held out her hand for the feather, saying, 'My maid told me you must have had a crow or raven in your hut. Let me look at that feather.'

I handed her the feather, and as she took it, a strange look of contentment came across her face. She brushed it up and down against her cheeks, as if caressing something lovely instead of an ugly black feather. When she came to herself, she said, 'Sorry, but I love the feeling of feathers on my skin. I always have. I am sorry if it concerned you, it probably blew in through the door in the night. Did you sleep well, Mia?'

Just for a split second I felt she knew that I had not slept well, and had had a dark dream. But I pushed the thought aside, explaining it as my silly imagination. Not wanting to make a fuss, I said, 'Yes, I slept fine, thank you. I am really hungry now though.'

Inja laughed and told her women to bring our first food, which we both devoured with relish. And I completely forgot about the feather.

10. THE TREE

After about six suns, more and more messengers were coming back from the forest, with news of the great lime tree that Kemit and the men were moving towards the settlement. When the tree was only a sun away, Inja said we should go and meet them and walk the last part back with them.

As we walked to meet them, I realised that the men would want to take the tree to the beach to work on it. Which would mean that I would be going home in a matter of suns too. What would happen to Brigit then? Even if she was allowed to live in my hut and work with Inja's women, she would still be very much alone. I walked ahead a little and caught up with Inja, and asked her, 'Is it possible that Brigit could come and live with me on the beach, when I go back there? We are such good friends now, and I would really miss her company.'

Inja glanced at me as we walked, and replied casually, 'Of course Mia, but it is not up to me who lives on the beach, is it? You will have to ask Kemit. But do not trouble him with decisions about Brigit now. I want him all to myself today!'

I smiled at her, and I went back to Brigit, deciding to say nothing to her about my conversation with Inja. It was no use getting her hopes up until Kemit said it would be all right. I also thought Kemit would only have thoughts for Inja that day, too.

After a while we could hear nothing but the shouts of men, and the cracking of shrubs and trees in the forest ahead of us. I was trying to imagine just how they were moving the tree, if it was the size of the tree our last log boat had been made of. It was not long, however, before I found out! We were just winding our way through a narrow path between some bushes, when someone called out, 'Keep clear, you in the bushes!'

Inja took my hand and pulled me sideways, away from the path, just as a small birch tree came crashing down, just where I had been standing. For once I did not mind her icy grip, and she looked at me and said, with bright and sparkling eyes, 'I think we have found them!'

She darted over the fallen tree and through the tangle of briars, and disappeared instantly from view. The other men in our party just smiled at each other to see their queen so happy, and we carefully followed her. Then we saw it! A huge river of destruction, leading on into the distance, where the men had moved the tree. What a tree! I had seen large lime trees on our island before, but nothing like that! Teams of men were chopping the trees in its path with axes, and others were carrying large logs from the back of the destruction to the front.

The men in front must have noticed our arrival, for they all stopped and came over to us. They were all filthy and covered in sweat. On that cold day too. I was trying to find Inja and Kemit, but they were nowhere to be seen. I wandered through a group of men who were greeting each other and talking excitedly about their adventures, when I saw Uin and rushed over to him.

'Greetings, Uin, you have a fine tree there!' I shouted formally to him.

'We do that, Mia. How goes it with you this fine day?' he replied stiffly,

'I am well, and you?' I replied smiling.

Then he lunged towards me and picked me up in his strong arms, holding me above him, saying, 'Enough of this formality. It is good to see you, sweetness, come and give me a hug.'

I laughed and we hugged, and suddenly it felt as if I was at home again. I could hardly remember what it had felt like, all those winters spent on Dogger Island without any show of affection from my family. I decided then, that maybe you were born with one family, but find your true family when you are older, as I had. As Uin and I walked over to where a fire was being made, we laughed and joked about his adventures in the forest.

'Where is Kemit?' I asked Uin. 'I have not seen Inja since we found you, either.'

'You'll like as not find them for a little while yet, I'll wager. Come, let's eat, and you can tell me all about living over a lake!'

I realised what he meant about Kemit and Inja, and felt a little stupid for asking where they had gone. We spent a pleasant few hours by the fire talking, then Kemit and Inja appeared as if from nowhere. They both looked happy, and I could not imagine Kemit ever wanting to leave her side again, he looked so contented. I wondered though, if he found her hands as cold as I did.

'Sweetness! Come over here and give me a hug!' he shouted at me.

I ran over to him and he held me tightly. I felt such a bond with him, I knew that it would be with me throughout my life. He was the father I had never had. Inja stood by his side, and we all walked back to the lake, leaving a small group of men with the tree. Kemit told me that they would take it from where it was, straight to the beach the next day. I was puzzled by that, and began to wonder just where we were.

Kemit must have noticed, and said, 'You see, we are in fact very close to the beach now. It is just over there. If we took the tree to the lake, and from there to the beach, we would have moved it twice the distance. We will leave some men with it tonight, and tomorrow we will get everyone to help us move it to the beach. What do you think of our fine tree then?'

I replied instantly, saying, 'I have never seen such a big tree in all my life!'

All the men around us started to laugh, and I laughed with them when I realised that as my life was not that long, I was not really the best judge of tree sizes. So it was a happy group that entered the settlement that night. They made a huge fire in the central clearing for us to all sit and eat around. I introduced a very timid Brigit to Kemit, as my best friend, and he said to her formally, 'I am honoured to meet any good friend of our Mia. Your queen has also told me that you wish to stay with us in our humble home on the beach. Is that true?'

I thought Brigit would never answer; she just stood there before Kemit, looking up into his eyes, with a completely blank expression on her face. I prodded her in the back, and she came to herself and replied, 'I would be very grateful if I could stay with Mia, a little while longer, my lord.' Her voice tapered to almost a whisper.

'No!' he boomed at her, and she went as white as a sheet. 'We are grateful to you, Brigit, for being a good friend to Mia. Of course you can stay with us, we would be delighted to have you, hey men?'

The men all held their fists towards the sky and cheered. Brigit instantly went from having a white face to a bright red one.

'Enough of this formality, we are all family here. Come, let us eat,' Kemit said, and the rest of the evening was spent with a wealth of funny stories being told, about their finding, then chopping, the great tree down. Kemit came over to me when it was quieter, and asked, 'Is there any news of Borg yet?'

I looked at him, and could hear the concern in his voice. I too was getting worried, as he should have been back days before Kemit.

'No, but I wish he were here. It frightens me to think he could be in danger.'

'They probably found some good hunting along the way and forgot about the days. I remember when I was his age, we would hunt for weeks, following trails, and completely forgetting about life back at home.'

I looked at him and smiled, but I was not smiling inside. Now that Kemit and the crew were back safely, all I could think about was Borg.

That night I slept in my hut with Brigit, in the lake settlement, for the last time. I kept waking up, thinking I could hear strange sounds, but when I sat up and looked around there was silence. The third time it happened, I was sure I had heard the flapping of wings. Just before first light I heard it again, and jumped up. When I looked at my pillow in the pale morning light, I saw three large black feathers. I decided not to say anything about it that time, and pushed them under one of the stones that surrounded the fire. I must have fallen fast asleep again, as I was woken by one of Inja's women, saying, 'It is time for first food, and we are all needed. Hurry!'

I leapt out of my bed, and ran out of the door straight into Kemit, who was just passing. He laughed and asked, 'Hey! Is there a fire loose?'

I looked up at him, relieved that he was close, and replied, 'We have to hurry, Inja's woman said. Is something wrong?'

He looked at me searchingly, then answered, 'Only that it is another day, and there is much tree to be pulled!'

I looked at him, and realised that I had got entirely the wrong impression from the woman's urgent words. After my experiences of the night before with the feathers, I must have been sleeping very lightly in case of danger.

'Oh, that is a relief! I am hungry! Come on Brigit, we have to help soon, so let us get some food.'

We both went into Inja's hut where we usually ate our first food, and started to eat quickly. Brigit still could not get used to sitting in the queen's dwelling for first food. Usually she would sit by the wall, dreamily stroking the thousands of swan feathers that lined it. She moved to sit by the wall again, and I said, 'Come on. The feathers will still be there tomorrow. We have to get that tree to the beach!'

I ran out not long after, and could hear Kemit and Inja laughing at my enthusiasm as they followed me. I turned to Kemit and said I needed to get something from my hut, and I would follow them. So I went back into the hut and sat by the hearth, lifting the stone that I had put the three feathers under, during the night. I don't know what I was expecting to find, but I was still surprised to see nothing but fire ash underneath it. I knew I had not dreamed it, or at least I thought I knew. I decided it was no use sitting there worrying about it, and ran out of the hut to catch up with Kemit and Brigit again.

Even though the tree was not far from the beach, it still took all the settlement men and crew all day to move it. Brigit and I got to the clearing ahead of most of the crowd, and I introduced her to the rest of the crew before they started work. It was really a huge tree, and I could see why it took so long for them to bring it back that far. They found the tree on the first day of their expedition, they told me later, and spent the next seven suns cutting it down before they could start to move it.

As soon as Kemit arrived, the men started work. A team of the crew and settlement men went ahead in the direction of the beach, to cut the trees in their path. I thought that that would take a long time, but soon they were back and the men started untangling the bark ropes, ready for pulling the tree. I went over to Uin, who was standing close to me, and asked, 'How have they cut down all the trees on the path to the beach so soon?'

He smiled at me and replied, 'They don't actually cut down the trees. They just chop wedges in the base of the trunks, so that the trees will fall in the direction we are pulling the big tree. As we move closer, the men with the log rollers loop string onto the top branches, and pull down on them until the trees snap. This way, the forest becomes a river for our tree to glide across.'

I looked back at him, and still must have looked puzzled as he continued, 'They can only do that in this type of forest of small birch, hazel and willow. If the forest was dense, like the forest where we found the big tree, then each tree would have to be felled completely. But these scrubby trees will snap nicely,' he patiently explained.

They stopped pulling for a while, so that the men could get the logs from the back of the tree and place them at the front. Uin and I went over to the tree to get a closer look at it. It was only then that I noticed there was a great big hole in the tree. Seeing us there, Kemit came over and said, 'Mia, I see you are taking a closer look at our wonderful tree! See the crack running down the trunk?'

I looked at the gaping hole in the tree and wondered if they had picked such a good one after all, then replied, slowly, 'Yes…'

I was trying to understand why they thought the obviously rotten tree was so good.

'It is the perfect tree for a boat. Lime trees of this size can get this type of disease, which creates a hole in the trunk that runs for most of its distance. The tree somehow stays alive for many years after this happens. To help it stand up in the winter storms, the tree builds a hard skin around the inside of the hollow. All we have to do is cut the tree down, and finish off the job that the disease has started. Then we have the hardest, strongest log boat, but only half the work in hollowing it out!'

I looked back at his sparkling eyes and understood that it was truly a wonderful tree. 'Is this type of hollow in a tree rare then?' I asked

'Yes, sweetness, it is rare to find one this tall that is still standing. Usually you find them on the ground after storms. But this one was protected by two huge pine trees, so it just kept on growing with the hollow trunk. Now we will have a boat at least a man's height longer than the one we lost. Come, I think I just saw the hunters bringing in our midday food. Let's go and sit for a while, and you can tell me what you have been doing while we have been gone.'

He walked ahead of me and Brigit followed, and we sat together around the fire and ate strips of deer meat, which had been cooked on sticks hung over the flames. I told Kemit about how I felt about living over the water, and how I had finally got used to it enough to sleep well at night in my hut. I did not mention the feathers though, as I thought he would think me silly. I also told him about Brigit and Rae, and the other maids. Then I confessed how I had told tales about my status to impress them. He laughed out loud at my confession, and thought it was a good way to make friends with that type of maid. He was glad however that I had found a real friend in Brigit, someone that I did not have to lie to. He did say something that puzzled me though, that I could not get out of my mind.

'I have a feeling you might not have been making tales up as much as you think.'

I looked at him and asked, 'Why?'

He looked down at me quite seriously, and said in a low voice, 'Do not speak of this now, Mia. We will talk together when we have more time, and there are not so many listening ears around. I have been thinking about where your father might have come from, and if I am right, you were a very precious cargo indeed that we took from Dogger Island!'

He put his finger to his lips before I could say any more, and put his hand on mine and held it tightly. I could see by the serious look on his face that I should just leave it at that for then. We continued to eat our food, and before long we were watching the tree being pulled through the scrub onto the beach. Our job was to untangle the ropes while they were moving the logs from the back to the front. As I did that, I did not feel like chattering to anyone. My mind was full of

Kemit's words about my father. Over and over again I kept repeating them. *I might not have been making up tales as much as I think!* What on earth could that mean? Did I really have noble blood then? Because that was what my tales had been about! It could not have been about my life on Dogger Island, as I was well aware of my family's standing, and my cousin Karn and grandmother. No, it must be to do with my father's blood. But how did Kemit know about him? And what did he mean about me being a precious cargo?

It was, in a way, every maid's dream, to suddenly discover her parents were not the people she thought they were, and that she was really a chief's daughter in disguise. I had dreamed of that many times on the sand cliffs, as I grew up. Particularly when my grandmother was cruel, or Karn's father would not have me in his hut. I would imagine that I was really the daughter of a powerful chief, and that my father, who conveniently left before my birth, was a Brit Land chief's son. That one day he would come back to the island and take me away from the drudgery that was my life. But then I would remember that my grandmother had told me that he did not even know my mother was with child before he left. So how would he come back for his child, when he did not even know he had one?

In that far away land, when my life was suddenly filled with real adventures and family, my old sand cliff dreams had come back to haunt me. I knew by the look on Kemit's face, that there was something very serious connected with his thoughts about my family. Maybe, when he had his new boat made, then he would tell me.

That afternoon went swiftly by, and when I suddenly heard the surf breaking over the rocks at the edge of the beach, I knew we were home. I had not seen Brigit for most of the day, as she had been helping sort ropes on the other side of the tree. I decided it was time to go home ahead of the tree and tell the men to start cooking food for the workers. I walked over to Brigit and noticed she was looking very sad, almost tearful. I asked when I sat next to her, 'What is the matter? Have you hurt your hands on the rope? I did that a while ago and it really pinches.'

She looked up at me and tried to smile, but I could see she was really upset. I looked over to see who she had been working with, and saw Rae sniggering with Lazdona as she watched us together.

'What have they been saying to you? You should know not to take any notice of them. You will be living at the beach with me from now on, and it doesn't really matter what they think, does it?'

She looked up at me tearfully and asked, 'You… you still want me to live with you at your home on the beach?'

I looked at her sternly and replied, 'Of course I do! I thought it was all arranged. If you do not want to, I will be sad because I was looking forward to having you there. I will understand if you have changed your mind though. After all, you will have to leave your lake.'

Then she put her hand on my arm and whispered tearfully, 'They said that you must have changed your mind, now that your family is back, as you have looked very serious all afternoon, and have not said one word to me since midday food.'

I looked back at her, and realised how it must have looked to her. I was so preoccupied with what Kemit had said, that I had been in a world of my own all day. I had been back on the island, on the sand cliffs dreaming, and there were those strange feathers to think about too. I leaned over to her and pulled her up from the tangle of rope she was working on, and said, 'I am so sorry, I just had a lot to think about. Please forgive me if I gave you the wrong impression. Leave that, we are going home right now!'

She stood up and looked at the pile of rope she was supposed to sort out with a shocked expression, and said, 'But I must finish my rope. The others will get cross if I do not do my piece too.'

'Who cares what they think. Rae,' I shouted. 'Finish off this rope will you? Brigit and I have things to do at my hut.'

The look on Rae's face was a picture, and before she could answer, we just walked away through the trees. Within minutes we were on the beach. I looked at Brigit's smiling face then and said, 'Now we are home! Come, let's get inside out of this cold.'

We ran the rest of the way over the sand, skipping and dancing with joy at our escape from Rae and her friends. The men inside had a good fire going in the hearth, and I told them that the tree movers were almost there. One of them went outside with a burning stick from the fire, to light the bonfire on the beach that they had prepared to warm all the people. We asked if we could do anything to help, and they gave us two huge platters of meat, asking us to cut it into strips with the blades they gave us. It was nice work, sitting by a fire cutting the meat up, warm and contented in each other's company again. We had just about finished when we heard a crashing sound, and the cheers of the crowd.

'They must be on the beach!' I said, and we rushed out, just in time to see the huge tree roll over the edge of the forest clearing and onto the sand. When we got close to it, I realised just how big it really was! It would make the biggest log boat I had ever seen.

Kemit and Inja were standing next to it, arm in arm, and when Kemit saw me they waved for me to come over to them, saying, 'Well, is that not a fine tree, sweetness?'

I smiled back and replied, 'It is not a tree! It is part of an island!'

At that comment they both burst into laughter, as did the crew that were within earshot.

'A fine description, and I think the name of our boat will have to be *Mia's Island*.'

I said that surely they would want to give it the same name as the one they had lost, which was the *Estergard Arrow*. I knew that was what the fishermen did on Dogger Island. When they made a new boat, they just gave it the same name. Kemit told me then that the tree would make a very special boat, and that it would not have existed had they not met me. So *Mia's Island* it would be! I was so proud that they were going to name the boat after me that I must have been grinning all evening.

That night the settlers had a chance to look around our hut. They mostly said that it was very strange, but also very nice. Each family that had helped move the boat were given a decorated bone necklace from my island by Kemit, They were all delighted with the gift; they did not really expect any reward, because their queen had told them to help. The women of the settlement then sent for some of their special plum mead, which we all drank and enjoyed. Brigit and I had ours watered down of course, as it burnt our throats when it came straight from the bag. Around the fire I kept noticing Rae looking at me, and talking to Lazdona. She was not at all happy at Brigit's new status as my close friend. I imagined she had planned to make her life miserable when they went back to the settlement that night. So I thought it was time to tell her what had been arranged.

I told Brigit to come with me and we sat down next to Lazdona, who made space for us and said, 'You have a wonderful home here, Mia. I love the coloured cloths on the walls. I have never seen such colours. You must be glad to be at home again. I am sure Brigit will miss you.'

There was a note of glee in the last part of the sentence, so I replied casually, 'Oh, did you not know? Brigit is coming to live with me on the beach now. She is to be my companion.'

Lazdona and Rae looked back at me in complete shock. Brigit had a home and chores there to do.

'How could she just leave her work and live on the beach?' Rae asked sarcastically, and went on to say, 'I imagine Brigit's mother will have something to say about it, she always has so much work for her to do.'

'That does not matter,' I replied. 'Your queen has said it is fine, so I suppose Brigit's mother will have to do the work herself from now on.'

They were looking exceedingly cross then, and Rae said, 'When you leave next spring, Brigit will have to go home then, will she not?'

Without thinking or even looking at Brigit, I just stated, 'No, as Brigit will be coming with us when we leave. It is all arranged.'

No sooner had I said that than I noticed Kemit had been listening to our conversation, and looked at me quizzically. I looked back at him and widened my eyes, as if to say is this all right? He smiled back and nodded, and I looked back at Brigit and smiled. She was looking at me as if I had taken leave of my senses completely. I took her by the hand and walked her towards the hut and away from the fire.

As soon as we were out of earshot Brigit asked, 'Did you really mean it? Can I leave with you in the boat next spring? I know you were trying to get back at

Rae for her comments, but please, do not promise me something you cannot keep.'

She was looking at me with desperation in her eyes.

'If I said you are coming, you are coming. Unless, of course, you want to stay in your own settlement. Do not let me pressure you. I know what it is like to leave your whole world behind, and Inja did say you could be one of her servants if you wanted.'

She sat down on the cold sand and said, 'I would spend hours as a child by the lakeside, hoping I would leave the settlement one day. As it is unheard of for people like me to leave, I did not have much hope. We live and die without sometimes even travelling more than a day into the forest. I am so happy, Mia, that I met you, you have changed my life completely! I will always be grateful to you.'

I pulled her up and said, 'Nonsense! Kemit rescued me, and now I rescue you. I am just passing on my good luck to another, and one day you can do the same for someone else. Let's go home and sit by the hearth and get warm. This sand is very cold! I want to hear the crew tell us their tree finding story again too.'

We disappeared into the hut and out of sight of Rae and Lazdona. Out of their world and into one where they could not hurt Brigit anymore. The rest of the evening we laughed and talked with the crew around our fire, and after a while some of the settlers came in and told us they were going back to the lake. Kemit went with them too to spend the night there with Inja. He gave instructions to the men that they were to make a start on the boat at first light, and that he would be back not long after. At that statement the men smiled, and said they would start at first light, but they would expect him back when they saw him. Kemit laughed and walked out, and we could hear him laughing in the distance as he walked back to the fire on the beach.

I showed Brigit where we slept and sorted some of the nicest furs I could find for her bed, and within minutes of her lying down, she was asleep. I settled myself down to sleep too, but suddenly all I could think about was Borg. Our room suddenly seemed strange without him there to snuggle up to. I hoped and prayed the Gods were looking after him, and wished he would come home soon.

I woke the next day to hear the chip, chip, chipping of stone axes on the tree. It was a sound that I would hear every day from then on, until the next moon. I looked over to Brigit's bed, but she was gone. I suddenly got worried that she had had second thoughts about staying on the beach, and had gone back to the lake. I needn't have worried though, as she was by the hearth, chatting with the crew and cooking first food for me.

'It is a wonderful day Mia!' Brigit said with sparkling eyes.

'Is it? I feel a little tired. I think I should not have had that last cup of mead by the fire last night,' I whispered.

'A nice slice of boar meat will sort you out! Come, drink some water. I have heard it is good to drink a lot if you have had too much mead the night before.' She handed me the water bag, and after drinking a lot from it, I did begin to feel a little better, as Brigit had said I would.

MOUNTAINS OF THE HEAVENS

INJA'S

BEAR

RITUAL POND

KEMIT'S HUT

BORG's ADVENTURE

11. BORG'S ADVENTURE

We opened the door of the hut a little while later to be completely dazzled by the bright sunshine. It was the sort of day you only get in mid-winter, a bright pale blue sky and crisp clear air, and warm sun on your face. It was only during those kind of days that you realised how much you missed the warmth of the sun, in the cold of the winter. I flopped down on the dry sand, shut my eyes, and absorbed the heat on my face. I don't know how long I lay there, or even if I had fallen asleep, but I woke up to the sound of a voice just above me.

'This is a fine way to start a day's work!' said the voice.

I knew immediately. It was Borg! I leapt up and hugged him, and did not stop holding him until the tears of relief streamed down my face. He looked at me and knew it was best not to say anything, just to keep on holding me until I was ready to speak again. When I eventually let go of him, he said, 'I am glad to see you missed me so much! Are you going to introduce me to your friend?'

I composed myself, and noticed Brigit standing next to us. 'This is Brigit,' I said. 'She has come to live with us on the beach.' Brigit smiled shyly, and I turned to Borg and said, 'And this is Borg who, as you know, is like my brother. Come into the hut, Borg, and put some dry clothes on. You look drenched!'

He agreed that he had better change, as he was a little cold, and I asked, 'How did you get so wet, it has not rained for days?'

He looked away from me and said, 'It might have something do with falling from a waterfall, and nearly drowning in a swollen river, I expect.'

I looked at him searchingly, for I instinctively knew that he had been in danger all along.

'Do not look at me like that. I am all right now, which is unfortunately not the case for the rest of our expedition.'

I looked at his face as we walked, and he looked grimly back at me, saying nothing. After he had warmed himself by the fire and changed into some dry clothes, he said, 'I had better go and speak to Kemit.'

I told him that Kemit had not come back from the lake settlement, and surely he had seen him as he passed the settlement on the way back. He shook his head and told me he had not come back that way. He had walked from downstream, where the river had carried him. I did not want to ask too many questions, as he was obviously very disturbed about something. I was just glad to have him back. I said I would like to walk with him to see Kemit, as I did not want to let him out of my sight again for a while. I asked Brigit if she would like to come with us too, but she said that as she had spent all her life there, she had no desire to visit so soon. She said she would like to watch the crew start on the boat, and anyway, she had better help prepare midday food for them as they would be very hungry after working all morning. I could see she wanted to get to know the crew by herself, so Borg and I walked towards the lake alone.

We had made it almost up to the reed beds, when Borg stopped and said he wanted to sit down for a while on a fallen tree trunk we were passing.

'Are you all right Borg? If you are hurt you must tell me.' I was starting to get concerned; it was not like Borg to want to rest like that.

'I am not hurt Mia, at least I am not injured in any way. I am hurt in my soul though, at the thought of the news I have to give, when we reach the lake.'

I looked at his grim face and asked, 'Would it help to tell me about it first?'

He looked down at me and smiled a little, saying, 'Yes, I think it might. Oh Mia, I was so happy to be going on our trip to the mountains. Little did I know my first real adventure would end in such disaster.'

I looked up at him as he had stopped talking, and I was sure I could see his eyes were welling up with tears. Could Borg be that upset? I thought. I had never seen him like that, so I said gently, 'Go on.'

He pulled himself together and told me about the outward trip to the mountains, and how they were all in such good humour. He told me of his particular friendship with Vehn, and how they seemed to think in the same way about most things. Borg had never had a brother, and he felt he had found the nearest thing to a brother in Vehn on that journey. Their expedition led them to cross a river over a ravine, by walking over a fallen tree bridge. They spent two days walking from there until they came to the slopes of a great mountain.

The trees changed to mainly pine as they climbed, and before long they noticed the little grey leaved bushes that produced the juniper berries. They camped by a clearing that night, and the next morning they filled all their bags with the fruit and were ready to return home. Then they heard a noise coming from the slope of the hill just a little way ahead of the camp. It sounded like some sort of large beast, and the men thought they might be able to get a good pelt to take home with them, as well as the berries. So they packed up the camp, leaving their bags behind a fallen tree, and set off to find out what it was. Just a little way up the slope they could hear the sound of a waterfall, and as they climbed over some large rocks, they saw what was making the noise. It was a bear. Not a normal sized bear, but a huge, brown bear, the height of two men.

I looked at Borg and asked, 'You have hunted bear before, haven't you?'

He looked blankly at me, as if he could hear me, but was looking at another picture in his mind.

'Yes, Mia, I have hunted bear before, with Kemit in Scan Land, on one of my trips with the crew. This was no ordinary bear though, Mia. It was huge, and it was wounded. Someone had lodged a spear in the back of its shoulder, and it was obviously in great pain. We thought it could not see us watching from the top of the rocks, but the wind must have blown our scent over to it, and it turned and charged straight at us! Rasa was ahead of us, and it moved so quickly it was on him before he could even think of running away. With one swipe of its great paw it crushed his skull against the rocks below...'

Borg looked at me tearfully, and suddenly it was me who was the older one. He looked at me like a little boy, hoping I would make the bad picture in his mind go away. As I looked back at him I could not fight back the tears either, at the thought of not seeing Rasa again.

'What did you do then?' I asked.

'Before we could collect ourselves, the bear had killed the other two men, and started to climb the rocks to get at Vehn and me. We fled, as we could see the others were dead, by the position of their necks as they lay on the ground at the bottom of the ravine. The bear was wounded, but that did not seem to have affected its ability to run after us. We ran to our camp and climbed a tree, and waited for the bear to go on past us.'

'But it just sat at the base of the tree, Mia. It knew we were up there, and it just sat down and waited for us to come down again. We spent that night, and the next, in that tree, wedging our bodies between the branches, so we would not fall if we slept. We did not get much sleep the first night, as we were thinking of our dead friends lying on the rocks at the bottom of the ravine. Vehn told me how he had known the two men from the lake settlement all his life, and how they were with him at the festival, choosing their maidens too. So we talked quietly for most of the night, and at first light we thought the bear must have gone. But as soon as we stirred, it let out a bellow to let us know it was going nowhere.'

'Could you not get onto another tree and escape?' I asked.

'No. We tried to jump to the next tree, but they were set too far apart, and each time we moved the bear would reach up the trunk on his hind legs and try to shake us out! We decided that as it was wounded, we would wait for another day and see if it got tired of waiting. Its mind as well as its body was wounded by that spear in his shoulder. That night, Vehn said we would have to take our chances on outrunning it. So we waited until it was dark, and then Vehn, without warning, just leapt over the bear and ran. The bear chased him immediately, and I jumped down and ran in the opposite direction towards the river. Our plan was that Vehn would double back and meet me there. We would then follow the river down the mountain slopes, till it met the low lands and eventually the lake. I had not gone more than a few feet when I heard a scream. It was Vehn. The bear had caught up with him, and all I can say is, it must have been pretty bad for Vehn to scream like that.'

Borg's face was wet with sweat, and his eyes looked dark and blank. I whispered, 'What did you do then?'

He did not reply for a while, then he said, 'I ran, Mia. I just ran. I could do nothing but run as fast as I could, in the opposite direction to the noise of Vehn's screams. I could not have saved him. I only had one spear on me, and the bear was huge. Mia, I really could not do anything but run.'

I could see he was tormenting himself for not going back to try and help Vehn, and I said, 'How could you have helped him? He was lost as soon as the bear got his claws into him. You knew that. Do not punish yourself, Borg. You were saved, and you can tell the men's families their death tale; they need to know how they died. Come, tell me how you got away as we walk. It is cold here next to the marshes, and you were very wet and cold when you got to the beach.'

I held his hand, and we walked slowly to the reed beds. Borg told me how he was stalked by the bear for days, and every time he waded for a while in the river to put it off the scent, the bear would pick it up again and follow him. After about three days, he made his way back to the tree that they had crossed on their way to the mountains. He crossed the ravine and was just about to try to dislodge the tree, to stop the bear from crossing too, when it was on the other side of the river, looking straight at him. Its fur was covered with dried blood, and its eyes were wild. Borg said he saw his own death reflected in its eyes.

The bear then made a lunge onto the tree bridge, and without thinking, Borg knew that his only hope was to jump down the waterfall into the gorge below, and take his chances with the river. He knew the bear would never give up on him if he just ran ahead into the forest. It would only have been a matter of days before it would have got him in the end, just like the rest of them.

So he jumped...

As he told me that, I asked, 'How high was the waterfall?'

'It was as high as the high cliffs on the promontory of the north lagoon, at home,' he said.

I stopped and looked at him. We both knew the height of those cliffs well. When you stood at the top of them, people on the beach below looked like ants.

He described the feeling of pain when he hit the water below, and how he went so deep under the water he did not think he would ever rise to the surface again. His world became a fast moving picture of avoiding rocks, as he was swept along at speed in the current; falling down and down, waterfall after waterfall, until he collided with a floating tree trunk and grabbed hold of it. He floated all that day on the log, and was eventually beached on a sandy bank, many days' walk down stream. Even though he was wet and bruised by the river, he could not stop, in case the bear was following the river downstream too.

After a little while he decided it was best to stay in the river, and got onto the tree trunk again, pushing it into the middle of the river. He stayed on the trunk for the rest of that day, until the mountains were just a speck in the distance. That night he waded towards the bank, at a point where the river was smooth and shallow. He knew he could not be far from the settlement, and started walking through the night. It was not until first light that he heard the chipping of the men working on the log boat, and knew he was close to home.

I held his hand tightly after he had told his story, and we walked the rest of the way to the lake in silence. We did not need the men to guide us past the swans anymore, as they knew us by then, and just ignored us when we approached them. We were almost up to the first hut before we were spotted. A boy saw us, and ran off in the opposite direction to tell people that Vehn's expedition was back. By the time we were approaching Inja's hut, there was quite a crowd following us. With each step Borg took his shoulders became more hunched, and by the time we reached Inja's hut his steps had started to drag. The settlers had noticed this, and what had been a crowd of happy, chattering people had become a silent one as they followed us.

Inja's woman gestured for us to go in when we reached her hall. The scene we met inside was a happy one, as Inja and Kemit were eating their first food together. They looked up at us as we approached, and could see from our faces that we had grave news.

Borg told his grim tale to them, and at the news of Rasa's death Kemit bowed his head, for he had known the old man all his life. As Borg related his tale, Inja began to cry silently too at the news of Vehn's heroic death. For Vehn would have known that the bear would catch up with him when he jumped down from the tree. He did it to give Borg a chance to escape.

I really felt for Borg at that moment. He was so very guilty that he had survived, when everyone else in his party had died. Inja could see that, and casting aside her grief, told Borg it was not his fault, and that the gods would say when and how people were taken. He had given Vehn the opportunity to die a hero, which his family would be grateful for. She told Borg to sit down, and went with Kemit to tell the young maidens and families of the men the sad news.

Borg and I just sat by the fire, and waited silently for their return. It was more than an hour before they came back. The two, who had looked so happy when we arrived, looked burdened with the grief of others. Kemit said that he should take Borg and me back to the beach, as the men would be wondering why he was not there to supervise the boat making. Inja told us that we would be expected at the frozen pond by the time the sun coloured, to bid farewell to Rasa and the young men of the settlement.

We walked in silence back to the boat, and on the beach the crew knew instantly that something was wrong when they saw Kemit's face. They stopped working and came over to us, and Kemit told them the sad tale. The men immediately put their tools away and walked down the beach towards the hut. They went straight to the store and got some bark containers full of their best masha, which was what they called mead. They sat around the fire, and started to tell their own tales about Rasa. Each time they ended a tale, they would drink a bark cup of mead in his honour.

By the time it was midday food they were quite drunk, and were becoming morose and depressed. They all went to their beds, so Brigit, Borg and I just sat there, looking into the fire as they slept and snored around us. Kemit sat next to us after the last man had gone to sleep, and said that that was their way of saying goodbye to a member of the crew. While they slept, they may if they are lucky dream of their old friend, and share one last experience with him, before he is taken to crew the great trading ship of the heavens. Kemit said that he too was going to go to sleep then, and say his final goodbyes to Rasa.

He told us to prepare a good meal for the later part of the afternoon, and that we were to wake them all up then, as they were all expected at the frozen pond before the sun lost its colour. Brigit and Borg set about cutting the meat, and I stoked up the fire. It was a strange and sad time that we spent, during those hours while the crew slept. It was Brigit's first contact with Borg, but it was so very sad. She did not know the light-hearted Borg that was so close to my heart. But the time went very quickly, and before we knew it the men had woken and silently started to eat their food.

Hardly a word was spoken, as the crew's thoughts were with the soul of Rasa. It was a quiet and sombre group that entered the arch of the enclosure around the frozen pond later that day. The interior was crowded with all the settlers, even the smallest children and babies. We were taken to our seats next to Inja, but that time the crew sat in a place of honour with the families of the dead hunters. How different that scene was from the one just a moon before, when it was the time for those young men to pick their mates.

Vehn and the two men from the lake had been part of that very ceremony, and now their prizes, the young maidens of the festival, were clothed in sombre black furs as they grieved for their young men. As soon as we sat down, Inja asked the maidens to come forward, and told them that even though they grieved, they were young women still and it was fitting to take another husband at the next festival. They all looked at her, and shook their heads in denial, that they would ever want another. Inja told them that she could understand how they felt, but she bade them to attend the next festival the following year. That time Inja would give them the first choice of the eligible men. They all looked shocked at that suggestion, as it was not heard of for maids to do the choosing. But Inja explained that there was never a time that young men were taken so close to them finding their mates, either.

As we sat there, I wondered how they were going to say farewell to their young men, when they did not have any bodies to dispose of. I then noticed that some men were coming through the archway, carrying three swans under their arms.

The swans were held down on the ice before Inja, who stood up and said, 'May our friends, the swans, take the souls of our lost young men to the hunting grounds they wish.'

As she said that she lowered her hands, and the men slit the swans' throats with the flint blades they held. As the birds fluttered their wings one last time, the women of the settlement wailed and cried the names of the three men, until the birds stopped moving. Kemit told me that the lake people believed that the swans, in those dying moments, would carry the men to wherever they wished to go in the heavens; when the swans stopped moving, the fallen men had finally departed.

The birds were then plucked just in front of us, and their carcasses were carried to the fire that was lit on the edge of the pond, where strips of their meat was wound around small sticks and cooked. As soon as they were cooked they were handed out to the waiting crowd, until every person in the settlement, including us, received a small piece. After eating the swans, people started to go home to their huts, to mourn their young men in private.

We left shortly after, and walked quietly back to the beach, sleeping not long after reaching our beds. It was a day I was glad to see the back of. The joy of Borg's return was completely masked by our grief for Rasa, and the bright young lake men. As I slept, I wondered who had injured the bear with the spear that had made it so intent on killing the first humans that it saw. I cuddled up to Borg that night, as I had done so many nights before, and hoped it would be a long time before he left me again.

The next day, all sadness seemed to have gone from the crew, and they chatted and joked with Borg as they worked on the tree, to make it into their new trading boat.

Over a moon went by as we all busied ourselves, helping to make the new boat. It was not just a case of hollowing out the tree; it had to be shaped, and all the seats and cargo stores had to be made. Also, because that boat was so much bigger than our old one, the traders' stall partitions were too small, so they had to be made again.

Borg, Brigit and I became firm friends during that time, so much so that it was as if Brigit was a part of us, the part that we had not known was missing. She was straight and sensible, but not averse to playing jokes on us either, and having fun. Borg was not the same boy I knew though, since the expedition to the mountains. There was an edge to his smile that I noticed from time to time. His experience had left a mark on his soul that I thought would take many winters to heal. Kemit and Inja were rarely apart then too; either Inja was with us for days on end, or Kemit would disappear to the lake settlement, sometimes for as long as half a moon.

12. INJA'S BINDING ANNOUNCEMENT

The winter was rolling on, and the huge pile of wood that the crew had stored when we first arrived on the beach had long gone. So wood gathering expeditions were carried out whenever the weather was clear and dry. It was after one of those expeditions, that I had tagged along with, when we arrived back at the hut, to find a group of lake people sat around the hearth with Kemit and Uin. I bounced into the hut, but stopped in my tracks when I saw the serious faces of the group in front of me.

'What is the matter?' I asked anxiously. 'Has someone been hurt?'

I looked around to check that Borg and Brigit were in sight, which they were, sitting at the edge of the room and also looking very quiet. Kemit looked at me but did not answer, he just stood up with the settlement men and followed them to the door. When they had gone I looked at Kemit, and was starting to get very worried. He came over to me, and taking my hand, led me back to the fire. Then in a very sombre voice, he said, 'Sweetness, we have grave news. The tribes to the south of us are threatening Inja's people with war, if she is not bound to their young chief. A few moons ago the young chief took control of many southern tribes, and now the fragile peace that had existed between his and Inja's people has gone. They sent a group of men to tell Inja of the new chief's wishes. They are a violent people, and want access to the lake and the fishing there. Their lands are in deep forest, with no open water, and their tribe has grown so much, they need more land. Inja now has to make a hard decision, for the safety of her tribe is at stake. If she offends these people, her own will become almost prisoners of the lake, for they would be attacked if they strayed too far from its edge and the swans.'

His voice was quiet and calm, but I could see his eyes betrayed his real feelings.

'But Inja is yours though, surely? She could not be bound to a stranger now? You are both so happy together,' I pleaded, not understanding why he was taking the news so calmly.

'Life is not that simple, Mia. Inja cannot make a decision about something like this so lightly as it affects all her people. She is a queen. She must not put her own feelings first.'

I could not believe he was saying that to me, and I said, 'How can you sit there and give her up? We will go and fight these other people! We will tell them they have a crew of traders to contend with too, not just soft lake settlement men!'

I could see the crew stirring, and nodding in agreement as I spoke, which fuelled my argument even more. 'I can throw a spear too, you know! Borg, tell them. We could set traps for them all around the lakeside.'

I saw by the look on Kemit's face, that my words were not having the desired effect, and he replied calmly, 'Yes, we could fight them. Yes, we could beat them too,' he said firmly.

'Well then?' I asked.

He stopped me before I could continue, and said, 'That is just not enough, Mia. There are hundreds of them. We are talking about two tribes to the south, maybe three or four. We might win the first battle or two, but they would keep on coming, and the settlement here is full of children. Inja knew this was coming. We both did. It was just a matter of time before the new chief took over the additional tribes.'

I sat down, realising then that what he was saying was the truth. If the tribes to the south were that big, they would win in the end, as Inja's settlement men were soft and not battle hardened like the crew. I could see from Kemit's face that he had very little hope and had come to terms with the situation.

'How long does she have to decide?' I whispered to Uin, who was sitting next to me.

'Just one moon, and the chief will want to be bound to her, or the tribes will send in their warriors.'

'Just one moon?' I whispered back, as the tears started to flow down my cheeks for the love that Kemit was losing. Uin put his arm around my shoulder, and said, 'It is the way of the world, sweetness. One day you are singing with the birds, the next you are falling in the mud of a swamp. We know enough to take what happiness we can, and cherish it, because we know it can be taken away as quickly as it comes. Kemit has spent his life waiting for someone such as Inja, and at least he has had a precious winter with her.'

I looked up at him and asked, 'But can't love last forever? Does it always have to be lost?'

Uin smiled back at me, and replied, 'It depends on the kind of love, sweetness. Some is so bright and sweet it would drive a person to madness, if it lasted too long. Some love is quiet and comfortable, and that is the kind you can grow old with. What Kemit and Inja had was the bright kind. It could not last. They both have responsibilities – Inja, the lake people, and Kemit to his crew. He could not have stayed here much more than a moon after the thaw anyway. Tashk will be out there looking for us when the thaw comes, and we need Kemit to steer us into prosperous trading waters again.'

I smiled, and leaned my head on his shoulder, as I watched Kemit's stricken face reflected in the firelight. We spent a quiet time that evening, and none of us were very hungry for the boar stew Brigit and I had made. I even put some of the red spice sticks in it, and some honey to make it sweet. We might not have bothered though, as lots of them left their bowls and went early to their beds. It was clear that the whole crew felt for Kemit. They had known him for many winters, and had never seen him as happy as he had been with Inja, and so they shared his loss.

I do not know why, but I had not thought about us leaving so soon. I knew we were making a new boat, but I thought we would just sail up and down the coast in the north to trade. It could not be more than a moon away to the thaw, too. I looked over to Borg and Brigit, sitting together on the other side of the fire, and signalled to them to meet me in our room by the store.

As soon as we were all sitting down I asked, 'Did you know we would be leaving come the thaw, Borg?'

Borg looked at me, and I could sense he knew I was frightened at the thought of going to sea again.

He replied, 'I had an idea we would not be staying long into the spring. The men need to trade, if they can, and in a way that makes it easier for Kemit to leave.'

'How could you say that! At least if Inja were still his, he could come back again for the winter. Now he will never be able to come back, he will never want to see her bound to another, will he?'

I saw Brigit's face and realised what the new situation meant for her. She would never be able to come back either, if she came with us. I said to her, 'Brigit, you must think very carefully now, if you want to come with us. It looks like we will not be coming back for a very long time, if ever.'

'That makes no difference to me. You two and the crew have been more of a family to me in the last moon than my real family were all my life. I am going with you, and no mistake now,' she said forcefully.

I knew how she felt, for I had been in the same position not that many moons ago myself, and I could not imagine a better family than Kemit and the crew. We decided there was no point just going over and over it, and went to our beds.

When I awoke the next day, everything seemed normal. The men were working on the boat, and Borg and Brigit were stoking the fire up after first food.

'I must have been tired if you have already eaten first food. Why did you not wake me?' I asked.

'You had a restless night last night, and we thought you needed your sleep,' Borg said quietly.

'What do you mean?' I asked, a little puzzled at his expression. I did not remember having a bad night. Borg came over to me and put his arm round me, and looked into my face with such concern that I started to get worried. 'What is it? What is the matter? Please tell me!'

'You kept shouting out in your sleep, and whimpering like a wounded animal. We were afraid to wake you. You...'

'What did I say?'

'Mia, you kept talking about some black birds, and the Shaman, and you kept on crying in your sleep. It must have been the talk of leaving here and going south again. Uin should have thought that the mention of Tashk looking for us would frighten you. Our adventure is not over yet Mia, but you will be all right. Do not worry. There is not a man in the crew that would not give his life to defend you. But I was wondering what the black birds meant?'

I looked up at him and shook my head. I had not realised I still had the Shaman on my mind so much. And what did the black birds mean? It must have been the mention of Tashk looking for us, as Borg said, that triggered my fears again. I shuddered to think that the Shaman was still in my head, but at the same time I was grateful he was only invading my dreams and not my waking thoughts. I asked where Kemit was, knowing the answer would be that he was with Inja. I wanted to go and see her, but felt that it would be an intrusion to anyone sharing their last moon together.

Why did it seem to be that just when life got into some sort of settled order, it was turned upside down again by events totally beyond our control? Then again, I had thought my life very tedious and uneventful for the first eleven winters, until the Shaman's announcement. It suddenly occurred to me that if the Shaman had not made his wishes felt, I would probably still be in my grandmother's hut crushing the last of the small nuts. So in a very strange and frightening way, the Shaman had set me free from the island, and led me into my wonderful adventure. I had suddenly found a totally new way of thinking about those horrible times. Looking back on the events that happened, I could, for the first time, see it as if a guiding hand had been directing everything. Making even the bad things work out for the best. Those thoughts, that day, gave me a great sense of peace, that somehow everything would turn out all right in the end.

My new understanding of the twists and turns of fate made me smile, and when I looked back at the concerned faces of Borg and Brigit, I smiled even more. They looked at me then with even more concern, as they must have thought I was losing my mind. They could not see what I had to smile about, having just had a nightmare the night before.

'Do not worry, I am not losing my mind. I have just gained a little wisdom, I think,' I said.

'Whatever do you mean?' Brigit asked.

I explained my new way of thinking, and they could both see the sense in it. After a moment's thought, Borg said, 'It is true what you say, Mia. If it were not for your desperate plight, I doubt that I or the traders would have risked what we did to save you. The Shaman did do you a great favour! I find it unbelievable, though, that that wizened old devil could do any good. But his evil intentions certainly put you on this adventure, sure enough.'

Brigit then said, 'And if you had not come here, I would still be living at home, being bullied by my family and those horrid maids. So your Shaman, evil though he sounds, did us all a favour.'

As soon as she said that, a shadow fell over Borg's face, and we realised her words had brought back the memory of recent events.

'Borg,' I said, 'you have to stop feeling guilty because you were spared, when the rest were lost. The gods must have had a reason to spare you. There is something in your future that is calling you. It was not your time to leave this world we live in. Hey, let's go and sit on the log on top of the cliffs and look out to sea.'

Borg looked down at me and smiled the clear, sweet smile of the old Borg, and shook his head, saying, 'You are amazing, Mia. You always seem to turn every bad situation around, to make it somehow good. I am glad you are my little sister, but no, I think I had better get to work on the boat with the men. I have wasted enough of this day chatting to little maids!'

At that comment I rushed forward to slap him on the back, but he was too quick for me, as he was out of the door in an instant. Brigit and I laughed, but then suddenly felt we shouldn't laugh out loud today, for Kemit's sake. We collected our furs and walked out into the bright sunlight too. I still wanted to go to the top of the cliffs, and asked Brigit if she would come. But she told me she thought she had better take the water bags to the men working on the boat. I hesitated, and thought that maybe I should also be doing some useful work, when Brigit noticed my wistful glance towards the cliff top and said, 'You go, Mia. I think you need to be alone with your thoughts at the moment, and there is nothing in particular for you to do anyway. I will see you at midday food, when you can help me twist the meat around the sticks.'

I smiled back at her, and realised what a good friend she had become. I walked up the path we had made behind the hut to the top of the cliffs. It was a cold day; even though it was sunny there was no warmth in the sun, as there was quite a breeze coming from the sea. I sat on the log and wrapped my furs around my body till there was only my eyes exposed to the weather, and looked out to sea. My mind was full of thoughts of my life on the island and the adventure it had taken to get me where I was. I kept thinking about my first sight of the Lonely Pine rock, at the end of that first day at sea. It was such a strange place, it seemed so alone in the middle of the open sea. The next day it had looked even stranger in the daylight. It made me think about the rising waters, and I wondered, where was all that water coming from? And why did it never go back? It just always kept rising. I had no doubt that my sand cliffs on Dogger would start to be undermined in a few more winters, too. The water at high tide was not far from them, and as soon as the waves could get under the cliffs, they would just fall down. It was strange to think that my sand cliffs one day would not be there. When they were gone, the settlement itself would be exposed to all the storms in the winter.

My mind wondered happily from thought to thought, until I remembered Kemit's words about where I might have come from. I knew that it was no time to ask him about it, with all that he had to think about. I looked down at the men in the distance, chopping away at the boat, and Brigit and Borg chatting about something or other next to it. I wondered if one day they might fall in love. It was only after that thought that I said out loud to myself, 'Stop right there Mia. If you are not careful you will end up like Lusa and Mayni, seeing love and bindings in every friendship!'

I suddenly felt some sort of brooding presence in the back of my mind. I could not put my finger on it, but it made me feel cold inside, and I found myself subconsciously clutching the crystal I wore around my neck. I shook myself vigorously, and told myself I was just being silly. And with one last glance at the distant horizon, I walked briskly down the path and into the hut below.

The rest of the day was uneventful until after last food, and we were all sitting around the hearth when Kemit came in. The men greeted him respectfully, realising he needed to be a little distant from them at that time. He nodded to them sombrely, and walked over to me and said, 'Mia, I would like you to come outside with me for a minute.'

I stood up and followed, glancing back to Brigit and Borg with a puzzled expression on my face. Outside I saw a group of the settlers holding torches around Inja, who was wearing her white feather cloak over a thick white fur cape. We walked over to them in silence, and Inja took a torch from one of her men and gestured for me to follow her to the other side of the beach. When we were out of earshot of Kemit and her men, Inja stopped and looked down at me in the torchlight, saying, 'Mia, you have heard the news that the chief of the southern tribes wishes to be bound to me?'

I looked up at her face, reflected in the torchlight, and just nodded. My throat was getting sore at holding back the tears, and so I did not trust myself to speak.

'I can see by your face, that you have. Do not say anything at the moment, Mia, just listen to what I have to say. I love Kemit dearly, as you know, but I have to put the safety of my people first. This is the price I have to pay for being their queen. I have to meet this man in his settlement before the next moon, and give him my decision. But I am in a very difficult position. I cannot take any of my own men with me, as I am sure they will not be able to control themselves if this chief humiliates me in any way. I also cannot take any of my women with me, as news would get back to the lake if I was treated disrespectfully, too, and there would be war between our peoples without a doubt.'

I looked up at her then and asked, 'Why do you think they will humiliate you? Surely, if he wants to be bound to you, he will be good to you, will he not?'

She put her hand on my shoulder and replied, 'He is not being bound to me because he likes me. It is all about more land, and lake fishing, not me. He knows the position I am in, and he also knows how my tribe has humiliated them over the years, when their warriors were chased away by the swans. He would want to redress the balance. He has taken over the other southern tribes

139

now, and he is far too powerful to be frightened by a few swans. I am afraid he will try to humiliate me, from what I have heard of this man.'

She looked down at me and saw I was crying, and put her arm around me, saying, 'Do not cry, Mia. I have had the precious gift this winter of being with Kemit. I fell in love with him when I was a child, and now that I have known him as a woman my life is complete. He would have had to go, for the sake of his men, come the thaw anyway, and now we have the precious memories of being together. I can take a lifetime of humiliation from this man, because Kemit is in my heart and my mind, and he will never leave me again. Also, I have a secret that you must swear never to tell Kemit.'

I looked at her, and I could guess what it was.

'Yes, I am with child! Kemit must never know, or he would never leave, and then disaster would befall all of us. This way, I will always have a part of Kemit with me.'

'But could this chief not harm your child when it is born?'

'No, my dear. He can control me and take my lands, but he could not touch my child. That he knows would tip the scales with my people.'

We walked along the beach for a while, and looked back at the group with the torches that stood outside of our hut. Inja said, 'I am going to ask you if you would come with me as my maiden, when I meet this chief before the next moon. Kemit has agreed to let Uin and some of his crew accompany me too. That way, if there are deeds that need forgetting, I can trust the crew and you to keep it to yourselves.'

Then I asked her, 'Could Brigit and Borg come too?'

She shook her head and replied, 'No. Brigit is a settler, and after Borg's recent experience, I feel he would need to prove himself by defending my honour, and that, too, would be a disaster.'

I nodded in agreement, and we slowly walked back. I realised she was right. Borg would not have been able to restrain himself, as Uin would. Uin was a kind and sensitive man, and slow to anger. When we reached the group of men waiting by the hut, Inja had a few words with Kemit and then they went back to the settlement.

Kemit and I walked along the shore on our own, and after a while he said, 'Thank you Mia, for doing this. If I had not taken you from Dogger I would never have met Inja again, and we would not have had our time together. It was inevitable that she would have had to be bound to the young chief, she knew that. But thanks to you the time we have had will keep our hearts warm in the winters to come, wherever we are.'

I stopped and looked back at him, and asked, 'Do you ever think, that you are travelling down a path that somewhere, in some place, you have trodden before?'

He stood and looked at me for a while before he spoke, then replied, 'Your wisdom is far greater than your winters. When this is over and we are preparing to leave, we must talk about where your father might have come from. I think you must have a lot of the strength of character of his people in you. I am sorry you cannot travel with your friends when you accompany Inja, but you can see the wisdom in it.'

I nodded saying, 'Yes, I do not want Borg, out of a sense of honour, to put Inja's people in danger. I cannot imagine how you feel about not going with her.'

I looked at his face, and saw him wince as if in pain at the thought of what she might have to endure. So I said quickly, 'Sorry, it is best if we do not speak of it anymore.'

He smiled at me and nodded, and I felt suddenly very old, imagining the burden he carried.

When we entered the hut the conversations of the crew stopped, and they all looked at us. Kemit ordered some mead from the stores, and the atmosphere lightened at the prospect. I left Kemit and sat down next to Borg and Brigit. They looked at me expectantly, as if I was going to tell them what Kemit had wanted, but somehow I could not speak of it to them then. I said I was tired and would tell them the next day, and went to bed. As I tried to get to sleep, my mind was full of thoughts of the journey ahead. I heard Borg and Brigit come in and settle down to sleep. They started talking to each other in whispers which, due to the fact that they were trying not to waken me, actually had the opposite effect. I kept my eyes shut and listened to them.

Borg spoke first, saying, 'What do you think that was about then? It is not like Mia to keep anything from me. It must be pretty serious.'

After a few moments Brigit replied, 'Mia looked very strained when she came back into the hut. It must have something to do with the queen and the chief of the southern tribes. Do not worry, she will tell us all about it tomorrow, I am sure. But from what I have heard about that young chief, he is a vindictive sort of man. They say he practises the dark arts, and is in league with devils. They also say that is how he has taken over so much land so quickly, and that he worships some huge snakes, and visits the underworld every moonless night.'

Borg whispered back, 'Such tales are to frighten little children. You do not believe in such things, do you, Brigit?'

Brigit mumbled back, 'No, of course not! I was just telling you what they say at the lake, that is all.'

As I heard her words I shuddered, wondering if he might have something to do with the feelings of darkness I had been having in my dreams. I certainly believed in such things! I do not know why, but I knew such dark practices existed. Then I wondered to myself how I knew? Brigit and Borg said no more, and not long after that I must have fallen asleep, as the next thing I remembered was Borg shaking me and saying,

'Mia, it is first food. Get up and eat something!'

I slowly stirred, and looked up into his anxious face, asking, 'What is the matter?'

'Nothing, I just think you should eat first food with us. You keep missing meals, and it is not a good thing to do in the winter.'

I smiled at his obvious concern and followed him over to the fire. The men were just leaving to work on the boat, and they greeted me before they went in their usual kind way. I smiled back at them and wondered which ones would be coming with us to the south.

I sat down by the hearth and Brigit handed me some crisp boar meat, which smelled delicious, saying, 'Here, I have saved the best pieces for you. When you have eaten you had better tell us what happened last night, if you can, before Borg and I go mad with curiosity!'

I laughed at her frankness, and after swallowing the piece of meat I replied, 'It has been decided that some of the crew and me are to accompany Inja, when she visits the southern tribe with her answer before the moon is out.'

They both looked at me in amazement. Brigit, because she had assumed that Inja would travel south with her own men and women, and Borg, because he could not understand why Kemit did not tell him last night too. Borg then asked, 'When are we to leave?'

I waited for a moment, to think of the right words to say so as not to hurt him, but I knew they would sound bad to him anyway, so just said, 'You are not to come with us, Borg. Kemit wants you to stay in camp. Maybe he thinks you have had enough adventures this winter.'

I felt that was the best approach. If he knew that both Kemit and Inja thought he might not be disciplined enough, and that he would let his feelings get the better of his judgement, he would have been devastated.

'I cannot let you go into danger without me, Mia. I will speak to Kemit.' He got up and stalked out of the hut. I looked at Brigit and smiled weakly.

'There is more to this than you are telling us, is there not?' she said, and I nodded but said nothing.

'If you cannot tell us, do not worry. I know you would if you could. When do you think you will go?'

I told her that I did not know, but I knew it would be soon. I asked her what she knew about the journey we would take. She told me that the forest was very dense south of the lake, and the only way to travel was by boat. Apparently, the journey would involve a trek through the forest for half a day, until we reached a small stretch of open water at the base of a great waterfall. She imagined that if the visit was at the request of the chief of the southern tribes, they would send boats there to wait for us. She had heard from hunters that it was at least two or three days' river travelling from there until we would reach the first of the chief's settlements.

When she said that, I asked, 'You said the first of his settlements. How many are there?'

'Oh, now they have taken over the other southern tribes, there must be at least eight or nine large settlements under his control, I would imagine.'

I looked shocked, and she went on to say, 'This is not a minor chief we are talking about. There must be thousands of warrior hunters under his command. He is treated more like a god in his country. His father before his death was a cruel man, but his son, from what I have heard, is truly vicious.'

I could see by the way Brigit talked about the chief that she was very much afraid of him. So I asked her, 'How do you know so much about this chief, if he has just come into power?'

Brigit looked a little uneasy then as she told me, 'You see, when he was a young boy, he came to our lake on a raiding party, to capture some of our young women. I was not born then, but I heard the story from my brothers, who saw it. They came in the night, and did not know about the swans, and were taken totally by surprise by them. As I said, he was only a young boy of maybe ten winters, and as the swans attacked he tripped and fell, and a swan caught up with him. The swan bit off most of his ear before he could escape into the forest with the others. A friend of my brothers saw it all from one of the platforms on the lake. Of course, we did not know it was the chief's son then, until about six moons later when some of our hunters who were out in the southern forest were attacked. They were all tortured and killed, apart from one man, who they let go to tell the our people what had happened. He was told that the chief's son had become very ill as a result of his wounds, and had nearly died of the fever. He had lost his ear completely, and the chief had said that if any of our hunters were ever in his forest again, they should expect to be killed. From then on we have been their sworn enemies.'

I looked at her intently and replied, 'If that was the case, then why would this young chief want to be bound to Inja?'

'The young chief could do nothing about our tribe while his father was alive, but once his father died and he became chief, he could exact his revenge on our people. There is only one thing certain in this proposal of binding. It is not for the love of Inja!'

The tone of Brigit's voice said it all. The situation was worse than I had thought; if the young chief was bent on revenge, then it was Inja that would pay the price for his disfigurement. I had no doubt that after his binding he would enslave the lake people too, as that was usually the case when a strong tribe took over a weak one.

I thought then about Rae and Lazdona. Their natural beauty would make them the first to be taken into slavery. I suddenly felt sorry for them. For all of their cruelty towards Brigit, they did not deserve that. Such is the life for maids and women in our world though. There should be tribes where women were in charge, and men were not the rulers, just to balance things up, I thought. (*Little did I know then, that there were such tribes, and that I was connected to them by blood…*)

During the next few suns, the crew seemed to work twice as fast as before on the boat. They all knew that Kemit would want to be gone as soon as the moon was up, and Inja was bound to the young chief. Borg threw himself into helping the men, and spent most of his time stripping wood to make the extendable partitions needed for trading. He did not speak to me again about my imminent journey south, after he spoke to Kemit. He was not his usual self with me during those days either. He was casual with me, and a little distant. I talked over my concerns about him with Brigit, who said it was probably that he was worried about my journey, and he did not want to make me nervous about it. I was not so sure though. I was worried that he thought I had taken his place in Kemit's heart, so I decided to have it out with him before it went on for too long.

I caught up with him on the edge of the reed beds, where he was cutting straight nut tree branches to make more partitions. He saw me coming, and busied himself stripping the knots from the branches he had cut with his blade. I was right next to him before he looked round, and asked me if I wanted him for anything.

'Yes,' I replied. 'I want you to be my brother again! What have I done to make you so distant with me? Do not answer. I know it is because I am going south with Inja in a few suns, and you are not. Do you not think I pleaded with Kemit and Inja to let you come with me?'

He looked round at me and asked, 'You did?'

I replied immediately, 'Of course I did! I do not relish the journey without you, but I have no choice. Inja needs a woman who is not from the lake to accompany her. That leaves me as the only option. I cannot let her down, after she has been so good to me, and for what she means to Kemit. Kemit saved my life, for I would have surely killed myself by now if I had stayed on our island. Even if I lose my life on this journey, it will have been a life worth having.'

I knew as soon as I said that, it was a mistake, and he shouted, 'What do you mean, lose your life? Are you going to be in danger? If that is so, I am certainly coming, even if I have to follow behind you on my own!'

'Do not be ridiculous,' I said. 'You would not get within sight of the chief's settlement before you would be caught, and without the traders' protection you would be killed. I am sorry, I should not have said that. I will not be in danger if I am with the crew. Kemit told me that this new combined tribe has a great need of trade goods, and he knows that I will be all right with Uin and the crewmen that are coming with us. There is always danger; I might fall from a boat, or be hurt on the journey in some way. You cannot come, you know that. Kemit wants you to stay with him. Do you not think he wants to go too? He knows he cannot come, as he knows he will not be able to see Inja humiliated by this chief and not challenge him. He knows also, that you would do the same thing.'

Borg was looking at me intently by then, and asked, 'Is that why he does not want me to come? When he told me of the trip, and said that I was not going, I thought that he thought I was not man enough, after my last journey.'

I could hear the anguish in his voice, and realised what he had been going through over the last few suns. He thought Kemit thought him a coward, and not brave enough for the task. Instead, it was because he knew Borg was too brave, and would challenge unimaginable odds for the sake of Inja's honour.

'Borg, for someone so wise in many ways, you are really stupid sometimes! Kemit knows you will not let Inja be dishonoured. He knows you will take on all the tribes of the south, without fear for your own life. He knows you would react in just the same way as he would, and it is for that reason he is not going himself. If this marriage does not take place, the lake people and Inja are lost. Brigit must have told you how big this tribe is, and the story of the young chief and the swan. Inja knows it is going to be bad, but she is the only hope for her people. You do Kemit a discredit if you think he is not letting you go because you are weak. He knows your heart, as I do.'

When I said that, Borg came over to me and hugged me, and I knew he shed tears, but I looked away when he let me go, so that he could wipe them away.

'Mia, how did I live all those years on our island without spending more time with you? I know I took you out on my boat a few times, but you used to spend all your days with Karn and Simi. I knew when I watched you, sometimes playing camp in the hollow tree, that you would one day become someone special. Little did I know you would become the rock that I would lean on. May the gods always bless you, Mia. You have given me back my self-respect. I look forward to the day when we paddle away from here, and continue our adventure together. I suppose you need to have an adventure of your own too, like I did. I will catch a sea bird every day you are gone, and offer it to the gods for your safe return.'

We hugged again for a long time, and then I helped him carry back the wood to the beach.

After we had eaten midday food Brigit came over to me and said, 'I do not know what you said to Borg this morning, but he is a different person because of it. Look at him running about and helping with the partitions. I have not seen him look this happy since I caught sight of him at the festival, when you first came to the lake.'

I gave her a knowing look, and said, 'So you noticed Borg then, did you?'

She immediately blushed, and I realised that my thoughts of a relationship one day between them was not so wild, at least from Brigit's point of view. If Borg's feelings for her were the same I could not say, but somehow I did not think he felt as she did. I could see she was still waiting for an explanation for the change in Borg, so I said, 'Oh, I just told him he was a brave young warrior. Somehow it just seemed to perk him up!'

She looked at me with a shocked expression, then realised that I was joking and we both burst into uncontrollable laughter. So much so, that the crew looked round from their work, and they laughed with us too.

13. INJA'S JOURNEY SOUTH

The time seemed to go so quickly those next days, and Kemit's mood became more morose with every passing day. Borg had not left his side since our conversation, and I knew it comforted Kemit to have his company during that time. Then the day arrived when Uin and I, and some of the crew, waved our goodbyes to Kemit and walked the short way to the reed beds to meet Inja.

As we approached Inja and her men we could hear raised voices coming from the reeds. When they saw us they stopped, and it was a chill silence that finally met us. Inja, of course, was all smiles, even though she seemed a little strained. Then she turned to one of the men and said with some annoyance, 'It is no use going over and over it again. I have made up my mind. I have chosen my escort, and I have chosen them with good reason. There are dangerous times ahead and the least waves we make at the beginning, the easier will be our passage. It is not what I want, but you know there really is no other way unless I condemn our people to slavery. Say your farewells, for we have a good walk ahead of us if we are to be met at the waterfall after midday food. Please do not make my last moments with you angry.'

When she had finished, the leader of the group came over and knelt down before her, and said, 'We have no wish to cause you more pain, my queen. May the gods be kind to you, and we will keep our torches alight until you return.'

She held out both arms to him and made him stand up, saying, 'Thank you. We will survive, my friends, if we use our heads and not just our hearts. Till I return.'

As she said those last words she turned and walked ahead of us down the path into the deep forest. I followed her, and we walked for the best part of the morning without stopping, or saying a word to each other. When we came to a little clearing in the forest, Inja requested we stop and rest for a while. We were very close to the waterfall apparently, and she needed to compose herself.

I sat next to her, a little distance from the others, and she said quietly to me, 'I wanted to have a word with you before we met the others, just in case we do not have the chance again before we reach their settlement. Mia, I know I am asking a lot of you, but you must be strong and help me when I ask you to. Or not help me, if I do not ask. Whatever happens, do not tell Kemit. Promise me now. And do not tell him of the child that grows inside me, or it will be the death of him. The fact that I know he is in this world of ours somewhere, will make the long winters sweet with his memory. If in any way I were to cause his death, then I would lose my will to live too, and that would mean disaster for my people. I must try to make this young chief feel that I wish to be bound to him. If he believes me, then I do not think it will be so bad for me.'

I looked at her as she quickly told me her thoughts, and realised then how strong she was. I told her she could trust me, and she hugged me tightly and we walked on.

We could hear the waterfall some time before we came upon it. When we were just a few paces away from the clearing, the sound of it was deafening, and we all stood speechless as we looked up at the magnificent sight in front of us. The waterfall was so high, its mist seemed to form small clouds halfway down. I had never seen anything quite so beautiful. A row of small rainbows shone from the spray in the pale sunlight, and it was as if we had entered the land of the gods. Yet there was a darkness there somewhere too. I felt the darkness rather than saw it, for my eyes saw nothing but beauty.

As I looked up, I also realised how close Borg must have come to falling, on his log, over that drop. He was very lucky to have got out of the river when he did, or I may never have seen him again. I doubted anyone could survive that fall, as I could see sharp rocks just under the surface of the pool of water in front of us.

When we finally took our eyes off the waterfall we saw four boats waiting for us on the sandy beach. Next to the boats were about sixteen or more men standing motionless, waiting. They were really tough looking men. They had long black hair, which was plaited tightly behind their heads, so from a distance it appeared as if they had no hair at all. Their faces and arms had a mass of tiny blue dots on them that formed some sort of pattern. When we got closer, I could see that the dots made the shape of a snake that wound around their arms, ending with the snake's open mouth and teeth on their cheeks. I was never that fond of snakes in any form, even the ones that we were taught were not dangerous. I thought at that moment we were all in great danger!

As we approached the seemingly arrogant warriors (who, by the way, did not seem to worry the crew at all, judging by the looks on their faces), they behaved with the utmost courtesy to Inja and myself. They prepared some food for us and politely fed us first, before giving the rest to the crew. Inja looked at me as if to say that their behaviour was not what she had expected at all. I still felt very ill at ease though. I caught a glance that Uin gave one of the crew, and I could tell he felt the same.

After we had eaten we were shown into the boats; Uin, Inja and I in one, and the rest of the crew in the others. The river was very slow moving as we left the waterfall, and so we made swift progress, not having to battle through rapid water.

After a while, I noticed some large, black birds that seemed to be following our boats, and I immediately thought of the black feathers that I had found on my pillow. At first it was just one bird, then another, and before long it was a whole flock! I had never been in that part of the world before and wondered if birds there were in the habit of following boats. No one else seemed to notice them, which made me think that maybe it was not odd at all. There was a little breeze too, out in the middle of the river, and I felt as though I could almost hear a whispering within it... just as when you almost catch someone's conversation, you can hear they are speaking, but you can't quite make out any of the words. I convinced myself I was imagining it and listened to the conversations of Uin and Inja, and tried to forget about it.

We travelled down river that day until it was almost dark, and then the men stopped paddling as we approached a little inlet. I thought to myself that they were leaving it a bit late to light a fire and make camp, but as we glided into the inlet I saw a fire already lit, and a group of people were cooking something that smelled really delicious. As we got out of the boats, we were immediately given food and drink. I looked back at the river, and noticed that the darkening sky was free of our bird companions. They must not have been following us after all, I thought, and smiled at my stupidity. But then I heard the sound of fluttering wings. Looking up into the trees above, I saw them all perched on the branches there, looking straight down at us. I jumped at the intimidating sight, for I knew somehow that they were not just ordinary birds.

I got up and sat back down next to Uin and the crew, a little way away from Inja, and whispered to him, 'Have you seen those birds?' I pointed up with my finger.

Uin followed my gaze and looked up, smiled, and replied, 'I cannot see any birds, sweetness, but birds have to sleep at night, just like we do you know.'

I leaned closer to him and said, 'But they have been following us since the waterfall!'

Uin looked at me with concern in his eyes, and said gently, 'Mia, they are just birds, wherever they are. It was probably just the same kind that you saw at the waterfall. There are many birds in the forest, and they all look the same to me.'

I looked up at them, and was sure one of them was looking straight at me. But I could tell Uin really could not see them and thought I was imagining it, so I replied, 'You are probably right. May the gods bless you with good dreams.'

Uin smiled and replied, as I went back to my seat next to Inja, 'And you also.'

Inja and I were shown to a small shelter, covered with bark and lined with furs, and left to ourselves while the crew were shown to their beds. Inja leaned over to me and whispered, 'This is a pleasant surprise! At least we are being treated with some respect. I must say, by the look of the snake marks on those men, courtesy is the last thing I would have expected from them.'

I nodded and replied, 'I have never been all that fond of snakes. They do look terrifying, don't they.'

She whispered back, 'I think that is the idea, my dear. You are supposed to look at them and be terrified. It makes attacking other tribes so much easier, when your warriors look like that. I do not want to get too confident, but I do feel a little better than I did before we met them. Their chief has obviously thought about our journey in every detail, and he has taken great care to see that we are well looked after. They are not the actions of the spiteful, evil man that we have heard he is.'

I could see the way she was thinking. She should be able to make this man think she wants the binding, especially if he was going out of his way to make her happy and comfortable.

The rest of the two days journey down river was uneventful, apart from the growing flock of birds that still followed our boats. Each time we stopped they disappeared into the forest, as we were given food by the people that were waiting for us. Even the crew visibly softened their grips on their spears and daggers, as they could see we were in no danger on that journey.

Uin came up to me on the last night of our journey and said, 'I think my lady Inja will be all right after all. These are the actions of a man trying to please a woman, not one trying to humiliate her. We will not drop our guard though, and mind you do not stray far from us when we reach the settlement. I believe you are to be introduced as Kemit's daughter, for your own protection.'

I looked up at him, and smiled happily to be thought of as Kemit's daughter. And then I hesitated, but had to ask, 'Have you really not noticed the black birds that have been following our boats?'

Uin frowned and looked concerned again, and asked, 'Show me these birds.'

I looked around, but they were nowhere to be seen. I could see that I was starting to worry Uin, and he said gently, 'When you see them again, just signal to me and I will see if I know what kind they are.'

I nodded to him, and was starting to wonder if I was perhaps just imagining it. They were just birds, I thought. Maybe creepy large black birds, but just birds. I was just being silly.

The next day we knew we must have been approaching the settlement by the small groups of people waving to us every so often. As we passed, the small groups turned into bigger groups, until a continuous line of people waved at us from both shores of the river. It must have been at least an hour after that, that we saw the first huts ahead of us. I had never seen so many people in one place. There were at least four times as many as in my entire tribe on Dogger Island!

The men paddled the boats towards a line of wooden jetties, and just as they were tying them up I heard a whoosh of feathers flying just above our heads. The whole flock of black birds flew over us, and disappeared amidst the roofs of the huts of the settlement. I looked around to see if Uin had seen them, but he was busy talking to one of the crew. He must have heard them, even if he had not seen them, I thought! But if he had, I was sure he would be looking at me, which he wasn't. I decided not to mention them again to him, and clutched my crystal tightly to make me feel better, which it amazingly did.

When we stepped out of the boats, we could finally see the extent of the settlement on the gentle slopes of the river bank. I felt that there should be another name for it, as it just did not seem right to call it a huge settlement.

And, as much as I strained my eyes, I did not catch sight of the birds again. They seemed to have disappeared completely.

We were soon met by a group of women all wearing pale blue dresses. They too had marks on their faces, but their dots made delicate spiral patterns on their foreheads, not snakes, and I thought they looked very pretty. They were all smiling, too, as we followed them into the heart of the settlement. Inja was wearing her white swan feather dress and cloak, and I wore my grey and black heron feather dress. I really felt like I was royalty by the way we were being treated as we walked to meet the chief. But at the same time I felt a pang of guilt that I was enjoying myself, when Kemit and Borg must have been beside themselves with worry. From the few glances Inja gave me, I could see she was feeling the same way.

We were shown into a large hut, and asked if we wished for anything while we rested. The women told us that their chief would see us when the sun coloured, as he was away at one of the eastern settlements and would not be back until then. We said we would like some water, which they quickly gave us, and then left us to ourselves. I popped my head out of the door to see what had happened to the crew, only to find them all sitting in a line in front of the hut entrance. I smiled, realising they were certainly not going to let their guard down, until we were safely home.

Inja and I sat down and talked about the journey, and the size of the settlement. After a pause I said to her, 'Those women did not look like they were badly treated, apart from the patterns on their faces, which is probably just the custom with these people. What do you think?'

After a moment's thought Inja replied, 'I know what you mean. These are not a people living in fear of a tyrant. The old chief died sometime last summer, so the new chief has had time to rule in his own way. I do not want to be too optimistic until I have met him, but I am feeling a little happier, having seen his people. If he rules my people in this way, we will all prosper from our binding.'

I must have looked a little shocked at Inja's words, as she continued, 'You must understand, Mia. I was brought up to rule, and I was also told from when I was a child that I would have to be bound to someone from another tribe one day, to make my people strong. I was frightened by the stories I had heard about this man, but maybe they were exaggerated just to frighten us. Do not worry, I know what I am doing. If he wants to be good to me, I am not going to object. If I have to be bound to him it might as well be pleasant, if it can be. I am flattered that he has gone to such a lot of trouble to please me!'

I still thought she was a little callous, and I was glad Kemit could not hear her obvious pleasure at being wanted by this powerful man. We did not have to wait long before one of the women came in and said the chief was ready to see us. We followed the woman through a walkway lined with crowds of people, all cheering and waving at us. I wondered if they always greeted their enemies like that. Maybe they were rejoicing at our coming doom? But I stopped that line of thoughts in its track, before I scared myself to death! Uin and his men followed me, as I walked a few paces behind Inja.

We approached a large open space, in front of a huge round hut with a very steep, pointed roof. At the entrance there were two of the snake warriors, and they were about to stop the crew from following us in, when someone told them to stand back and let us all go in together.

As we entered the hall we saw a blazing torch lit room, and a high seat at the far end with a man sitting upon it. As we approached he got up, and walked briskly towards us. He was dressed in a black fur tunic, and wore a necklace of black shiny beads and rough golden ones. His face was tanned and his hair was dark and long, and fell over his shoulders covering his ears. I thought that was probably a good thing, as I would not have been able to resist looking at the missing ear the swan had bitten off when he was a boy. Apart from a line of dots on the top of his arms, he had no other marks on him. His face was so handsome, and his eyes sparkled as he looked at Inja. He gently took her hand and led her to the seat next to his. I was shown to a seat just below hers, and the crew sat next to me.

The chief did not sit down, but walked up and down, looking thoughtfully at me and the crew. Then he said, 'Greetings, Inja, Queen of the north lake. And greetings to you, traders from the south. This is a great day for my people, for we are now strong, and have need of trade with the tribes of South Brit Land and Scan Land. Your leader did not come, I hear. That is a pity, for I would have liked to have met him. But his beautiful daughter has come in his stead, and that is a great honour.'

He leaned towards me, and from the corner of my eye I caught sight of Uin reach for his blade. In the same instant the guards at the door took a step forward.

'Calm down! I only wish to kiss the hand of this fair maid!' he said laughing, and everyone visibly relaxed. He kissed my hand, and was it not for the rumours about the man and the circumstances of our coming, I would have fallen head over heels in love with him. He was so very handsome, yet he was also very frightening. I tried to smile naturally at him, but I suddenly felt very, very cold. I realised that it was not my whole body that felt cold, just the back of my hand, where he had kissed me. I held it in my other hand, and rubbed and rubbed it to try to warm it up.

He went back to his seat, and poured all his charm onto Inja, until she was laughing and giggling like a young maid. I could see by the look on Uin's face he was glad Kemit had not seen that, for he too thought that she loved him. Inja was not just being friendly with the chief; she was, after a drink of mead or two, almost throwing herself at him. I looked at him as he spoke to her, and for a split second noticed a fleeting glance of seer evil in his eyes. I realised the whole scene was for our benefit, and he was not being honest with us about his true feelings.

The hall began to fill with people, and after we had eaten he said it was time for the entertainment. Before that, his servants brought round many bags of honey mead for everyone to drink. I shook my head when it was offered to me, but Inja leaned forward and said, 'Come, Mia, you are old enough to have some mead to celebrate my future binding!'

I smiled and replied, 'Oh well, maybe just a little.'

Inja got down from her seat and took the bag from the servant. Handing it to me, she said, 'I insist, really I do!'

Uin had been watching us closely and said, 'Maybe Mia would like some water with her mead? She is not used to strong drink. Here is my water bag. Take a drink from each, it will be easier to swallow then. But you do not have to drink a lot to wish our lady well, does she?'

He put his question directly to Inja, who left us, shrugging her shoulders, to sit next to the chief again. Uin leaned over and whispered, 'Give me the mead. You just drink from my water bag, she will be too drunk to notice soon.' I nodded gratefully, and sipped the water slowly.

A little while later, when many bags of mead had been drunk, the centre of the hall was cleared and a group of women dressed in blue led two maidens, who were dressed in white, towards two stakes driven into the floor. They tied their hands behind their backs and poured some sort of drink down their throats. The maids looked a little drugged when they came in so they did not seem to resist. I was getting a very uneasy feeling about what was happening by then, and so were the crewmen by the look of it. I looked at the crew again, and they seemed to have a glazed look in their eyes. In fact, I noticed everyone in the hall had the same look on their faces. I covered myself in my furs, and decided to pretend to be asleep, as I sensed something terrible was about to happen.

Before I saw them, I heard the flutter of wings and a horrible, spine chilling kaar, kaaring noise. First one swooped in through the open door, then another, until the high roof of the hall was spinning with the black birds that had been following us since the waterfall. I shut my eyes as I was too frightened to look, but still could not resist peeking from under my furs at the strange scene before me. The birds had stopped flying and had arranged themselves in a tight ring around the maids tied to the stakes. The chief stepped down from his seat, with Inja closely following, and as he raised his arms the birds fluttered their wings, as if in some sort of answer to him.

He started to shout some strange words to the watching crowd, and they all dropped onto the floor, including the crew! He turned suddenly and looked directly at me. I shut my eyes tight, but in the split second before I shut them, I felt an arrow of ice start to fill me from within. I was getting colder and colder, and he took a step towards me, to see if I was really asleep. I could not see him walking towards me as I had my eyes tight shut. I just felt it. It was the same as if I was walking towards an ice sheet. I felt truly terrified, and suddenly I remembered the crystal I wore around my neck. I could feel its warmth as the cold began to envelope me. I moved my hand slowly under the furs and held it tightly, instantly feeling better. The tighter I held it, the warmer I felt, and suddenly I heard the footsteps walking away from me. I peeked out at the chief, who had turned his attention to the two maids tied to the stakes. It was then that I heard a strange crackling, like the sound of distant thunder, and the room was suddenly filled with a large, black shadow. As I watched in horror, some sort of cobweb seemed to pour from the roof into the chief's outstretched arms, and then started covering the poor maids. They did not seem to notice it. In fact, they seemed to like the blackness surrounding them. Inja started to giggle like a young maid at the spectacle, and reached her arms up to the sky also. At that point some sort of blue smoke filled the roof of the hall. Just then the birds rose and started to fly round and round the roof space, swirling the smoke as they did so, until it looked like blue threads floating above us. When I looked back at the maids they were gone, and in their places were two large black birds. After a few hesitant hops they joined the others, and flew out of the door.

The chief smiled, and standing with his hands on his hips turned to address the crowd, saying, 'Those maids were the daughters of the chief from the eastern tribe. I brought them back with me today, to teach their father a lesson. He needs to understand that when I own the land, I own all that live on it too. They have passed into the other realm now, and will live only to serve me until they are consumed by the flames of our lord Zundal on Ispa!'

At that the crowd roared, and even the crew started to cheer. I lay so still, as I was terrified to move in case anyone noticed that I was not drugged, as the rest of the room seemed to be. Even my breath seemed to me to be too loud. I saw Inja kiss the chief passionately, and then burst out laughing with delight at the poor maids' fate. The crowd then started a slow chant – 'Laguz, Laguz' – and I realised I did not even know the chief's name until that moment. A group of men in the corner of the room started up a slow beat on their huge drums. Then the whole room came alive, with people slowly moving to the beat, around and around. Including Uin and the crew! The drums began to beat just a little faster, and the people moved their pace in time to their rhythm. Inja and Laguz stood arm in arm watching them, seemingly immune to the beat. The beat became faster and faster, until the whole room was almost running in one huge circle around the two stakes in the middle of the floor. I watched in amazement as some of the older people seemed to tire and fall to the ground, and the others just danced over them until they lay still.

Inja suddenly turned and looked at me, and I thought she saw me looking at the scene through my eyelashes, but after a moment she turned back to Laguz and said, 'Our little trader maid is fast asleep. No matter, she might have fallen in the dance, and we would have had some explaining to do at first light to Uin.'

Laguz looked at me, and I tightly held my mother's crystal. He looked away, sneering, then said in a harsh voice, 'I really do not see why we care about these traders. We have all we need here, and the power to bring more to us with our black friends.'

Inja replied in a very subservient tone, 'That is as may be, but how much can a bird bring to us? We need links with the settlements of the south if we are to capture their people's souls too.'

He reached over to her and kissed her again, replying, 'You are right as usual, my love. We can save their fate for another day when we have no need of them. But they must be gone by midday food, for I have to visit the Caves of Marr again, and be bathing in the waters of sight by then.'

Thank the gods Kemit could not see her with Laguz, I thought. For all she said about the need to help her people, I could see she was in love with him. That was also an Inja none of us knew, and I looked at Uin and the men dancing in increasingly fast circles, unaware of what was happening to them. I realised just how powerful Laguz and Inja were.

Then I must have really fallen asleep, for the next thing I remember was Inja gently touching my shoulder saying, 'I think I will be going with the chief now. You just go back to your hut with the crew, and I will see you at first food'.

I just nodded and reached over to Uin, who was standing in a daze next to me. As we walked back to the hut I asked Uin, 'Do you remember dancing all night?'

Uin looked back at me, puzzled, and replied, 'Dancing? I do not dance, sweetness. What do you mean?'

I explained to him what had happened, and he was horrified to learn that I had been defenceless while they were all drugged by the mead. I missed the part out about the maids turning into black birds, as I really did not think he would believe me.

'How could she behave like that? I thought she loved Kemit?' I asked him.

He leaned over to me and replied, 'You have to remember, she was a grown woman when Kemit met her again. Rumour at the lake has it that she has had many men friends over her life. This chief is obviously more to her real taste, than our good Kemit. It is good we travel south on our return before he sees her with him. I think Inja and this chief are very well suited to each other, and there need be no fear for her safety here, make no mistake.'

I looked up at him and nodded, but was worried. I was in a settlement so far from home, and I could not get those birds out of my mind. He must have sensed my fear and said, 'Fear not, sweetness. He will not harm you, or let any other. He wants our trade too much for that.'

We then reached the door of our hut and went inside. Uin said, 'We will sleep in here with you tonight. I doubt Inja will be back, and two men will stay awake all night to keep watch.'

Uin made up his bed near the door and we all went to sleep. I woke up wondering where I was, and when I remembered I jumped up and looked around me. There was still a faint glow in the hearth, and I could see some of the crew asleep near the door. I dressed quickly and carefully, so as not to wake anyone, and went out of the door. One of the crew that was on guard turned round and looked at me, and smiled. His name was Kas, and though I had known him as long as the rest of the crew, I had never really spoken to him before. He was usually on his own somewhere, and although he was always polite to me, he kept his distance.

'How are you this first light, missy?' he asked.

I arranged my furs around my shoulder and sat down next to him. 'I am fine. This is a huge settlement, is it not?'

As we looked down the main pathway towards the river in the distance, we could see the dozens of huts below, where there was complete silence. The only signs that they were inhabited were the wispy streaks of smoke seeping through the reed roofs into the morning sky.

'More what they call a town in the east, than a settlement. They say the chief has an even bigger settlement between here and the eastern one. I was talking to one of his men last night, and it sounds very similar to the Lady Inja's settlement, but it is five times bigger, with the lake it is next to being more like the Inland Sea!'

I looked at him thoughtfully and said, 'I was told by Inja that they did not have any stretches of water. That was why they wanted the binding, to have access to some inland fishing.'

As soon as I spoke, I knew then how ridiculous her story was. Kas looked down to me and smiled, but it was not a smile of happiness. It was a smile as if to say I had put too much trust in Inja's words. I continued then, 'I cannot believe she has deceived us like that.'

He patted me on the knee, and said quietly, 'Hush now, do not speak too loudly, we might be overheard. I could tell there was something afoot the way we were treated on the journey up. That was not the way you treat someone you are planning revenge on. It was more the way you treat an old friend.'

I was going to blurt out what I had seen the night before, when he put his finger to my lips to silence me, and drew my gaze to the passageway at the side of the hut. I could then hear what he had, which was the sound of footsteps walking slowly towards us. We sat in silence and waited to see who it was. In a few moments a small boy walked by, and jumped when he turned the corner and saw us looking at him. He looked completely terrified, but when we just sat there and smiled at him, he relaxed and smiled back at us. It was a sweet smile, and had his face not looked so thin, he might have looked like a boy from my home on Dogger Island that I knew. Kas gestured for him to come over and sit with us, and I thought by the terrified look that he gave us he was about to run in the opposite direction. I held out my hand to him, and he slowly came over and sat down next to us. He kept looking from side to side though, checking that there was no one about to see him talking to us.

'Hey lad, what is the matter? We mean you no harm. My name is Kas, and this is Mia. What is your name?' Kas asked gently.

'I am Torin, and I will be in great danger if anyone sees me talking to you!'

I put my hand on his and said, 'We are here with Queen Inja…'

At the mention of Inja his eyes widened, and he looked absolutely terrified again.

'What is the matter, boy?' Kas said. 'You cannot be that afraid of Inja? She has never been here before, and she is nice enough.'

He looked at us as if we were completely mad, and said quickly, 'Nice enough is not what I would call our Queen Inja! She lives here most summers with our king. She has a wicked soul, and she has been the cause of so much suffering for my people. If she knew I had spoken to you, I would be the next person sacrificed to her evil gods. You seem like good people. How is it you travel with such a person?'

Kas and I looked at each other and wondered the same thing. The minute we took our eyes off the boy though he was gone, like a frightened deer in the forest.

'What do you think that means?' I said.

Kas looked at me seriously, and replied, 'I do not know, but we need to talk to Uin about it straight away.'

He went inside, leaving the other guard on the outside of the door alone to keep watch. Kas went over to where Uin slept and woke him. Uin was awake in seconds, and listened to the news the boy had told us. Then I told him what I had seen the night before, and the whole crew just looked at me in amazement. Uin put some wood on the fire, and looked into the flames for a moment. Then he said in a hushed voice, 'I have heard of such dark craft being practised in the north, but always thought they were just stories to scare children into not going out at night alone. We are going to have to be very careful what we say and do from now on. It looks as though our leader has been doubly betrayed by that woman. I had my suspicions last night, but this confirms it. I think she is trying to manipulate the trade route to include these people. If we are to get away safely, we must go along with this falsehood.'

He looked over to me and said, 'Mia, it is up to you to make her believe that we suspect nothing.'

I looked and him and replied, 'But surely Kemit has told her that because of me, we have no links with Scan Land, or the Dogger trade, any more?'

He looked at me and smiled. 'You are thinking ahead of me Mia. Good girl. Yes, she will know that, but she does not know what other lands we have access to for trade, and this is where you can help.'

I leaned forward and listened to what he said.

'You have to convince her that you are our link with one of the wealthiest tribes in Southern Brit Land, and that we are travelling straight to your father's homeland when we leave the beach. The part about your father is only the truth, anyway.'

I sat back and looked at him, and wondered how he knew about the tall tales that I had told the lake settlement maids. I had wanted them to think that I was of royal blood, as I knew they would never find out that I was just a poor orphan on my home island. I looked guiltily at Uin, and said, 'You do not understand. When I told Rae and Lazdona that I was from noble Brit Land blood, they were just lies I told to impress them!'

Uin and the men looked back at me blankly, and said nothing. I could not stand the look of shock on their faces, so I said, 'What? Did you never tell a few lies to impress anyone, when you were boys?'

Uin put his hand on my shoulder and said gently, 'But Mia, sweetness, they are not lies! Kemit believes you are of noble blood, and not just any noble blood. You are an Icin Lander!'

I looked back at him, and said in a whisper, 'An Icin Lander? There are no such people! They are just a story to tell children by a winter's fire.'

We were all told stories of Icin Land when we were little. It was a land which was ruled only by women. The men in that magical land were only there to produce children for the warrior women, and to tend their homes and look after the children when they were born. No one believed such a people existed! How could there be a land where women were the warriors and hunters, and men stayed at home and cared for the children? Uin must have really had too much mead last night, I thought to myself!

Then I said in a very annoyed tone, 'I thought we were being serious. What are we going to do about getting out of this dreadful place?'

Uin looked at me and replied quietly, 'Mia, I am sorry to have to tell you about this in this way. Kemit planned to talk to you when we took to the water again, but you have to know now or we might not get out of here so easily.'

I looked back and him, and decided that he must think that if he tried to make me believe the tale was true, I would sound more convincing when I told Inja. He needn't have worried. I am a good liar, when I want to be. So I just pretended to take it in, if it made him feel happier, saying, 'All right, all right. Even if it were so, how would it help?'

He spoke then, quickly and concisely. 'You should convince Inja that Kemit is taking you to your father's land, to form a new trade link with them. You must also tell her that we plan to travel from there, down the great southern river, the Dan, to the tribes of Vir Land. Have you got that?'

I replied, 'Yes, I have that. You go from my homeland, down the river Dan, to Vir Land. Is there such a place?' I looked around at the faces of the crew, and they all nodded back seriously at me.

'Yes, sweetness. We have travelled to Vir Land many times. They are important people, and are the link between the cold wet lands of the north and the warm dry lands of the south and east. Tell Inja that when you are alone, in confidence, pretending that you thought Kemit would have told her all about his plans beforehand.'

'Let her know that Kemit plans to make a trade link with her settlement, so that he has the excuse to keep coming and visiting her every season. She will believe that, because she knows how Kemit feels about her. Now, we must not appear to be talking to each other like this. So go back to bed and wait for one of the women to wake you.'

I did as Uin said, and it was not long before I felt someone touching my shoulder. I looked up at a young maid about my age, wearing one of the pale blue dresses. She smiled sweetly to me, and said that Inja wished me to take first food with her in the great hall.

I got up and put on my feather cloak, and topped it with my fur, as there was a really cold chill in the air. I followed the maid to the hall, with four of the crew as an escort. Uin stayed behind, to make Inja feel that they saw no real threat to my safety. I entered the hall to find Inja, and a group of women wearing the blue dresses, chatting happily together. When she saw me she gestured for me to come over and sit next to her. The table in front of us was spread with crispy pieces of boar meat, cooked with wild plums. It looked delicious.

'Good morning, Mia. Here, I had these kind women make your favourite first food – boar meat and plums, crisped over stones.'

I smiled and looked at the bark platter, my mouth watering at the smell. I thought it best to just eat the food first. It certainly looked good, and tasted even better. I had almost finished the whole tray before Inja spoke again, saying, 'Well, you were certainly hungry! Did you sleep well last night?'

I replied, after licking my fingers thoroughly, 'Yes I did. I had some mead last night and do not really remember much about it. What happened after we had eaten?'

She looked at me searchingly, and then her face lightened when she had convinced herself I was telling the truth. 'You do not remember the two maidens being brought in?'

I looked at her blankly and replied, 'No. Did they dance for us?'

She smiled back and said, 'Yes, they did a wonderful forest dance for us. It is a shame you do not remember it. That is what comes of drinking too much mead at a feast!'

I looked at her then, and wondered how I could have been so taken in by her. I tried to look worried, and replied, 'I am sorry. Did I offend the chief by falling asleep?'

'No, in fact he knew you were not used to the mead and understood that. Do not worry, you did nothing to offend.'

I smiled and said, 'I am glad I have not offended him, as he is being so nice to you. I do not want to be the one to spoil it. What is his name, by the way? Everyone just refers to him as the "young chief"?'

Inja looked back at me and said, 'Yes, I suppose they do. His name is Laguz.'

Her voice went quiet, ever so slightly, when she said his name, and I replied, 'That is after one of the water gods, is it not?'

'Yes, it is. Laguz is one of the river gods. All this tribe's settlements are situated on the river, and his father thought the river gods would look kindly on him if he took one of their names.'

I said that it was a shame they did not have a lake on the river, as she does in the north. Then they would have enough fishing of their own, without having to join the tribes to get access to hers. She looked at me casually, and agreed. I was amazed at how easily she lied to me. I asked where Laguz was, and she said he had business with the old leader of the eastern tribe.

I asked then, 'Oh, was he not there yesterday, when we arrived?'

'Yes, that is right,' she replied. 'He had some news to take back after last night.'

She actually smiled then, at the thought of those poor girls being turned into black birds for her entertainment. I thought about what I had seen the night before, and started to feel cold inside. I pulled my fur up around my shoulders, and Inja said I must be cold, and told one of the women to make up the fire. The way she spoke to those women gave her away completely. She knew them all, and they were used to doing as she asked.

After a while, I said, 'He does not seem as bad as we thought, does he? Kemit will be happy to know you are going to be well cared for, at least.'

She sighed then and replied, 'Yes. Dear Kemit. I have spent so many happy days with him since he came. I will always treasure the memory of our union. So what are your plans, when the new boat is finished? You cannot go home to your Island, and Kemit cannot return to Scan Land, by the sound of it.'

I looked at her, and was glad that Uin had prepared me in the hut that morning. If he had not told me what to say, I would have been lost. I sat up, feeling warmer by the fire, and replied, 'We are returning to the home of my father, Icin Land, to the south of here first.'

I saw the look on her face, for she seemed to know the name, and looked suddenly very serious. I continued, 'My family will be so grateful to him, for saving me from Dogger. He thinks they will agree to let him trade with them and the Vir Landers.'

She butted into my flow, asking, 'Vir Landers? Who are they?'

I was enjoying myself by then, as I loved to tell a good tale. 'Oh, they are the people that live far south on the river Dan. They are the link between the northern tribes and the people of the warm south and east. Apparently Kemit has a good trade agreement with those people, which is not that easy to get. Most traders would love to trade with them. Kemit used to live there when he was a young man, and he has the friendship of their chief.'

She was glued to my every word by then, and I went on, 'Yes, you see, the traders in spices from the dry lands of the east trade with the Vir Landers. So you can get eastern trade goods without having to travel there to get them yourselves!'

Inja asked one of the women to bring me a drink and some dried plums, and we spent a pleasant time talking about wonderful things that came from far off lands. I had almost forgotten that she was really my enemy, until she said quite casually, 'Do you think Kemit will come back here next season, and trade with me and my new chief?'

I could hear the strain in her voice, as she tried to make her words sound casual. That was what the whole charade was all about, trade! She had engineered the whole thing. I could see it then quite clearly. She made Kemit think that she loved him. Then told him about her binding, so that he would go away, but in the hope that he would start trading again and keep coming back with goods, thinking that each season he could see her again. If she had not told him about the binding, he would probably have not left. He would have given the boat to Uin and the crew, and been no use at all to her and the evil Laguz. As it was, she could keep enticing him back for many seasons. She would probably have made sure she was alone when he visited, so he could meet her secretly on each trip and keep his love for her fresh.

She was starting to look a little concerned at my silence, so I replied, 'Sorry, I must still have a little of the mead in me!' I smiled at her and asked, 'What did you say?'

'I asked if you thought Kemit would come up here again, to trade after my binding?'

I looked back at her as if to say, what a question! 'Of course he will come back!' I said. 'The men were saying last night when we got back, that they will probably be returning to our home on the beach every season, so Kemit can stay in touch with you. He did say that he wondered if some of your people could keep the hut dry and the roof repaired, so that it would always be ready for their return. You know how huts tend to fall down quickly, if no one is living in them.'

She looked at me and smiled broadly, saying, 'Of course we will look after your beach home. It is the least we can do. I might even make one of my families live in it while you are away, to keep it really dry. I will tell the men to send that message back to Kemit when you return.'

I looked up at her, feeling a little shocked, and asked, 'You are not returning with us?'

She was just about to speak when Laguz strode into the room. She stood up, and I could see she tried to look demure and also regal when she caught sight of him, but her face could not hide her love for him. I stood up and bowed my head in respect. He came over to me and put his hand under my chin, and lifted my face to his. That instant the four crew men took a pace forward, and Laguz took his hand away, and laughed.

'You certainly have a good bodyguard, little maid! Do not worry, men. I mean her no harm. I just wanted to look at her beautiful eyes. They are green and brown, are they not?' he asked.

I looked at him in a bewildered way then. I had not thought to ask anyone before what colour my eyes were.

'I do not know. Are they?'

He laughed, and replied, 'She is not just beautiful, she is modest too. A rare quality in a young maid, in my experience!'

He turned to the women that kneeled before him, with their heads facing the floor, and said, 'I hope these women have been taking good care of my future wife and her charming companion?'

One of the women stood up and nodded, and it was not difficult to see the fear in her eyes as she looked at him.

'Good. Good. Tell me, where do you come from, little maid?'

I could not help looking at that handsome man, and wondering how he could look so good, and be so evil. But I replied softly, 'My mother was from Dogger Island, in the south, but my father was of noble blood of the tribe Icin, in South Brit Land.'

He raised his eyebrows at the mention of the Icin. Then he asked, 'I thought you were the trader Kemit's daughter?'

His face was suspicious then, and I replied, 'I am sorry for the deception, my lord, but Kemit thought it best not to tell you of my noble blood, until he knew you were a good chief.'

He looked back at me and nodded, confirming that that was a sensible decision on Kemit's part. Then I continued, 'Kemit is going to take me to my father's home, and make a trade link between them and the Vir Landers on the Dan.'

He looked puzzled and asked, 'Vir Landers? I have not heard of them.'

Inja then interrupted, saying that they lived on the River Dan, and explained all about their trade with the warm lands of the east. She sounded as if she had always known about those people. She was trying to impress Laguz, and it was working, too.

'When do you start your journey home?' he asked.

'The new boat should be ready by now, so as soon as we return we will go, I think,' I replied.

He looked at me in silence for a while, and I was beginning to feel uneasy when he asked, 'I expect you will not be returning to these waters again, will you?'

His voice was becoming steely, even though he was obviously trying to be nice. I could see it was very difficult for him to keep up the pretence. So I looked at him and smiled my sweetest smile, and replied, 'The traders and Kemit are planning to return next season. I was just talking to Inja, about the need to keep their home on the beach repaired, ready for their return. I will not be coming back though, but as they intend to loop the trade from Vir Land via my people, the Icin, to Inja's lake settlement, I will probably always get news of you.'

He positively smirked to himself at the news, and was just ordering more food and mead from the women when Uin and the rest of the crew came in.

'Come in men, and make yourselves comfortable. You must eat well before your return journey!'

I looked at Inja, not realising that they expected us to leave that day.

'Yes, I think you had better get back, as Kemit and Borg will be worrying about you. All the boats and stages on the journey have been prepared for you.'

I looked at Uin and said, 'Yes, I would be glad to get back to Borg and Brigit. I am sure they are worried about us, as you say.'

Uin looked at me very respectfully, as you would a noble, and replied to Inja, 'Whatever you wish, if we have the leave of yourself and Laguz. We will prepare to leave within the hour.'

Laguz looked at Uin long and hard, and decided he was just what he looked like – a simple trader, and replied, 'Of course. My men have the boats ready. They are waiting for you as we speak. I hope we will see you again next season?' he said, to check their reaction.

Uin replied, 'We are always happy to make new trade loops. We will certainly be back next year, with your permission.'

'Permission granted! I look forward to many seasons of trading! I will let you say your goodbyes to my future queen.'

He strode out of the hut, and the tense atmosphere lifted as he left us there. Inja looked a little uncomfortable for an instant, and then said, 'Please send my best wishes to Kemit, and tell him I am going to be all right here. We were misinformed as to the character of Laguz completely. He has treated me with great respect, and I am sure our two tribes will prosper.'

Uin thanked her, and made a move towards the door. I got up and followed him, thinking Inja would follow me too. When I reached the door I realised she was not behind me, and I called over to her, 'Are you not going to wave goodbye to us at the river?' I tried to make it sound as if I was a little hurt.

She then rushed over to me and replied, 'I would rather not. I hate waving goodbye to the people I love. We will just say it here. I hope we will meet again one season, but I doubt the Icin will let you travel the seas again, once they have you safely home with them. May the gods smile on you always.'

She hugged me then, and I muttered, 'And may they also smile on you.'

I did not look back, or my face would have betrayed the contempt I felt for her. I stopped for a second, as I was sure I heard the flutter of wings in the darkness above. Inja looked at me keenly and asked, 'What is it?'

'Oh, nothing,' I shrugged and replied, 'I thought I heard a bird or something.'

Inja looked about her blankly, so I said, 'I must have been mistaken.'

We walked down the path to the jetty in a tight group. Uin walked next to me, and the rest of the crew both ahead and behind. It was obvious the crew were taking no chances with my safety until we were on the river again. I was wondering why Inja did not walk to the river with us to say goodbye, and whispered so to Uin as we walked. He whispered back, 'Do not speak of it now. We will talk later. I think I know her reasons.'

I nodded, and was content to wait until we were alone. The crowds were out again in force, waving and saying farewell. I imagine they were ordered to do that by Laguz, as most of them had not even seen us before. As we approached the jetty I could see Laguz was waiting for us, with a group of his snake warriors. He walked up to us, and held out a bark container to me. I stepped forward and smiled. I knew he must have no idea we did not trust him.

Laguz then said, 'I have a gift for the fair Mia. Send greetings to your father's family, of our goodwill!'

He handed me the container, which I took, and nodding, I replied, 'You are too kind. I will not hesitate to tell them all I have learned about you and your people.'

I looked into the container, and was amazed at what I saw. The container was lined with the same pale blue cloth that the women wore, and nestled in the middle was what looked like a pile of pure white, tiny stones. I put my hand in and took some of them out. They shone in the sunlight like frosted dewdrops. They looked like they were coated in the pure white silk that Kemit had in his store, for they had the same sort of sheen. I had never seen such stones before, and they were so light, too.

I looked bewildered by them, and Uin stepped forward and whispered in my ear, 'This is a very generous gift. Do not show that you are unaware of its value. They are called pearls.'

I nodded, and walked up to Laguz and said, 'You honour me with such a gift of pearls, my lord. I can see that our tribes are at the beginning of a great friendship.'

He nodded back to me, and looked very pleased with himself. Then without another word we got into the boats and headed up river again. I turned and waved back at Laguz, who was standing on the jetty watching us. He raised his hand in reply, before turning and striding through the parting throngs of his tribe. It was then that I saw the birds again, flying in tight circles above the great hall, and wondered what it must be like for those poor maids to suddenly have become a bird. Uin saw me staring and asked, 'What are you looking at Mia?'

I pointed to the birds circling the hall roof, and replied, 'The black birds, of course.'

He looked to where I was pointing and replied softly, 'What black birds, sweetness? I still cannot see them.'

I looked at him and realised that he really could not see them. A chill took over my body at that moment. I suddenly became aware of the bag of pearls in my pocket, too, becoming heavy and very, very cold. I carefully took them out and looked at them. My eyes just saw their beauty, but I felt something completely different. I felt a blackness, and a decay and sadness, and knew that I did not want to carry them anymore. So while the snake warriors were not watching, I gently dropped them, one by one, into the river.

The sensation I felt as the last one disappeared into the green river waters was unmistakable. I felt suddenly lighter and warmer, and as I smiled to myself, Uin saw me and smiled back at me.

I was lost in my own thoughts as we travelled back up the river. How was it that Uin could not see the birds? And why did Laguz suddenly turn away from me, when I held my mother's crystal in my hand in the hall? I somehow felt very different then; not older, just different. As if an old self that I had forgotten about was awakening. I felt I knew a lot about a world I had never known existed until then, and somehow, as well as frightening me, it excited me. It was a world I knew, and belonged to.

14. THE BRINGERS OF BAD NEWS

The journey up stream was harder on the men paddling, as the river currents were strong, but the snake warriors seemed to be used to it and did not want any help from the crew. We did not talk to each other much on the journey to the first camp as our thoughts were all with Kemit, and how he had been deceived by Inja. As on the journey south, a fire and food were waiting for us on the river banks, just before dark. I kept looking around for the birds, but there was no sign of them on the river, or in the forests. After we had eaten and the men were sitting by their boats, we had our first opportunity to talk out of earshot of the warriors. I sat down next to Uin and asked him why he thought Inja did not walk to the jetty, to say goodbye to us. He whispered in my ear,

'Think about it. Inja has already been his queen for many summers. She is a big part of that settlement life. She would not risk someone letting out her secret as we walked to the jetty. It would have ruined their plans completely. As it is, they think they have deceived us, and that is the way we want to keep it until we are at sea again. With Kemit, that is.'

I nodded that I understood, and started a conversation, about the amazing size of Laguz's settlement, with one of the snake warriors. I also made an effort to talk to the women that had cooked our food, asking them if they lived nearby and if they had many children and so on. Doing that seemed to make them all relax, and the rest of the journey was much the same. When we stopped at the second night camp, I made a point of chatting to everyone we met, about anything I could think of. Hopefully, I thought, when they went back to Laguz they would tell him I was completely relaxed in their company, and they would not have any suspicions that we knew of their plans. I did find it quite a strain though, and noticed Uin smiling a few times as I searched my mind for mundane questions to ask our guards.

We finally heard the sound of the waterfall by mid-morning on the third day, and the going became quite slow up the river from then on. The force of the falls made the currents strong against us, and the crew finally gave the men a hand with the paddles, which they eventually seemed very grateful for. We turned the bend in the river and our last meal was waiting for us on the clearing, as it had been before. We ate quickly, as we wanted to get home as soon as we could. The men could understand that, and bade us farewell. We waved to them as they and the cooks left the clearing and headed back downstream. We stood and watched as they disappeared, and it was some minutes after they were out of sight before we spoke.

'Well, I am glad to see the end that journey. If I had to think of something chatty to say to anyone any more, I think I would have gone completely mad!'

The men looked at me, and laughed the hearty laugh of relief, relief that we were alone again in each other's company. Uin said we had better be on our way, as we still had a long walk to get back to the beach and we wanted to get there before dark. So I walked in silence for a while, happy not to have to speak, until we reached a clearing and Uin said we should rest for a few minutes. I sat next to Uin on a fallen tree and asked, 'Just what do we say to Kemit, when we get back?'

He looked back at me and just shook his head, and replied, 'I have been thinking of nothing else since we left Laguz at the jetty. We have to tell him straightaway, I know that much. The sooner he gets over her betrayal the better. It will not help at all to delay the truth. It might even make it worse. For at the moment he is grief stricken at the thought of his fair Inja being subjected to the brutality of a vicious man. Better he has hatred for the she-devil she really is instead.'

I looked up at him and saw the anguish in his face. I could see he did not want to give this news to Kemit. He was right though, it was no use keeping it from him. He would get over her more easily if he could begin to hate her. I knew also that he would vent his anger on the messenger of such news, until he believed it to be the truth. I thought about that for a while, then I turned to Uin and said, 'I think I should tell him about her.'

Uin stood up and shook his head, and was about to speak when I said quickly, 'No, do not stop me from speaking. I have thought about this. Kemit will want to lash out at any messenger who gives him this news, but he will not lash out at me. Also, I have been very close to Kemit since his friendship with Inja, and I feel as a maid that I should tell him. He knows how I felt about Inja, too, so he will know that I would not say such things, if they were not the truth.'

Uin could see that what I was saying was true, as any member of the crew might have another motive for putting him off his relationship with Inja, whereas he knew that would not be the case with me. He put his hands on my shoulders and looked at me hard and long, and eventually said, 'Thank you, Mia, I am sure you are the best person to tell him this dreadful news. You are doing me a great service, as I had no wish to be the one to hurt my friend so, and I really do not think he would believe me, not at first. He has thought about Inja since he was a boy. He has put her up on the clouds with the gods in his mind, and he will reject any move that, in his eyes, knocks her down.'

We walked home from then on in silence, and it was almost dark when we saw the beach and the row of torches next to the hut. My heart, instead of rejoicing to see home again, was suddenly very heavy. A few days ago Kemit waved goodbye to the love of his life, and now I was going to have to shatter that sweet memory. My steps seemed to drag more than usual in the soft sand as we walked towards the door. Uin put his arm on my shoulder and asked, 'Are you sure about this, Mia? I will understand if you want me to tell him.'

Just as he spoke, I heard Kemit's voice right next to us, saying, 'Tell him what?'

I must have jumped out of my skin, as I had not seen him leaning against the wall of the hut under the roof.

'I thought we had an agreement before you left, that you would not tell me what happened on your journey down river.' His voice was harsh and bitter, as his spirit had become morose while we had been away. He was doing his best to not think of Inja at all.

Uin could tell by the tone of his voice that his mood was dark, and he replied, 'This is news you have to hear. Let us walk along the beach a while...'

Kemit looked at him curiously, for he had known Uin most of his life and trusted his judgement completely. So the fact that Uin had said he needed to know something stopped him from objecting. They were just starting to walk along the beach when I finally regained my composure and shouted, 'No, Uin, we agreed!'

Kemit turned round to me, and looked a little taken aback by my tone. Kemit had never heard me shout at anyone in that way. He walked back to me and asked, 'What is it Mia? It is not your duty to tell me this news, whatever it is. Stay here. We will be back in a while.'

His voice was soft and kind, like I was used to, but I stood as tall as I could and replied instantly, 'No! I must tell you about this! Inja was close to me. Closer than she was to Uin, so it is my duty, and not Uin's, to speak to you.'

Uin looked at me with a mixture of pride and relief. Kemit saw that and replied, 'Very well then, come on.' He led me slowly along the shore until we were next to the now finished log boat, far enough for us to feel our conversation was completely private. Then he asked calmly, 'So, what is this news that my good friend Uin cannot tell me about?'

His voice was calm, but I could hear the tension in it so I said, 'Can we sit while we talk, for I have been walking since midday food?'

He looked at me then with concern, and gestured for me to sit on one of the logs which the crewman use to sit on.

'I do not know where to begin, so I will just tell you what happened as it happened. It is not going to be anything akin to the story you are expecting though.'

Kemit looked at me curiously, but waited patiently for me to speak. I told him about the argument we interrupted at the reed beds, and how Inja had had her little talk with me before we reached the waterfall. He nodded sadly when I told him what she had said. I described the men waiting for us at the waterfall, their fearsome tattoos, but how they had food ready for us and were very courteous.

At that point he looked at me a little puzzled, and asked, 'They were not even a little brusque with Inja?'

'No, not at all. They were very respectful, and even thoughtful of our comfort during the journey downstream. It was getting dark, and they told us we would travel down river for two days. I thought we were going to sleep in the boats, but when we turned a bend in the river there was a fire and shelter, and food waiting for us.'

He looked a little surprised at that too, but said nothing and I continued, 'Yes, there were even women attendants for us. They must have dropped them off on their journey up stream, and told them to have everything ready for our return. Inja also looked amazed at the hospitality, and told me so. Our every wish was seen to, and we were treated as honoured guests, certainly not enemies.'

Kemit interrupted then and said, 'That is a strange thing for them to do indeed. I could imagine the chief wanting you to arrive safely, but I would not have expected a man like him to be so thoughtful. Go on.'

I told him about the approach to the settlement, and the crowds cheering us as we got nearer to our landing. He was silent then, and I could see he was more relaxed at the thought of his beloved Inja being treated with respect. I described the size of the settlement and the women in their pale blue dresses, and our walk to the hut where we were to stay. I told him all that Inja had said about needing the chief to think that she wanted him, so it would be easier for her people when she got home. Kemit looked sad again, and I knew he was thinking what a noble person she was. As I had, when she spoke to me about it. I described our entrance into the hall, and the feast.

Kemit asked immediately, 'What does this chief look like?'

I had to answer honestly. It was no use describing him as ugly, when he wasn't. 'He was the most handsome man I have ever seen!'

Kemit sat back and stared at me, not expecting me to speak so frankly. I continued, 'Yes, Kemit, he was wonderful. He was tanned and had the most brilliant bright eyes, and a kind...'

Kemit started to fidget then and said, 'All right, you do not have to rub it in so much.'

'Yes, I do! You will know why when I finish.'

'I am sorry,' he said, 'continue.'

'The feast was wonderful and the mead was strong, so Uin swapped a mead bag for one with just water in for me. Which is why I saw what happened, for the mead had been drugged. When the food was cleared away, two stakes were driven into the floor in front of us. Then two young maids were brought in and tied to the stakes.'

I looked at Kemit and said, 'Please do not interrupt me now, as it is going to be difficult enough for me to describe what happened. I know it will sound unbelievable, but it is the truth.'

He nodded, and I continued, 'Laguz, that is the chief's name. He walked over to one of the maids, and told the crowd that they were the daughters of the leader of the eastern settlement. He said that this chief needed to know that when he, Laguz, took over a land, all the things on that land were his to do with as he wished.'

Then I described the glazed look on everyone's faces, even the crew's, due to the mead, and the birds flying in. I described it all in detail, including the strange cloud that poured from Inja's fingers that the birds flew through.

I turned to Kemit and he said softly, 'Sweetness, you must have dreamed all this.'

I looked at him, and the desperation in my eyes made him wait for me to continue.

'No! I was not dreaming! I did not drink the mead, as the crew had done. Then the drummers started, and everyone paced around and around the hall to their beat. Including Uin and the crew. Inja and Laguz laughed, while they watched people who had fallen being trampled on by the crowds.'

I looked up at him, and something in my face made him stop and wait for me to speak.

'There is more for you to hear, before you know the whole story. Inja came over to me much later, and said she needed to see Laguz alone for a while, and we were to go back to our hut to sleep. She said she may or may not be back that night. The men escorted me back to our hut, and I asked Uin what he remembered of the dancing. He had no memory of it at all!

'I could not sleep well then, so I got up early and sat outside the hut with Kas. He told me that during the feast he had been talking to some of Laguz's men, and they had told him of the great inland sea on Laguz's land to the east, and how Inja's lake was small by comparison.'

Kemit looked at me curiously, and I know he was thinking about what Inja had said, about how they had no inland stretches of water. I looked back at him knowingly and nodded.

'Yes, there is lots of inland water on their tribal lands, much more than Inja's small lake. Do not stop me now, for I am getting to the heart of my story. Then we talked to this boy, Torin, and when we told him we were with Queen Inja, and he had no need to fear us, he looked at us as if we were mad! I then asked him why he was so afraid of Queen Inja, when that was the first time that she had been to that place. He said that that was not the first time she had been there at all, and that she had lived in his settlement every summer for many seasons. She had been made Laguz's queen not long after her first visit there.'

Kemit stood up then and looked like thunder, and said to me with a voice full of venom, 'That is a lie! Why do you repeat such tales, Mia?'

I looked up at him, and my eyes filled with tears and I cried, 'Oh, that it were a lie! I would give anything to say it were not true. But please let me finish, then you can shout at me all you want.'

Kemit sat back down and looked at the ground. I told him what the boy had said would happen to him, if he were found talking to us; that he would be sacrificed to Inja's evil Gods. I described the terror in the boy's eyes, too, as he ran away. I told Kemit what Uin had said, when we gave him the news, and what he had told me to say to Inja the following day. I related the whole scene in the hall, with Inja and Laguz, and the talk about new trade loops. I told him everything, especially the part about her not waving goodbye to us, and Uin's explanation for that. I finished my story, ending with my telling Uin, before we reached the beach, that I would relay the bad news to Kemit.

We sat in silence for a long while after I had finished my tale. Every so often Kemit would ask a question, about what Inja and Laguz had said. After answering, he would be silent again. I do not know how long we sat there on that log, but it was long after the first of the forest birds had started to tell us that another day was upon us.

Eventually, Kemit looked at me and said, 'You are a brave young maid, to tell such a tale to the man that loved that woman. I am sorry if I frightened you last night. I cannot believe I have been such a fool, to think she had been waiting for me all those summers. You must think me an idiot indeed.'

I looked straight into his eyes and replied, 'You will never be a fool in my eyes. I believed her lies too, and I had no past memories of her. She was very good at telling lies, and I thank the Gods we found out before we left. If it were not for that little boy, we would have thought she was just being brave for the sake of her people. I would probably have thought that I dreamed the whole episode of dark magic too. How was I to know of such things? Their plan was for her to always be here for you, when you visited to trade, so that she could get the best trade goods for Laguz.'

Kemit smiled and replied, 'Never have wiser words come from such a child. Of course, you are right. I thank you for telling me. If Uin had told me, it would have cast a shadow between us that would have stayed with us. Let us get back and get warm, and have some food. Borg and Brigit will be beside themselves with worry by now, wondering what is wrong. I have taken my pain out on you, and I am sorry. Mind you, if it had been anyone but you that had told me, I might have used my fists a few times before the end of the telling!'

I looked at him with feigned fright, and he laughed at my expression. As we approached the hut he said, 'Keep this to yourself for now. I will talk to everyone this coming night about what has happened.'

I looked up at him and nodded gratefully, as I did not want to have to go over it all again with Borg and Brigit. I stopped just before the door and asked, 'Kemit? The tale about my father, and the Icin?'

He looked suddenly serious again, and said, 'Give me a day or two, and we will sit on your cliff up there and talk about it.'

He smiled at me in his familiar, kind way, and I knew it was probably not the best time to talk about it. We entered the hut, and as soon as I popped my head inside, Brigit ran over to me and hugged me, saying, 'We were so worried about you! How did it go? Was Inja all right?'

I just looked at her, and she immediately stopped her questions and asked in a low voice, 'It was that bad, was it?'

'Yes,' I replied, 'but not in the way we expected. I must sleep now, Brigit. I did not sleep at all last night, and I have been travelling since first light yesterday. Kemit is going to tell everyone what happened at last food.'

She looked back at me a little surprised, and said, 'Kemit will speak? I thought the whole idea of Uin going was so that he did not have to know the horrible details?'

I suddenly wished I was in my bed, asleep, but I did not want to hurt Brigit's feelings. It looked like she had been genuinely worried about me while I was away, so I said, 'You will understand about it all when Kemit speaks. I am sorry Brigit, but I must sleep.'

She nodded and led me back to my bed. She had already freshly fluffed up the furs to make it comfortable for me. As soon as my head hit the fur I must have gone to sleep. If I had lain on a floor of wet grass, I would probably have slept just the same. I couldn't get the thought of Inja's deception out of my head. All the time she had been friendly to me, it was only to find out information that could be useful to her and Laguz.

When I opened my eyes again I saw it was late, and looking straight at me was Borg. As he noticed I was waking he smiled, and leaned forward to hug me. It felt so good to be held by Borg again. I felt as though all my worries just dropped and fell away from me as he held me. He said gently to me after a while, 'I think we should go to the hearth now, as Kemit is about to speak, and he wishes you to be there when he does.'

I nodded and followed him to the main hearth. Kemit held out his hand to me when he saw me, and I sat next to him instead of between Brigit and Borg, as I usually did at meetings. He stood up and said sombrely, 'We have unwelcome news from the party that went south with the Queen Inja.'

The crew started muttering then because, like Brigit, they thought the whole idea of him not going was because he did not want to know the details.

'Yes, I know what you are thinking. Why am I telling you this, when I made such efforts to avoid knowing what happened to Inja on that journey? The fact of the matter is, is that Inja has betrayed us! She led us into thinking that she had not met this chief of the south before, and that he was going to exact a revenge on her for his boyhood injury. There is no easy way of telling you this, other than to be straightforward. Inja has in fact been bound to this chief, Laguz, for the past two summers at least.'

The crew looked really shocked at the news, and Kemit continued, 'When we arrived here in the near winter, she was spending a few months with her people before returning home to the southern tribe lands. She took advantage of the fact that she had met me as a child, and wove the web that finally ensnared me into thinking we were meant to be together.' He hesitated, and then said, 'And that she loved me. I feel such a fool, to have been taken in by such wishful thinking. Her story of the chief and his revenge were to stop me from staying here with her; I would have left, and started to trade again, and so she and Laguz would have become one of our trade loops in the north. Yes, men, it just comes down to trade! That is all she wanted. I will not go into the details of her position in that tribe, for it shows a side to Inja that I would rather not put into words. Let us just say that thanks to Uin and Mia's quick thinking, we may get out of this situation with at least a damn fine boat to trade in!'

When he said that, the men cheered at the prospect of taking their huge new boat to sea and starting to travel again. Kemit raised his hand to silence them,

'There is one thing though, that is important if we are to leave in safety, and that is that the settlers here must think we suspected nothing. If any of them visit, we are to tell them that we intend to return each season to this hut, to trade with Inja and her new king. We are also to say how happy we were that Laguz was indeed kind to Inja, and that we are sure the two tribes will prosper because of it. It is vital we all tell them the same tale. Understood?'

The room erupted with shouts of unity. Kemit looked at Brigit, and gestured for her to come over to us. The rest of the men started to eat, and talked amongst themselves.

As Brigit walked towards us I could see she looked very nervous. The talk of Inja betraying us must have frightened her, and made her think that she, too, might be implicated in the deception.

'I need to ask you some questions, Brigit.' Kemit said sternly, and Brigit nodded as the tears started to brim in her eyes,

'Yes, I… I… understand. What do you want to know?'

He leaned forward and looked straight into her eyes, and asked, 'I want to know what you knew of this deception? I also want to know if you too have been lying to us, and are a spy in our midst?'

Brigit sat down and looked up at him, directly in his eyes, with an expression of complete horror on her face. 'I would never betray you, any of you. I love you all as my family.'

Kemit did not stop his gaze and asked, 'You did not know she was bound to this king of the south? I find that very hard to believe.'

Brigit collected herself then and replied, 'I knew she travelled from our lake many times in the summer months. I thought she travelled to a tribe in the east, and that she had friends there. I am from a very lowly family, and although I used to talk to the settlement maids and overhear the conversations of my brothers' women, I never heard of her knowing the southern tribes. Her father hated those people, and forbade any of our people to travel south or make contact. If she had been bound to the chief of the southern tribe two summers ago, I am not surprised she kept it from our tribe. Even though she is queen, a great many of the elders are still loyal to the memory of her father.'

Kemit interrupted, saying, 'Yes, I understand that he was a fine man. I am sorry to have pressed you so hard, but we had to know where your loyalties lay.'

I put my arm around her and said, 'I knew she could not be dishonest. Look at her! Have you ever seen such an open face in your life, Kemit?'

At that comment Kemit laughed, and replied, 'Come to think about it, Mia, no, I have not! It is good to have you with us Brigit, and if you still desire to travel with us, you are very welcome.'

'Oh yes, please,' she replied, then said thoughtfully, 'I cannot imagine what the tribal council would think if they knew.'

Kemit then said in a low voice, 'They must not get this news from us, or we will not get away in safety with our fine new boat!'

She smiled and nodded, and we went over to the hearth and ate the remains of the stew that the crew had left.

The next few days were full of preparations for leaving the beach. All the goods had to be sorted and stowed, and Brigit and I got the job of sorting out and packing all the cloth and bead necklaces. We delighted in that job, as it gave us the chance to open up containers we had not looked at before, in order to re-pack them. We had just opened the last of the silk bundles when I said to Brigit, 'Do you ever wonder what kind of world this cloth came from? It is so fine and soft, and the colour is so rich. I had never seen anything like it before I met the traders. When they traded cloth on my island it was usually plant fibre cloth, and although it was beautiful and soft, it was nothing like this.'

Brigit looked at me in her usual, thoughtful way when she was asked a specific question, and eventually replied, 'I did not even know such a cloth could exist, until you showed it to me the day we visited the beach together. As to where it comes from, I cannot imagine, apart from the fact that the people who wear cloth like this every day must live in very fine warm homes.'

I looked back at her and laughed. Trust Brigit to think of the practical side of the question, I thought.

'Of course they live in warm homes. It comes from the dry hot lands of the east! In that world it is never winter, and they live in great towns, and have earth on the roofs of their huts. Or so Uin once told me, but I can't imagine having earth on your roof instead of thatch. It must rain sometimes, or the people would die of thirst. So how does the earth stay on the roof when it rains? The first time I saw this type of cloth was when Kemit asked me to choose a colour to give to Inja, that very first day he met her on the beach. That seems so long ago now. So much has changed since then; Borg had his horrible adventure, and I met you and stayed at the lake. Which, I might add, caused me many sleepless nights, sleeping over the water like that!'

Brigit laughed at the thought that it had worried me so much, and I went on, 'Then we lost the boat, and the crew made a new one. And I went south with Uin. I still find it hard to believe Inja lied to us so well for so long. It must have hurt Kemit deeply.'

We were both silent for a while, thinking how terrible it must be for Kemit. Then I said, 'We had better get on with this packing, or Kemit will want to know what took us so long.'

We continued to carefully pack the cloth into new tight bundles for stowing in the boat. When we had finished, the sun was almost down in the pale winter sky. We decided to walk over to the boat and see what they were doing before it got too dark. We had sat on the floor of the store room all day, and our legs were feeling stiff. Almost all the crew were doing something in or around the boat. Borg was helping Kas to pack the partitions he had been making, and we walked over to talk to him.

'Hey, Borg. How goes it?' I shouted as we approached him.

He turned round and smiled and replied, 'It goes very well, sweetie!'

He laughed at my reaction to his new name for me, and I replied indignantly, 'I am not your sweetie, or anybody's sweetie! My name is Mia to you! Only Kemit and the crew can call me sweetness, but never sweetie!'

He laughed back at me, and Kas said, trying to keep his face straight, 'You tell him, Mia!'

I looked at Borg and nodded, saying, 'There. Kas agrees with me too, so do not say it again!'

Borg came over to me and put his arm around me and said, 'Whatever you say, sw… Mia.'

I punched him in the ribs, and then walked over to the other side of the boat to see what the others were doing. Uin and Kemit were watching two men put sand in the end of the boat, before the stones for the hearth. They smiled at me when I walked up to them, and asked if I had done the packing. I told them we had finished the last bundle a few minutes before, and had come to look at the boat being packed. It was amazing just how much sand was put into the boat to go underneath the hearth. No wonder it was never in danger of getting too hot and setting the boat alight.

I remembered that first day on the boat, when the men caught fish and cooked it on the fire. I remember how it tasted, like the best fish I had ever eaten. Maybe because it was cooked within minutes of being caught. I was just telling Brigit about the fishing and cooking at sea, when a man started calling to us from the clearing next to the path to the lake. We all stopped talking and looked, as a group of people started walking towards us across the beach. As soon as they were halfway across the beach, I could see that Inja was with them. Kemit stiffened, and said quietly to us to remember our tongues. He then walked towards the party, smiling and holding his arms out to Inja, as I had seen him do so many times during our stay there.

That time I knew he was acting though. Inja held her arms out to Kemit too, and they embraced each other. After a few words they came over to us, and seeing me she shouted, 'Mia! It is good to see you again. How are you?'

I smiled back at her and replied, 'I am fine. And how are you getting on with Laguz? He is still being kind to you?'

She looked back at me and hesitated before she replied, 'Yes, thanks to the gods. He is not the cruel man we were told about. He values our lands and has been nothing but kindness itself to me.'

She could see Kemit watching her, and turned to him and said, 'Kemit, my dear, if only it were you I was being bound to. You will return here again, will you not?'

Her voice was sweet and humble as she waited for the answer she knew she would get, and Kemit smiled and replied, 'You know I would not go at all if you were not being bound to this chief. I promise I will be back every season, for as long as you still wish it. I will bring your new tribe such trade goods as you could not even imagine! Come, let us not be sad, it will be no time before you will see us return to this beach again. If we are successful at Vir Land, we could be back in a matter of months. Borg, run ahead and get the mead, for we have a farewell party to give!'

Borg ran, as did Kas, as he had just caught a boar that morning, and it needed to be prepared before we could roast it that night. Inja took my hand and Kemit's, and we walked slowly back towards the hut, which made me feel very uncomfortable. Kemit and Inja talked about the journey we would take. Then she asked me how I felt about seeing my father's people. Kemit looked at me and said in a low voice, 'Mia is a little sad to be leaving our wonderful company, I am afraid. She knows she will not be allowed on an adventure at sea again, once she is home. She will almost certainly be groomed for her first binding.'

Inja looked at him curiously and asked, 'First binding? They have more than one bound man in the Icin?'

Kemit replied casually, 'Yes. It is a tribe run by women, and women can take as many men as they choose. It is a strange country, as it has all of our rules about how to live turned upside down. Let us not speak of it now, as we will embarrass Mia.'

'Yes, yes, I can see she is embarrassed already. Let us be happy tonight, and bid you farewell. You leave at first light?'

I looked at Kemit then, because I did not know exactly when we were leaving. He replied, 'Yes, we leave on the morning tide.' He threw a glance at me, and we went inside to celebrate.

I do not know how Kemit did it, but you would not have guessed his feelings for Inja had changed at all by the way he was treating her. It was quite late by the time Inja and her party left to return to the lake. It took a long time for all the farewells and good wishes to be exchanged, and I saw my dear crew in a completely different light. To look at them you would never have suspected that any of them knew of Inja's betrayal. Maybe it came from years of trading, and haggling with merchants over the price of goods, but they certainly would have fooled me if I had not known the truth. Inja was absolutely delighted, as she obviously thought she had been very clever in manipulating the traders, and adding her people to a very lucrative trade loop in the north. She kissed me endlessly, and even shed a tear at our departure. Then eventually she was gone, into the night with her men.

15. MIA'S INHERITANCE

I stood at the doorway with Kemit and watched, as the little speck of light their torch gave finally disappeared beyond the clearing on the far side of the beach. I could imagine Kemit's heart being heavy at the thought of the months of happiness he had spent with Inja, and how it had been just an illusion. I thought about how happy I had been, when we arrived, to find a friend in Inja too.

We stood in silence for a while, lost in our own thoughts, when Kemit turned to me and said, 'Mia, I think it is time we talked. Get another fur and we will go and sit on your precious cliffs, and I will tell you who I believe your father was.'

I looked up at him, and was suddenly filled with dread for some reason. I did not know why, as I had always longed to discover where my father had come from. I was now going to be told, and suddenly I did not want to know anymore! I stepped inside and took a fur from the pile by the door, and followed Kemit up the path that Borg and I had made, to the cliff above the hut. I loved that spot, and it was hard to imagine that it would probably be the last time I would sit up there. It was a far superior place to sit than the sand cliffs of Dogger Island, as it was a cliff made of rock. I would sit on a fallen tree trunk, so I could just see the roof of the hut below me. The view of the beach and the cliffs on the other side, stretching into the far distance, was magnificent. It was a sheltered spot too, as there was a dense screen of furze bushes behind the log to protect me from any off shore breezes.

As I followed Kemit I remembered when I first scrambled up there with Borg, when the men were building the hut. The furze was in full bloom then, and the air was filled with its sweet scent.

Kemit and I sat on the fallen tree and just looked out to sea, marvelling at the scene before us. The moon painted a white river on the sea that glistened in the dark, and above the sky was a blanket of brilliant stars in the clear air. Every so often, as we sat, we could hear laughter from the hut below, and now and then we could smell the wood smoke as it drifted like a thread through the hole in the roof.

Kemit eventually broke the silence, and said, 'This is a wonderful place you have found for yourself Mia, and this is also the kind of night that is filled with wonder. I have seen the moon on the sea like this from many different shores in my lifetime, and yet I never seem to get used to the beauty of it. But, we must talk of your future now, and what you want to do as we leave these shores.'

I looked at him in amazement and said, 'I did not think I had a choice?'

He smiled and replied, 'Of course you have a choice! You are a member of my crew, not my slave! I believe I know who your father was, and after I have told you, you must then decide if you wish us to take you to his homeland or not.'

'What do you mean, you think you know who my father was? Is he dead? And why would I not want to go to his homeland, if I have family there?'

My tone must have seemed a little harsh, but I was a little annoyed that he might think I would not want to find my family.

'Hey, slow down now. It is important that you get the whole picture before you start jumping to conclusions. Are you warm enough, because this is a long tale I am going to tell you.'

I nodded and he continued, 'When we first met Borg, on that insane raft he would take to sea in, we would spend many hours talking about your island. Although we had traded there for many seasons, we never really got a chance to speak to any of the islanders for any length of time. Borg told me the story of your mother and you, and how a Brit Lander had promised to take her away from the island, and also how he had abandoned her before knowing she was with child. He told me about you, and how he liked your bright, strong spirit; how you were so different, not just in looks, but in character, from the other island maids. He also told me your father's name…'

I looked up at him and gasped, and asked, 'I have never known his name! My grandmother would never speak of him, so how could Borg know it?'

Kemit patted me on the shoulder and replied, 'Hold on! If you stay quiet for more than a minute I will tell you.'

'Sorry,' I said.

'Borg used to be great friends with the son of Danz, the hunter, and it was Danz that had been a friend to your father while he was on the island. He had met your father in Scan Land, after a hunting trip. Your father had been living in Estergard, and asking everyone if he could get a passage on a boat travelling to Brit Land. He had been trading for his family when he was set upon by thieves. All of his companions had been killed, and he had only escaped by hiding under the roof of a hut behind a woodpile.

'At that time Danz thought he was just another Brit Lander looking for adventure, for the people of Brit Land were well known for their adventurous spirit. His name was Thoreall, which Danz thought was a little grand for a simple Brit Lander at the time, but thought that maybe his mother was of noble stock. To cut a long story short, Danz and he got on very well, and he talked the other members of his group into giving him a lift, to Dogger Island at least. Then he could perhaps wait until the next traders came to the island to take him on to Brit Land. There is little to say about his stay on Dogger, apart from the fact that he met your mother and fell hopelessly in love with her.'

I looked up at him, with eyes filled with tears, at the thought that my father had loved my mother after all, and had not just taken her for pleasure and then left her alone with child.

'Yes, he loved her all right! So much so he had to leave her before it was too late, and his past caught up with him. Apparently, he was not supposed to have gone on the trading trip, but had disobeyed his mother and gone anyway. In the same way as women of your island are not allowed to leave, it is the same with certain men of the Icin tribe. He knew it would not be long before they would come looking for him, and he did not want them to find him with your mother. If they had discovered him with your mother, then she would have had to return home with him.'

I had to stop him there. 'Was it not the dream of my mother to leave the island? And to have the man she loved take her to join his family? That would have made her short life complete.'

'Please, Mia, let me go on. You will understand it better when you hear the whole story.'

I nodded, and looked out to sea as he continued.

'You see, the Icin is a tribe ruled by women, as I said, and the men born to their noble line are treated more like slaves than noble sons. They have very strong beliefs about the line of their blood not being mixed with that of common people, not just from outside of their tribe, but also from within. The son of the queen of the Icin is almost a prisoner from the day he is born. He is destined to mate with the daughter of one of the tribe nobles, and his first daughter would then automatically become the next queen on reaching adulthood. Therefore, it was vital that the son of the queen did not take any woman other than those chosen for him, as any daughter he had would eventually become ruler.

'I believe your father was such a man. His mother was Queen Esha. As soon as Borg said his name, I knew it was he, for I had heard that he had gone missing. All traders were told at the time, and there was even a reward for information about where he could be.'

'Being a male for him in his homeland was like being in a cruel prison. When he heard tales of how different it was for men in the rest of our world, he knew he had to go and see for himself. He always knew that he would have to go back; as an heir, it was expected of him. But he just wanted to have an adventure before he returned to his life of wealthy imprisonment. That was why he left your mother. If his mother had found out that he had taken her, she would have had her brought back to Icin Land until it was clear whether or not she was pregnant. If she was found not to be pregnant, then she would have been killed for violating royalty. If she was pregnant, after you had been born you would have been taken away from her, and brought up as the future queen, just in case your father had no daughters from his arranged bindings.'

I looked up at him, trying to take in the fact that I was suddenly royalty. 'What would have happened to my mother, if she had given birth to me there?' I asked.

Kemit looked away and said, 'She would have been killed, not long after you were born. That is the law in that country, to stop maids from thinking that if they let a royal son take them, they might then get a life of privilege.

'So now you see why he left her, before he thought she was with child. He knew that if she was carrying a child, the islanders would have made him stay and look after her. It would have only been a matter of time before the Icin came looking for him, and if they had they would have found you and your mother. You would have been taken away, and your mother would have been dealt with, which was far from anything the Dogger Islanders could do anything about.'

I had to butt in then, as the reasons for my very existence were suddenly falling into place.

'You keep talking about my father as if he were dead? Did he not take another woman, and have daughters, after he returned?'

It was a while before Kemit talked again, but eventually he replied, 'Mia, he is dead, I am afraid. I was trading just along the coast from the Icin, when I heard the tale from a friend of my father's who had just returned from there. He told me of the rejoicing of the queen, because her only son had returned safely. There was a great feast in his honour, on the cliffs of Doonay. That is where they held their festivals, and sometimes offered sacrifices to the gods. They would make young boys jump to their deaths from a raised platform over the edge of the cliff. For men, apart from the first sons of the women that were needed to produce the blood lines, were not valued at all.'

'Your father was sitting next to his mother, when he suddenly got up and walked to the platform. Without a word to anyone, he jumped to his death. There is no easy way to tell you, Mia, so it is best to come right out with a truth like this. It must have been only weeks after his return to the Icin that he did it. Nobody knew why. And the queen then had only one other child after him, a daughter called Leena.'

I felt no sadness at that moment, as he told me about my father's death. Maybe it was just the shock, I do not know. I just asked, 'Kemit, why would he do such a thing?'

Kemit put his warm arm around my shoulder and replied, 'I could not understand it myself, nor could any who heard the tale. But when Borg told me about you, and your father, it all seemed to make sense. He must have guessed that your mother was with child. Maybe she had even told him, and that was why he left, to protect you both. As I said, he would have been made to stay by the islanders, and the Icin would have eventually found him. The reward they offered to find him was great. So he knew he had to go, and maybe he told your mother that he would never take another. And maybe your mother knew that to be true. When she was carrying you she probably knew that he had killed himself, as the story had spread throughout the trading community by then, because it was so strange. When you were born, looking so much like him, she probably could not bear to be apart from him any longer and just pined away. They could then at least be together in the heavens.'

I was crying by that point, at the thought that my parent's love for each other was so great, that life itself was not worth living, for either of them, without each other. Then I asked, 'So what would happen if I were to travel to the Icin Lands, and say who I was?'

Kemit looked at me thoughtfully before he spoke.

'I imagine, when the queen saw you, she would know it to be true. From what I remember of your father when he was a boy, you look so very much like him.'

I stood up then and said, 'You knew him when you were a boy?'

'Yes. We traded with the Icin often, for they are a very rich people. I met your father many times, and we were friends. He was a very kind boy, and was always careful to put me at my ease when we were in the presence of his mother, the queen.'

'So what would happen to me if I went there? You said that my father had a sister. Will she not be the next queen?'

'No. It is the daughter of the first born son that should become the next queen, and that, my dear Mia, is... you. Queens there usually give over their rule to their grandchildren, not their children. They often live to a good age, and do not wish to stop ruling after their child grows up. Your grandmother was still well, or so I heard, the last time I travelled that way. If you returned you would never be allowed to leave again, and you would most certainly become queen when your grandmother died. Your life would be full of privilege and wealth, but you would not be able to choose your mate. That would be for the women's council to decide.'

I thought then, why was it, that when I was offered a life of such privilege and ease, it always had to be at such a price? The last time it was as the Shaman's Pure One. Now it was as a princess of the royal line of the Icin. A people I thought had only existed in stories for little children. Why was it also, when I was offered such privilege, that the other more uncertain and possibly dangerous alternatives always looked so appealing to me?

Kemit was silent, as he knew I had a lot to think about, but after a while he asked, 'Well, Mia, is it home to the Icin, to take your place as rightful heir or...?'

I butted in quickly, saying, 'Or!'

He smiled and said, 'Or come with us and travel. I cannot say where we will go, as we have to avoid Scan Land for a few seasons at least. So it is not a certain future that I can offer you.'

'Who ever needs certainty? I do not!' I replied 'The only time my life was certain, was when I was growing up at the beck and call of my grandmother. Quite frankly, if that was certainty, the only certainty was more boring days ahead of me! Take me with you, Kemit. I do not care where we go. I certainly do not want to be trapped in a life of privilege with the Icin!'

He looked at me and laughed, saying, 'How did I know you would react in that way! Most maids would love to find out that they would one day be queen of a wealthy land, but not you! You are a breath of fresh bright air in my life, Mia. I would sorely miss you if you were gone. I know the crew will be glad to keep you with them too, as your attitude to life makes us realise that you were well worth saving from the clutches of that sad old man on Dogger. Come, we must try and get some sleep now. We have a busy day ahead of us tomorrow!'

He held my hand and led me down the path. I did not need his help as I had walked down it many times on nights darker than that one. It felt good to hold his warm strong hand though. I felt a closer bond to Kemit then than ever. He was the father I had never had, and I was very proud to be his adopted daughter.

As soon as I put my head through the doorway of the hut, Brigit ran up to me and asked, 'Is everything all right? You were so long in coming back that I was worried something had happened to you!'

I looked at her and smiled. It was good to have friends that really cared about me, I thought. I still found it strange though, after fending for myself for so long. Apart from the times I played with Karn and Simi as a child, I had led a very lonely childhood with my grandmother. She seemed to think it was her duty to make me as cold and as insensitive as she was. Maybe she thought I was less likely to come to the same, sad end as my mother. Maybe she just disliked having to care for me in the first place. It was strange thinking of Karn and Simi, and my grandmother again, as they then seemed so very far away from my life.

Brigit and I sat together near the hearth, and Borg, noticing I had returned, came over to join us asking, 'So, where are we to head for at first light then? Do we travel to the Land of the Icin, or not?'

I looked at him curiously and asked, 'How do you know about my connection with the Icin?'

He looked positively sheepish as he replied, 'I have known for some time. In fact, ever since I first met Kemit and the crew.'

I jumped up immediately, and with my hands on my hips said, 'What? So why did you not tell me then?'

He pulled me down so that I was sitting next to him again, and said quietly, 'At first I did not believe it, but when Kemit told me about the search for your father I knew it was true. I... I suppose I did not want you to leave the island. I liked you, and I enjoyed the times we spent together on my boat. Then the longer I knew, the harder it became to tell you at all. When we had to leave the island and Kemit volunteered to take you, I thought he would tell you as soon as we were safely away. In fact, I asked him why he did not tell you. He said the right time would come, and you needed to find yourself a little, before he burdened you with the truth.'

I looked at him blankly, and then looked into the fire. I thought that maybe he was right, as the whole episode with the Shaman took a lot to get over. On our escape, to be confronted immediately with the news that I was the royal heir of some strange tribe of women, would probably have tipped my mind completely over the edge.

Brigit broke the silence, asking indignantly, 'I know I am a new friend, but I think I might be told at least a little of this truth!'

We both looked at her and realised she knew nothing of this, and must have felt very left out of our conversation. Trust Brigit to come straight out with it though, I thought!

'Oh Brigit, I am sorry. Of course you should know. But I have only just found out myself. Even though I knew a while ago that Kemit had some news of my father, he would not tell me until just now.'

Brigit looked at me in that serious way of hers, when she knew she was going to have to concentrate on something. Then I told her what Uin had said to me, when we were in Laguz's settlement, and finally I recounted all that Kemit had just told me. Her expression changed from one of serious concentration to outright amazement.

When I had finished she said quietly, 'So, you are the heir to the Icin throne! My gods! Do you know how powerful the Icin are?'

I looked up and shook my head, and said, 'I thought the Icin were just a tribe invented to tell a good tale around the hearth in winter. I did not believe such a people could exist. A tribe ran totally by women!'

She looked at me with utter amazement and replied, 'You did not think they existed? You really were brought up in a backwater! I thought everyone knew about the Icin. They parade up and down the coast at various times of the year, paying homage to some sea goddess or other. Their warriors are all women, and a frightening lot they are to see! They are very rich as well. They wear a beautiful type of necklace, made of stones that shine like the sun, and they...'

I interrupted Brigit's detailed description asking, 'How did you get to see them? I thought you never left the shores of the lake?'

'That is true, except when the whole settlement went down to the beach in the summer for a week to boil sea water, to get salt for the winter.'

'Sorry, I forgot about that,' I replied, 'you told me about your salt festival before. Go on.'

Brigit settled herself in her furs and continued, happy to be the one telling us some news for a change, rather than it always being Borg or me that told her the stories.

'It was four summers ago, when one of their boats was passing our bay as we were celebrating a good salt harvest. It was a long and sleek looking boat, painted inside and out with red ochre and some sort of bright white paint. It was not a log boat either. It was made of many, many strips of wood, all joined together in some way. They saw Inja dressed in her swan dress as they passed us, and decided to find out more about our people. As the ship beached and the tribe ran over to look at it, six women warriors holding spears immediately jumped out of the boat and onto the shore, threatening to attack us. They looked very fearsome, and the men were totally taken aback by seeing women with weapons in hand, ready to fight. We all stepped back from the boat, and the women relaxed their grips on their weapons. Then Inja walked through the crowd and hailed a greeting to the women in the boat. As soon as they saw our chief was a woman they started to smile, and their leader was helped to shore by the warrior women.

'It was the princess Leena, who we now know is your father's sister. She was dressed in fine cloth, and wore a wide necklace of the bright yellow stone I told you about. It was a sunny day, and the light reflected off her necklace and blinded us all for a second, so that we had to bow our heads in order to see at all. It looked as though we were all bowing to her, but we had to as the light from her necklace was so bright, we could not see.'

I could see it really upset Brigit to think that she and her whole tribe bowed in the presence of this woman, so I said, 'That is amazing! So the sun reflected off her necklace, and created a little sun around her face! I would love to have seen that. Sorry to interrupt, go on.'

'As I said, we all bowed our heads, which pleased the princess no end. Also, the fact that we had a woman for a leader made them like us as a people. Inja, too, had to bow to stop from being blinded, and that really annoyed her to say the least, as you can imagine. But she never showed it and was very welcoming to the visitors. She ordered her women to prepare some of the fish they had caught that morning for the guests, and they followed us to our camp and shared our food. Even though they seemed to be friendly, the warrior women never left the princess's side and always held their spears ready to defend her.

After they had eaten, Inja said she would like to make some sort of trade loop with them, but they just laughed at her! The princess said that they could not imagine that Inja would have anything they would want to trade for. At that insult, Inja was so keen to impress them that she started to tell them about the furs and cured fish we made. They looked very uninterested, until one of the women whispered something in the Leena's ear. She then asked Inja where she got all of the swan feathers, to make such a dress and cape. Inja happily went on to tell them all about the tame swans, and how they were fed to keep them close by, so providing a constant supply of feathers. Leena thought that was an amusing tale, especially when she was told about the swans chasing away men from the tribes to the south. She said they would be very interested in learning more about how the swans were tamed. Inja, stupidly, was so delighted to finally find something to impress them with that she told them exactly how to tame and care for them. She even told them how her women made her dress!

'My brother told me that later that night, that a few of the settlement men were very angry that she had told them everything, as they could have perhaps traded the knowledge for some of those yellow stones. They would not have said that in front of Inja though. The Icin stayed a few more hours, and told

Inja a little about their land. It seemed they had everything they needed, lots of hunting and fishing, white and red rocks which they used to paint their homes with, and an endless stream of trading fleets stopping to trade with them for the yellow stones. Then they just got into their boat, promising to visit again, and had gone.

'Our tribe spent the rest of the day talking about the Icin, wondering when they would return. They passed us each year after that, when we had our festival, but they never landed again. The only thing they were interested in Inja had given them for nothing.'

Borg then said, 'I bet a lot of your tribe are still annoyed at Inja, for telling them your swan secrets.'

'They certainly are,' Brigit replied. 'It was not long after that, that Inja started travelling to visit her friends in the east, or so we thought, each summer. Now we know she was meeting up with Laguz in the south. If my people knew of her betrayal of her father's wishes, she would have lost her status long ago. What I do not understand, is why she keeps coming back to the lake each winter?'

'She probably likes to keep a little independence from Laguz, as he sounds like the kind of man that could tire easily of a woman that was with him all year round,' Borg said, and we both looked at him and nodded. He continued, 'Anyway, now we all know Mia's tale. Where do we head for at first light?'

Brigit answered before I had a chance to speak and said, 'To the Land of the Icin of course! Mia will one day be a queen of unimaginable power and wealth. What a stupid question, Borg!'

Borg looked at me and asked quietly, 'Was it a stupid question, Mia?'

I looked back at him and smiled. Then I said, 'No, I am afraid it was not, Borg. I have no intention of travelling to the Land of the Icin at first light, or ever!'

Borg laughed and patted me on the shoulder. 'I knew it! So we head for adventure and the unknown then!'

I laughed back at him and stood up, holding up my water bag in a toast, saying, 'To adventure, and the unknown!'

We were both beside ourselves with laughter and delight, until Brigit regained her composure and said, 'What are you both taking about? Are you mad? You are not going to claim your rightful place with the Icin?'

Borg and I looked at Brigit's incredulous expression, and collapsed into fits of giggles. When we finally composed ourselves, after intoxicating half the crew in the room with our laughter, I turned to Brigit. It was very painful though to keep a straight face, and I said, 'I am sorry Brigit, but I am very happy not to be travelling to the Icin Land. I have no wish to exchange one life of privilege on Dogger, for another with the Icin. For although it would be a comfortable life that I would have, it would come at too high a price. That price would be my freedom to live my life how I want. To visit strange lands and have adventures. To finally fall in love with a man of my choice, and not one chosen for me, simply to make an heir with. If the Icin ever find me, I will be a prisoner for the rest of my days. Come, let's see if we can get Kemit to let us have a little of the good mead to celebrate our next adventure properly!'

She looked at me seriously and nodded, saying, 'I can see what you mean, but I still think you are mad to give it all up. But who am I to know the best course? I have not even set foot in that boat yet. A prospect that, I must admit, fills me with dread. Wherever you go, I will go Mia. If it is adventure and the unknown, then so be it!'

We both looked at her and smiled, and I was sure I saw something in Borg's eyes that betrayed more than just friendship for Brigit. Could Borg be falling for Brigit? That would be just too perfect! I smiled to myself, and Borg asked me, 'What are you thinking? You gave me a very strange look then Mia!'

'Oh, nothing,' I replied, thinking I would keep my thoughts to myself about that.

We went to our beds soon after, and the next thing I remembered was the noise of the hut contents being moved to the boat. The crew were working at the task with such efficiency that I felt I would just be in the way if I tried to help. So I prepared some food for our journey. Kemit and Uin were directing the stores to be stowed on the boat, and were meticulously seeing that everything was put in the right place. Borg disappeared not long after we woke to help the men carry the partitions he had so lovingly made during the winter. I was just putting the cooked boar meat into a bark container to take with us for food on the boat, when I noticed Brigit looking decidedly worried.

'What is the matter Brigit? Are you ill?' I asked.

'Ill with fear, more like. Oh Mia, I am so frightened at the prospect of getting into that boat and leaving sight of the land.'

I realised then that Brigit had hinted earlier that she was not happy about travelling at sea, but I just thought she was joking. I could see she was really frightened, as we were just about to leave. I put my arms around her and hugged her, and said, 'Really Brigit, you have nothing to fear. This is one of the best trading crews in the northern seas. The route we took through the southern straits of Dogger was the most dangerous sea any boat could navigate. The crew told me at the time that there were only two men that could safely take a log boat through the straits, and they were Kemit and his grandfather. So if you think about it, if they can safely bring a boat though the straits, they are hardly going to sink it in other less dangerous waters.'

She looked up at me with tear filled eyes and asked, 'But what if a storm comes, and a big wave sinks us?'

I could see I was getting nowhere. Although she trusted me, she knew I was hardly an experienced sea goer myself. I held her at arm's length and said, 'Come on, I think you should talk to one of the crew about this.'

She shook her head and replied, 'No. No. They are all too busy, and if they think I am going to be a problem, they might leave me here!'

I did not reply to that, I just led her out of the hut and pulled her along the beach, protesting all the way. Uin was just walking towards us and asked, 'What is the matter? Are you not well, Brigit? You look terrible.'

'She is fine,' I said. 'She is just a little frightened about taking to the sea.'

Uin smiled and said, 'I think she is more than a little frightened, by the look of terror on her face. Come here, Brigit.'

Brigit meekly obeyed, for she knew that Uin was second-in-command of the crew, and she had not really spoken to him much before.

'I do not want to be any trouble, really. It is just…'

'I know, you do not like the thought of leaving sight of the land in a carved out tree trunk. And that is very sensible of you. If I were you, I would probably feel just the same. What you have to understand is that this crew is one of the best in the northern trade routes. The reason they are the best is because Kemit would have nothing but the best crew working for him.'

Brigit was looking a little more relaxed then, but still replied, 'What about storms though?'

Uin laughed and replied, 'You really have been worried, haven't you? Kemit will take to the nearest shore if it looks like a storm is brewing. Although we are out of sight of the land sometimes, we are never more than a few hours paddling from it at any time. I will sit you next to Kas on the journey, and he will tell you anything you want to know. He is one of the most experienced crew members that Kemit has ever traded with.'

'Thank you. I feel a lot better now.'

Uin patted Brigit on the shoulder, and said as he walked away, 'After a few trips, you will feel just as happy on sea as on land.'

'There, you feel better now, do you not?' I said.

She looked up at me and nodded. I could still see the fear in her eyes, but at least she was controlling it better.

It was almost midday food by the time the boat was loaded and we were ready to leave. I tried not to make eye contact with Brigit, or she would see the look of fear in my own eyes as we were finally about to travel the seas again. Borg lifted me into the boat and jumped in after me, and we watched as four of the strongest members of the crew pushed the boat on rollers into deeper water. After the grating sound ceased, as the bottom of the boat scraped along the gravel, it was suddenly silent, and we began to float. The crew then let out a loud cheer, to herald the boat's first floating.

16. AT SEA AGAIN

The boat we left the beach in was huge, compared to the boat we had arrived in. We were comfortable before, but the new boat was luxurious. We even had a permanent covered area in the middle, to sleep in. I saw Brigit sitting next to Kas four or five paddles ahead of me and smiled at her, and she smiled back. It looked like once the boat was afloat, she was beginning to enjoy herself. She would probably be better on the water than I was, I thought to myself. Once the men started to paddle we made good headway out of the bay. As there was no raging surf on that bay, it was just a matter of paddling normally for us to leave the shore.

I leaned over the edge of the boat, and looked at our home, getting smaller and smaller as we paddled away. Then I could see the whole beach, and my cliffs above the hut. I could not get the conversation that I had had with Kemit the night before out of my mind, as I tried to take in the enormity of it all. I was so keen to not be taken to the Icin lands, that I had not really thought about my father, or my mother, that much. I had always tried to think well of my father as I grew up, but I always ended up feeling a mixture of disappointment and sometimes hatred for him, for leaving my mother like that. All she wanted to do was leave Dogger, and for the first time, I could see why he could not take her with him. He knew the Icin would eventually find him wherever they went, especially as his mother, the queen, was going to give such a reward for news of him. If the Icin had found them, they would have taken me and killed my mother, probably in front of him.

The more I thought about the Icin, the more I did not like the sound of them. Yes, I could see the justice in having women in control of a tribe for a change, but did they have to be so very cruel to their men? Maybe they felt they had to be harder in their treatment of their men to show how strong they were. I knew I was only young, and had a lot to learn of the ways of men and women, but I wondered why it always had to be such a battle between the sexes.

As I was lost in thought I looked ashore, and saw that a group of people had appeared on the cliffs, and were standing watching us. I turned to Kemit, who saw my gaze and nodded, 'Yes, I can see them Mia, and by the looks of them they are not lake people either. They look like warriors.'

I looked again, and could see what he meant. They were, even at that distance, very different to the lake men. It could only have been Laguz and Inja, watching us leave. I could see another group of warriors too, gathering on the shore, maybe as many as thirty or forty of them. What could it mean? I turned and found Kemit had come forward and was standing next to me. He whispered, 'It looks like Inja has decided to show her hand with her people after all. I fear Brigit's tribe have a surprise waiting for them this day. Laguz has obviously got tired of keeping their binding a secret. I fear that any loyal followers of Inja's father will not live to see another day.'

We both looked at Brigit, who was preoccupied with talking to Kas and looking out to sea. Then Kemit said, 'It is best we do not mention what we have seen to Brigit. Even though she never intended to return, it would do no good to imagine her home in flames tonight, and all the people she knew either dead or enslaved.'

I looked up into his eyes, and realised that my own were filled with tears. There were some very kind people that I had got to know at the lake during that winter. How life could change so suddenly, I thought. Just as my own life changed with the announcement of the Shaman, the lake people's lives were also going to change, due to our landing on their shore.

'Kemit, is it our fault this is happening?' I asked.

'No, sweetness, it would have happened sooner or later, as Inja felt more secure in her relationship with Laguz. I doubt he would have let her have her own bolthole much longer anyway. He sounds like the sort of man that has to have total control over everyone he comes into contact with. No, do not trouble yourself. If anyone is to blame, it is that harlot Inja.'

I heard the bitterness in his voice, and just nodded my head without looking at him. He patted me on the shoulder and walked to the front of the boat, giving orders for the whole crew to paddle. He tapped time on his staff, and suddenly our leisurely pace instantly became a fast rhythm of paddling. It was as if all the crew had become one paddle, and the speed at which we travelled from then on was amazing.

I would have thought that the larger boat would have been slower, but Kemit had made the front of the new boat more of a wedge shape. He said at the time when I asked him about it, that he had seen a boat like that in a river in the east, and had always wanted to have a tree big enough to try it out on a boat for himself. By the looks on their faces, the crew were also amazed.

Borg, who was paddling next to me, said excitedly, 'What do you think of this? We cut through the sea like flint through flesh!'

I looked at him and laughed at his comment, saying, 'Flint through flesh, eh?'

He laughed and said, 'You know what I mean! Isn't it amazing? I believe we could outrun any boat in the northern seas in this!'

As he said that, a shadow came over my thoughts as I realised that in all the excitement of getting away from Inja and Laguz, we were also heading straight into possible danger, and not just danger from the sea. Borg had not intended to worry me with his comment, but he had, nevertheless. His thoughts were already taken up with the need to outrun other boats. As it was spring, Tashk and the Scan Land traders would be taking to the seas soon to look for us again. His vow to the Shaman that I would be returned to him for the Dogger trade, would be foremost in Tashk's mind I thought. I did not think I would need to worry about the Icin looking for me, because I did not see how they would even know that I existed. (I did not know it then, but the Icin search for me had already started.)

That first day on the water flew past, just as the shores of the northern lands did. We stopped a little before dark, when the men started to fling their hooks and lines over the sides of the boat to fish. A fire was lit at both ends of the boat, so that we could sit round one while the other was used for the cooking. Brigit came over and sat next to me. Her eyes were bright with excitement, and I could see she had taken to the boat with a passion.

'Was it not amazing, the speed we travelled? I cannot imagine why I was so frightened. Now look at them fishing! Curiouser. Curiouser. But they just seem to put the line over the side, and just pull it straight back out with a fish on it!'

I laughed at Brigit's enthusiasm and replied, 'Yes, apparently there are so many fish in the sea, it is always like this. They also grow a lot bigger in the deep water than by the shore. Look at that one!'

I pointed to a huge fish that one of the crew was bringing into the boat. The rest of the crew cheered the lucky fisher, and they all stopped fishing, as with that fish and the ones they had already caught, there would be more than enough food for that night. Brigit made her way up the boat to get a closer look, and I followed her. It was a beautiful fish, so big that it had to be cut into steaks, as you do with meat, to cook it. I asked Uin who was standing next to me, 'What kind of fish is that?'

He looked back at me and replied, 'I do not know its name, but it is common in the deep northern waters. Just wait till you taste it. It is really sweet, and has such flavour.'

We all waited in anticipation for the first piece to be cooked over the fire, until finally one piece was ready. Kas placed it onto a bark platter and handed it to Brigit, who was so taken aback she nearly dropped it. Kemit laughed at her and said, 'The first food caught on any boat always goes to anyone who is on their first sea journey. It is a tradition of ours, Brigit. So come, tell us, how does it taste?'

Brigit was really embarrassed, but sunk her teeth into the fish and beamed with delight as she chewed it, saying between mouthfuls, 'It has to be the most delicious fish I have ever tasted!'

The crew in turn patted her on the shoulder, as they took a platter for themselves. Those kind of traditions were really good, I thought, but I wondered sometimes if Kemit made them up as he went along! We all ate our fill of the delicious fish, and I said that I thought we should name it, as it was too good to swim the seas nameless. The crew thought that was a fine idea, and we spent the rest of the night thinking of names. We finally misheard a crewman taking to his bed, saying he was cold. As he was from the eastern tip of Scan Land, people very often could not understand his accent. We thought he said the fish was cod, and so that is what it became.

As we travelled south again the next day, my heart became heavy, and I kept thinking that I had caught sight of the black birds again. I kept looking at the sky behind the boat, but I never actually saw one. I somehow felt they were still following us, even though I could not see them. We were paddling far out to sea at that time, so no one would see us from the land. I would have thought it was too far for the birds to fly, so I could not understand why I felt that Laguz's presence was suddenly so very close.

That night, before I went to sleep in my furs, I felt the darkness envelope me, as a heavy fur would in mid-winter. It was a suffocating feeling, and I found myself clutching my mother's crystal so tight that I cut my hand with my nails. I watched the crew laughing and joking with Brigit around the fire, and I suddenly felt more alone than I had since being rescued from Dogger. No one seemed to notice my distress, so I thought I would try to go to sleep early. No sooner did my head touch the fur than I started to dream. Or was it a dream? I thought. Where was I? Was I asleep, or not? I could not tell. I was enveloped in complete blackness, apart from the tiny glow coming from my mother's crystal as I clutched it in my hand.

It was suddenly quiet too, no sound at all, even of the water lapping the sides of the boat. Where on earth was I? Or was I in the other realm that I had heard Laguz talk about? It felt like no place I had ever been before. Then I heard it, a whooshing noise from beneath the boat. And again, until the water around the boat rippled in the blackness. I shouted out, who is there? But no noise came from my lips.

Then I heard the whispering, softly at first, then louder and louder, saying, 'Come, Mia. Jump into the water. It is so nice in here. Come, Mia. Jump!'

I sat up and leaned over the side of the boat, to see what was speaking to me, but the water was still and calm. Then I saw them! There must have been ten or twenty big black eels swimming under the boat. They were huge! And as they passed they looked like they were smiling at me, as I caught sight of the glint of their white teeth. I looked at my mother's crystal, and saw that the light in it was becoming dimmer and dimmer. Then I heard the flap of wings, and suddenly the boat was surrounded by the black birds.

I looked down the boat both ways, and there was no one to be seen. I was completely alone. When I looked back, the birds that had been perched on the edge of the boat had jumped down and were starting to hop slowly towards me. I screamed as they reached the edge of my furs, then the whispering started again.

'Jump in, Mia. Jump in and join us. You belong to us, and we belong to you.'

Then I saw, gliding over the surface of the black water, a golden beam of light. My eyes were immediately drawn to it, so much so that I forgot about the birds at my very feet. As it got closer I could make out its shape. It was a golden figure of a woman holding a staff, with a crescent moon dangling from it that, flashed with light like lightning. She was so beautiful, and somehow so familiar, that I was overwhelmed by it, and silent tears began to stream down my cheeks. Then I heard a gentle voice, more in my head than in my ears, say, 'Mia, Mia, you are not for them. You belong on the side of the light, and always will.'

As I watched the figure hover next to me over the dark waters, I heard the birds start to hop backwards. As I looked at them, they somehow started to shrink in size until they were too small to see, and had disappeared completely. I looked over the boat at the water, just in time to see the last eel swimming away. I turned back to look at the golden figure again, but she was gone, and immediately I heard the crew chatting around the fire. Had I been asleep? Or had I been somewhere else?

I shuddered just as Uin passed me, and he gently covered me with his fur cloak and said, smiling, 'Be careful you do not get cold, sweetness. It is a clear night, and it is always colder out at sea.'

I smiled at him and snuggled under the furs, clinging on to the crystal, and fell into a dreamless sleep. The next morning I wondered whether I had imagined it all. I kept looking over the boat, and every so often I was sure I caught sight of an eel, out of the corner of my eye.

For the next few days as we travelled south I could not stop thinking about the eels following our boat, and my dark dream, which I was not sure had been dream at all. I had certainly been awake when I saw Laguz and Inja turn those two poor maids into birds. Had I visited this other realm of theirs? Or had the other realm visited me? The normality of the boat trip had somehow heightened the abnormal experience that I had had too. Who was it that had told me I did not belong with the eels? Was it my dead mother? Somehow I knew it was not my mother, but someone I had not yet met, but at the same time already knew. The golden figure with the crescent moon staff came into my mind, and the more I thought about her the more she seemed familiar to me. Not familiar to me now, but familiar to some other me from a distant past. I had thought that travelling to strange and different lands was an adventure, but eels, black birds, and other realms, and glowing golden figures were almost too much of an adventure. Yet at the same time, and for the first time in my life, it made me feel really alive.

The next day I awoke to a flapping of the cloths covering our partition roof. There was quite a wind blowing, and the waves were lapping noisily at the windward side of the boat. Kemit's men had put two huge rocks tied with bark rope over the side to stop us from drifting in the night. Two men at each end of the boat were now struggling to pull them back into the boat, so that we could turn away from the wind. Kemit ordered the men to take to the paddles, and we were soon racing through the choppy seas with the wind at our backs. If we thought the boat was fast before, it was nothing to the speed it travelled then. Brigit sat next to me, and we both hugged each other to keep out the cold, and to keep from falling over, as the boat sometimes rolled as it sliced though the waves.

'This is really something, Mia. I love the speed we travel. It must be like this if you are a bird flying through the skies. I can't imagine why I was ever frightened! I even like it when the boat rolls about.'

I glanced at her, and wished I enjoyed the boat rolling about too. Still, I was glad she was happy, as it had worried me that she would ask to be taken back home. To a home we suspected was no longer there. The speed of the boat and the stops to fish and cook food took up most of the next three days, until, on the morning of the fourth day, I saw in the distance the Lonely Pine on its little island. I gestured to Brigit, who was deep in some discussion with Kas, to come and look as we approached the tiny island.

'Look Brigit. There is the Lonely Pine I told you about!'

She leaned forward and stared at it, as it grew larger and larger as we approached it with speed.

'Well, you said it was a small island, but I did not imagine it was quite that small!'

We both laughed, then sat quietly looking at the huge pine tree getting closer and closer. Then I noticed something hanging from the tree, and immediately became worried that someone had been there since we had last passed. I waved to Kemit and he came over, asking, 'What is it Mia?'

'Look, there is something hanging from the tree!'

I looked up at him, and saw the grave look on his face as he stared at the tree.

'What is it?' I asked.

'I do not know sweetness, but I have an idea. Let's wait until we get there and have a closer look,' he replied, thoughtfully.

Kemit walked back to the end of the boat and started to talk intensely to Uin.

'There is something wrong, I know it. Borg, come and look at that thing hanging in the tree.'

Borg put his paddle down and came over.

'Can you see what it is?' I asked.

Borg stood on the very end of the boat and shaded his eyes from the morning sun, and replied, 'It looks like some sort of clothing, and a paddle!'

I looked at him and asked, 'Why would anyone leave a paddle and some clothing on the tree like that? Oh Borg, I am getting worried that we are moving towards a trap.'

He looked back at me and smiled, saying, 'Some trap! We can see for leagues in every direction! And there is certainly nowhere behind the tree to hide. Come Mia, do not worry. Maybe it was left by some passing trader last winter. Although I would doubt anyone would leave such a paddle behind anywhere.'

As the boat neared the sandy shore of the island, the paddle could be seen quite clearly.

'By all the gods, that looks like Kemit's paddle! I would know it anywhere. He had it specially made to his own design. He told me all about it when I first met him.'

Borg turned and shouted to Kemit, 'Kemit, it is your paddle, by the looks of it!'

The boat slid onto the sand that surrounded the tree. Kemit came over and nodded, and jumped into the shallow water with Uin, going over to inspect it. We were just about to follow when he said sharply, 'Stay where you are!'

We sat down and watched. It was not like Kemit to use that tone of voice with us, so I became even more worried. It seemed like an age before Kemit and Uin came back to the then silent boat. They had been in deep conversation as they looked at the cloth and paddle, but they did not touch it. Kemit was first on the boat, and called for the crew to come forward so that he could speak to them all together.

'We appear to be dead, my friends. According to the governors of Estergard!'

There was a murmur amongst the men, and he gestured for them to be quiet and continued, 'The cloth was my old cape, and the paddle, as Borg so rightly said, was my old one. The tree is decorated with charms to help our poor dead souls return to land, from our watery graves. I think I know what has happened. It seems that our old boat must have reached the shores of Scan Land, before it broke up. My old paddle and cape must have identified it as our boat. Some of our families must have travelled here within the last moon, to place those charms there for our souls.'

The men did not look too happy to be thought of as dead, but then they realised that they might as well be, as they could not return to Scan Land for many winters. Kemit went on, 'This could not be better news for us, because the search parties that would undoubtedly have started looking for us soon will not now go out. The Shaman from Dogger will be satisfied, and the trade there will continue. So when we do eventually return to our homes and families it will not go so badly for us, as the Dogger trade will not have been lost because of rescuing Mia.'

They all looked at me, and I was suddenly very embarrassed. A sight that Borg took particular delight in seeing, from the look on his face.

'So I think it is best we make our way now, as we do not want to meet any traders until we are out of Scan Land trading waters. To your paddles men, let us put some distance between us and our shrine!'

The men immediately went to their places, and after two men pushed the boat back from the shore, we set off at a good pace southwards. I went ahead and asked Kemit where we were heading.

'We will follow the river to the western channel, and eventually into the great western sea. Not many Scan Land traders go that way, as the passage is bad and the people of the west trade mainly with the Iberi and the Galli from the south.

There is going to be a little rough water as we enter the river though, so you had better get Brigit tied onto the hooks with you.'

Kemit's smiling yet knowledgeable face was so reassuring; if anyone else had said we were going into rough water I would have been worried. I made my way to Brigit's seat and told her we had to be tied down when we entered the mouth of the river, after midday food. She took the suggestion with surprising distaste, saying that she was not a piece of cargo to be lashed onto the boat, and that she was sure she could hold on tight enough. I told her that Kemit had said she was to be tied down, and if she wanted to complain she should do it to him. She went very quiet, and said she was sure that if Kemit wanted it, then who was she to complain.

I smiled and realised that Brigit, though brave and independent, had spent most of her life obeying unquestioningly those of higher stations than herself. So as Kemit had the highest authority, she would do his bidding, but definitely not mine.

After midday food we continued our journey at the same fast pace, and just before it was getting dark I saw a tree lined river mouth in the distance. I asked Kas just where we were, and he replied, 'Well, sweetness, we are just about to go down the Brit Land passage. It divides Brit Land from Galli Land to the south. It is constantly widening each year and some say that there actually was a time when it was not there at all. The passage is rough at this time of the year though, as the melting snow in the northern lands swell the already full river and make it a dangerous passage. It is not that far before we reach the edge of the Great Western Sea, and calm waters again. Do not be afraid though, we have Kemit to guide us, and he has made this journey many times in his lifetime.'

I nodded and asked before he left, 'How long before we are through, did you say?'

'Well, with the wind behind us like this, not more than a day at best.'

He returned to his seat and started to paddle with the rest of the crew. Within an hour of us entering the river, Brigit was glad she was tied in. The journey through the southern straits was nothing compared to the raging waters we now travelled through. I was not surprised the Scan Land traders did not trade the other side of those waters, if they had to navigate that river. Especially as it would have been even more difficult to travel back against the current after their trading. I wondered if we would be coming back that way too, and was not looking forward to the prospect if we were. But we were at least out of the northern sea, and out of the reach of not just the traders, but the Icin Landers too. I felt a great sense of peace in thinking that. We did not stop during that night, as there was no shore to shelter the boat in. The edges of the river were covered with dense forest that overhung the water from the rock-lined shore. The crew must have been getting tired, I thought, to keep up that pace through the night. I must have drifted off to sleep, and when I awoke it was almost dawn, as there was birdsong coming from the forests on either shore. We were heading onto a gravel island in the middle of the river, where it seemed we were going to stop for a while. I looked around for Brigit, and saw she was next to the fire at the other end of the boat, hanging a fishing line over the side. I made my way forward and asked her how long she had been awake.

'How long have I been awake?' she replied indignantly. 'I have not been to sleep at all. I do not know how you could have slept through that passage; you must have a wonderfully pure heart to not have been frightened by those raging waters. Either that, or you are just plain stupid.'

I was a little taken aback by her tone and harsh words, but put it down to tiredness. Borg, however, took exception to it. 'What right do you have to call Mia stupid? Take that back, or our friendship will be at an end right now,' he said, in a steely but hushed voice.

She looked back at him in shock and said, 'Oh, forgive me, Mia! I do not know what came over me. Whatever possessed me to call you stupid? It is just that I have never been so frightened, and it annoyed me so much to see you sleeping peacefully through it all. I am so sorry.'

I smiled at her, and said in a hushed voice, 'Enough of this, you two. We have all been under a great strain. I am not offended, so do not be offended for me, Borg.'

He looked back at me and smiled, but I could see he was still annoyed by Brigit's words, and I was worried it might put a distance between the three of us. I needn't have worried though, for by the time we had eaten first food, Brigit and Borg seemed to be getting on well, as usual. Still, I had seen a different side to Brigit, and realised that she might not have been as open with me as I had been with her. She had had a difficult life, and spent most of it being overly friendly and helpful to people that I knew she disliked intensely. A thought occurred to me, that she might have been doing the same thing with me, but I hoped I was wrong.

I was brought abruptly back from my thoughts by Uin standing next to me, holding a piece of bark with a hot steaming fish on it saying, 'Here Mia, you must eat quickly, as we cannot stay on this gravel bank long. We have a long way ahead yet, to the western sea.'

I took the fish and asked him, 'Is the passage as fierce ahead as it has been?'

'No, my dear, it is much calmer, yet more treacherous in a way, as there are many submerged rocks to navigate around along the way. If we make good time we should get through before the moon rises.'

I nodded, and took my fish back to my seat to share with Borg. The rest of the day we did not stop; as soon as one difficult passage was navigated, there were two more ahead of us. The land on either bank of that huge river was the same all the way along; rock cliffs and dense forest to the very edge of the water. There were no shores to land on, or any signs that people lived nearby at all. No huts or fish traps, or rising smoke in the forest. I asked Kas, who was paddling near me, about the land. 'Kas, does no one live near here? I see no smoke in the forest, or traps in the shallows.'

He smiled and replied, 'Aye, my sweet, you won't see anything of them. There are people about, right enough, but they will have nothing to do with this river. They are forest dwellers, and they live as far away from the river as they can. It is constantly rising, you see, and at certain times of the year it floods with such force, that any huts round about would be crushed by the waters. It is very different ahead, on the edge of the western sea though. The land there on both shores is teeming with people.'

I nodded, and looked back at the dense forests. I must have drifted off to sleep again, and it was almost dark when I woke. The crew were paddling gently, hardly making a ripple in the calm waters. I sat up and looked at the shore, only to see that it was just a thin, dark line in the distance. The river had widened so much that I thought we must have entered a sea. Borg noticed that I was awake, and crept over to sit next to me. He immediately put his finger to his mouth to tell me to be silent. I nodded and followed his gaze, towards the north side of the river. There were patches of mist between us and the shore, but every so often, if you kept looking in the same direction, you could see the glimmer of firelight. The crew were paddling towards the south shore, which seemed to be devoid of light, and I wondered why. There was much tension in the air too, until we eventually grounded the boat on the shore.

Kemit came over to me and said, 'We will spend the night here, Mia, and cross the estuary at first light, to the Mount Land settlement over there.'

I looked at him curiously and asked, 'Why do we not just go to the settlement now? It has only just got dark, and it certainly looks more welcoming than this deserted shore.'

'I know these people Mia, and they do not take kindly to strangers arriving after dark. They are not naturally suspicious, but they have been raided in the past and they now take no chances of it happening again. They would have attacked us before we were in reach of the shore with fire arrows, and asked who we were later. We will be fine here for the night, and at first light we will arrive to a fine welcome. For they are good people.'

I nodded and he went to the other end of the boat with the crew, who were going to light a fire on the shore. Brigit came over to me with some cold fish from midday food, and we talked for hours about the people we were going to meet the next day. Brigit had some strange ideas of these being wild people, not averse to eating men and women. I asked her where she got such stories from. She told me that when she was a child, they would be told lots of stories about the people of Mount Land, and how strange they were. I told her that stories told to children were designed to frighten them into not straying from home. I recalled the stories I had been told of the Icin, and marvelled that there actually was a tribe run by women. I thought too about the events I had experienced, in no more than seven moons, and it took my breath away. I certainly did not feel like I had only twelve winters, as I had done more since I left Dogger than most women do in their entire lives.

Borg touched me on the shoulder, and I was so deep in thought he made me jump. 'Hey, it is only me! What were you thinking about? You looked like you were dreaming while you were awake,' he said.

I replied, laughing, 'That is exactly what I was doing. I was travelling through my life over the last seven moons, and marvelling at all the adventures we have already had.'

'Our adventures are just beginning, Mia. I have heard of the land of the Mount, but never thought I would be just a river mouth away from it. They say they are a strange people, and either take a liking to you or hate you on first meeting. The fact that Kemit has been here before looks like they don't hate him, at least.'

I smiled at him, which seemed to make him look nervous and on edge suddenly. 'What is the matter with you, Borg? You do not treat me the same way as you used to. I hope we are still friends, for you are the brother I never had.'

He shrugged and looked a little put out by my words. Then I heard him mutter, 'Huh, brother.'

I put my hand on his shoulder and pulled him round to face me, asking, 'What do you mean by that? Borg, tell me! What is wrong? For I feel in some way that you have become more and more distant from me.'

'Come, let us go on shore. We need to talk,' he replied. He jumped out of the boat, and stretched his arms out to catch me when I jumped after him, so that I did not get wet. He carried me to the shore, and kept carrying me long after we had left the water's edge. I somehow liked him carrying me, so I did not protest, as I would usually do if he treated me like a frail maid instead of his equal. He put me down under a tree on the edge of the beach, and sat next to me. I do not know why, but I felt I had to say something, anything, as he was just sitting there looking at me, making me feel uncomfortable.

'So,' I said loudly, 'what's all this about then? Is it about you and Brigit?'

He sat back and looked at me with stark amazement. After what seemed like an age, he replied, 'What on earth do you mean? There is no "Me and Brigit", and there never will be!'

I replied in a hushed voice, 'There is no need to say it like that. I have seen you looking at each other. I know you were a little annoyed with her, about the way she spoke to me. But that is what happens when...'

Before I had a chance to say '... people are in love' he put his hand over my mouth and pushed his face close to mine.

He said in a whisper, 'When nothing. You must know how I feel about you. I know you are still too young to think about bonding with me, and I am happy to wait for you. But you must know how I feel?'

I felt a sudden chill come over me, as if a cold wind had just blown over us both. It made me pull away from the rock I was sitting on. Oh, why did he have to speak of such things? I knew it would never be the same between us now. I turned away, not trusting myself to hide my feelings of regret and sadness.

He asked in a pleading voice, 'Mia, are you all right?' He tried to pull me round to look at him, but I shrugged my shoulder at him, and he said with deep regret in his voice, 'Have I offended you? That was the last thing I wanted to do. I just had to tell you how I felt, especially after you suggested I had feelings for Brigit.'

When he said Brigit's name, he could not disguise the distaste in his voice. I turned and looked at him crossly, and said, 'Why do you dislike her so? I thought you were good friends, at least.'

He looked me straight in the eyes and whispered, 'I believe she deceives you, Mia. She is not a true friend, and is just using you for her own reasons. And I do not say that just because of the way she spoke to you the other day. That just confirmed what I suspected.'

I stood up and brushed the moss off my clothes, and said indignantly, 'This is really too much, Borg! Brigit is a good friend. What are you suggesting? That she is in league with Inja, in some sort of spying plot?'

He looked away and then replied, 'No, of course not! She did not know anything of Inja's schemes. She is just out for herself. She makes herself useful to the people around her, until they do not know what they did without her. I do not believe she has any genuine feelings. She has spent so much of her life not quite fitting into settlement life, and that is why I think she has developed a way of using people to improve her life.'

I turned and looked at him and said, 'Well, that was a long and well-formed opinion. How can you say that about Brigit? She has been so good to me.'

'That is just what I mean. She wormed her way into your affections, so that you would take her away from a life she really hated.'

He was really annoying me by then, so I said, 'So what you are saying, is that no one can have genuine feelings for me. They only make friends with me so as to use me in the future. Is that what you have done Borg? Made friends with me and rescued me from the Shaman, only to take me for yourself at some point?'

He jumped up and grabbed my arm as I was walking away, and said angrily, 'How could you think such a thing of me? I love you, Mia. I think I fell in love with you when I used to take you fishing on my boat, all those winters ago. I would give my life for you, without wanting any reward. To compare me to the Shaman. Mia. You have gone too far now.'

He started to stride back to the boat, and I just fell onto the sand and sobbed. I do not know why I cried, whether it was for Borg, or for me, or for some lost innocence that we had had between us. Why did it always have to turn out like that? I thought. Would that I were ugly, and did not have red hair. Then I might not have such attention to confuse me. Oh, what have I done? I wanted to call out to Borg to come back, but he was already at the boat, and it would only draw the crew's attention to us. I do not know how long I lay there on the sand, but I was starting to get cold. Then I saw someone coming over towards me. It was Kemit, who asked, 'What are you doing here on your own, sweetness? Although this shore is deserted, we must always be careful, as there might be bears about.'

Kemit pulled me up, and I just leapt into his arms and started to sob again. He just stood there and held me for a moment, then held me at arm's length and looked at my tear stained face, saying gently, 'Sweetness, what is it? Has someone upset you? Tell me who it is, and I will have words with them!'

I looked up at him and told him what Borg had said, about Brigit, and his feelings for me. Then I told him what I had said in return.

After a moment he replied, 'Oh. That was not a very nice thing to say to him, Mia. Borg is only trying to protect you. He is very good at judging people too, as I have also seen a side to Brigit that is not entirely honest. As for his love for you, surely you knew he adored you?'

I looked up at him in amazement and whispered, 'No, I didn't know he had those sort of feelings for me. If I had, I would not have snuggled up to him in the night for warmth and comfort. Oh Kemit, is it my fault?'

He put his arms around me and said gently, 'No, of course not. Borg's feelings for you are genuinely loving. He is not like the Shaman, desiring your soul. He loves all of you, and he would never try to persuade you to give him more than you were happy with. You must apologise to him, Mia, for you have done him a great injustice.'

I nodded and he said, 'Come, it is cold here and we have another adventure ahead of us tomorrow.'

As we walked back, I asked him what the people at Mount Land were like. He stopped in his tracks and said, with a beaming grin on his face, 'They are the best kind of people! They are slow to like you, but when they do there is no better friend in all the known world. I think you will like them, and I know they will like you. However, we must not tell them of your origins, for they have no love of the Icin. I have told the crew, and Brigit and Borg that we are to say you are my daughter from Scan Land, who has decided to trade with me for a few seasons.'

I looked up at him and laughed, and said, 'A fine story too, as you are the father I have wished for all my life!'

At that he hugged me tightly, and then held me at arm's length and said, 'In my heart you have been my daughter from when I first saw you, looking at my amber goods in the boat that day. It is no lie, when we tell these people that you are my daughter; for you are, and always will be.'

I let him lift me into the boat, and I went over to the fire to warm myself a little before I went to sleep. Borg and Brigit were sitting on either side of the fire, and Brigit asked immediately, 'Where have you been? I have been worried about you. Here, take this fish. I saved it for you.'

I reached over and took the fish, glancing at Borg as I did so. He looked away and got up to go to his bed.

'What is the matter with him? He has had a face like thunder since he came back from the beach. Have you two had an argument?'

'Oh, it was nothing, just a little disagreement about something,' I replied.

'I wouldn't mind a little private meeting on the beach with him. You can be sure he would get no disagreements from me!'

I looked at her, and could not disguise the shock in my face and asked, 'What exactly do you mean? Would you let him kiss you? Surely not, you are not much older than I am.'

She smiled to herself and replied, 'I am two winters older than you, actually, and well old enough to have been kissed already.'

She suddenly looked like she had said more than she wanted to, as I asked, 'What? You have let a boy kiss you? When? Who? Was that why you wanted to leave the settlement?'

Brigit leaned forward and whispered to me, 'It was one of the crew on the beach, when you were away with Inja. He wants to kiss me again, but I have told him he is too old for me, so he has not pestered me for some time now. Borg now, he could kiss me anytime, on any terms!'

I moved closer to her and whispered, 'You are telling me that one of the crew kissed you, on the lips, on the beach, while I was away? A real kiss?'

She leaned forward and said quietly, 'Very real. More than once, too.'

There was a gleam in her eyes, and I had to ask her, 'Who?'

She leaned back and smiled, and replied, 'I think I will keep that to myself for now, as I don't think he wants anyone to know about it. He did not force me mind, he just said I was the most beautiful thing he had seen in many a season, and told me he would be honoured to be the first man to really kiss me.'

I sat up and whispered in her ear, 'You have to tell me who it was.'

She pulled away from me saying, 'Why? I do not see why you have to know all my secrets!'

I stood up then and said firmly, 'We will see about that. Kemit has to be told.'

She grasped at my cape as I started to move to the end of the boat, and whispered, 'No, do not tell Kemit! Please, Mia!'

I looked down at her pleading face, and asked gently, 'Tell who it was then?'

'I… I am not sure of his name. I… it was Kas. Yes, it was that nice, friendly old Kas. He is really not as nice as he seems, you know.'

I stopped in my tracks and sat down, staring at her. She thought that was a good reaction and continued, 'That is why he has been so close to me on the boat. He just wants to hold my hand now and then, and I let him because he likes it so.'

I did not know what to say! How could she have been so stupid as to expose her lies like that? Of course it was not Kas. He was with me on the trip south. She was lying, and she had not realised that I knew she was lying. Oh Borg, you were right, I thought to myself. She was not the person she pretended to be. How could I have been so stupid? What do I do about it now? I could not expose her, just before we were about to visit the Mount Land people, as she might betray us and tell them about my connection with the Icin, simply to gain their friendship. I decided that I would have to pretend I believed her, until we were on some other shore. I could not tell Borg about it either, or he would not be able to help himself from exposing her. I just looked at her and said gently, 'Maybe we should keep this to ourselves Brigit. You must promise not to let him kiss you again, not until you are a little older at least.'

She nodded and replied, 'You are right Mia, as always. It will be our secret.'

She smiled, and we went to our beds, but it was a long time before I finally got to sleep that night. Poor Kas. He would have been devastated if he knew what she had said about him.

17. MOUNT LAND AND THE PRIESTESS

Kemit woke me at first light, and asked me to stand by him as we approached the beach at Mount Land. It was a bright, clear spring day, and the mood amongst the crew was noticeably happy. There was no mist by the time we left the south shore, and I realised why that place was called Mount Land. The land ahead of us was very low lying, no cliffs or hills, just vast stretches of scrubby forests as far as the eye could see. And right in the centre of the wooded plain was what they called the Mount. It just seemed to stick out of the land, on its own. A huge, craggy rock, big enough for the few homes I could see on the top, but nothing else.

I pointed to it and looked at Kemit, who smiled and said, 'It is magnificent, is it not? That, as you can guess, is the Mount, of Mount Land. I think you will like it here, sweetness, these are good people.'

I smiled at him, trying to forget what had happened the night before with Borg and Brigit.

'Who lives at the top of the Mount? Is it the chief?'

Kemit was silent for a while, then replied in a hushed voice, 'No, that is where the priestess, Iona lives.'

He spoke her name with a whisper, and I wondered if she was another bad Shaman. 'Does she have a dark heart, like the Shaman on Dogger?' I asked.

Kemit turned round instantly and held my arm tightly, and said almost harshly, 'In no way does she belong to the same world, as your Dogger Shaman. She is all that is good in this world, and if she requests to meet you, you will be truly blessed!'

The shocked look on my face made him release me and say, 'I am sorry Mia, but the thought of Iona and the Dogger Shaman being spoken of in the same breath was just too much for me. I owe a lot to her prophesies in the past, as she has always steered me in the right direction. Just the thought of her bright soul has brightened some of the darkest hours of my life.'

I looked at him and asked, 'Will I meet her while we are here do you think?'

He patted me on the shoulder as we slowly approached the north shore and replied, 'I have no doubt she will want to meet you, sweetness. She will probably know more about you than you do yourself, even as we speak. For she can see not just into the future, but also into the past.'

I had never heard Kemit speak in that way about anyone before. The priestess of Mount Land had obviously had a great influence on his life. I knew

Kemit's heart was full of goodness, so I thought she must be very special for him to think so much of her. As we approached the shore I could see that we were entering a small bay with a gravel bank in the middle, which formed a low-lying island. On the gravel bank was a line of log boats, and lots of racks for drying fish and repairing nets. It was a very familiar scene to me, as the boats and racks were just the same as the ones on my island at home. The shore however, and the huts were very different. The huts were all round, not a square hut amongst them, and they all had a sort of cloth covered doorway, held up with two stout poles. I imagined it was so that you could sit protected from the rain or the sun, in your doorway, but I had never seen it before. It looked very strange, but it looked like a good idea too. It was always so dark in a hut, and the covered places outside were probably very good to sit or work under.

There was a wonderful smell drifting over the water as we approached the shore, and I asked Kemit, 'What is that delicious smell?'

'That, Mia, is the best thing you will ever have tasted, I have no doubt! It is the smell of sea spiders cooking!'

I looked up at him with a puzzled expression, and he continued, 'You will see soon enough. Look, there is a group of people who have come to greet us.'

I looked in the direction he was pointing, and saw an extraordinary sight. A group was gathering at the end of the beach, wearing very strange clothes. They looked, from that distance, like a group of brightly striped butterflies or bees, until we got closer and I could see what they were wearing. They were wearing furs. But instead of the furs being worn as usual, they must have cut the furs into lots of very small strips, and sewn them back together again. Each strip was a different colour, so that their cloaks were covered in white, brown, red and black stripes. They looked magnificent, but I was amazed that anyone would go to so much trouble, cutting and sewing back the fur to get that effect.

'Don't their cloaks look wonderful? They are so proud of them, that no matter how much I offer for them, they will never trade them. I could sell them for a fine price in any port, even in the Far East, but they say they make them for themselves, and for no one else. That is the kind of people they are. They have some very strange values too, but you have to admire them for it.'

The boat was grounding on the sandy shore as he spoke, and suddenly the settlers surrounded us.

'Hail, Gimble! How goes it with you this fine morning?'

A tall man with a twisted staff called back, 'Kemit, you old rogue! It is good for my eyes to see your smiling face on our shores again! You have left it too long!'

Kemit jumped out of the boat and waded through the surf to embrace his old friend. It was a heart-warming scene, with many people coming up to him and either hugging him or patting him on the back. We just stood in the boat and watched, not wanting to intrude in the greetings of old friends. After what seemed like an age, as the huge crowd of people all seemed to need to greet

Kemit individually, Kemit turned round and gestured for me to come over to him. Kas jumped overboard and reached out to me, so he could carry me to shore, and within minutes I was amongst the crowd of welcoming tribes-people.

Kemit took my hand in his and said to Gimble, 'This, my dear friend, is my daughter, Mia. I do not think I told you about her. She has been living with her mother to the north of Estergard, and now has a taste for adventure with her father before she is to be bound.'

Gimble stood and looked at me, and after a while said gently, 'It is an honour to meet one of the family of my dear friend, Kemit. For all the gods, I did not even know he had a family!' He turned and patted Kemit on the back with a playful gesture of reproof, then said, 'Come, my honey, let me take you to my home for refreshments!'

He led me ahead of the crowd of settlers, leaving Kemit and the crew to beach the boat on the shore. Gimble's hand was warm and strong, and yet he held me so gently that a fragile flower would not have been crushed.

We approached a large hall with a huge cloth roof at its entrance. The cloth roof was so large, that it had furs and grinding stones, and even looms under it, leaning against the entrance of the hut. It was obviously a place for daily chores, and I wondered why my own people had not thought of such a simple idea. As we passed through the settlement I noticed that some of those outer rooms even had low wattle walls around them, to give them protection from the wind.

When we reached the entrance to Gimble's hall, all his family came out and stood in a line to greet me. They were certainly a people that thought much of very formal greetings, I thought. A tall woman, with hair not unlike my own, came over first and held out her arms to me. I thought that was very strange, as I had not met her before, but it was obviously a greeting they had, even for strangers. I walked up to her embrace and she hugged me, and then held me at arm's length before hugging me again. That procedure continued until I had been hugged by the entire line of his family, ending with a little boy of about five winters. Gimble then gestured for me to go inside, which I did gladly, as I was not used to such a display of affection from perfect strangers. Nice though it was, I found it a little unnerving.

'Raffi! Fetch a hot drink for our guest,' Gimble shouted, smiling. His wife then brought out a bark container and set it by the hearth. I could not imagine what sort of drink she was making for me, but it was probably hot honey water, like my grandmother used to make. I sat down on some furs, happy just to watch her prepare the drink. She took some herbs out of a bag dangling from her waist, and put them into the container; then she poured in some water from a leather bag hanging on one of the roof beams. She picked up two sticks and poked them into the fire hearth, eventually bringing out a red hot stone which she immediately put into the bark container. The whistling and hissing noise that it made was very loud, and she looked back at me and smiled. Within a few moments the water was boiling, and she took out the stone with the sticks and put it back into the fire. She then got another stick and stirred the hot liquid for a few moments, before pouring it through a cloth over a bark cup. A huge platter full of honey was brought over, and she gestured to it. I nodded happily, for honey was one of my most favourite foods. She spooned some honey into the cup, and after stirring it again handed it to me.

I had never seen herbs used in that way before, as we only ever used herbs on my island in order to heal you if you were sick. I could recognise one of the herbs from the smell though; it was an herb usually used to cure sore throats. The other was definitely water mint, which was not used at all by Dogger Islanders. I knew I would have to drink it all, as she had so carefully prepared it for me, so I hoped it did not taste too bad. I took a sip, as the water was still quite hot, and then another, and before I knew it I had drunk it all! It was delicious. Sweet and warming, and I knew at that moment I was going to like it there a lot! Raffi was delighted by my reaction, and so was Gimble. I had not realised it until then, but the whole family had been watching me intensely, as if I was taking some sort of test.

Gimble sat next to me grinning, and said, 'You are truly the daughter of Kemit, and now an honorary daughter of Mount Land too! I do not think I have seen anyone take to our drink with such delight. We have many strangers passing by, and we always, on first meeting, give them our special welcome drink. You would be surprised at how many not only do not drink it up, but will not even take a sip!'

I looked at him in amazement and replied, 'Really? But it is the most delicious drink I think I have ever tasted. How foolish of them!'

Gimble and the whole family laughed at my remark, and I suddenly felt as if I had known those people all of my life.

'Now you have met my family, you must come and have some first food with us.' Gimble led me out of the hall and down to the beach where the boat was pulled up onto the gravel, and the crew were standing in a group, with Brigit and Borg at the front, watching our approach.

'Well,' Kemit shouted, 'did she pass your test?'

Gimble replied heartily, 'Not only did she pass our test, my friend, but she is now my daughter too!'

Kemit laughed and looked at me proudly.

'Time for first food now, I think, as your crew look very hungry!'

Kemit came over to us and held out his hand to me, whispering, 'We think of nothing else but the first food of the Mount Landers, during our seasons away. There is no finer food in all the known world!'

Hearing this, Gimble said, 'Kemit, you jest! For it is a simple food, not one of your exotic eastern dishes. Come, let us go and eat, and stop talking about it, for I have a good hunger myself today.'

We walked together with the rest of the tribe to a long table covered with a skin roof, situated on the edge of the shore. Just to the side of it, on the stony part of the beach, were many raging fires. We all sat on the long log seats next to the table, so that we could watch the fires in front of us. Borg and Brigit sat next to me, and we watched in fascination, wondering what the amazing food was going to be. Next to the fires were lots of wooden lined pits that were filled with water, which was boiling and steaming. The men kept adding hot stones from the fires to keep the water boiling, and Gimble shouted to one of them,

'Are they ready, Safn? For you have a large party for first food this day!'

Safn prodded one of the pits, and pulled out on his long hooked stick a steaming sea spider, and replied, 'They are as ready as they will ever be!'

Safn's team of cooks were all men, which I thought was odd, as usually only women cooked in my settlement, apart from on hunting trips. They started to fill huge wooden platters with cooked, steaming sea spiders, and another type of spider that I had not seen before. They brought the platters over to us and placed them all along the table. The crew immediately grabbed the hot sea spiders, and started ripping their limbs off and sucking out the contents. As I looked at them I knew they must be good, for I had never seen the crew so enthusiastic about their food.

Kemit pulled one of the strange long legs off and handed it to me, saying, 'Be careful, for it is still a little hot. This is a sea king, and the tastiest of all the sea spiders. Here, let me show you how to eat it.' He picked up a stone from under the table and cracked the legs with it, and pulled them apart to reveal pure white flesh. 'Here, taste that!' he said enthusiastically as he handed it to me.

I took it from him, and sunk my teeth into one of the best taste sensations of my entire life. It was wonderful, and after eating it I enthusiastically joined the rest of the crew in cracking open the shells. Gimble looked at me and said, 'Mia, you do not have to eat so quickly, we are not going to run out of sea spiders, I promise you!'

I looked up at him and laughed, saying, 'You mean you eat them every day? Surely not!'

He nodded and replied, 'Every day, and somehow we never get tired of them.'

'I am not surprised,' I replied, and went on eating.

Brigit was not eating at all. I turned and asked her if she did not like them, and she replied, 'I am sure they are good, but we were told in my settlement that sea spiders are poisonous to eat.'

Suddenly a hush came over the gathering, as they had all heard Brigit's words. Then Gimble said, 'What is this? You think we are trying to poison you?'

Gimble's tone had changed completely, and was sharp and cold. Brigit looked around and saw everyone looking at her. She replied apologetically, 'No, no, of course not. It is just that in my settlement we were told that if we found a sea spider washed up on the beach, we were never to eat it, as it would poison us.'

Brigit was near to tears by the time she had explained herself, and when she had finished a huge roar of laughter went up from the crowd. Gimble came over and said, 'I am sorry if I misunderstood you. Yes, your people are right. If ever you find a dead sea spider on the beach and eat it, you could become very ill indeed. You could even die. The secret is to catch them alive in the sea, and cook them while they are alive, so that you know they are really fresh. It is then, and only then, that you can eat this delicious food without being ill. Come, sit next to me and I will get you some of the best pieces.'

Brigit got up and sat down next to Gimble. Borg and I looked at each other as if to say, how is it Brigit always seems to end up as everybody's friend? I smiled at Borg, and thought that I must speak to him soon, to clear the bad feelings between us.

The first food meal of sea spiders seemed to go on most of the morning; as soon as the crew finished their platters, they called out for more! Gimble was delighted that they were enjoying it so much, and after watching them eat through their third platter, he decided he had watched them enough and took a walk along the shore with Kemit. I watched them for some time, and from the look on their faces as they stood a little way away from us, I imagined Kemit was telling Gimble all about our winter's stay on Inja's shore. Gimble kept stopping as they walked, to shake his head.

At that point I felt that I could no longer stand the distance between Borg and myself, and I asked him if he would take a walk along the shore with me too, to talk. His first reaction was to make excuses, that he was needed by the crew. But when he said that, I just looked at the crew tucking into another platter of sea spiders, and then looked back at him. He knew it was no use pretending they were going to do any work that morning, so he agreed to come.

He followed me down to the shore. Usually when we went for a walk, Borg would hold my hand, or if it was cold he would put his arm around my shoulder. But that time we walked apart, and in silence. As we turned around a small headland at the edge of the beach, out of sight of the crew, I stopped and turned to him.

'Stop right there, Borg! This has gone on long enough. I cannot stand this coldness between us!' I said.

'I do not know what you mean,' he said flatly.

'Well, really! I thought you might have at least given me some sort of excuse, but to pretend that things are as they usually are between us is ridiculous. Borg, I am sorry for the things I said on the south shore last night. I really did not mean it. I was just angry and confused, by you telling me how you felt.'

He looked up and was about to say something, but I held my hand up and continued, 'No, do not say anything. Let me speak first. I love you, Borg, you know that, but I am too young to even think about that other kind of love, between a boy and a maid. I do not know how I will feel about you when I am ready to bond with a man. Those feelings are winters away from me. I do not want this to spoil our friendship, and I cannot say what will happen in the future. It is now that I care about.'

Borg reached out to me and took my hands in his, saying, 'I was foolish to tell you what I was thinking. I too do not want to spoil what we have together. I did not sleep last night for thinking about it. You are right though, by the time you are a young woman, we might both have found another we would rather be with. So it is stupid of me to try and predict what will happen. Forgive me, Mia. By all the gods, let it be the same as it was between us, for you are the only family I feel that I have.'

I pushed his hands away and leapt into his arms, hugging him tightly, as tears of relief streamed down my face. When I eventually released him I could see his eyes were wet too, and I said, 'I really did not mean it, when I said you were like the Shaman! I was just angry with you, for putting me in a situation I did not want to be in.'

We sat down on the gravel beach and he said, 'I can see that now. Let us not talk about it again, all right?'

I just looked at him and nodded. Now we were friends again, I thought of Brigit and said, 'Borg, I have another thing to apologise for as well.'

He looked at me with an expression of fake shock on his face, and replied, 'Oh?'

'Yes, and do not look like that. This is serious. It is about Brigit.'

As soon as I said her name his face changed, and he looked stern and attentive.

'You were right about her not being what she seems.' I said. I then told him what she had said about Kas. Borg jumped up, and with a red face full of anger, he started striding down the beach.

'Stop! Borg come back!' I shouted to him. He was walking so fast, I had to run to catch up with him.

When I did, he turned to me and with a face like thunder said, 'No Mia, she has gone too far now. Blackening the name of a kind man like Kas. I must speak to Kemit of this!'

He started to stride away, but I shouted to him, 'Stop!'

The fear in my voice must have cut through his anger. He turned and walked back to me asking, 'Why? What is the matter?'

I pulled him back along the beach, and said to him urgently, 'Kemit does not want these good people to know I have any connection with the Icin, for they are their enemies. Even though I have never met the Icin, it might cause a shadow to be cast on Kemit's friendship with them.'

Borg nodded and replied, 'Yes, I can see that, but what does that have to do with Brigit?'

As soon as he said that, I could see it had dawned on him what she would probably do, if Kemit reproved her for her lies about Kas.

'By the gods you are right! She would tell Gimble about you, to gain favour, and have a new shore to stay on. But Mia, she cannot just get away with this!'

We sat down again, and I said, 'Do not worry, she will not get away with it. We just have to play her at her own game for a while, until we leave these shores and make sure she comes with us. When we are away, we will tell Kemit everything and let him deal with her.'

Borg looked at me and nodded in agreement, and said, 'For a maid of only twelve winters you certainly have a wise head on your shoulders. Thank the gods you stopped me in time. I was determined to ignore you and tell Kemit, you know.'

I looked at him and asked, 'What stopped you?'

'I do not know, it was something in your voice when you shouted stop. I heard the fear in it. Come here, you little beast, give me a hug again.'

We embraced again, and it was good to have him back to his old self, so I said, 'Hey, less of the beast, Paddle Boy!'

I jumped up and ran. Borg chased me until we rounded the headland and were in view of the settlement again. We started to walk, as we noticed the crew and the Mount Landers were watching us. We laughed as we walked back, happy to be comfortable again in each other's company.

'Where have you two been? I have been looking for you everywhere.' Brigit shouted as she ran up to us. Borg tightened his grip on my hand when he saw her, and I had to pull it away because he was hurting me.

He said quietly, 'Sorry, I did not realise I was holding your hand so tightly.'

'You weren't, until you saw Brigit.' I said quietly.

Brigit bounced up to us, smiling from ear to ear. 'Isn't this place wonderful? And the sea spiders were the best first food I have ever had! Have you met Raffi yet? She is really nice, and she is going to show me how they make their wonderful fur capes.'

I could not help feeling a little annoyed that she had asked Raffi about the capes, as I had intended to ask her about them when I went back to her hall. Brigit's forthright attitude was starting to annoy me intensely. I would have to be very careful that I did not show my annoyance with her though. I have always found it hard to conceal my real feelings about people, when they annoyed or upset me.

'Really? I was going to ask her about that too,' I replied.

Brigit smiled and said, 'Well, why don't you come along with me? I am sure she will show you as well!'

I was gripping Borg's hand so tightly that my knuckles went white. He looked at me, and smiling, raised his eyebrow as if to say now you know how I feel. Then I said, 'All right, I will meet you at Raffi's hall in a little while.'

Brigit looked at me, puzzled, and asked, 'You know where she lives?'

I smiled sweetly back and replied, 'Yes, of course. I had a drink with her and her man, Gimble, before we came down for first food.'

'I did not know she was the woman of the chief! She was so very friendly. In my settlement you would never have been so friendly with the chief's family, so soon after meeting them. So you have already been to their hut?'

'Hall. Yes.' Then I whispered, 'Watch out for the special drink they give you. It is very bitter. If I were you, I would say you do not like hot drinks.'

'Thanks, I will remember that! See you later.'

I looked up at Borg and could not help laughing out loud.

'What are you so happy about?'

'Oh, just a little joke at Brigit's expense. You see, the people here have a particular love of certain herbs steeped in hot water, and it is a sort of test, to see whether they are going to like a newcomer or not. They told me that they did not trust people that did not like it, or even try it. So I told Brigit it was really bitter, and to avoid drinking it at all costs!'

We both laughed, but then Borg became serious and said, 'Be careful Mia. You are no match for Brigit's devious nature. She will soon see through you, if you try to play her at her own game. Just be yourself, but keep your confidences to yourself from now on.'

'Yes, you are right. I know it was a foolish thing to do, but hey, how is she going to find out that I lied to her?'

'She will know next time you are with Gimble's woman, and she offers you the drink. You will take it and drink it up and Brigit will wonder why, if it is so horrible.'

'You are right. I am going to catch up with Brigit and tell her I was joking. Nothing must spoil our relationship with these people, as Kemit loves them so, and he has already given up enough for me.'

I ran along the main path through the settlement, and caught up with Brigit and Raffi just as they were about to enter the hall.

'Oh, I thought you were going to follow later,' Brigit said. Her tone was a little put out, as I think she wanted Raffi to herself for a while, once she knew how important she was.

Then I replied, 'Oh I just had to run up and tell you about the joke I played on you.'

'What joke?' Brigit said, looking suspiciously at me.

'Oh, nothing important, it was just about the drink. It is not really bitter, it is actually wonderful and sweet. Sorry, it was silly of me to pretend you had to avoid it. It is really good.'

Brigit laughed and looked relieved, and I wondered what joke she thought I had played on her. We went inside, and Raffi immediately brought out the bark container and offered us both a hot drink. Brigit laughed and said she would love one, and her mood was happy and relaxed after that. After we had drunk, and Brigit had duly praised the drink, Raffi went over to the corner of the room and brought over a basket full of strips of different coloured furs. She sat down in front of us and laid out the strips, so that the colour of the furs alternated.

'You have to make sure they are all the same type of fur, as you could not sew a young bear skin next to a fox skin, or it would not look right,' she said. 'Here is a basket of bone needles. Take one each.'

We did as she said and marvelled at how fine the needles were. The ones we used on Dogger were twice as thick.

'They have to be very fine, so as not to rip the soft leather. We find it best to make these needles from goose bones, as they can be made very sharp. Now, after working out the order of the colours that you want, it is time to sew them together. Plant thread or sinew can be used, it doesn't really matter. Come, it is time to get started. Pick your furs and choose your patterns.'

I became so absorbed in making my cape, that I forgot where I was for the best part of the morning. I chose the red fox fur and white goat fur. I decided to make alternate stripes of both colours, leaving a trim around my neck and at the bottom edge in the red fox fur. It was so long since I had done such a simple task, that I delighted in the monotony of it. Brigit had decided to make a cape of every type of fur that could be found in the basket, and the result looked a little mixed up, although it would still be a wonderful cape. We were totally absorbed in our task when Gimble and Kemit came in, and Raffi set about making the drink again.

'What do we have here?' Kemit asked me.

'Raffi is showing us how to make a cape like the Mount Landers wear. Look, what do you think of mine so far?'

He reached over and took the half-sewn cape, and laid it out on the floor. 'It is very fine, Mia. Are you following a pattern?'

'No, I just worked it out myself from the strips in the basket.'

Gimble came over and looked at it, and said, 'Mia, you have a fine eye for cape design. It is so simple, but really very good. Well done! What about you Brigit, what have you done?'

Brigit spread her mismatched mixture of pelts on the ground, and Gimble rubbed his chin and said, 'Mmm. I think you may need a little more practise in the art of matching the furs, Brigit dear. Still, it is only your first, and you should see some of the first cloaks that our children make! We have a rule here too, that all first capes must be worn for the whole year, before they can be let loose on the pelt basket again. You would be surprised at how much more care they take in matching them, after wearing their first one for a whole winter.'

We all laughed, and although Brigit laughed too, I could see she was annoyed that her cape did not meet with the same approval as mine. I would have to be very careful not to annoy her, I thought, or she might not want to leave with us, and that would be disastrous for Kemit's friendship with Gimble. It would only be a matter of time before she told them about my father's past.

Borg came in, and Kemit introduced him to Gimble as his adopted son from Dogger. Borg looked surprised at that description of him, but I could see he was also very proud.

'From Dogger, eh? That is a strange place, or so I have heard. I do not know anyone that has been there. Except for Kemit, of course. He always talks about their wonderful decorated wood and bone goods. In fact, I have a link of beads from there that I bought from him on his last visit. Tell me Borg, how do you get the resin in the holes so neatly?'

Borg stood next to Gimble as he showed him his beads. He could see they were some of the finest that he had ever seen, and he replied, 'I am afraid you are asking the wrong person about the making of these beads, for I am just from a humble fishing family on my island. These goods are made by the women of the cliffs, in the centre of our island. There is a strange tale about how those women came to be making such work, which I will tell you if you have the time.'

Gimble gestured for Borg to sit next to him by the hearth, and said, 'If we have the time for a good tale on a cold spring afternoon! Of course we do! Raffi, make this young man a drink.'

Borg sat down amidst an ever filling hall, and told them all about the law that stopped the women of the island from leaving, and how there were eventually more women than men. He then explained how that became the origin of the cliff women, and their trade. When he had finished, he looked around to find the entire hall was brimming with people, delighted to hear a tale from Dogger Island, and especially from one who was born there.

Gimble leaned back when Borg had finished and said, 'Well, young Borg, that was a tale and a half all right. Who would have thought that by imprisoning their women, they would have fostered such a wonderful craft. Hmm… maybe we should lock up our own women for a while, and see what they come up with, eh Raffi?'

Raffi leaned over and hit him on the head with her stirring stick, and the whole room roared with laughter.

'On second thoughts, maybe not!' Gimble said laughing. 'I doubt we could make a prison strong enough to keep them in anyway, eh men?'

Raffi was just about to attack him again, but he leapt up and ran out of the door, to the delight of the watching crowd.

Kemit came over to me and said, 'That really is a fine cape you are making for yourself, sweetness. I can see you are already feeling at home with these good people.'

I looked up at him and smiled, saying, 'Yes, are they not wonderful?'

'You will have to leave this work for a little while though,' Kemit said, 'for we have to sort out where we are to stay before it gets dark. Come, leave it there. We will come back in a while.'

Raffi gestured for us to leave everything as it was until we returned. As we went outside we could see that Gimble was waiting a little way along the path from the hall, and laughed as we approached, saying, 'You have to be quick if you offend our women, or they will take a stick to you at the least provocation!'

Kemit thumped him on the back then, and laughing said, 'You don't think talk of locking your good women in prisons could be more than a little provocation?'

'Maybe, my friend, you could be right! Let's get you sorted out for the night, for although it is spring, there is a hard frost at night still. Come, I have just the place for you.'

We followed him down the path to the beach, then we veered to the right, past a few more huts, until we were at the edge of the forest itself. Two huts were there, overhung by a great oak tree. It was not until we were almost up to the huts that I realised there was also a hut in the tree itself! A rope walkway from a bank behind the huts went straight into the tree. I just stood and looked at it in amazement. Borg was also without words, as we walked underneath the platform that rested on the huge oak boughs far above us.

Gimble smiled at our expressions and said, 'What do you think of our old look out hut? It was the idea of our priestess, to build it there so that we could see if any boats were approaching from out in the bay. That way, we would be warned if we were under attack. During my days as chief we have not been threatened so much anymore, and people prefer to sleep on the good earth rather than in a tree. And so it has been empty for many seasons. Apart from the illicit meetings of some young men and women, that is,' he said, and winked at Borg then continued, 'You, Kemit, and your family, can stay in the tree hut. The rest of your men in the two huts below.'

Kemit smiling, replied, 'You do us proud, good friend. I know these youngsters are dying to run along that rope bridge and explore. Go and take a look at the view from up there, you three.'

We did not need any more encouragement as we ran around the huts and up the bank and stood at the end of the rope bridge. Holding onto the rope rail we carefully walked along it until we had all reached the platform in the tree. We had to step over a thick branch then we were inside the first room. It was just like a normal hut, with wattle and daub walls and a thatched roof, but there were lots of holes cut into the walls, to look out from. Above the holes were reed blinds that had been dropped down to keep the weather out. Brigit walked over to one of the blinds, and rolled it up and tied it with the string above. Immediately we realised just how high above the settlement we were. Down below us the rooftops stretched down towards the bay and the sea spider fires. We turned and walked up a covered flight of wooden steps to another room even higher in the tree. When we rolled up those blinds the view was breath-taking. You could see the roof tops way down below, and the bay with the island of nets and boats. You could even see the south shore from there, and the sea stretching far into the west.

I turned to find Kemit standing behind me, and asked, 'Have you ever seen such a view from a home before? It makes the view from my cliff last winter seem like nothing. Oh Kemit, I love this place, and these people.'

I said it with sadness, as I knew, and he knew, that we could not stay there for long, as we were too near to the Icin and Dogger Island. Kemit smiled and put his arms around me, and gestured to the others to leave us alone. They went down to the other room, and Kemit walked me over to one of the log seats next to the hole in the wall.

'Mia, I know you like it here, and these people are very dear to me too, but we cannot stay long. No more than one moon, as I fear the Icin might have heard of your existence and will start to look for you soon.'

I looked at him in amazement and asked quietly, 'How do you know this?'

He was silent for a while, then replied,

'Gimble knows that you are not my daughter. I told him all about you the first morning we arrived. I decided I could not keep anything from my dear friend after all. So… when I was talking to him earlier, after first food, Gimble told me that at the time that Tashk was looking for you, to keep the Shaman happy and the trade alive, he had sent out a description of you to all of the trading boats. Apparently, one of those boats came here, not more than a moon ago, with news from the Icin. A trading boat visiting the Icin settlement had asked if they had seen you. One of the Icin Landers asked why you were so special, and was told that it was due to the strange colour of your hair, which was not unlike Icin hair. The trader was then asked if he knew of your parentage, to have such hair, and he said that you were the product of a passing Brit Lander and Island woman from Dogger, from around twelve winters ago. He told them, too, how your father had disappeared, not long after realising your mother was with child, and how she had died soon after your birth. When the trader told the Icin when this Brit Lander had been on Dogger, the Icin became very interested indeed, and gave him a bag of their gold stones as a reward. He then asked the trader to send word to them if he heard any more about your whereabouts.'

I simply stared at Kemit at first, then said, 'But will they not think that we were all drowned, because our boat was lost?'

Kemit nodded and replied, 'Maybe, and maybe not. If word gets back to the Icin from Laguz and Inja, saying that we wintered there, they will pay all the traders in the northern seas to stop trading and look for you!'

I stood up and said, 'How can we stay here as long as a moon then? Should we not leave immediately?'

'No, we will be all right for half a moon, as the spring tides are running and there is the winter snow melt to flood the river. No one will travel the way that way for at least a moon.'

'But what about over land?'

Kemit shook his head. 'The forest is very dense in this part of the world, which is why the river trade is so important. Also, you have to wait to be called to see Iona before we can leave'

'Why?' I asked.

He was silent for a while, and then said gently, 'She will help you to see the patterns in your life to come. I cannot explain it, but she is a light in this dark and dangerous world. Once seen, it can stay with you for all of your days.'

I looked at Kemit's serious expression, amazed to hear him speak of such things. This was a very different Kemit. A Kemit I would never have imagined before. He was always such a practical man, and talk of a shaman had always made him comment in some sarcastic way or other. The priestess Iona must be very special if he believes in her powers, I thought to myself.

'When did you see her last Kemit? I thought you did not believe in the powers of prophets. You have always been cross when any of the crew has talked about the lucky charms they carried, that shamans had given them. What makes Iona so different?' I asked.

He smiled at me and replied, 'You have such a wise head on your shoulders Mia. Were you ever just a child?'

I looked at him blankly, not knowing how to react. Then he said, 'I am sorry, sweetness. I do not expect you to answer that! It's just that, for a maid of twelve winters, you seem to have more wisdom than most old people I know. Maybe we do not come into this world as innocent babies, as some say, but as old spirits with many lifetimes of experience. The priestess Iona was like you when she was a child too, for she had no more than nine winters when I saw her first in her temple on the Mount. That was in the days when I was a young lad of fifteen winters, travelling with my grandfather in his trading fleet. We stopped here to trade Dogger beads, and my grandfather was a great friend of Gimble's father. When we were on a long trip to the land of the Galli, we would often stop here on the way, and again on our return. I had heard of the young maid priestess that lived on the Mount from the people here, and was determined to see her for myself.

'The Mount, as you know, is such a striking place seen from out at sea, and even more so when you travel farther down the southern coast, as you will see when we leave here. Gimble and I became good friends too, and I told him I wanted to see the young priestess. He told me that to travel up to the Mount without an invitation was forbidden, and that he himself had never actually seen her in all the time she had been there.'

'How did she come to be the priestess?' I asked. 'Was she born on Mount Land?'

Kemit smiled, and said he had better start at the beginning of her tale.

'No, she was not born on Mount Land. Apparently the young maid was washed ashore after a violent storm. She must have been travelling with her family, when the spring flood was about to purge the river and their boat was wrecked on the rocks in the river channel. Gimble told me that the boat must have been very strange though, for some of the wreckage was finely carved and painted, and the boat must have been made of many strips of wood that were joined together, not a log boat like ours. Parts of the boat were covered with the same yellow stone as the Icin have too, beaten so thin that it covered the wood and made it gleam like the sun. Are you all right there Mia? It is getting cold in here, let's sit back away from the cold air.'

I quickly moved to the other side of the room, where the icy wind blew away from us, and waited for the next part of his tale. I nodded that I was fine and he continued.

'Apart from the strange wreckage there was only a small child and a tall man that were washed ashore. The man was drowned, but the child was sleeping in a sort of basket made of wood, which must have been her bed on the boat. The people took her in and cared for her, and made a funeral pyre for the strange tall man.'

I interrupted then, asking, 'What was strange about him?'

Kemit paused for a moment, then said,

'His face was black like the half burned wood in the fire. There was even a shade of blue to his skin too, and he had very tight, black curly hair. He was dressed in a cloth of what I now know to be silk, and he wore bracelets and a headdress of the beaten yellow stone. The people initially thought that he must be some king from a strange land, but they later thought that he might have just been the servant of the child's parents.'

'In my travels I have seen many people like him since, and I know they come from a dry land called Atta Land. That is to the south of the great Inland Sea, through what we call the Dubek Straits, a narrow passage that divides the great cold Western Sea from the warm Inland Sea. They must have been blown out of the Inland Sea and through the Dubek Straits in a storm to travel this far north. Sadly, they would have been almost safe, when the spring flood waters must have caught their boat just off the shores of Mount Land. So the little maid was saved, and Gimble's father and mother took her into their home, to raise as their own daughter.'

'Did she have black skin too?'

Kemit looked at me, as if thinking that was a silly question saying, 'No, of course not. Her skin was golden and her hair was long and fair. She was strange as a child too, by all accounts. She seemed to know what people were going to ask her before they spoke. She would also have dreams that would come true. She was a happy child, but always kept herself separate from the other children, preferring the company of the elders of the settlement. At the age of eight she told Gimble's father that she had to live on her own, away from the settlement, so that she could protect her new family from harm. Gimble's father said that she was just a child and could not possibly live on her own, that it was ridiculous she thought he would let her do such a thing. But the little maid kept saying that she could not help them if she lived with them, and she became more and more withdrawn. Then one night she woke up, screaming and shouting about danger near the settlement. Gimble's father sat her down and tried to calm her, but she kept saying that a tribe from the west was travelling up the coast to attack them. These people had lost the land they lived on due to the rising waters and wanted land on higher ground. She described the sharp pointed spears they held, and how they were going to attack the settlement the very next night while they slept. She had dreamed things before that were true, and she looked so frightened that the elders decided to prepare for an attack, just in case.

'The next day they dug traps on the beach, and prepared their spears and arrows for the coming night. No sooner had the moon risen than they heard the movement of boats being pulled ashore on the gravel, and footsteps slowly walking up the beach. When the first man fell into the trap, the Mount Landers let fly with everything they could, and the bewildered and shocked attackers just ran back to their boats and paddled away.

'The following day there was a council meeting with the elders, to decide what to do about the child that had undoubtedly saved all their lives from the surprise attack. They brought the child in and asked her how she knew in advance of the attack, and she told them that in her dreams she had seen it all. She said she must not live in the settlement any more, as it confused the spirits that talked to her every night. She asked if a home could be built on top of the Mount for her, and that if she could have one of the women to care for her she would be happy there. The elders would have overruled such a suggestion outright if it had not been for the previous night's attack. The Mount had only ever been used as a temporary camp for hunters in the forest, so no one would have to leave their homes for her wishes to be granted. It was flat on the top too, and it would not be difficult to build a hut for her there. So the elders agreed to Iona's wishes, grateful to have such powerful spirits in the child to protect them.'

'When did they build the hut for her?' I asked.

'They sent some men into the forest below the Mount the very next day, to cut trees down to prepare for the making of it. After a week or so Iona went to the Mount and climbed the steep path to the top. She told the men that she wanted her home to face out to sea, and that she wanted a platform of stones to be laid in front of the hut, on the edge of the sheer rock face. She then asked for a seat to be made of stone at the edge, so that when sitting on the seat, you would see only the forest below and the sea ahead. By that time the men were treating her more as though she was a young goddess rather than a child, and did everything she wished them to.

'When the hut was built she asked Gimble's father to do one more thing, and that was to build the hut we sit in now, in this tree.'

I was puzzled, and asked him why she would want them to do that when she was going to live on the Mount. He smiled and said, 'Come here, and I will show you why!'

He took my hand and led me to a cloth covering the wall in the far corner of the room. He pulled the cloth back and revealed another set of covered steps. He led me up them until we were standing on a platform, right on top of the hut. There was a rail around it so you could not fall off, which I was glad of for it was very high up. I stood there and gasped at the view of the sea, and the bay bathed in the colouring light, as the watery sun went down like a red fruit into the western sea.

Kemit put his hand on my shoulder and said, 'That is a wonderful view, is it not? Turn now, and look inland!'

I did what he said and nearly lost my balance. I was so surprised! From where we stood, on top of the great oak tree, we looked straight at the Mount in the forest. There was the great stone seat, on the edge of the cliff face, as Kemit had described it, and on either side of it there were bright flares burning. In front of the hut, (or was it a temple?) I was sure I saw someone move across the stone platform.

'Is… is that her?' I stuttered.

'I should think so, for she sits on her seat every night to watch the sun go down. The Mount Landers say she sees her homeland to the south in the red reflections on the sea. She can signal to the settlers on this rooftop, or they can signal to her at this time of day too.'

I was getting really cold then, but I had to hear the rest of the tale and asked, 'So did you go and see her?'

Kemit pulled his fur over me and we sat there, looking over the dark forest at the flaming torches on the Mount platform.

'Yes, we went, and I might add it took some persuasion to get Gimble to show me the way at all. When we knew that his father and my grandfather were busy talking about trading, we set off to see the young priestess. She had only been there for a season, so the pathway to the Mount was not that clear, and we got lost a few times before we reached the base path up to the top. Gimble refused to go any further, and no amount of persuasion would make him change his mind. So, I set off up the path to see her for myself.

'As I said, the path was not well worn, and I stumbled and slipped in my eagerness to reach the top. When I got to the top I was a sorry sight, covered in dirt and mud from the path, and my good tunic had been ripped in the forest. I walked onto the platform, wondering what I was doing there, until I saw the view. It was breathtaking, so I stood just behind the tall stone chair, gazing out to sea, when a voice just in front of me said gently, "Welcome, Kemit, trader's son." I was so surprised that I actually fell over onto the grass that surrounded the platform. I said I was sorry to intrude, and she said that she had been waiting for me all day, and wondered why it had taken me so long to get there.

'I spent the rest of the afternoon with her, and after that day she has travelled with me in my heart, on all of my adventures. Whenever I have been lost, or unsure of what to do, I would think of Iona and I would immediately seem to know.'

I saw the dreamy look in his eyes and wondered just what Iona could be like, to have such an effect on him.

'How do you know she will want to see me?' I asked.

He looked at me very strangely, and eventually said, 'Because she told me, all those many seasons ago, that I would bring you to these shores, and that she would need to talk to you.'

I looked at Kemit, and a shiver came over me. Suddenly I felt that I was a part of some great story, but that it was somehow a story I had already heard. His words seemed so familiar, as if we had sat on the tree top platform, and had the same conversation many times before. Kemit knew when he saw my face what I was feeling, for he said gently, 'You feel you have been here before. I felt just the same, when she spoke to me that day when I was a young boy.'

I could not speak. I just nodded, and Kemit held me close. Suddenly I felt safe and strangely light headed, as if I had just had some terrible weight lifted from my shoulders, and I was now truly becoming myself for the first time in my life. Kemit stood up and said we had better go down, as Gimble would be waiting for us to start the feast celebrating our arrival.

I looked the same, I was sure, but I felt that I was somehow changed, as I walked along the walkway with Borg and Brigit to go to the feasting that night.

'Where have you been all this time?' Brigit asked when we went down to meet them.

'I have been talking to Kemit, about when he was young,' I replied.

'Oh?' she said, waiting for me to elaborate. But I did not say anything, so she just followed me.

'Here, take some of these furs,' Borg said.

'Thank you. It is getting cold, is it not?' I replied.

'Yes, I think it might even snow tonight,' Borg answered. 'I was talking to one of the settlers when we were pulling the boat on shore, and he said they often get snow this late into spring.'

'Let's hurry then,' I said. A biting wind was getting up, and my ears were hurting.

Gimble's hall was full to the brim with people, all laughing and singing silly songs about hunting and tripping into the marsh. What was actually funny about the stories and the songs I did not know, but the laughter in the room was infectious, and we could not help laughing at everything until our faces hurt. Wooden bowls of a wonderful fish stew were constantly being passed around by Raffi's team of women and maids. It was full of bits of sea spider, and fish, and shellfish of all sorts complete with shells. Kemit showed me that the shells could be used as a tool to scoop the juice of the stew up, and so drink it without having to drink from the bowl itself, which was a much better way to drink it as it would not dribble down your front, as it usually did when you drank straight from the bowl. There were also some bits of meat in the stew too, but I could not recognise them in the fishy juices. It was so cosy and warming in the hall that I was very soon stripping off my layers of furs. Kemit started to sing after a while; I had never heard him sing before, and he actually had a good voice.

We had a wonderful night, but before long people were drifting away to their homes, and it was time for us to leave too. We wrapped up well, remembering how cold it had been when we came in. I was certainly glad of my furs, as when we opened the door we were confronted by a world bathed in whiteness. It must have snowed very heavily while we had been inside, and for as far as the eye could see everywhere was clothed in soft fluffy snow. I never liked snow very much when I was a child, for it meant doing my chores with very cold hands and feet, but there it was just beautiful. I ran out of the hall and down the hill to the path to our tree home, with Borg and Brigit running after me. We glided on gentle slopes, and even picked up snow and threw it at each other. But before long we were all drenched and cold, and then it became a race to get to our hut, hoping that the fire had not gone out while we had been away.

As we clambered over the rope bridge we smelled the sweet smell of the herb drink that Raffi had made for us, and found one of her maids sitting by the fire making drinks for us. We all beamed at the welcoming scene before us, and as we sat down by the fire the maid handed us all a hot drink. She was about to leave when I asked, 'Do you have to go now? Why do you not stay with us for a while, and have some of your wonderful drink too?'

She smiled, but said that she had to get back home. I realised that she was one of Gimble's daughters, called Thriffy, and I asked, 'Will you come and see us in the morning then?'

She smiled and replied, 'If you would like me to, I will walk with you to first food on the beach.'

I smiled back and nodded as she left us, and within a few more minutes Kemit came in and said, 'This is a welcoming scene. Is there any drink left for me?'

I laughed and handed him the last one, saying, 'It is not our doing. Thriffy was waiting for us when we arrived, with a hot drink and a good fire.'

'They really are good people. It is a shame we cannot stay longer.'

Brigit looked at him then and asked, 'Are we going to leave soon?'

'Yes, Brigit,' Kemit replied. 'We will be leaving in a few suns I am afraid, as I have urgent trading business with the Iberi. I have to sell some of my goods to them before the Galli get to them, or all their trade goods will be gone. In these seas we have lots of competition for the trade, you see.'

Brigit looked thoughtful and said, 'Maybe I will stay here with these people, until you return, if you do not mind, for I am not used to travelling so very much.'

Borg and I then said simultaneously, 'No!'

'Do not stay, Brigit,' Borg said, 'we would miss you so much if you did not come with us.'

Brigit's face went bright red, and I knew what she was thinking. That Borg wanted her more than she thought he did.

'Well, if you feel so strongly that you want me to come, Borg, of course I will.'

Kemit looked at Borg and me quizzically, and said, 'Well Brigit, it seems you will be missed far too much if you do not come with us. You will like the Iberi. They are very hospitable too, and have very handsome young men, I might add. You might find you have some competition with Brigit there, Borg.'

I looked at Kemit curiously, wondering what he was thinking, for he knew Brigit and Borg were not really suited.

When I eventually got to sleep that night I dreamed of the Mount, and Iona the priestess. I saw myself walking through the forest on the path to the Mount, then being followed by something I could not see. I stopped and looked around in the darkness, and saw in the bushes three pairs of eyes looking straight at me. They were wolves' eyes, as I had seen them before as a child. I had no fire with me, which was the only protection against wolves, so I started to run. I could hear my breath booming in my ears as I heard the noise behind me getting louder and louder. I knew that if I tripped and fell I would be lost. Then I fell, but instead of falling, I was lifted gently to the roof of the forest by the claws of a great white owl. I looked down into the darkness, to the forest floor, to see the eyes looking up at me. As we rose through the canopy my relief turned to terror, as I saw what was moving across the treetops towards us.

In every direction I could see hundreds and thousands of large black birds, flying at speed directly towards us. The owl kept rising higher and higher, and the black birds left the treetops and as one, moved higher to intercept us. I shut my eyes tight, and through my closed eyes saw a bright light. I opened my eyes then to see that the owl was now being circled by hundreds of white swans! After they had surrounded us completely, they turned on their wings and flew directly at the oncoming darkness. As the swans reached the birds they flew through them like straight white arrows, and the black birds just fell to the ground. I could hear them as they hit the treetops, then as suddenly as the black birds appeared, they disappeared again with the swans. All I could then hear was the steady wing beats of the owl, as it carried me gently to the platform and lay me on the stone chair that Kemit had described. I saw myself holding out my hand to a shadowy white figure… then I awoke in our hut, and I just wanted to go back to sleep to meet her. It was as if the nightmare, with the wolves and the black birds, was not important anymore, compared to meeting Iona.

Suddenly Brigit was tugging at me, saying, 'Come on, Mia, everyone has already gone for first food, and I am very hungry for sea spiders today!'

I got up and walked behind her as we followed the path down to the beach. I heard Brigit's chattering as if from afar, even though I was right next to her, as if I was still in some faraway place. Brigit did not seem to have noticed, and she chattered away about how much she now liked sea spiders.

Gimble greeted us and sat us next to his family, to watch the fires and sea spider pits steaming. It was a strange sight, for the grey stony beach was covered with a blanket of snow, and the steaming pits and fires looked out of place. Gimble was looking at me strangely, when I suddenly realised he had been speaking to me.

'Oh, I am sorry,' I said. 'I seem to be in some sort of dream today. What did you say?'

'I just said, honey, that you have the look of a person about to visit Iona.'

I was wide awake then and asked, 'What did you say?'

He smiled and replied, 'Do not worry, my dear. We see it often in people before they are called to the Mount. We had word this morning that you are expected there, when the sun colours tonight.'

I looked at him and smiled, suddenly feeling wide awake and so very happy. Brigit shouted to me across the table, 'I am looking forward to seeing the view from up there, I must say!'

Gimble interrupted, quickly saying, 'Sorry, my dear, but only Mia is invited.'

Brigit looked very put out as he continued, 'We really have no say in it, as it is the priestess who decides who visits her. But do not worry, I will take a party to the western cliffs to watch the dolphins race as the sea colours. You will like that just as much, and Borg must come too.'

Brigit looked a little more relaxed then, and seemed happy at the thought of being entertained by the chief instead of seeing the priestess. I saw Gimble look at Kemit, and knew something had been said between them about Brigit, but I could not imagine what. After we had eaten Kemit said he would like to talk to me, and we went for a walk together along the shore. I took this chance to mention something that had been bothering me.

'Kemit, I know that Gimble's people and the Icin are enemies. Everyone here has been so good to us, and I am worried that the knowledge of my Icin blood will ruin your friendship with him.'

'Mia, Gimble likes you, and knows the deeds of the Icin can hardly be put at your feet. He saw a dark side to Brigit though, not long after we landed, and he warned me against her.'

'Really?' I looked up at him amazed.

'Yes. He only tolerates her because of our friendship, and she certainly would not be welcome to stay alone.'

'Why? What has she done to make him think that, in such a short time?'

Kemit stopped and reluctantly replied, 'I did not want to tell you this, but she was trying to turn Raffi and Gimble against you when you were not there. Nothing too obvious, just little hints and suggestions, that you were not to be trusted.'

'I do not believe it! How could she? When I have tried to be such a friend to her?'

'Do not be cross, she is just jealous of you.'

'Jealous of me? Why?'

He laughed out loud then and replied, 'Now you are just being silly! Look at you. You are not only beautiful to look at, but you have a beautiful spirit too. It is not surprising that she resents the ease with which you seem to be good at everything you do. Take the cape yesterday. I thought she was about to leap over the room and strike you, when Gimble praised your cape but obviously had to try to be polite about hers!'

Kemit stood still and held my shoulders, and continued, 'Listen Mia, just try to understand the way that she sees the world, and be kind. She has a good heart, amidst all of that resentment. Come, enough of this. We must prepare for your visit to the Mount.'

My attention suddenly switched from Brigit, and I asked, 'How did the priestess know I was here? And why does she want to see me and no one else?'

Kemit laughed and replied, 'You cannot expect me to answer those questions? How do I know what is in the mind of Iona? You have dreamed about her, have you not? Do not look at me like that. I know you have dreamed of her, as each time I have visited these good people, I have dreamed about her too, every night before seeing her.'

We walked the rest of the way in silence, and I spent the afternoon sewing my fur cape, to wear when I went to the Mount. The skins were so soft that it was easy to sew quickly, and I finished it before it was time to leave. I left the hall wearing the cape, and Gimble came over to me to wish me a good visit, saying, 'That really is a fine design you have on your cape, Mia. I hope the priestess sees a good future for you.'

He turned and led a group of settlers, with Brigit, to the western cliffs to watch the dolphins. Borg insisted that he come with us to the base of the Mount though, and Kemit did not object. I did not know it then, but Kemit would not climb up the path to the top of the Mount, and he was glad of Borg's company while he waited for me.

The path we walked was wide and well worn, and whenever it crossed a stream or skirted a pond, wooden trackways or bridges had been made. So we were a happy group that walked that path, which was a world away from my terrified run down it the night before in my dream. When we approached the base of the cliff, I saw that there was a little hut there, for people to rest while waiting for their loved ones to return from the top. I looked at Kemit and Borg, and wondered what I would see when I got up there, and suddenly felt a little nervous. Kemit kissed me on the cheek, which he rarely did, and said, 'Fear not. She has been waiting for you for a very long time, and you have a bond between you already. I do not know how, but I feel that you do. Now go on, for she is waiting.'

Next to the door of the hut I noticed an old woman dressed entirely in white, not unlike the dresses of the cliff women on my island at home. She greeted us, and held out her hand to me to lead me to the steps which led to the top of the Mount.

I had such a strange feeling, of meeting my own destiny head on, as I walked up to the top of the Mount that night. As if I was not going to be the same person, when I walked back down it again. It was not a bad feeling, but it felt momentous, as if I was going to find out who I really was. Growing up, I had always felt different from the people around me. Not just because of the colour of my hair, there was more to it than that. I felt that I was not connected at all to my grandmother and cousins. As if I had been a baby from some distant land, found on the beach, just like the priestess I was about to meet.

I used to dream as a child, that I would eventually find out that my grandmother was no relation to me. It would all make sense then, the feeling of my difference from her. I did not know what it was about me that was different, I only knew that it was a profound difference. That might make it sound like I was a lonely child, but that was far from the case. I never felt that I was truly alone, it was as if there was always some presence with me. It was a good feeling, and whenever life took a turn for the worst, it was then that the presence enveloped me and gave me a feeling of wellbeing and peace. When I was troubled, perhaps about a decision I had to make, I would sit on my sand cliffs and talk to the distant horizon. I always knew what needed to be done when I walked home.

As I walked behind the old lady, up the steep steps to the top of the Mount, I began to marvel at the ease with which she walked ahead of me, as I was breathless by the time we were only halfway up. The top of the Mount was just how I had imagined it to be. In fact, it was exactly how it had looked in my dream. I walked towards the platform and stared at the view of the snow covered forest below, and the sun colouring as it dropped into the western sea in the distance. As I approached the great stone-backed seat, I knew she was sitting there before I saw her. She stood, and held out her slender hand to me.

She was dressed like the old woman, in pure white, and her figure glowed in the light of the sun behind her. As soon as I saw her, and before she spoke, I knew that it had been Iona that had pulled me back from the other realm, on the boat that night. She smiled as she saw me and said, 'Sweet Mia, it is good to see you!'

She spoke to me as if we were old friends, not people just about to meet.

'Was it you who spoke to me on the boat?' I blurted out, but had to ask.

She just smiled at me as if it was the most natural question in the world, saying, 'You were not actually in the boat, Mia. You were at the gateway to the other realm. If you had left the boat as they wanted you to, even I might not have been able to pull you back.'

'What do you mean, I was not in the boat? And how did I get to this gate?'

The priestess smiled and replied, 'They drew you in with your mind. A mind I need to teach some protection rites to, before you leave here.'

Then she laughed, and her laugher sounded so sweet and kind as she took my hand and led me to the front of the seat.

'Come,' she said, 'sit next to me on my chair.'

The chair was lined with white furs, and looked warm and inviting amidst the snow covered mountains behind, and the forests below.

'I have waited for this day for so long, Mia of the Icin. I saw your visit here in Kemit's future, when he first visited me as a young man more than thirty winters ago.'

I looked at her beautiful face and replied, 'Why? I am not so special.'

'I think you know you are special, Mia,' she replied. 'You have a relationship with the gods that most shamans spend all of their lives praying to obtain.'

I looked at her and asked, 'What do you mean, I have a relationship with the gods? I have never prayed to them in my life. I usually left that sort of thing to the Shaman.'

She smiled back and replied, 'Who do you think you were speaking to, when you spent most of your spare time in your childhood sitting on those sand cliffs?'

I could not believe she knew about the sand cliffs. Of course, Kemit must have told her. But as far as I knew, he had not been to see her himself since we arrived.

'No, Kemit did not tell me, for I have not seen him on this visit. I saw you Mia, and I heard your longings, to leave and travel to far off lands. I first knew you existed when I met Kemit, and saw your visit here this day. I have been dreaming of you for many winters, during the time you have been growing up. I also know how close your spirit came to being lost, if the Shaman had got his evil hands on you last winter. But well, Kemit came and rescued you, as I knew he would, and now you are on the brink of a wonderful life, showing the power of the Goddess to all the known world!'

After that, we sat there in silence for what seemed like a long time, as we watched the sun finally dip into the distant western sea. While we sat there the torches had been lit, although I did not remember seeing the old woman light them. I thought about what Iona had said, about the power of the Goddess. I had never consciously thought about any particular goddess in my life, but I somehow knew exactly what she meant.

After a while, she touched my hand and said gently, 'You are going to be the means that changes this world that we now live in. You are going to bring the Goddess into the world of men. Our world is changing, not only with the rising seas, but the need to settle, and make claims on the land. The power of the Goddess will be needed, and the power of the women that she works though will also be needed.'

She smiled, as she could see I was thinking of the women of the Icin.

'No, not the ways of the Icin women. The ways of motherhood, and fertility, and the ownership of lands. As land becomes claimed and the soil tilled, it will be important to want to pass on that work to the children of a tribe. Who can really say who their father is?'

I looked at her, not really understanding what she meant at first. Then I blushed, and she smiled, saying, 'Yes, but you can always say who your mother is, can you not? So land will be passed down the female line, and a great time for women will cover all the lands. All women will become close to the Goddess then. Women will bear the children to work the land, and women will pass the land on to the next generation.'

I was enthralled by what she was saying. In my world, women had always been treated with lesser importance than men, because they could not hunt the wild bull or elk. Women were left to scrape the greasy skins, and keep the fires going. Their only hope was that their man treated them well when he returned from the hunt. I relished the thought of such a new world, but really did not see what I could have to do with it.

The warmth of Iona's hand seemed to fill my whole being, and I turned to her and asked, 'What of this other realm, and why do they want to pull me into it?'

Iona was silent for a while, then she said, 'Come, sit in my temple, for we can be watched too easily from here.'

I looked around at the darkening forest below, and was glad to be going indoors after she had said that. We entered the hut, which was not like a hut, but more like a temple or holy place. I wondered how I knew what a temple or holy place would look like, as there were none on Dogger Island. I became increasingly aware of a memory I had, but not a memory Mia of Dogger had, but from some other Mia. I pushed those confusing thoughts to the back of my mind, and marvelled at the walls that were smoothly covered with white clay, and painted with strange symbols in red ochre. The room was round, and there were three torches attached to the walls, so that it was as bright as day inside. There was a round table in the centre, and white furs around it to sit upon. Iona gestured for me to sit opposite her, and gave me some water to drink and berries to eat. I realised then how hungry I was, and ate all of the berries before looking up again.

When I had finished Iona said, 'Now it is time you knew a little about the world you live in.'

I looked at her curiously and she continued,

'Not the world you can see, but the other world, the world only a few can see. It is the world we belong to, Mia. For people like us live in two worlds. The world of the material that you can touch, this is the world of most of the people you will meet. The other world is the world of the Goddess, and the Devils of the Dark Lord. In this world there is great light and love, but also great darkness and hatred.'

As she told me about those other worlds that ran parallel to the ordinary world, I felt she was somehow reminding me about them, rather than telling me about them anew.

She smiled as if she was reading my thoughts, and said, 'You are remembering, I can see. This is not your first life, Mia. You are a very old spirit, older than I am, in fact. Each time we are born we have a lesson to learn, and each time we die we find out if we have learnt it, or not. The constant cycles of life make us who we are. Some take the easy road and help the darkness. They get all the power they wish in this life, but they pay for it by losing their way in the darkness when they die. You will soon remember this, as you are coming of an age when the memories of who you really are will come to you, if they are going to.

'I must warn you though. There is the greatest darkness trying to pull you towards it, and you will have to pull your memories from the past in order to help yourself. I can only guide you, I cannot fight your fights. Know only that you will succeed. You have to, or we will all be lost for many lives to come.'

We sat in silence for what seemed like only a few moments, but by the dimmed torches I knew it must have been some time. Iona pulled the heavy cloth from the centre of the table to reveal a pool of water. I looked at her, and she smiled and asked, 'Is there anything you wish to know about, Mia?'

I thought for a moment, then asked, 'Will I ever find a man when I grow up, to love me truly?'

Iona smiled at me and touched the water in the pool. Suddenly it looked like it was frosted over with cold. She looked into the centre, and it looked like she was seeing something, but to me it still looked frozen.

Then she said softly, 'You will find your true love, Mia, when you are entering your sixteenth winter. And he will make you very happy, for the time you have together. You will know you are near to him, when you see the rollers that carry boats across the plains. You will always find companions that will love you, and care for your precious spirit. For it will be recognised by the most unlikely of people. You will have a long and full life, and you will see many great changes in our world. Some you will help to change, and some you will not. I have one more thing to say to you, before you meet dear Kemit and return to the settlement. As you enter your thirtieth winter, you must beware the temple of women with the snake-handled dagger on the temple shrine.'

She then put the cloth over the pool, and said, 'Before you go, I must show you how to protect yourself from the creatures of the other realm, until you remember how to do it yourself. Sit before me.'

I sat on the furs before her and looked into her pale blue eyes, and waited. She smiled and said, 'Shut your eyes, and imagine yourself on your sand cliffs, looking out to sea. Now see with your mind's eye a beam of light from the distant horizon, growing larger and larger, until you are bathed in it. Hold that picture in your mind, and whenever you feel you are being pulled into the darkness, cover yourself with that light. Do you still have your mother's crystal?'

I looked at her in amazement, wondering how she knew about the crystal.

'Yes, here it is,' I replied, and held it out to her.

She put her hand up to stop me and said, 'No Mia, you must not let anyone touch your crystal, as it is full of your energy and that of your mother. You may have seen a light in it when you were in danger.'

I just nodded and she continued, 'This is where your horizon light will come from. Hold it tight as you have been, then open your hand and let the light envelope you, and you will be all right.'

I did not say anything for a moment, and then I asked, 'When Laguz became aware of me, he stopped when I held it. Why was that?'

She smiled and replied, 'I hardly need to tell you anything, as you already know what to do. The energy in the crystal makes your own energy invisible, as it is too bright, for those that would want to take it. I have something to give you now.'

She turned and pulled something out of a little leather bag next to her. I could not make out what it was, as the lights from the torches caught it and made it shine so brightly. When I saw it in her hand, I knew it was the golden figure that had come to me, that night on the boat, and saved me from the black birds. But what I had seen that night was just an image of the figure. In Iona's hand was the actual figure itself! It was as golden as the petals of a flower, and the crescent moon she held on her staff. Flashes of light were emanating from it, as if it held lightning within. Then she placed it in my palm, and I could for the first time see the detail of the little figurine.

I whispered then, more to myself than to Iona, 'It is the Golden Goddess.'

Iona smiled at me and said, 'It was yours many lifetimes ago, and it will be yours again in many lifetimes to come.'

I looked down at its beauty, and was overcome, as the waves of love poured out from it to me. I knew she was speaking the truth, as cradling the Golden Goddess in my palm seemed the most natural thing in the world for me to do.

Iona then said gently, 'This has returned to you, Mia, but not for you in this life. It is for a Mia that will be born many thousands of winters from now, when the Mount itself will be surrounded by the sea. There will come a time when the Goddess is forgotten, and women will begin to feel that loss. They will try and draw her back to them, but they will not know how to do it. They will need you then to show them. When you find her again in that life, it will help to bring back your memories of this time, when the Goddess was the most powerful energy in the known world.'

I nodded and listened to her, knowing that what she was speaking was the truth. She continued, 'You must listen very carefully. Take it, and journey at first light to the Hill of the Two Seas. Gimble knows where it is. To hide it you must sit alone, after the sun has gone down, on the Rock of the Two Seas, above the forest. It will be picked up by some old friends of yours, and hidden until you return.'

Puzzled, I looked at her and asked, 'Why must I leave it there, if it is so important? Will I not need it in this life?'

Iona smiled and replied, 'I know it seems strange to you now, but you will understand why when you leave this life.'

I still did not understand why I had to leave it, and had to ask again, 'But why can it not remain on this hill? I so want to keep it, now that I have seen it again. Why do I have to leave it on that hill?'

'That is a very good question, Mia,' she replied. 'You must sleep with it under your pillow in the little hut at the bottom of the Mount, and every night until you reach the Hill of the Two Seas. During those nights your energies will be drawn into the crystals the Goddess holds. It will be that energy of yours, as you are becoming yourself again, that will sleep in the crystal for thousands of winters until it is found again by you. That energy will help you to remember who you really are, in that future life when you are needed again.'

I somehow understood what she meant then, and placed the beautiful little Goddess figurine in the bag hanging from my belt.

'Go now, my sister Mia, and enjoy your adventures!'

She stood up and walked back to her seat on the platform, and was gone from view. I became aware of the old woman standing next to me, waiting to guide me down the path again. I do not remember walking down, or even meeting Kemit and Borg, or falling asleep on the piles of furs left for us in the hut at the bottom of the path. I do remember, however, taking my bag off my belt, and putting it underneath my pillow before I went to sleep.

18. THE HILL OF THE TWO SEAS

I awoke the next day to the sound of a crackling fire in the hut at the bottom of the Mount. Borg was sitting next to me, cooking some dried boar meat on sticks in the flames. He turned to me and said quietly, 'I thought you would wake up when first food was almost cooked!'

I looked up into his smiling eyes and felt really happy. I felt like I was smiling inside, somehow, too. I sat up, after wrapping a fur around my shoulders, and watched him as he cooked the meat.

'Where is Kemit?' I asked.

'Oh, he had to go back to get Gimble and some supplies,' he replied, without turning round.

'Supplies?'

Borg slid the crisped boar meat onto a piece of bark and handed it over to me, saying, 'For when we to go to this Hill of the Two Seas, of course. Careful now, the meat is hot.'

I smiled, and was so glad we were friends again. Then I remembered what Iona had said, about leaving the little Goddess figurine on some distant hill, and marvelled to myself that it wasn't a dream after all. I reached under my pillow and pulled out the leather bag that held it.

I was about to take it out when Borg put his hand on mine and said urgently, 'No Mia! We were told you must not let anyone see what is in your bag, whatever it is. Kemit talked for a long time with the priestess's woman last night after you had gone to sleep, and she said under no circumstances must you take it out of its bag and show it anyone.'

I looked at him blankly, then tied the leather bag onto my belt and started eating the meat Borg had cooked for me.

We sat for some time by the fire in silence, waiting for Kemit to return with Gimble. I spent that time thinking of Iona and what she had said, as Borg seemed content with his own thoughts and keeping the fire going. It was a good job too, as there was an icy cold breeze coming from the door to the hut. Before long we heard someone coming, and suddenly Gimble burst into the room, brushing the snow off his cloak and making a flurry of snow fill the air. Kemit came in immediately behind him, stamping his feet on the floor to shed the snow from his shoes. Then two warriors came in, and our quiet fireside was turned immediately into a mess of drying feet and dripping furs. When they finally settled themselves down around the fire Gimble said, 'Well, this is a bit of a turn up, isn't it, Mia honey?'

I just looked at him, not really knowing what to say, and he continued, 'Yes, it is that. So we have to take you to the Hill of the Two Seas on some errand of Iona's? Hmm... you obviously have been told to say nothing about it too.'

I opened my mouth to tell him I knew not much more than he did, but he said, 'No, you must not say anything. Iona knows best, she always does. We need to leave this lovely fire though, if we are to make it to the first hunting hut before dark.'

He stood up again, and I quickly got my shoes on and wrapped some more furs around my shoulders, and left our cosy hut for the snowy woodland outside. Kemit put his arm around my shoulder as we waited for Gimble and his men to organise their packs, and whispered in my ear, 'This is a bit unexpected, isn't it? In all the seasons I have visited Iona she has never asked me to go on a quest!'

I looked at him curiously and asked, 'Quest?'

He smiled at me and replied, 'Yes, sweetness, the quest to find some sort of object she has left up there, of course!'

I was about to say we were not going to find anything, we were in fact leaving something, when he stopped me by putting his finger to his mouth saying, 'You must not tell me about this. Iona's woman was very firm on that fact. It is between you and Iona alone.'

I looked at him blankly and nodded, thinking who was I to question what Iona wanted? I did think it strange though, that they thought I was looking for something, and not leaving something. So, as we walked through the snowy forest that day, I thought about why Iona wanted them to think that I was finding something. A thought occurred to me, that if people knew I was leaving something on the Hill of the Two Seas, they might one day go and see if they could find it. If they thought I was looking for something, and I pretended I had found it, then there would be nothing to hunt for in the future.

The snow kept falling, and it was a cold two suns' walk through the forests to the foot of the Hill of the Two Seas. The only comfort was the well placed and stocked hunters' huts that Gimble's men had built, many winters before. I did think it a little odd that they had built them though, as usually hunters would travel light, never staying in the same camp twice. The Mount Land people obviously believed in having comfort when they hunted, by making the huts a day's walk away from each other. So that night, around a roaring fire in the last hut before the hill, I asked Gimble about the huts.

'Why sit under a dripping tree when you can sleep on warm furs, I say!' was his reply.

I laughed at his answer, and thought how much my people on Dogger could learn from him.

The next day, we set off at first light up the slopes of the Hill of the Two Seas, having had our first food when it was still dark. Gimble said we had to get to the top in one day. There were leopards on the slopes, so it was best to make it to the top as quickly as we could. I made sure that I walked in the middle of the group after he said that, too.

The sun was just starting to take colour when we finally got to the top of the Hill. I could see immediately why it was called the Hill of the Two Seas, when we looked down on the vast dark forest below us, sweeping as far as the eye could see. If you stood at the edge of the cliff, on a large smooth stone, one way you could see the Mount, and in the far distance the smoke of the fires of Gimble's settlement, with the silver sea beyond. If you looked the other way you could also see the sea far in the distance, at the end of a vast, flat grassy plain.

Gimble stood next to me and asked, 'Well, honey, what do you think of this then?'

I looked back to Gimble's settlement, and then to the other sea, and replied, 'I think that whoever named this hill named it well! Why is there no forest over there?' I pointed over to the grassy plain.

'Ahh, that is because the sea washes over it on every tide, so trees do not grow there. It is a good place to hunt though, as many elk and deer roam the lush grass at low tide. Come, we are making a fire to sit around, let's hope it does not snow tonight, for we will all be very cold by first light if it does!'

I turned to him and asked, 'Do you not have one of your nice hunting huts up here?'

Gimble looked at me strangely and whispered, 'We do not come up here at night usually, as they say spirits live here after the sun goes down. So come and sit next to me by the fire, for the sun will be gone soon.'

I followed him back to the fire, and as we walked, I looked behind me at the lengthening shadows and quickened my pace.

That night, as Borg, Kemit and Gimble laughed and joked around the fire, it seemed that they were forcing themselves to be light-hearted and somewhat loud. I could detect fear in their laughter too, and that made me feel very uneasy. I thought that Iona would not have sent me to that hill if I would have been in danger; yet danger was what I could feel all around me that night. When it was very late I tried to go to sleep, but whenever I shut my eyes, I could see faces looking at me from the blackness. So I opened my eyes again and noticed that none of the others were settling down to sleep as they usually would.

I tugged at Kemit's fur and whispered, 'Is no one going to go to sleep this night?'

Kemit lifted his fur up for me to snuggle under, and when he had his arm around me he said quietly, 'No, not this night, sweetness, not here. You can sleep though, as we will watch out for you and keep the fire bright. No leopard will come near us while you sleep.'

I looked up at him and whispered, 'It is not leopards that frighten me here.'

I expected Kemit to ask me what I meant by that, but he just nodded and said nothing. Borg had gone very quiet too, and suddenly, for no reason, I needed desperately to stand up. All the men looked at me as I started to step backwards into the darkness and away from the fire.

'Mia!' Borg shouted. 'What are you doing? Come close to the fire again. There are leopards on this hill!'

I looked at him and shook my head, saying, 'I need to be alone for a while.'

Kemit stood up and walked up to me, saying, 'He is right, sweetness, this is no time or place to be alone. Wait until first light, and then you can wander around the top of the hill all you want.'

But Gimble interrupted, saying gently, 'Leave her Kemit, she will be all right. Do not ask me how I know. I just do. I feel Iona is near her. Come, friend, let us open that bag of mead and lighten this mood of ours!'

Kemit looked at him, and then at Borg, and sighed and said to me, 'Do not be gone long, and take this torch with you,' handing me a flaming torch from the fire.

I wished then that I had not said I needed to be alone. That was the last thing I really wanted at that moment, but I somehow felt I had no choice. I carefully made my way amongst the smooth rocks at the top of the hill, until I was on the rock above the small cliff, the one that you could see both seas from. I sat there holding my torch, and looking over the dark forest below. I was sure every so often I could see lights moving in the tree tops. I thought it must be my imagination, but then I saw them again. Slowly the lights were getting closer, until they were in the tree tops directly below me. They were like wisps of light that moved and danced on the leaves at the top of the trees. I was so absorbed as I watched the lights below me, that I did not notice a light appear right next to me. I could see it out of the corner of my eye, and marvelled at what I saw. Then I slowly turned my head and looked at it directly. It was like a beautiful butterfly, with wings that you could see right through, but at the same time were glowing in the pale moonlight. It was no butterfly though, for it had a beautiful face and a fine thin body. It was what I had always imagined Syfs, the tree or flower spirits, would look like when I was a child. I had no fear of the darkness then, as more and more of them came up from the forest and sat on the rock in a circle around me. Their faces were neither male nor female, just beautiful and kind.

The larger one that stood next to me started to speak to me, but not to my ears. To my mind it said, 'Welcome, Mia, to our Hill. Iona tells us you have something for us.'

I wondered at first what it meant, then realised that she must have been talking about the Golden Goddess figurine. So I wedged my torch in a crevice in the rocks and untied my bag from my belt, and opened it. As I did so, the little spirits all moved closer until the area around my bag was as bright as day with the light from their wings. I took out the little figurine, and they all gasped. The noise was like a sharp intake of breath, and I did not know why, but it made me cry just hearing that sound. I placed the Goddess on the rock in front of them, and they all moved towards it and, together as one, they lifted it up and flew away with it, into the rocks below me.

Moments later they returned without it, and I heard them say, again to my mind, 'It is safe now, Mia of the Icin, until you need it again. We will watch it until you return. No one else will find it, but you...'

Then as soon as they had come, they were gone. I became aware of the flickering torch next to me, and that I was alone. I sat there for some time, as warm tears rolled down my cheeks at the feelings the little plant Syfs stirred in me. I stared across the dark forest, and felt suddenly at one with it all. The trees, the rocks, and the sea; I felt the timelessness of it all. I thought of the me that would come and find the little Golden Goddess again, thousands of winters into the future, and wondered what my world would be like then. I somehow knew that the rock I sat upon would still be there, and the view of the two seas. And in a way, I knew that some the forest below me would also be there.

I do not know how long I stayed there, but suddenly my mood was shattered by a terrible sense of foreboding. I picked up the torch, and was about to turn and walk quickly back to the fire when I saw a dark shadow move from behind a rock. I looked behind me, and there were many large, dark shadows, moving from behind the rocks towards me. I instinctively grasped my mother's crystal from under my tunic, and held it high above me. Then I visualised the golden light coming from within it, as Iona had taught me, and in moments I was engulfed in its warm glow. So much so that I could not even see the shadows as I made my way back to the fire. When I climbed over the last rocks I saw Kemit and Borg, and Gimble and his men around the fire. But they were not sitting around it as they had been when I left them, they all had their backs to the fire and held their spears in their hands, as if they were warding off an attack. They saw me coming, and I put my crystal back into my tunic and jumped over the last rock, walking casually over to them.

They looked at me as if I was a ghost myself, until I spoke, saying, 'Is everything all right? Are there leopards about?'

Gimble then said, almost trembling, 'Leopards I would take on any day, rather than those evil spirits that have just been watching us. You are without doubt one of Iona's people, for they vanished as soon as you jumped over that rock.'

Kemit looked at me keenly and asked, 'Have you found what Iona wanted you to look for?'

I smiled at him and replied, 'Yes, but for the most part I have just been sitting on a rock, looking at the two seas.'

Then Borg came over, and almost shouted at me, 'You have been sitting on a rock, looking at the two seas? Do you have any idea how worried we were about you, especially when those dark shadowy things would not let us leave the fireside?'

I looked at Kemit then and asked anxiously, 'You could not leave the fire?'

Kemit put his arm around me and covered me with his fur, saying gently, 'Let us talk about it no more, you are safe now. You are cold too. Come, sweetness, let me get those hands warm.'

Everyone relaxed then, and started cooking some of the deer meat they had over the fire, and passed around the mead bag again. Gimble and his men started talking about hunting, and the atmosphere lightened considerably. No one slept much that night though, so we headed down the hill at first light, and were in the forest well before the sun coloured.

Our journey back to Mount Land was uneventful, just very cold. My thoughts kept drifting back to the beautiful Syfs on the hill, and by the end of the second day I was doubting whether I had seen them at all... apart from the fact that I did not know where the little Golden Goddess figurine had gone. Surely I would have remembered if I had hidden it myself.

19. ESCAPE TO IBERI LAND

It was late when we finally reached Gimble's settlement, and we went straight to the tree hut where Brigit was waiting for us. She greeted us with a barrage of questions, not in a very friendly way either. She was not too happy with one of Gimble's men showing her the dolphins that night, because Gimble had had to go to the Mount to meet us. She was also not happy, when we briefly told her that we had been to the Hill of the Two Seas – she said it sounded wonderful, and she would like to have seen it too. By the time Kemit came into the hut, Borg and I were both exhausted with her questions, and Kemit, seeing what was going on, told her to go to her bed and to leave us alone. Although she was probably furious at being told to go to bed, she would not have said so to Kemit. However, we fell asleep happily that night, glad to be home at last.

The next day I woke suddenly, to the sound of drumbeats on wood. But then I sat up with a start and looked around, realising that I had only dreamed of my initial waking. Brigit and Borg were sitting next to our hearth talking, and Brigit said slightly sarcastically,

'I see you are awake at last, Mia. You certainly slept a long time. It is nearly time for midday food. Kemit told us to let you sleep. Did you drink too much mead on your way back from this Hill of the Two Seas? You looked like you were in some sort of daze last night.'

I looked at her, and said in a voice that sounded sort of distant, and somehow not my own,

'No, I did not have any drink. At least I don't... I must see Kemit! Where is he?'

Borg came over to me, looking suddenly concerned, and replied, 'He is down by the boat. What is the matter?'

I got up and ran out of the hut, calling back that I just had to talk to him about something. I was not sure what I needed to talk about, but I knew I had to see him, and quickly. I ran down the path, passing startled looking people. It must have been something in the way I ran, or maybe in my expression, that made them stand back and watch me pass. I eventually reached Kemit on the shore, talking to Uin, and ran into his arms. I was so breathless that I could not speak for a few minutes, and he asked,

'Calm yourself, Mia. Whatever is it?'

Kemit's voice was full of concern, and I replied, 'I had a dream, or I think it was a dream. In fact it was so real, I thought I was awake!'

'Mia, come and sit down, and then tell me what you dreamed, or thought you did.'

I sat down on a log and Uin left us, but I could see from his face that he, too, was concerned about me.

'I woke up, or dreamed I woke up, to the sound of drums beating. Oh Kemit, it was just drumbeats, but it put such fear into me. I wanted to run, but then I woke up properly and realised that I had been dreaming. I knew it was urgent, that I tell you about it straight away too. What does it mean? Has my visit to Iona made me lose my senses?'

Kemit hugged me for a while then said quietly, 'No, she has not made you lose your senses. She has heightened your own awareness of your future. I think the drumbeats sound like the drummers of an Icin warship. I have heard it before. I do not know of any other people that beat a drum like that in the northern seas. Their men slaves paddle their boats, and the drum makes them paddle together to gain speed in the water.'

'You do not use a drum to make your men all paddle together.'

'No, but then my men do it because we are a crew of friends, and we choose to work together. The slaves of the Icin are not willing to paddle, so they need a drum to keep them in step with each other. Look Mia, I think maybe we should leave now. It could be that the Icin are braving the river in flood in order to catch up with us. Maybe the events of your dream will take place tomorrow morning. I do not know, but I do not want to take any chances of the Icin catching up with us. We would not be able to protect you here if they did, and I do not want Gimble's people to shed blood on our account.'

'Can we leave so soon?' I asked, and he smiled back at me and replied,

'We can go as soon as we wish! Uin, get the men together. We leave on the next tide!'

Kemit pulled me up to my feet and said, 'We must go and see Gimble straightaway.'

I half walked, half ran behind Kemit to Gimble's hall, to tell him our news. Gimble was sitting by his hearth, with Raffi and his daughter. As soon as we entered his hut, Raffi got up to collect the bark container to start making the hot drink for us. Kemit put his hand up to stop her, and she stopped what she was doing and looked at Gimble.

'What is this, friend, you do not want a drink? Is everything well?'

Kemit walked over to the fire and sat next to him, and said urgently, 'No, my friend, all is not well. We must leave on the next tide.'

Gimble looked at him with concern, for he knew that Kemit would not make such a rushed decision if it were not absolutely necessary.

'It saddens me to hear that. Can I do anything to help?' Gimble asked.

'Yes. If you could let us have some dried food supplies for a few days' journey, for I do not expect we will have time to fish or hunt.'

Gimble's face was very grave, and he gestured for his wife and daughter to leave us. I sat down next to Kemit and Gimble replied, 'Of course, my friend, just take what you need from the store. What has happened to cause this flight? For flight it must be, if you are not able to fish or hunt on the way.'

Kemit smiled and replied, 'As usual Gimble, your senses are sharp. Yes, we are in flight. Mia had a vivid dream on waking, so vivid that it has the feel of Iona in it.'

Gimble was leaning forward, as if some unseen force might overhear us, and asked, 'What did you dream about honey?'

His voice was gentle and concerned, so much so that I felt tears welling up in my eyes at his kindness.

I replied, 'I dreamed that I woke to the sound of drumbeats coming from the river. It was so real that I thought I was actually awake. Then I woke and found that I was in the tree hut with Brigit and Borg. There was such a fear in me that I just had to run and tell Kemit. He thought we should heed the warning, and so we came straight here. But I do not understand how any dream could be so real.'

Gimble leaned over to me then and said, 'You have just seen Iona, that is how. Kemit and I know that she affects people long after they meet her, heightening their own awareness of their own futures. They are usually particularly sharp if there is any danger around. Kemit is right to leave, for what is the use of having such a powerful priestess, if we do not heed her warnings.'

He turned and looked at Kemit and said, 'You think it is the Icin, do you not?'

Kemit nodded, and Gimble jumped up and shouted to Raffi, 'Send for Sefn! We have need of him!'

Raffi ran from the hall, realising by his tone of voice that it was urgent. Gimble then turned back to us and said, 'We had better make haste. Mia, could you tell in your dream what time of day it was?'

I looked at him, amazed that he took every detail of my dream so seriously.

'It was early in the morning, for it was only just light and very cold.'

He nodded to Kemit and said, 'That would be right, for they do not like to fight in the dark. They usually like to make a surprise attack. They will probably sleep just a little way up river this night, and come in at first light.' He put his hand on Kemit's shoulder and continued, 'I do not think you should wait for the tide tonight, as they will probably have a scout on the edge of the bay by then, watching for any night flights.'

Kemit nodded and replied, 'I think you might be right. We must make haste if we are to leave straightaway.'

'Look, I think it is better, just in case the Icin are already about, for your boat to leave in the middle of our fishing fleet, until you cross the bay at least. There is no time to lose, my friend.'

Kemit grabbed Gimble's arm as he started to leave the hall and said, 'I am sorry to bring danger to your shores, good friend.'

Gimble looked at him intently for a while, then replied, 'It is better to bring it to the shores of a friend who wants to help, than to strangers. Do not speak to me of sorrow. We are family. Come, we must make haste.'

We left the hall, and Kemit told me to run up to the tree hut and tell Borg and Brigit to come down to the shore straightaway, with all of their things, and also to tell them that we were to leave within the hour. I ran down the hill, up the path to the tree and across the rope bridge. I had to stop halfway along it to stop it swinging, I was running so fast. As soon as I entered the hut, I said hurriedly,

'Borg! Brigit! Make haste, we are leaving!'

Brigit met me at the door and asked, 'What do you mean, leaving?'

I pushed past her and said as I gathered up my furs, 'Leaving! Now! Where is Borg?'

She quickly replied, 'He is on the top platform.'

I ran up the connecting stairways towards the platform, but Borg was already rushing down, asking, 'Mia, what is it? Did I hear you say something about leaving?'

The look on my face was answer enough, and he said, 'I will get my things!'

He ran down the stairs ahead of me, and collected his furs and spear. We walked quickly along the rope bridge, pushing the bewildered Brigit ahead of us. As we ran down to the shore, it seemed that the whole settlement was rushing and running about on some urgent job or other. The shore was alive with people, and already our boat and three or four of the Mount Land fleet had been brought over from the gravel bank. Borg immediately ran over to our boat to help the men tie down our goods, and load up the baskets of dried food that Gimble had had brought from his stores.

Brigit just sat down on the stony beach and watched in amazement at the frenzied activity all about us. She came over to me after a while and said, 'Mia, I do not really want to go. I think I will stay here, if you do not mind?'

I was just about to say something when I noticed Gimble had been standing behind her as she spoke. He replied to her question, 'That will not be possible I am afraid, honey.'

He spoke firmly, and Brigit jumped up as she had not seen him standing behind her.

'I will work hard if I can stay, I promise!' she pleaded.

He looked at her with a stern expression, that I had not seen on him before, and replied, 'It is nothing to do with you working. You do not belong here, and anyway, we can have no one here that shows we have had any visitors since the last moon. You do not look like a Mount Lander, and would be spotted straight away as a stranger. And you would not want the Icin to question you! Now, I think there is work you can do for Kemit, so go and do it.'

His tone was harsh, and not at all friendly as it had been before. I was just about to follow Brigit, thinking that he was talking to both of us, when he put his hand on my shoulder to stop me. I turned around and saw his usual smiling face again, looking down at me.

'No, not you, honey. Come, I have gifts for you.'

I followed him to a hut on the edge of the beach where Raffi and Thriffy were waiting. They both hugged me and wished me well, and then Raffi turned and brought out a full-length fur cloak. She held it out to me, and I turned and looked at Gimble in amazement. It was one of the famous Mount Land cloaks! Not a cape, but a full-length cloak with a hood. It was one of the cloaks that Gimble would not trade with Kemit for any price, too.

Gimble looked at me and nodded, saying, 'Yes honey, it is for you. It is our gift for you, and may it keep you warm on your travels. And, if needs must, you could trade it for a good sum, if you have to.'

Gimble took the cloak from Raffi's outstretched arms and put it on me, and I could not help tears streaming down my face at their generosity. Gimble hugged me, and so did Raffi, so that I was in both their arms together, feeling all their love for me. After they let me go I said, 'I would never trade such a gift. Oh, thank you. You have both been so kind to me. I do not know how to repay you.'

Gimble took my hands in his and replied, 'Just keep safe, and we will be repaid in full. Iona sent this for you too, just a little while ago.'

He held out his hand, and revealed a bright sparkling cord made of beaten gold stone wrapped around fine plant string. I looked at it as it caught the sun, and was dazzled by it.

I looked up, and Gimble said, 'She told me to tell you that this came from her homeland, wherever that is, and that you might like to put your mother's crystal on it. She also said to remind you that perfection is not everything. It is the flaws in the crystal that makes the rainbows. She said to remember that.'

I took my mother's crystal from its leather thong and put it onto the golden cord. Raffi came over and tied it around my neck.

'I think you are just about to leave. When you are older, maybe you will visit us again. May the Gods watch over you!'

I ran down to the boat, as the crew were waiting for me before they pushed off. Kemit was in the boat, and Uin was waiting to lift me in. He saw the cloak I was wearing, and raised his eyebrows saying, 'They gave you that? In all the winters I have known them, they have never let one of those cloaks leave their shores. They must think you are a very special person indeed, for them to actually give you one!'

I looked up at him, and the tears welled in my eyes again at the thought of their generosity. Within minutes I was sitting in the boat, and we were steadily paddling amidst the fishing fleet towards the great Western Sea. The boat had been draped with fishing nets like the settlement boats, and when it was in the middle of the other boats it did not look quite so big. The crew paddled in silence for the best part of an hour, until we were out of sight of the land. Sefn brought his boat alongside ours, and stepped into our boat.

Kemit clasped his arms, then hugged him and said, 'Thank you, good friend. I hope the Icin do not detect our presence at your settlement, for I fear for your people.'

Sefn said as he jumped back into his boat, 'Fear not for us, for we have the Priestess to protect us! We will paddle on to the west for a few more hours, before returning home. I do not need to tell you the way from here!'

Kemit smiled and replied, 'That you do not, my friend. Farewell, until we meet again.'

We all watched motionless, as the fishing fleet paddled away from us, until they became a speck on the horizon.

We were then alone on the calm sea, out of sight of any land. Kemit turned to the crew and said, 'Well men, we have a few choices ahead of us now, and I feel you should have as much say as me as to which one we choose. We can go south to the Iberi coast, or travel down one of the great rivers of Galli Land. Either way, we have to put as much sea between us and Mount Land as we can before first light. So, which is it to be?'

The men looked at each other, and there was much discussion as to which option to take. Kemit came over and said to me, 'I have to ask the men which route they want to take, as it is their lives that are at stake, just as much as ours.'

Brigit's eyes widened as she overheard him, and she said, 'What is it we are running away from? No one told me why we had to leave so quickly!'

Her tone of voice did her no favours in Kemit's eyes, I thought, and he coolly replied, 'We believe that a morning raid is planned by the Icin to look for Mia.'

She looked at him then and, detecting his tone, said nothing more. But I could tell she wanted to know how he knew that something was planned, for he had said nothing the night before about leaving. I caught her glancing at me through the corner of my eye, and saw the distaste in her eyes as she looked at my cloak. I turned to Kemit, who had also seen the glance, and asked, 'What are our options then?'

He sat down next to me and said, 'Well, sweetness, if we follow the coast of Galli Land we can find the mouth of one of their great interior rivers to travel up. Or we can travel directly south, keeping far out into the western sea, until we hit the west coast of Iberi Land. If we travel down the coast from there, there is also a great river that we can hide in for a while.'

I felt a little concerned at the thought of being far out into the western sea, for it frightened me when we were out of sight of land.

'Why do we have to travel far out to sea, to go to the Iberi Coast?' I asked. 'Can we not just follow the coast until we reach it? Or is Iberi Land an island?'

Kemit smiled and replied, 'No, Iberi Land is not an island, but the seas between the Galli Coast and the north coast of Iberi Land can be fierce. It has something to do with underwater rivers, I think. Let me just say that I would never travel across it unless it was a choice between that, or certain death. But do not worry, we will be fine out at sea, for the western sea is calm at this time of the year, and we have plenty of food and water with us if we need it.'

I leaned towards him and whispered in his ear, 'Which route do you prefer?'

He looked at me, then he looked at the crew and replied, 'I prefer the route my crew pick!'

He winked at me, and I looked at him and smiled, knowing that that was the only answer a man like Kemit could give. The crew had stopped muttering between themselves, and Uin stood up and said, 'We have decided to take the Iberi route. The men feel that though the Galli River would be easier, it would leave us no place for escape if the Icin blocked the river mouth. It would only be a matter of time until they found us, as that river only goes to the mountains and there are no forks to take along the way. If we travel along the western Iberi coast we could take the Dour River, and stay with the Sannis for a while. Then later in the year, when the water is low, we could go through the Dubek Straits and into the Inland Sea from there.'

Kemit stood with his hands on his hips, and looked at each of his crew individually with a stern expression, then his face cracked into a wonderful smile and he said, 'The choice I would make myself! We think as one, as usual, men. So let us get going!'

The men smiled and took their paddles. They started to paddle as fast as they could, and soon we were racing far out into the west. We did not stop to catch fish, so Brigit and I walked up and down the boat every so often, with water and smoked fish and meat for the men. We did not stop at all until dark, when Kemit told the men to tip over the stone weights, to stop us drifting too far during the night. We settled down to sleep, and Borg came over and lay next to me as he had always done. I was glad he did not feel the need to stop doing that, after our words the other day.

He whispered in my ear before he went to sleep, 'Nice cloak, Mia! Aren't you the lucky one!'

I looked at him and elbowed him in the ribs, and he laughed and turned over to go to sleep.

We did not sleep right through the night, for Kemit woke the crew when it was still dark. After pulling up the stone weights we were under way again, but this time we were travelling south, or so Kas who was paddling next to me said. I asked him how they knew which way we were going, as the boat could have turned in the night. I started to worry that we might be travelling at speed right back to the shores of Mount Land.

He could see that I was concerned and said, 'Do not worry. A trader always knows which way he is travelling. It is instinct. Anyway, when we have first light you will see that we are travelling south, as the sun will come up on our side of the boat.'

I nodded and smiled to show that I was happy with his answer, but I was still worried. I had never longed for first light so much in all my life. It seemed to take an age for it to come, and sure enough, the sun came up on our side of the boat, just as Kas had said it would. I was so relieved to know that we were travelling in the right direction that I must have fallen asleep again. I was woken up with a prod by Brigit, who was asking why I had not given the men on my side of the boat something to drink yet. I quickly went up to the men, apologising along the way for being late. They did not seem to mind, and some of them said that I was not late anyway, and even if I was they thought I was a sight worth waiting for.

I returned to my seat, my face beaming with the kindness of them all, and patted Brigit on the back and said, 'They did not seem to mind. But thank you for waking me. I was so worried in the night that we might have been travelling in the wrong direction, that I did not sleep at all. How are you this day?'

She looked at me with a glum face and replied, 'I am as fine as I could be, for being whisked away at a moment's notice into another distant sea. Why did we have to leave so quickly?'

I was about to tell her about my dream, but then I felt that if she knew we had left so suddenly, just because of a dream I had had, she would have been even more annoyed. So I just said Kemit had heard that the Icin war ships were in the area, looking for me.

She looked at me and said blandly, 'Oh, well I suppose we could not let them get you, could we?'

There was something in the way she spoke that made me suspect that she would have no qualms about telling them where I was, if she got the chance.

The day went by quite quickly then, as the men had their rests individually so that we did not have to stop at all. This meant that Brigit and I were always providing refreshments for the men who were resting. The next night was the same, and we slept no more than a few hours before we travelled again. It was well after midday food when Kemit shouted land was in sight. The stores of water were getting a little short, and I was glad we could perhaps put our feet on solid ground again, even if only briefly. We appeared to be heading towards a sort of headland, and by the time the sun was taking colour we had beached the boat on a sandy shore.

Kemit jumped ashore with Uin and Kas, and walked about the beach. After a while they returned, and said we had to take to the sea again, as it was not a friendly shore. We were also a little too far east of where he wanted to land. He ordered two men to fill our water bags from a small waterfall at the edge of the beach, and we were soon travelling up the coast again.

I was very disappointed that we could not land, but Borg came over to me later and explained, 'That was not a good place to spend the night, the men said. The tribes along the north coast of Iberi Land have a taste for shipwrecked crews.'

I looked at him curiously. Then it dawned on me what he meant, and I asked, 'You don't mean they really have a <u>taste</u> for shipwrecked crews do you…?'

He nodded and we both looked at Brigit, and then laughed at our wicked thoughts. She looked up at us both and said indignantly, 'What is so funny about taking to sea again?'

'Oh nothing, nothing at all!' we both replied in unison, at which we started laughing again until Kemit came over and told us to be quiet. He did not want anyone to know that we were passing, and sound carried far on a still night.

We nodded, but sniggered for a while longer thinking about Brigit, left alone on that shore, trying to make friends with people who have a taste for human flesh. It was a funny thought, although we would never really have done such a thing. After we had negotiated a rocky shoreline, we were safely out to sea again, and travelling at pace in the last of the light along the western coast of Iberi Land.

20. DEVILS AND DARK THOUGHTS

That night I had difficulty sleeping again, and drifted off into a strange grey world. I was sitting in the boat, looking at the north Iberi shore swiftly passing by, but there was no colour. It was all grey, yet I knew it was not night time. I looked at the crew paddling the boat, and suddenly did not recognise any of them. It was not Kemit and Uin at the front, but a red-haired burly man, and a short, dark haired man, whose arms were covered with tattoos of strange creatures. I looked behind me, to where Brigit usually sat, and there was another Brigit in her place. It looked like Brigit, but that maid was slim and very beautiful.

She smiled slyly at me and said, 'How is Mia the Wonderful now then? Yes, it is me, Brigit. The Brigit that is inside the other one. The one that has power over the men that she meets.'

'What are you talking about?' I whispered in a daze. 'Who are these people? And where is Kemit?'

She smirked and replied harshly, 'Oh, this is the crew I chose, for they are my kind of people.'

I looked around to see where Borg was, and saw that he was in some sort of trance in the seat in front of me. I touched his shoulder and he spun around. Although it looked like Borg, his eyes were somehow blank and distant. I shrunk back from him, and Brigit's voice said from behind me, 'Come and sit next to me, Borg my dear.'

Borg got up immediately, and sat on the furs at the feet of Brigit. He put his head on her lap and she stroked his hair, and said, 'Now this is how it should be, sweet Mia. You are no good for Borg. You would just crush him with your fine ways.'

I looked at her in amazement, and before I could ask again what was going on, she answered me.

'You should be more careful with those thoughts of yours you know, sweet Mia. You cannot laugh and joke about me being eaten by Iberi Landers, and not take a step into the Dark Realm because of it. That is where such thoughts belong, you see. You are not as sweet as you think, are you?'

I remembered how Borg and I had joked about Brigit, being a fine meal for the tribe there, and replied, 'But that was just a joke. We did not mean it. I could never wish for such a thing.'

'We had a saying at the lake, "Many a true word is said in joking".'

Then she stood up and pointed at me accusingly. 'You thought it, Mia. So you have brought yourself here. I know you have always hated me. Well, I have hated you too, from the day I met you, with your airs, and "… everybody loved Mia, she was so sweet!" Inja fooled you though, didn't she? Poor good Kemit. She betrayed him, but he deserved it. Did he really think she had been waiting for him all her life? What arrogance!'

I stood up then and demanded, 'Where is Kemit and the crew?'

She smiled and pointed into the distance, and said, 'Why, they are over there, paddling away to Iberi Land with the shell of Mia and Borg seemingly asleep. Oh, and that loser Brigit you took such pity on too!'

I looked to where she was pointing, and I could just see Kemit's log boat moving away into the grey distance. I thought about what Iona had said, about the light, but I could not focus on the horizon as we were enveloped in such a thick mist. The sound of the paddles stopped, and I could hear the boat grounding onto a gravel bank. Or was it a sandy beach, I wondered? I looked for my mother's crystal, but it did not appear to be around my neck.

'Looking for this?' Brigit whispered in my ear.

She held my crystal on its golden string in her hand, and laughed and laughed. And in desperation I jumped ashore, just to get away from her. The shock of the cold water stunned me immediately, and I think I must have fainted because the next thing I saw was the handsome face of Laguz in front of me.

We were in some sort of hall. No, not some sort of hall, Laguz's hall! I was tied to one of the stakes in the middle of the hall. I looked at the stake I knew would be next to me, to see Brigit tied there too. Inja was sitting next to Laguz and the strange crew from the boat were sitting below them.

Inja slowly got up and walked towards me, and asked, 'What did you do with the pearls I prepared so well for you, to take with you, sweet Mia?'

I looked at her smiling face, and felt an anger I did not know I possessed well up in me, and I replied, 'I threw them away. They felt very cold, like your heart, and your hands, Inja, Queen of… what are you exactly queen of now?'

She instantly slapped me on the face, thinking I would be shocked into submission. But she did not realise how often my grandmother used to slap me. I was not as soft as she thought I was. Laguz jumped down and came over, and caught Inja's hand before she could strike me again.

She shrugged and went back to her seat, and he smiled at me and said, 'Well Mia, you were a lot more special than any of us thought, were you not? If you turn to the Dark Realm you could be more powerful than that pathetic priestess Iona ever could be. You have taken a step into our realm, now take another and you can join us, and we will rule all the known world together.'

I looked at him and the dark shadowy figures in the hall, and wondered for a moment what I could do. Then I asked, 'Why have you tied up Brigit? I thought she was with you already?'

Laguz looked into the dazed eyes of Brigit and laughed, 'You thought she was already with us? That is interesting. No, she is just weak and jealous of you, Mia. She was easily turned. She is nothing, but she was useful in distracting you, so we could get you out of that boat.'

I realised the whole thing had been to trick me into leaving the boat. Which I had done, because I thought it was not our boat! How stupid I had been. Then Inja was back, whispering something to Laguz, and he answered, 'Yes you are right. I think it is time to bring in our feathered friends, to show them their new companion.'

I watched in horror as the birds flew into the hall and took their places, just as they had before when Laguz turned the two maids into birds. Laguz saw my face then and said, 'I thought you were awake on that occasion, but then I could not see you and thought I had been mistaken. So, you know what we can do. Do not worry, you will not become a bird. That is for your sad friend there. We have much more exciting things in store for you, Mia of the Icin.'

The familiar drum beat started, and the first of the shadowy figures started to dance around the hall. Laguz raised his hands to the roof, as I had seen him do before, and I could see the cobweb-like threads forming high up in the darkness. Brigit was just coming round, and looked at me and the shadowy figures dancing around us. She screamed, as they had no faces, just blank spaces where there faces should have been. Laguz laughed, and continued to spin the web above us. Brigit looked at me again, and because of her desperate, lost look I felt nothing but pity for her. Laguz had used her weakness to help trick me out of the boat, and I could now see that she was not really bad, just very insecure.

Then I realised that if the crew had been an illusion, maybe Brigit had not taken my crystal either. I could not see it, but as soon as I thought about it I could feel its warmth under my dress. I remembered what Iona had said, about the light on the horizon. I closed my eyes and imagined I was sitting on my sand cliffs, looking at the sun entering the distant horizon, as I had so many times before. I captured that image in my mind, and brought it in to cover not just me, but Brigit too.

Before Laguz knew what was happening we were both bathed in golden light, and the crowds in the hall instantly melted into the floor, as did the birds. Only Inja and Laguz stood before us, as we were bathed in the golden glow. They both took many steps back from us, so that the light could not touch them. I might have laughed at the astounded looks on their faces, if I had not been preoccupied by visualising our hands unbound. I do not know how I knew how to do that, but it worked, and Brigit immediately clung to me when she was free.

Laguz started shouting something to me, but I could hardly make out what he was saying as his voice was so faint. Then I heard his words, saying, 'Nice trick, but you will never get back to the boat from here with that light!'

He was right, I knew. How could I get back to the Iberi Land coast from north Brit Land? I knew also that there was no point in worrying about it, as I just had to get away from Laguz first. I pulled my crystal out on its golden thread, and saw them immediately fall to the floor in front of me. It was radiating a golden light, like a torch in a cave. Brigit watched as I tried to think of something that was in the back of my mind, something that had helped me in the past. No sooner had I thought about it, than I knew the owl would be outside, waiting for us. I grabbed Brigit and pulled her to the door. Our feet seemed to disappear into the floor with every step, as if the ground below us was not quite solid. It took all my strength to take each step, but before long we were outside. What kind of an outside was it, I thought, when I got there? It was a grey land, with grey sky, and grey trees. Apart from the brilliant white owl that stood before us. In front of the owl were two huge swans. The owl in my dream had been huge, but now the swans were huge, and the owl was of a normal size. I had no time to think about it though, as Brigit and I climbed onto the backs of the swans. The owl took off, and the swans gracefully followed.

In a few seconds we were high above Laguz's settlement, just in time to see them leave the hall and look up at us. Then we were gone, gliding amongst the clouds, heading south. I looked at Brigit, who seemed to be asleep. I could not sleep on such a journey, for I intuitively knew it was my mind that was taking us home, more than the swans. As we passed over Brit Land, I wondered which parts were the Icin lands. I quickly cast that distracting thought from my mind as we passed the Mount of Mount Land. I looked at the top of the Mount, but Iona's temple and seat were not there! Then I realised that it would not be in the Dark Realm. And I knew I had to concentrate, until we were home and away from all of that greyness.

Then I saw it! The boat was just at the entrance to a great river. We flew lower and lower, until we were flying alongside the boat itself. I shouted to Brigit. She woke up and looked at me in a daze, and I shouted again loudly.

'Jump into the boat Brigit! Now!'

She did as I told her, and with a smile to the owl and the swans, I jumped. No sooner had I touched the deck than the world was filled with colour again, and I knew I was back.

Borg turned to me and asked, 'Had a nice sleep? You two you have been asleep for hours. Kemit said you might like to see when we enter the river.'

I smiled at Brigit, who looked at me with a white face, and I asked vaguely, 'Which river is this?' But Borg had already gone back to his paddle, to help get through the river currents.

I leaned over to Brigit and put my hand on hers. She looked at me in a daze and asked, 'Did that really happen?'

I looked her straight in the eyes and replied, 'Did what happen?'

She looked at me searchingly and said, 'I had the most horrific nightmare. You will not believe it. You were in it too, like some sort of sorceress. Why is it, even in my dreams, you always get the best parts?'

I smiled and replied, 'It was your dream not mine. You obviously gave that part to me!'

She was silent for a while, then she smiled and said, 'They are right you know. You are special, Mia.'

I shouted back as I went to the front of the boat to watch the river mouth appear, 'We are all special, are we not?'

21. SANNIS'S LAKE

Kemit came over to me as I looked at the huge river mouth.

That is the River Dour, and on a lake that is at its source, lives a very old friend of mine. We will be safe there for a while. We will not be able to leave the centre of the river until we are a lot farther up though, as the tribes in this area do not take kindly to strangers. They tend to attack, and ask who you are afterwards. But do not be worried, I have travelled this way many times before. The river is deep and wide, and as long as we stay in the centre we will be all right.'

I nodded, and was about to go back to my seat when he said, 'I think the men need some more water along your side, sweetness.'

I took the water bottles along my side of the boat, and I was too busy to notice the small groups of people that were standing on the north shore, watching us. When I gave Borg his water he said, 'They do not look that friendly, do they?'

I looked up and saw the group and said, 'Kemit said the same thing to me just a while ago. This is a strange land though, is it not? There are trees here that I have never seen before, and look at that bird!' He followed my gaze and saw a bird fly past, with brightly coloured feathers.

After I had finished the row I went back to Borg and sat next to him while he paddled for a while. It was becoming very hot in the afternoon sun, and most of the crew had already stripped off to their fur tunics. Borg had done that too, and his skin glistened with the sweat from paddling and the hot sun.

I could not help commenting, 'Hey, look at your strong arms, Borg! All this paddling is making you look very manly!'

He laughed at my comment, as he knew I was trying to tease him into reacting, and kept on paddling.

It was wonderful to feel so much heat in the sun that early in the year. On Dogger it rarely got that hot at the height of summer, and I realised then how far south we must have been for the weather to change so much. Kemit waited until we were in the middle of a very wide stretch of river before we stopped for the night. But before I went to sleep I noticed that two of the crew were staying up on guard, just in case anyone paddled up to the boat as we slept.

The next day the land on either shore began to look very strange. There was little greenery to see, just red earth and rocks as far inland as the eye could see. No one was wearing furs at all by then, in fact they had been stowed away for sleeping on only. I had never felt the sun so hot, and Brigit was suffering more than most of us, for she came from the coldest climate of us all. She spent most of the time sitting under the cloth roof of the sleeping area, until the sun went down. I could tell the mood of the crew, and Kemit too, was becoming lighter as we travelled farther up river, and I wondered if we were nearing his friend's settlement.

It was not until first light the following day that the river widened into an inland lake, and far into the distance I could see the roofs of huts ahead of us. The edges of the lake were surrounded with the usual water reeds, and the low lands around the lake looked very lush and fertile, but behind the greenery were stark, bare mountain slopes. There did not seem to be anything growing on the slopes at all, apart from some grey shrubby trees. The tops of the mountain peaks were capped with snow, which seemed very strange to me when it was so hot at the lakeside. I pointed the snow out to Borg, and he said, 'I cannot understand why that snow has not melted in this heat!'

I nodded and replied, 'That was just what I was thinking. Look at the slopes too, they look so dry and barren. And have you ever seen trees like those before? There is some strange fruit on it that looks like the sun before it goes into the sea at night.' He followed my gaze, and shook his head at the strangeness of it all.

Kemit was just passing us while we spoke and said, 'Just wait until you taste that fruit! You will not believe anything that just grows on trees could taste quite so good.'

We just looked at him in amazement, that he should suggest we could eat such a poisonous looking fruit. He looked at our expressions and laughed to himself, as he continued along the boat. It must be wonderful, I thought then, to be a trader like Kemit; to know about so many different people in so many different lands.

We were almost at the settlement by then, which was constructed on stilts over the water, just like Brigit's home. The huts looked very similar apart from the colour of the daub on the walls, which was bright red like the setting sun. I wondered if they had painted them that colour, until I looked at the soil on the banks as we approached and saw that the bright red was the colour of the earth in that land. There were crowds of people gathering as the boat approached the jetty, near to the first huts of the settlement. The people all had very black, wavy hair and golden skin. Like the colour my skin used to go after a very hot summer. They were dressed in strange clothes too, the colour of the fruit that we had seen on the trees. I had never seen cloth dyed that colour before in the north.

Around their necks they work necklaces of bone and brightly coloured bird feathers, and I knew I was going to like these people. A tall man hailed us from the jetty, saying loudly, 'Kemit! My brother, you return at last!'

Kemit called back, 'It is good to see your eyes too, Sannis!'

Instead of waiting for the boat to come alongside the jetty, the man jumped into the boat and hugged Kemit so very tightly that I could not imagine he could breathe. There was then a stream of people jumping into the boat, and patting and hugging the crew. I began to worry that we would sink with all the extra weight. Sannis then shouted to his men,

'Look at this fine new boat our brother brings to our shores. You must have done well with the trade to come by a tree that size! Come, enough of this, let us eat!'

They all leapt back onto the jetty and tied the ropes securely, and jostled the crew out and along the walkway to a large hall that stood surrounded by its own stretch of water. Kemit gestured to Uin to bring us along, as he was carried on the shoulders of the people, laughing heartily as he went.

'They seem to like Kemit well enough here, don't they!' I said to Uin.

He laughed and replied, 'You could say that! It is always like this when we arrive here, even if we have only been away for a few moons. It must be at least two winters now since Kemit has been here, so this is to be expected. They will all be drunk within the hour, for the mead they drink here is made with a local fruit and is very potent. Come, Kemit will be expecting us to follow quickly, before they start drinking!'

I felt a weight drop off my shoulders then, as I thought that the Icin would not find us there, not when we were amongst such good friends. We quickly followed Uin to the hall in the lake, and as we walked all of the people smiled at us along the way. We crossed a long bridge to the entrance of the hall, and when we entered there was a hush in the room. It was a little unnerving as we walked through the silent crowd, all watching us until we reached Kemit and Sannis.

'Forgive me for not guiding you to our hall, my lady, but I did not know of your presence on board, and I have missed my brother Kemit so.'

I suddenly realised that he was talking to me – I had never been called my lady, before. Kemit must have told them about my connection with the Icin, and I wondered if that was such a good idea. But I thought that Kemit usually knew what he was doing, and I replied, 'Do not worry, I can see you were glad to see him.'

I laughed then, and the whole room laughed with me, which actually made me jump.

Then Sannis said, 'Come, Lady Mia, sit here next to me and let me give you some food, for you must be hungry after your long journey, eating nothing more than that dry fish Kemit keeps.'

I walked over to him and sat down on some wonderfully soft fur, and Brigit and Borg sat down with the crew. Brigit was not going to like that, I thought, then I stopped myself and thought, what did I care if she liked it or not. I looked at Kemit beaming across at me from the other side of Sannis, and it was good to see him look so happy again. A woman brought over a platter of the strange fruit we had seen on the trees as we paddled in, and Sannis said, 'This is a local fruit that I think, as a northerner, you will like very much. Kemit has told me you have nothing like it where you come from. It is called an orange, because in our land that is the name of the colour of the earth that it grows from. Come, let me peel one for you, my lady.'

He took the fruit and peeled the skin from it until it looked just like a white ball, then he broke it open to reveal the bright flesh, the same colour as the skin, and bursting with juice inside. I took the piece he handed to me and after smelling it took a little bite. The juice squirted all over me and into my eye. The room suddenly went silent as I chewed. Then I smiled happily, nodding that I loved it, and did not mind in the least being covered by its juice. The whole room thumped their fists on the floor, and cheered when I had finished. I was not used to getting that kind of attention, and whispered to Uin who was sitting next to me, if it was always like this when a guest tried their orange fruit. He told me that it certainly was not, but then it was the first time they had had a visit from northern royalty, and they were all very nervous about not offending me.

I looked up at him and whispered, 'Royalty from the north? Is it not dangerous to let them know where my father comes from?'

Uin leaned over and whispered in my ear, 'No, not really, for the Icin are only powerful in the northern seas, and the Galli that might look for you are not welcome here. So it does no harm for you to be treated like the heir to the throne of the Icin, which you actually are!'

I looked at him for a while then replied, 'What about the trade in the gold stone of the Icin, do they not care about that in the south?'

He smiled and replied, 'Yes they do, sweetness, even though there are many lands in the south with the same stone. In this land they have another stone, even more beautiful to my mind. It is the colour of the moon, called silver. And they have such contempt for the Galli that they would do nothing to help them, however great the reward.'

I looked at him then, trying to imagine a stone the colour of the moon. Sannis was starting to look at us with concern as we had been speaking in whispers. So I turned to him and said loudly, 'You truly have the best fruit in all the world here!'

He was delighted when I said that, and insisted I have some more before the rest of the feast was brought in. That consisted of wild piglet cooked over a spit while the orange juice had been poured over it, so Uin told me, which is why it tasted so wonderful. How lucky they were to live in a land with such fruits. The rest of that day was spent eating and drinking their strange dry mead, which was very strong, so I just sipped it. The gathering started to fall asleep after the sixth or seventh lot of food was brought in, and I decided I wanted to get outside, as it was very hot in the crowded room.

Borg saw me getting up and followed me, and I asked as we approached the door, 'Where is Brigit?'

He pointed to Brigit, leaning on one of the settlement men, fast asleep.

'She drank two whole bowls of the mead they have here, and after leaning on that man and saying how very nice he was, she fell asleep. He is just too drunk, or polite, to move her, I think!'

We both smiled and walked outside, just in time to see the last traces of the sun disappearing over the mountains to the west. 'This is a wonderful place, is it not, Borg?'

He nodded and replied, 'It surely is Mia, and a far cry from Dogger.'

I nodded and we gazed at the sun setting over the snow-capped mountains, marvelling that such places existed in the same world as Dogger Island and the cold northern coasts. We heard footsteps on the platform behind us, and noticed that it was Kas coming out for some fresh air too. I smiled and asked him, 'Have you been here before Kas?'

He nodded, and as he too looked at the last strip of sun descending out of view he said,

'Many times, my dear. This used to be one of Kemit's favourite places to over winter, for it never really gets cold here. Mind you, I have never been here at this time of year, for we are usually long gone trading by now.'

I still gazed at the mountains that were now totally black, fronting the most amazing coloured sky behind.

'Was it too hot for you too in there? Borg and I just had to get out, there seemed to be no air to breath.'

'That is right. Some find the heat difficult to cope with, particularly by a lake like this, for there is a lot of water in the air, and that makes you sweat. I do not mind it too much, but if you are asking, I prefer the dry heat of the desert lands to the east. It is much hotter there, but somehow easier to live with.'

He looked at Borg and me and said, 'I reckon to you two Dogger Islanders, this place is a marvel, eh? You have not seen anything yet!' Then he turned and walked away from us, along the platform in the direction of the boat.

I turned to Borg and said, 'I cannot wait to see more, can you?'

Borg put his hand on mine and squeezed it tightly, and replied, 'I surely cannot wait. Although this land will do me for a while, as it is such a strange country. The lake looks normal with the reeds surrounding it, but the barren red earth behind it is very odd. I would love to go up into the snow in the mountains and look down on this land from there.'

I pulled my hand away from him and said crossly, 'Trust you to spoil a nice moment, with talk of climbing mountains! When are you going to realise that mountains are dangerous places? After your last mountain trip I would have thought you would have learnt your lesson!'

As soon as I had uttered those words, I regretted them instantly. The look of hurt on his face made me feel as if I had stabbed him in the heart. He turned without a word and walked briskly away from me, as I cried after him, 'Borg! I am sorry, it was a stupid thing to say.'

He shouted back without turning round, 'Aye, but true nonetheless,' and he disappeared from view around one of the huts.

How stupid of me to bring that up. Would I ever learn to think before I spoke? Borg was just getting over it, and I had to bring it back into his mind again. My dampened spirits made me not want any company for a while, so I decided to walk to the end of the platform and sit on the boards, and watch the lake take on the colours of the sky. I knew Borg needed to be alone for a while, and it would just make things worse if I followed him. I sat there for some time, and the torches lit at the edge of the water made it a pretty sight. I was just getting up to see if anyone was still awake, when I saw Kemit walking over to me.

'How goes it with you, Mia?'

His tone was still happy, and I did not want to spoil it by mentioning my stupid comments to Borg, so I smiled and said, 'I am fine. I have been watching the sun's colours cast themselves onto the lake. But it is getting a little cold now. I think I should go and get my furs.'

He smiled and replied, 'They are not on the boat, as all your furs have already been placed in your hut. A serving maid is waiting to bathe you.'

I looked at him as if he had gone mad, then suddenly felt very worried and asked suspiciously, 'Why? Am I to be part of some ceremony?'

He laughed and whispered quietly, 'No ceremony, sweetness, just the normal nightly routine of royalty in this part of the world.'

I looked at him curiously, not believing that anyone would bathe every night! They would wear away their skin and become ill, surely! He held my hand and walked me briskly to a fine oval shaped hut, not far from Sannis's hall.

As we entered, I saw that my furs and my new cloak had been draped amidst many others on a low bed in the corner. A good fire was burning in the hearth, and a huge wooden container full of water was placed next to the fire. As soon as I entered a maid gestured for me to come and sit by the fire. I turned to Kemit with a look of abject horror, but he just laughed and said, 'Enjoy your new status, sweetness. I wager you will start to like it very soon. Remember, this is their settlement, and you must not offend their generosity.'

He was laughing as he said that, for he knew I would not do anything to offend, and I wondered just what he meant.

'Come, my lady, sit a while, as I have not got the water hot enough for you yet.'

The maid picked up a stone from the fire with two sticks, and dropped it into the huge container. I had never seen anything made of wood quite so big before, apart from a boat, and asked her if it was made in the settlement. She told me that most settlements had one or two of the bathing boats, as she called it, for the people of noble blood to use.

I then asked her, 'Where do the other people bathe, if bathing is a tradition here?'

She laughed and replied, 'Oh, we just jump in the lake after the midday sun! I hear you come from the cold lands to the far north, and are not used to bathing so much. I imagine if it was very cold, I would not want to bathe much either.

My name is Effy, after the bright coloured birds that fly in our land. What do you wish me to call you, my lady?'

I turned to her and replied, 'Call me Mia.'

She nodded and said, 'Very well, my lady Mia. I will just go and get the herbs and crushed olives to rub onto your skin.'

I was going to say 'not lady Mia, just Mia', but I did not want to contradict her, as her chief had obviously told her I was royalty. I did not like the sound of olives, whatever they were, being rubbed onto my skin, but I remembered Kemit's last words and said nothing. Effy added herbs to the bucket and took out all of the stones, then gestured for me to step into the steaming water. I did not know what she meant at first, for I thought she was going to dip a cloth in it and bathe me, as Sula had done before the ceremonies on Dogger.

She shook her head and said, 'No, my lady, you are to step into the bathing boat.'

I stood up and thought, well, why not.

I was just about to put my toe into the water when she screamed to me, through fits of giggles, saying, 'No, mistress, not with your tunic on! You must take your clothes off first!'

I looked at her and realised how stupid I must have looked, attempting to step into the hot water with my shoes and clothes on. I looked to the door sheepishly, and she nodded and went over to it and placed a bucket full of staffs with feathers tied onto them across the doorway outside. When she came back she said, 'That is our message, that no one should enter this hut. Come, my lady, or the water will get cold.'

I stripped my clothes off and stepped into the herb-scented water, and instantly loved the experience. I had never in my life submerged my whole body in hot water before, and it felt wonderful! I did not know what herbs they were, but the sweet smell filled my senses and the tension of the days before just dropped away from my shoulders. I thought then and there that I was going to like that custom, and every night too! Effy crushed some black berries on a stone, then placed them in some cloth and tied it into a little bag. She came over and started to rub my arms and shoulders with the bag, and my skin afterwards felt soft and smooth. It was almost like the grease young children were covered in during the winter, to protect them from the cold, but instead of being greasy and smelling foul, it was light, and smelt good too. I asked her as she was rubbing my shoulders, 'What are those berries? For they make my skin feel wonderful.'

She smiled at me and asked, 'Do you not have olive trees in your land?'

I shook my head, and she looked mildly shocked and replied, 'I cannot imagine a land without olive trees growing! There is a juice that comes from this fruit that we call oil. It is good for the skin, and for stone lamps, but it also tastes good to eat.'

I looked at her and smiled, and she finished rubbing my skin with the bag. I just sat there in the huge wooden container, not wanting to get out. Effy looked at me after a while and asked, 'You wish to stay in longer?'

I nodded, and she went over to the fire and put some hot stones into a bucket of water, then took them out and brought the bucket over, saying, 'Sit back a little, for this is hot water!'

I did as she said, and delighted as the hot water mixed with the cooling water, making the bathing boat water nicely hot again. A noise at the door interrupted the moment, and Brigit stumbled in saying, 'Kemit said that this was your hut, but someone left those sticks in the way and I nearly tripped over them.' Then she took in the scene in front of her, and stopped in her tracks, standing with her mouth wide open, but for once she was speechless. When she collected herself she said, 'What on earth are you doing in that huge bowl of water? Have you gone mad? It will wash all your skin away!'

Effy and I just laughed, which was not a good thing to do where Brigit was concerned, so I quickly said, 'I thought the same thing too, Brigit, but Kemit told me it was a tradition here, and I was not to offend.' I looked at Effy and said, 'I am so glad I tried it, for it has to be the most wonderful experience I have ever had! Come over and smell the herbs Brigit, and look at this bag of fruit. It actually makes your skin soft when you rub it on!'

Brigit came over and sniffed the water, and raised her eyebrows, saying it actually did smell nice. Then she rubbed the olive bag on her hand and marvelled at her skin afterwards, saying, 'Hey, maybe I will try it too!'

I was just about to say I would get out for her, when Effy interrupted, saying in a very stern way, 'I am sorry, Lady Mia, but your servant cannot step into the bathing boat. It is for people of royal blood only. I would be whipped severely if I let her use it.'

Brigit and I looked at her in amazement, and the mood suddenly became tense and full of bad feelings. Iffy thought she would be whipped, which I thought sounded a little much, just for letting Brigit get into my hot water. Brigit was suddenly annoyed that she had been demoted to my servant from my companion and friend, and I just looked at them both, wondering what to say to them.

I stood up in the bath, and Effy immediately covered me with some soft plant cloth as I stepped out. I sat down next to Brigit near the hearth, and put my by then wrinkled fingers on hers. As I looked down at my hand, I squealed with shock at the white rippling of my skin. Effy came over and smiled, saying it was normal for that to happen after being in the bathing boat for so long, and that in a few minutes it would return to normal. Brigit had by then forgotten her annoyance, as we both watched my wrinkled hands slowly become smooth again.

Brigit looked at me, and said quietly so that Effy could not hear, 'I do not think I want to get in there now, Mia, anyway, if it does that to your skin. I think you are a very brave person if you go into it again, for next time your skin will probably drop off completely. I reckon a few minutes more and you would have looked like a piece of meat, ready for cooking!'

I looked at her in horror at the thought, then dismissed it, for just as Effy said, my hands were normal again and so very soft. We sat by the fire for a while, then I dressed and said I was suddenly very sleepy. Effy guided me to my bed. I do not remember anything after that, until I awoke in the middle of the night to hear a strange howling noise. I sat up with a start, and saw that Brigit and Effy were awake too, sitting by the fire.

'What was that?' I whispered across to them.

Brigit answered, 'Effy says there are packs of wolves that hunt in this part of the mountains. The settlers keep fires alight all night next to the platforms, and the wolves usually keep away.'

That seemed like a sensible thing to do, I thought, and I lay down and drifted off to sleep again as Brigit and Effy talked by the fire.

I woke the next day feeling wonderful, and my skin felt silky and smooth. And I smelt good too. I leapt out of bed and woke Brigit and Effy, and said I was really hungry. Effy told me that her people tended to eat first food in their own homes, only sharing their midday or last meal together. I asked what we had to eat, and Effy brought over a bowl of strange looking fruits. Apart from the orange fruit, it all looked dried and unappealing. Effy picked up a piece the size of a hazel nut and offered it to me. I picked it up and thanked her, thinking it was so small that even if it tasted bad, it was not too much to eat. I tasted it, and it was sweet and chewy and had a seed inside, which Effy said you could either eat or spit out. She then gave me another larger fruit that looked like a huge dead spider's body and I hesitated. Effy took a bite of it and said that it was wonderful and sweet too. So I tried it, amidst looks of horror from Brigit, and it was the sweetest thing I had ever tasted, apart from pure honey. Effy then gave me a drink, which she told me was the boiled juice of many fruits.

I took the drink and said, 'Thank you, Effy. It is very good of you to care for us in this way.'

Looking a little puzzled, she said, 'But I belong to you, so it is my life now to tend to your needs. Just as Brigit does.'

I looked at Brigit, and before we had bad feelings again I said, 'Oh no, Effy, Brigit is my friend, not my servant.'

I could see Brigit looking at Effy then, and almost wished I had not said it. Brigit was now positively looking down on Effy.

'What do you mean, you belong to me?' I asked.

'Sannis paid my family with a lot of goods, to buy me for you, last night. So I belong to you now.'

I just smiled back and nodded, as I did not want to offend her by rejecting her. But I would have to speak to Kemit about that, I thought. It was strange enough to have people treating me like royalty, but I was not yet ready to have a personal slave, if ever. I had always thought it was not right for one person to own another, just because their family was better at fighting. We ate our food, and stepped out of the dark hut into blinding sunshine. It took a few moments for our eyes to adjust to the light, as it was so bright. Effy left us then to attend to her chores, whatever they were, and Brigit and I were left to stroll about and have a look around. After Effy had left I said to Brigit, 'Where was Borg last night? I hope he is all right. I said a stupid thing to him, and I am worried he is still cross with me.'

Brigit looked at me curiously, and replied casually, 'Oh, he did not say anything about it to me last night before I left him. He said to say to you that he hoped you slept well, though.'

I looked at her and said angrily, 'Did he? Why did you not tell me?'

She looked at me with that blank face she always pulled, to tell you that she really did not care, and said, 'I really did not think it was that important. He just said to tell you he hoped you had a good night.'

I could see she was getting annoyed by then, so I replied, 'Sorry, you were not to have known. Why did he not sleep with us, as usual?'

Brigit muttered back, 'Oh, something about these people's rules, he said.'

I stopped and made her repeat exactly what Borg had said. She then told me that young maids were not allowed to sleep in the same huts as young boys, unless they were bound together.

'That is ridiculous!' I said. 'Where is Kemit?'

I strode away from Brigit in the direction of the boat, only to find it empty, apart from Kas, who was sitting in it eating some fruit.

'Kas!' I shouted. 'Where are Kemit and the other men?'

'Bright morning, is it not, eh?' he shouted back casually. 'Kemit and the crew had a mind to go hunting at first light, with Sannis and his men. Something about a wolf pack hunting too near to the lake.'

I stood there on that bright morning, surrounded by snow-capped mountains and clear blue skies, and I suddenly felt deeply unhappy and sad. I sat down on the platform and stared blankly at the lake, feeling very alone. I could hear Brigit's heavy steps thumping along the platform towards me, but I did not turn around. 'Where are they then?' she asked.

I just replied flatly, 'Gone hunting after wolves with Sannis,'

Brigit sat down next to me breathlessly, and said, 'Oh, that is nice for them. So what shall we do?'

I looked at her blankly and said, 'I do not want to do anything. I just want to sit here for a while.'

She looked at me curiously and said slowly, 'All right, but you would not mind if I wander about a little, would you?'

'No, of course not. I will see you later, when we have midday food.'

With that she walked purposefully off into the settlement. I turned around a little while later and saw her talking to a group of women outside a hut, and they all started laughing at something she had said. What was the matter with me? I thought. Why did I feel so dejected? Kemit and Borg had been away hunting before. Maybe it was the fact that Borg could not stay in our hut with us, and had not said goodbye, that was upsetting me. Kemit usually left a message too, if he was going somewhere.

'Did Kemit or Borg leave a message for me?' I shouted down to Kas.

Kas shook his head and carried on eating his fruit. I did not like the royalty part either. I just wanted to be treated like one of the crew, and I certainly did not want anyone, however well intentioned, buying a slave for me. I hoped that my mood was just due to tiredness, as the night before was the first good sleep I had had in many moons.

22. FIRST LOVE

After a while of sitting on my own, feeling miserable, I decided to explore the settlement myself. I walked along the platform in the opposite direction to Brigit, as I did not feel like her company when I felt so vulnerable. I passed a small hut decorated with sticks in the thatch that had bright bird feathers attached to them. I was watching the fluttering feathers, and thinking what a nice idea it was, to use the feathers in that way, when a young man came out of the hut. I was not expecting anyone to come out of the black hole that was the entrance to the hut, and I must have let out a squeal of shock.

He immediately held out his hand to me, and smiling, said, 'I am sorry if I frightened you, my lady. Do you wish to enter my sister's home?'

I shook my head and replied, 'No, thank you. I was just looking at the feathers fluttering on those sticks.'

'Ahh, they are for good luck. Let me tell you my name. I am Sten, and my father is Sannis, the chief.'

He stood up straight with pride when he told me that, and I suddenly became aware of how extremely handsome he was. He had long black hair tied behind his head with some leather, and his skin was golden brown. He also had the darkest brown eyes I think I have ever seen. I must have stood there looking at him for some time before I collected myself, and said, 'My name is Mia.'

He smiled a wonderful smile and replied, 'Yes, I know, and you are the daughter of a great and powerful chief of the north.'

I had never heard my father described in that way before, and I supposed he actually was the chief. Except that in Icin law the only real chiefs were women. I did not think he would understand that, so I just nodded.

He stretched his arm out to me then, saying, 'Come. As the offspring of chiefs, we should be friends. It will therefore be my job to show you my lake.'

I smiled and nodded, and followed him through the settlement. He was so very nice, which was somehow heightened by his good looks. I asked him why he was not out hunting too, and he said, 'It is a law with our people that the chief and his heir must never hunt together, in case they both do not come back. If that happened, the people would not know who to appoint as the next chief, and they would fight. For we are a people that love to fight!'

I looked at him a little surprised, and he winked at me and said, 'Yes, sometimes we just fight for fun. Is it not the same in your land?'

I thought about Karn and Simi, fighting all the time, and I nodded. It was a long time since I had even thought of them, and I suddenly wondered what they were doing. Lusa and Mayni would probably have them running around after them, before they would be bound to them later that winter. I realised that I had been away from Dogger for no more than eight moons, and wondered how my grandmother was faring without her little slave. Then I noticed that Sten had been talking to me, and I said, 'I am sorry, did you say something? I was in a daze, thinking of my family at home.'

'It is of no matter, Lady Mia. I was just pointing to those specks on the distant foothills.'

I looked to where he was pointing and asked, 'What is it?'

'It is my father and your trading friends coming back, I'll wager.'

I looked again, and I could clearly make out a group of figures in the far distance. 'Oh good. Can we go out to meet them?'

'Of course!' he said. 'Come, if we walk along this path we will reach the edge of the plain, and then we can sit and watch them walk towards us.'

We left the lake and walked through a well-worn path in the reeds until we came to a group of trees, and an arid plane stretching out in front of us to the foothills of the mountains. Sten walked over to a fallen tree and sat down, gesturing for me to sit next to him. I walked over to him, and suddenly wondered if I should be there, in that deserted place, with that handsome young man, alone.

He must have sensed my hesitation and said, 'Fear not, Lady Mia. Even though you are the most beautiful maid I have ever seen, it would be more than my life is worth to make any advances towards you. Even though I might very much desire to!'

I blushed, and suddenly felt far too self-conscious. But I walked over and sat next to him, and we watched as the specks in the distance very slowly became bigger and bigger. Then we started to recognise people by their walk. I saw Kemit, and put my hand on Sten's shoulder and pointed to him, saying, 'Look, there is Kemit! I would know that walk anywh…'

I was about to say "anywhere", when Sten reached up with his hand and, cupping my chin, kissed me gently on the lips. When he kissed me, I felt that my very being would explode into a thousand pieces. I felt at the same time desperately happy, and yet desperately frightened, that the feeling would leave me.

He kissed me again, but that time for longer. I pulled away, trying to collect myself, aware of a new sensation. How could the touching of two sets of lips have such an effect? I thought to myself. Was it love? Was it that which makes men and women give up everything for each other? I knew in that instant that it was, but it was not the same kind of love I felt for Borg and Kemit, and the crew. That was a warm and comfortable place. Sten's kiss had taken me to a desperate place. The kiss had no warmth in it, just fire and desperation. Did Sten feel all that I was feeling too? I wondered. Somehow I knew he did not, yet at the same time I chose to deny those thoughts. Yes, he was in love with me too. He must be, I thought. Then I began to understand why these people were so strict about leaving boys and maids alone together. Especially if it only took one kiss to make your whole world turn upside down! I was suddenly not surprised by their rules. He let me go, and looked deeply into my eyes, and I was transported to another place, a place I had not been to before.

Suddenly he moved away from me and said, 'Please forgive me. I could not help it. When you touched me on the shoulder, I just had no control. Forgive me.'

He was about to say it again, when I put my hand on his mouth and said, 'There is no need. I liked it. I have never been kissed before. I never imagined it would feel so good, to touch someone else's lips with mine.'

He kissed my fingers gently, and I felt my very being melt before him. I looked into his dark eyes, and kissed him again on the lips. This time it was not gentle, but hard, and he held me tightly to him in his arms. But suddenly I became frightened and pulled away, and he reluctantly released me.

I could not look at him, yet I wanted him to kiss me again. My mind was racing with contradicting thoughts, until I almost burst into tears. He sat on the log, smiling smugly at me, as if he knew exactly what I was thinking and I said, as haughtily as I could, 'I think we should walk out to meet them now, as they are getting nearer.'

He nodded, and we walked out to greet the hunters in silence together. As we walked towards Kemit and Borg and the crew, I wondered if they would be able to tell that he had kissed me. I felt so strange, and yet excited! I felt they would surely notice the fire that now raged inside me, as I looked at Sten walking beside me.

It was not long before Borg saw us, and came running ahead to meet us saying, 'Mia! You should see what we have got!'

He pointed to the beast that was being carried on the backs of the crew. Then he suddenly became aware of Sten standing next to me, and I said, 'Oh Borg, this is Sten, Sannis's son. We have been waiting for you since you started walking on the plain.'

Borg looked at Sten and said, 'Thank you for looking after Mia, Sten. Your father is a great hunter!'

Sten smiled and left us to go and greet his father. Borg put his arm around my shoulder, and suddenly the fire in me went out, and I was my old self again, thank the gods! I felt more than a little disturbed by the sensations I had just experienced.

Kemit came over to me and asked, 'Did you like the bathing boat then, yesterday evening?'

I looked at the twinkle in his eye and replied, 'It was the best experience my skin has ever had! Have you heard of this fruit called the olive?'

He laughed and said he surely should have, for he had spent most of his adult life transporting the oil from it about the eastern seas. I looked at him, and realised how much at home Kemit was there. Sannis saw me then, and walked over and said, 'We went out hunting for wolves, and brought back a grand brown bear instead! Look, my lady!'

He pointed to the huge bear that four of the crew were carrying between them. Then went on to say, 'Your young friend, Borg, sent the second spear into it too. You should be very proud of him, he is a brave young man!'

I saw Borg's face as Sannis said that, and was glad that he had finally lain to rest the ghost of that hunting trip to the Mountains of the Heavens. He looked at me, and smiled so happily, I knew he would now be all right again, as he had proven his bravery with that bear.

As we walked together, Sannis started to sing some hunting song that everybody seemed to know the words to, so they repeated it over and over again, until we reached the edge of the lake.

Kemit came over to me then and said, 'Mia, I did not have time to explain last night, but this tribe has very strict rules about young maids and boys sleeping together in the same hut. It is to do with their fiery blood. The young men seem to find it more difficult than most young men to restrain their urges, when it comes to young women. That is why they have these rules. I am afraid Borg cannot sleep in your hut while we stay here.'

I nodded, and thought if he only knew Sten had been kissing me, he would be furious. I could appreciate those rules were not just for the men, but also for the maids. That is, if my own feelings were anything to go by, after Sten had kissed me. Kemit went on to say, 'I know your feelings for Borg, and his for you, are no more than brother and sister, but we must abide by their rules while we are here.'

I nodded and replied, 'That is all right, I understand, but I wanted to talk to you about Effy.'

He looked at me and asked, 'Who?'

'She is the maid that was preparing the bathing boat when you showed me to my hut.'

'Yes, but what about her? Is she not good to you?'

'She is fine, but she told me that Sannis had bought her from her parents for me, and that she is now my slave.'

Kemit took me aside so we were out of earshot of the others and said, 'Listen, Mia, this is their custom. You must not show you are not happy with the gift of Effy, or Sannis will be insulted and, good man though he is, he must not be insulted at any cost. He would like as not have her killed for displeasing you, and buy you another maid to replace her.'

I looked at him in horror and he continued, 'If he has bought Effy for you, then she belongs to you, and we will have to take her with us when we go, or her family will be shamed. I did not know he was going to do that, but now it is done, there is nothing that we can do to change it.'

'Very well,' I said, 'but as soon as we are away from here, I will set her free.'

Kemit sat down, and made me sit down beside him.

'You do not understand. You are responsible for your slave. You could not set her free, far away from her tribe and family. Where could she go, or what could she do? She could never go home again. Having a slave is not like having a servant; it is a responsibility of yours. One day, if we travel somewhere and she falls in love with a man that is prepared to be bound to her, then you can set her free, but not until. For it is your job to protect your possession from the world, and it is her job to try and make you comfortable at all times.'

I sat next to him for a while, then eventually said, 'I had no idea it was like that. Of course I will look after her. I like her actually, I think we will be good friends too.'

Kemit smiled and said, 'Do not be too friendly, or she will not know how to behave. Leave it as it is, that she is your servant. Royalty must always have servants.'

I laughed then and said, 'She described Brigit, while she was there, as my servant, which annoyed her greatly, to say the least!'

Kemit laughed and we walked back to the shore, where the men were already skinning the bear and cutting strips of its meat for cooking that night.

Brigit came running over to me and asked, 'Where have you been? I have been looking for you everywhere.'

'Sorry,' I replied. 'I went to the edge of the plain with Sten to watch the hunters return.'

She looked at me intently, and asked, 'Who is Sten?'

I tried to make my voice sound bland and said, 'Oh, he is the chief's son.'

'Really? Which one is he?' she asked with excited eyes.

I looked at the crowd in front of us, and saw he was talking to Borg and watching the skinning. As I saw him, it rekindled the fire in me, which was a little disconcerting to say the least.

'Look, he is the one talking to Borg.'

Brigit looked at him, then looked back to me and said, 'He is very handsome, is he not? Is he nice to talk to as well?'

'Yes, I suppose so,' I said. 'He seemed more interested in hunting than me though, if that is what you are getting at.' I could not believe I was lying quite so easily.

'That figures, as most young men his age seem to think of nothing else. He is very, very nice though. Shame he is the chief's son, or I might go and charm him a bit myself, now that I have had some experience with men.'

I did not really want to carry on that conversation, apart from her comment about Sten.

'What do you mean about it being a shame he is the chief's son?' I asked.

'Well, it is usually the case that the son of a chief has to be bound to whoever his father tells him, for the good of the tribe, you know.'

'Yes, I know what you mean,' I said blankly.

As I looked at Sten, he caught my gaze and smiled. I had to look away.

'Come on, let us go and see what they are preparing for food tonight,' I said to Brigit.

'All right. I have seen enough bear skinning anyway.'

We walked along the platform that surrounded the settlement, past Borg and Sten.

'Where are you two going? Do you not want to see them take the skin off?' Borg asked.

I shouted back, trying not to look at Sten, 'No, I don't think so. We are going to watch them cook the food.'

Borg nodded and replied, 'We will be along in a while,' and continued his conversation with Sten.

The cooking hut was a hive of activity, with what seemed like lines and lines of pit fires, all cooking various different dishes all at once. I sat next to a maid who was just outside of the hut, working with some water and what looked like mud.

'What are you doing?' I asked her, and she looked up at me sheepishly, but when I smiled at her she relaxed and said,

'I am preparing the clay for the bear meat tonight, my lady.'

I looked at the bucket and saw it was the local clay that she was mixing. It was a dark red colour, just like the earth in that land. I did not recognise it at first, for the clay in the north tended to be pale grey. I sat and watched her as she mixed it with the water, and made each piece pliable enough to use. Brigit soon got tired of watching that, and she walked into the cooking hut to watch the meat roasting. As I sat there I remembered the last time I had mixed clay, to line the tar pit on that fateful day when the Shaman had told the hunters that he wanted me for his next Pure One.

After watching her for a while I asked, 'Which pit are you going to line with the clay?'

'Pit?' she replied, looking puzzled.

I thought they must have some other name for it, and described the stone lined pit we used for making tar, or sometimes for cooking meat. She smiled and hesitated, not wanting to contradict such an important person, but eventually said, 'I am not preparing the clay for a pit, but for cooking the bear meat.'

She could see I did not understand what she meant, so she picked up her bucket and gestured for me to follow her into the hut. We passed pit after pit, either with meat roasting or fish cooking in leather bags suspended on wooden frames, as it is cooked on Dogger. Then I saw a long table at the end, and the maid pointed to it and I walked over to have a look.

At one end of the table were piles of the worked clay, and a woman was kneading it into flat round shapes. Next to her was a woman working with what looked to be a huge pile of green grass, and at the far end were two women tying chunks of bear meat with string into tight balls. I saw Effy helping the woman cut the string to tie the meat with, and I asked, 'What are you doing here?'

She jumped up when she heard my voice, and stood at my side looking very worried, saying, 'Did you need me my lady? I am sorry I was not waiting at the hut for you, but my mother asked if I could help with cooking the bear meat, as there is so much of it.'

I smiled at her and wondered if I was always going to get that reaction from her. Hopefully she would become more relaxed with me, when she got to know me a little better.

'No,' I said, 'I do not need you, I am just interested to know what you are doing?'

She took my hand and led me to the end of the table, where she had been working. Smiling, she said, 'Here we cut the string into certain lengths, to tie the meat into tight bundles. It does not have to be meat, it could be fish that we tie up. Then we give the meat or fish to Hessy here, and she will cover it with grass from the lakeside, tying it on tightly with more string. Sometimes we put herbs on the meat before we put the grasses on, to give it more flavour, but we like bear meat without them. The meat wrapped in grass is then given to Finnia, who covers it all over with the worked clay, until not a crack can be seen. Look how she smoothes it so that it looks just like a rock from the lakeside. Now the clay covered meat is put on a strip of bark and taken to the fire. Come over here, you can see one already there.'

I looked at the balls of clay sitting around the fire, and every so often a woman would turn them as they dried and steamed. Effy pointed to a woman lifting up one of the dried balls onto a bark strip and said, 'Now watch!'

The woman rolled the ball right into the middle of the fire, and covered it with lots of blazing sticks until it was lost from view. Effy could see my expression of amazement, and she laughed.

I stepped back from the fire, as it was very hot, and said, 'So, you take the trouble to hunt a bear, skin it, tie the good meat up in string, wrap it in grass, cover it in clay and then destroy it in the fire!'

She looked at me with a fearful expression, thinking I was cross, and then she laughed when she saw how the process must have looked to me.

'It may seem foolish, but when the clay gets hard in the fire it seals the meat inside, and cooks it without burning.'

I could not believe that the meat would not burn in the raging fire, and I asked, 'How long does this take to cook?'

'Oh, maybe two or three hours. Come, we were cooking some boar meat in this way today, before the men brought back the bear meat to cook. Let us see if it is ready.'

We walked to another fire that had almost gone out, and in the middle of it were three clay balls amongst the ashes. An old woman was moving the balls to the edge of the fire with two sticks, and she smiled at us as we watched her. She rolled one of the balls onto a stone platform next to the fire, and with a brush made from rushes dusted off the ash from the clay. The clay had changed in colour to a pale red. Then she started to hit it with a big wooden stick. After a few attempts the clay cracked, and steam and juices flowed out of the ball, which she caught in a wooden bowl she had placed to the side of it. The grass was still very hot and steaming, and she carefully cut the string with her blade and pulled the grass back to reveal a wonderfully cooked piece of boar meat. The smell was incredible, and it was not burnt at all.

I turned and looked at Effy and said, 'This is amazing! However did you find this way to cook meat?'

She shook her head and said, 'I do not know, we have always cooked in this way.'

The old woman touched my shoulder and gave me a piece of the meat on her knife to try. I picked it up and tasted it. It was wonderful, and so juicy. Although I loved boar meat I had always found it a little dry and chewy. I thanked her and walked outside again, as the heat of the fires in the hot afternoon sun was almost unbearable. Effy followed me and said, 'You look a little hot, my lady?'

I smiled at her and replied, 'You could say that. It is hot enough, without standing next to any fires. I am not used to the heat, I am afraid.'

She took my hand and led me along the platform and onto the shoreline. 'When we get hot we usually walk into the water along the edge of the lake, to cool ourselves. Would you like to do that?'

I looked at her, and thought what anyone in the north would have thought if you suggested dipping your toes in the icy lake waters out of choice. But I was so hot, I followed her through the reeds to the soft silver sand that surrounded the lake. We sat down and took off our shoes, and she ran ahead of me into the water. I ran in after her, and immediately my feet touched the water I felt cooler. So much so, I waded in up to my knees, holding my tunic up as I did so. I realised then that my leather tunic was totally the wrong type of thing to wear in that climate, and asked Effy as we splashed about, 'Could you get me a tunic like yours later? The cloth will be so much cooler than this leather that I wear.'

'Of course, but I am afraid we do not have much coloured cloth, only this red and a yellow one.'

I said I did not mind the colour, and she nodded then said, 'This weather is still very cool though, compared to the heat of the summer. Then it gets really hot.'

'I cannot imagine it hotter than this,' I said. 'I hope I get used to it soon.'

We spent the next hour or so sitting on the silver sand, every so often wading into the water to cool off. Then we suddenly became aware of a group of people on the bank above the reeds, watching us. I saw them first and asked Effy who they were, and why they did not come down and join us? She looked at them, and her face immediately changed, looking suddenly worried.

'What is the matter?' I asked.

'They are young men,' she whispered back, 'and they should not be looking at us in that way. We are unbound maids, and they know they should keep away. They probably think that because the reeds separate us it is fine to watch, but Sannis would beat them well if he knew!'

'Why do you have such strict rules about young men and maids? We do not need to have them in the North.'

'I do not know what young men in the north are like, but our men certainly cannot be trusted.'

'What on earth do you mean? Do they kiss young maids against their will?'

She looked at me in horror, then said vehemently, 'No! Of course not! It is just that they are so very handsome, and they can tempt you with their fine talk and good looks. Maybe it has something to do with the hot climate that we live in. We are quick to anger, as well as quick to show our feelings.'

I thought about my meeting with Sten, and knew exactly what she meant.

'How old are young maids when they kiss their first boy in this tribe?'

Effy looked at me quizzically, and replied, 'Well, usually in their thirteenth summer, maybe their fourteenth, but most maids are bound by the end of their fifteenth summer.'

It was strange, I thought, the way they added summers instead of winters, as we did in the north. Effy then asked, 'If you do not mind, could you tell me how many summers you have?'

I thought about it, and realised that although I had now only twelve winters, I was born in the spring and so that was going to be my thirteenth summer.

'This will be my thirteenth summer coming. In the north, we count our age by winters, and I have had only twelve of them.'

'How strange, to count winters and not summers. If you were a member of our tribe you would be watched very carefully now, to protect you from the young boys, and from yourself. For it is in the thirteenth summer that a maid can lose her head and think she is in love. Or so they say.'

'How many summers have you had, Effy?'

'This will be my sixteenth summer.'

She spoke the words in no more than a whisper, and I asked, 'Why have you not got a young man then, and perhaps even a child?'

She looked down at the ground, and I could see she had become very sad. I wished I had not asked her, and said, 'I am sorry, do not answer if you do not want to, if it is personal.'

'But a slave has no personal things!'

'This slave has! I do not want to hear about it, until you feel you want to tell me.'

She nodded with tear filled eyes and I said, 'Come, it is time we went back to the hut, as Brigit will probably be looking for me again.'

As we came through the other side of the reed beds the group of young men had gone. They must have run as soon as they saw we were going back to the settlement. We were about to walk along the bank to our hut when Effy put her hand on my arm to stop me. I turned, and she looked very serious and said, 'I thank you for your kindness, in not making me tell you of my shame, but I would like to tell you.'

She sat down on the bank, and I sat next to her. A little nervously, she began her story.

'It is a very simple story really; during my fourteenth summer I fell for a boy of one of the noble families of our tribe. He had a great love for me too, or so he said, but he knew his mother would not allow him to be bound to me. For the people in my family are only servants. It was a very hot summer, and we had taken to meeting each other in the reed beds on the far shore. One day he kissed me, and that became our special place together. I yearned to one day be bound to him, and have his children.'

Her eyes smiled at the thought of him, then she held her head down and continued, 'We were so much in love, it was as if we were the only boy and maid in the entire world. The settlement, our families, and the laws of our tribe just vanished from our minds as we met and kissed each other in the reed beds.'

She sat there in silence for a while then continued, 'Then one day I saw him kissing another maid. He seemed to have had enough of me by then, and each time I saw him from then on he just ignored me. I was desperate, and I went to his family and told them about our meetings. The chief was called and the boy and I were brought before him. He told us that we knew the laws of our tribe, and he asked the boy if he wanted to be bound to me to make it right. The boy said that he did not, and told the chief that I had lied, and that he had never kissed me. I thought the chief believed me, but the boy's family was powerful, and so I was to be punished for telling lies. They sent the boy to a settlement far south of here, to be bound to the daughter of another chief.'

I looked at her and she was crying bitterly by then. I waited until she could speak again, then she said, 'I was taken out before the whole tribe, and beaten for lying about such a thing, to try and make a boy be bound to me. No one would want to be bound me after that, the chief said, and he sent me to work in the kitchens. That was until you came and I was given to you as a gift, so that when you leave you would take me with you, and they would not have to see me again. So do not think I am sad to be your slave. I welcome it. The chief said before he gave me to you that I had a chance to make good all the bad that I had done. He hoped I did not shame myself again in another land.'

I listened to her tale, and realised how reckless Sten had been to kiss me in that way. I could easily see myself falling hopelessly in love with him too, if he kissed me again. What was it about these people, I thought, that caused such passion in others? I thought it could only be something to do with the climate, for I have never heard of such behaviour in the north before, apart from my mother and father. But then theirs must have been true love for him to kill himself without her, and for her to die, rather than be without him. I was lost in thought then, at least glad that I had the opportunity to take Effy out of the shameful life she was leading.

We walked up to the platform and saw Brigit running towards me, shouting, 'I am really getting tired of looking for you all the time, Mia!'

Her tone was so harsh that a few of the people next to us looked at her, amazed that she should speak to me so. I was in no mood to apologise to her for anything either and shouted back, 'Just who do you think you are, talking to me in that tone of voice?'

Suddenly we had an audience. Brigit, who was used to getting away with talking to me just how she liked, stood there and looked at me in shock. Her face went red, as she saw how the people were scowling at her.

'I will not be spoken to in that way. Get about your business, for I am sure you can find something to do without me,' I continued.

She looked at me with a mixture of fear and hatred as I strode past her with Effy to my hut. I glanced back, and saw that she had gone and the crowd was dispersing. I looked at Effy, who was giggling to herself gently.

'What is so funny?' I asked, as I started laughing myself.

'Oh, just the look on Brigit's face! I do not know why you have let her speak to you in that way before.'

'I do not know why myself!' I said as we went inside.

'Would you like a drink?' she asked.

'Yes please, like the one you made me at first food.'

She busied herself making the drink, and Borg came in and sat down.

'So this is your fine home the crew are all talking about?' he said.

'Yes, it is, and there is the bathing boat I am sure Kemit will have told you about, too!'

Borg got up and inspected it, and sniffed it too, saying, 'Mmm, it smells nice. You are really enjoying this treatment, are you not?'

I told him to sit down and have some drink, as I wanted to talk to him. He realised by the tone in my voice that it was important, and he sat down and looked at me and asked, 'Well, what is it?'

I looked at Effy, who was bringing our drinks, and asked her to wait outside for a while. She looked at me a little worried, but I said that Borg was as good as my brother and not to worry. She nodded, and I could see she was not happy but she did as I told her. As soon as she was out of earshot I said to Borg, 'I am going to tell you something now, and I do not want you to tell anyone else about it or do anything about it.'

He looked at me sternly and said, 'Now you have me wondering what on earth you are going to say. I do not know if I can make a promise before you tell me.'

I looked at him imploringly and said, 'You must! Or I will not tell you, and then I might do something stupid if I do not tell you. That I would not do, if I did!'

He smiled then and said, 'Well that makes a lot of sense, does it not! What on earth is it to make you so passionate…'

He stopped as soon as he said the words, and looked at me intently.

'Do not look at me that way!'

'Mia, is this about a boy? Is it? Tell me! Or I will fetch Kemit now!'

I screamed at him then as he got up, 'NO! Do not tell Kemit anything, there is nothing to tell!' Then I whispered, 'Yet.'

He looked at me seriously then, and sat down and said gently, 'All right, I will not tell anyone or do anything if nothing has happened yet. But if anything HAS happened I will break my promise.'

I looked at him keenly, and wondered if a kiss could be classed as something happening. I wished I had said nothing. He came over to me then and put his hand on my shoulder.

'Come on, tell me, or I will not sleep tonight for wondering what it could be.'

'All right, but you must promise you will speak to no one about it. Promise!'

'I promise,' he said reluctantly.

I told Borg about my meeting with Sten, and our kisses. At which point I thought he was going to get up and go and find Sten immediately. Then he sat down, and I told him of my feelings for Sten too. Borg looked into the fire, not showing any expressions, so I could not gauge what his reaction might be. I then told him Effy's story, and how I had realised that I was heading in a very dangerous direction, and how I needed him to help me resist the feelings I had for Sten.

He said nothing for a long time, then eventually he looked at me and held both my shoulders, and said, 'I am glad you told me, Mia. I am glad you felt you could tell me, too. You were right to talk to me about it. What is it about these people? They behave like animals! I can see why they have such strict rules, as the men, and the women, do not trust themselves without them. We cannot let this go any further though. You can see that, can you not?'

I nodded.

'One thing you must do is make sure you are never alone, in case you might meet him. Effy will see to that. She will have to stay with you at all times. After her own experience, she is actually one of the best people you could have for a companion. I will speak to Kemit about his plans tonight, saying that you do not feel you will be able to take the heat if we stay here all summer. He will understand that, because I was talking to the crew, and they do not like the lakeside summer heat in this valley either. On the coast of the Inland Sea it is hotter, but it does not make you sweat so much, so they say. Come here.'

He put his arms around me and held me tightly, and I suddenly felt all was well with my world again. I looked up at him as he held me and said, 'Did you know that this tribe counts their summers and not their winters? And that although I only have twelve winters, as I was born in the spring this is my thirteenth summer?'

He looked down at me and smiled, and said, 'I can see where you are going with this, Mia, but you are still twelve winters to me, and far too young to be having the feelings that you have!'

I pulled away then and he laughed, saying, 'Do not be in such a hurry to be older, it will come soon enough. Tell Effy to come in.'

I called Effy in and she stood in front of me, waiting for me to speak. Borg said to her, 'I have some instructions to give you, and you will have me to deal with if you do not carry them out, all right?'

The tone of his voice made her bow her head and nod in agreement.

'Your lady is never, I repeat never, to be left alone! There is someone making advances towards her.'

She shot me a quick, shocked look, then bowed her head again.

'Yes, you know more than any what happens when two young people allow their passions to take control of them.'

She nodded again.

Borg walked to the door and said he was going to speak to Kemit. Then he saw my look and said, 'Do not worry, I will say nothing, and I will not speak to the person we speak of either, or I might not be able to keep myself from hitting him.'

He left the hut, and Effy looked at me strangely and asked, 'You are in a turmoil over a young man?'

I nodded and she held out her hand.

'Do not worry, you have a good friend in Borg, and I will protect you from yourself, for as Borg said, I know only too well the price of such feelings.'

We walked then to Sannis's hall for the feast, and when we went in it was already half full of people patiently waiting for their food. I saw Kemit, and went over and sat next to him; Effy sat behind me. As we waited for Sannis to come in, I looked around the room for Brigit, and saw her sitting in the arms of the same man that she had been asleep on the night before. Maybe she had found someone that would make her want to stay here when we leave, I thought to myself. For I knew I really did not want her to travel with us anymore.

Borg was sitting at the table in front with Uin and the crew, and he laughed and chatted as if I had not told him anything. Sannis marched in and clapped his hands, and the women started to bring in the food. So many different dishes, cooked in so many different ways! I told Kemit about the cooking of the bear in clay and grass. He told me that in parts of the Inland Sea they made containers of clay that they baked in the fire, and they used them to cook stew in instead of leather bags. I asked him why he never had such things amongst his trading goods, as I thought they sounded wonderful. Leather bags very often dripped, and you could lose a lot of stew that way, I said. He said he had often thought about it, but the clay containers, which were called pots, were very heavy and could break very easily. He could travel halfway around the known world, but if a storm took them at the end of the journey, he would have nothing but a pile of broken pots to trade with. That is why he traded in fine cloth, spices, and small but unbreakable goods. I could see the sense in that, and wondered what the people of the north would give if someone from the east came and showed them how to make pots for themselves.

The meal went on into the night, and Sannis leaned over to Kemit and said, 'My friend, the maid Brigit seems to have taken a liking to one of my hunters.'

We all looked at where he was pointing to, just in time to see Brigit sitting on the lap of a man and laughing as he fed her with bits of meat.

Kemit frowned and said, 'I am sorry if she is offending you with her behaviour.'

Sannis replied, 'It is no offence to me, as the man is well into his thirtieth summer and beyond our laws for young men and maids. It is your maid I was thinking of.'

Kemit watched her, then said, 'I will go and speak to her.'

Sannis nodded, and watched as Kemit strode across to Brigit and the man. He whispered something into Brigit's ear, and she smiled at the man and left the hall with Kemit. They were gone for some time, and when they entered again Brigit was beaming from ear to ear. She went back to the man and whispered something to him, and he slapped her on her behind and sat her on his knee again, laughing heartily.

I wondered what was going on, and when Kemit sat back down again he said, 'She has taken a shine to that man, and wishes to be bound to him and stay here. He has had thirty summers, and he lost his first young wife when she had her first child. He sounds like a good man, and I think he will make her happy.'

I nodded and asked, 'When are they to be bound?'

'I do not know. I will ask Sannis what their customs are.' He leaned over and spoke to Sannis for a while, then Sannis stood up and clapped his hands, and the room fell immediately silent. He gestured for Brigit and the hunter to come forward and said, 'Our good hunter, Dennak, has the wish to be bound to this fair northern maid, Brigit. How do we like this?'

The whole room stamped their feet on the floor, which was apparently a gesture of approval.

'Good! They will be bound on the next full moon, which by my reckoning is tomorrow!'

The whole room let out a cheer at the prospect of another feast, and then turned back to their food and continued to eat.

I looked at Kemit and said, 'That is a little quick, is it not?'

He smiled and replied, 'They are always quick with such things here. I think it is in case the maid changes her mind.'

I looked for Borg, who saw my gaze and smiled, as we were both pleased Brigit would not be travelling with us again. I used to think Brigit was like me. When Lazdona and Rae were cruel to her, I remembered how Lusa and Mayni used to treat me. I thought that that made us the same type of person, but it just meant that we had experienced similar things, and that was all. Brigit needed to grasp every opportunity out of self-preservation, and she did not care who she hurt in the process. But then she did not have someone watching over her, as I did. It made me sad that Brigit and I had not become close, but somehow I knew that I was not meant to be close to anyone, as other maids were. I seemed to be somehow closer to things that I could not see, rather than those around me. I thought of the Golden Goddess figurine, that Iona had told me to leave on the Hill of the Two Seas, and wondered what I would be like when I found it again, thousands of winters into the future, and if I would remember the life I was living then. I thought of my experience in the Dark Realm with Brigit, and knew that it was only a matter of time before she would pull me into it again, even if not intentionally.

I gestured to Effy to say that I was ready to go, and she led the way after I had said goodnight to Kemit and Sannis. Borg was deep in conversation with Uin, so I just patted him on the shoulder and walked out of the hall. We strolled along the platform to my hut, and I marvelled at how it was still quite warm outside, long after the sun had gone down. While we had been eating, some of the other maids had been heating the bathing boat water for me, so that when we walked into the hut the strong sweet scent of the herbs pervaded our senses. It took no persuasion that night to get me into the bathing boat, and I slowly eased my body into the warm scented water. Effy and I were much more relaxed in each other's company then, especially after sharing our confidences. I think the thought that Brigit was soon going to be out of my life, as well, put Effy much more at ease with me. I asked her, as she rubbed my shoulders with the olive bag, what a binding ceremony was like in her tribe.

Then she burst out laughing, and it was some time before she muttered, 'Probably not the way you are bound in the north, I think!'

I told her to stop laughing and tell me, and after a moment she collected herself and said, 'Well, there is a wonderful feast by the lake in the evening. Which will mean the cooks are going to have to work all through this night to get things ready for tomorrow. The maid wears a yellow dress, and she will have yellow flowers in her hair. The man will be dressed in the same colour. They will sit on a platform on the edge of the lake, and be king and queen for the feast.'

'Well,' I interrupted, 'that sounds nice, so I do not see what you were finding so funny.'

'It is not really funny, I am afraid. I do not like Brigit too much, as you know, but she will not be expecting our ceremony. Our women know it is the way to become a bound woman, and do not mind, as every other woman in the settlement has to go through the same thing. For outsiders, I imagine you would think it a little humiliating for the maid.'

'Go on,' I said.

'Well, as I said before, the maid and man are king and queen for the feast, and can order the people to do anything they wish. But before they eat, Brigit must be prepared for the binding. The maid must kneel before her man and have a cord attached to her neck, the other end of which is attached to the belt of the man. He then sits at a table on the platform, and the maid must sit on the floor at his feet. Each time a dish is brought in, he sits at his table and eats while the maid kneels on the floor and watches him. At the end of each dish he will throw her either the bone or the gristle, or a very fatty piece of meat. She must then appear to be thankful and eat some of it. That goes on until the final ceremony.'

I looked her, and tried to imagine what could be worse. Then she continued, first asking me, 'Has Brigit a fear of water?'

I looked at her curiously and replied, 'No, I do not think so, her people often learn to move in the water. Why?'

'It is the next part of the binding. The man then leads the maid by the cord to the edge of the lake, and pushes her in. The cord is long enough and the water is not deep, but…'

'Yes…?'

'No sooner does the maid get out of the water, than the man pushes her in again, three times in fact. Then he leads her back to his hut, and they are bound. The rest of the tribe then has a very good feast. Sometimes they pretend to be the maid being pushed into the water, and spend many happy hours on the beach.'

'How did the ceremony come about?' I asked.

'It has to be something to do with a woman knowing her place in the relationship. She is equal before she is wed, but once she is bound she is the second person in that relationship. The man can lead her about the settlement on a cord for the rest of her days, if he wants to too. Though most men only do it for a few days after the ceremony. I do not know about Dennak, as he is older and might keep the cord round her neck for longer than most young men would do today. It was very common when Dennak was young for men to keep the cord on their wives necks for up to a winter or more, so my mother told me.'

I thought that I would not wish that on anyone, even the scheming Brigit, and asked, 'What about the eating at the table with him? Is that just for the ceremony?'

Effy looked at me oddly and replied, 'No, of course not, a woman must never eat at the same table as her man. She must always sit at his feet when he eats in the home.'

'But I sit on the high table, with Sannis and Kemit?'

Effy shook her head and replied, 'You are a maid, you are not bound. You are equal until then, at least with our people. Did you see any older women at the hall feasts?'

I thought for a moment, then realised that there had been no older women there at all. How could women spend the rest of their lives eating from the floor at the feet of their men? I thought. They were a strange people, on one side they worship women more than in the north before they are bound, but then they show them a lifetime of disrespect once they are bound. One thing is sure, I did not think Brigit would like it. Then I asked, 'What if a woman refuses to eat at her man's feet, or wear the cord round her neck for more than a day?'

Effy looked at me in horror saying, 'That is the worst thing a woman could do! It is our law, and our way! If Brigit refuses to sit at his feet, or wear the cord, then she would be beaten before the whole tribe every time she refused. I have only known one woman to refuse, after the first year, to wear the cord and sit at her man's feet.'

'What happened to her?'

'She was beaten at least four times before she gave in.'

I thought that I must speak to Brigit, as she must know what she is letting herself in for. They treated their maids totally differently to their women. I was feeling tired again after bathing, and when Brigit finally came in, flushed with her imminent binding, I was almost ready to fall asleep.

'Mia, is it not wonderful? He is so handsome, and he has a hut of his own already. So we will not have to live with his family while we build one! I cannot believe we are going to be bound tomorrow. Do you know anything about the ceremony, for no one would talk about it at the feast.'

'You will have to ask Effy, she will know. I must sleep Brigit, for the bathing boat has made me so sleepy I can hardly stay awake.'

'Hmm, all right. I will talk to Effy. After all, I am going to be part of her tribe soon.'

Effy and I exchanged glances, but we said nothing. Brigit had obviously not realised Effy would be coming with us when we left. Poor Effy was left to explain about the ceremony, about the cord around her neck, and sitting on the floor eating what her man did not want. I looked through the corner of my eyes at Brigit's expression, and saw she was horrified. I then heard Effy say, 'It is not embarrassing, for every woman in the tribe has gone through the same thing. If you think of that it will not be so bad. You have picked a good man in Dennak, he is not without influence in the settlement, and as his woman you too will have some status.'

I must have fallen asleep then, for when I woke the room was full of women fussing around Brigit. I was about to ask if she needed anything, but that would have been ridiculous, as these women had thought of everything. So I slipped out of the hut and walked along the platform to the boat. Kas was sitting in it with Tray, talking to one of Sannis's men. As they saw me he called over to me and said, 'Mia, come and meet my friend Bragn.'

I nodded and stepped down into the boat. Bragn looked a little uneasy as I walked towards him, until I said, 'It is good to meet you Bragn. Do you have a boat too?'

He relaxed, and went on to point out his fishing boat amongst the fleet.

'It looks like a fine boat. Do you ever travel out to sea in it?'

Bragn nodded and replied, 'Yes my lady, many times. My brother and I go along the coast to the south, to trade with the settlements there. It is a beautiful coast too, with many fine cliffs on the way. The people are kind and generous, and love to have visitors.'

'That is good to know,' I said, and he smiled at Kas. Not knowing what next to say, he busied himself sorting his nets.

'I think I have scared him off Kas. I am sorry if you were having a good conversation.'

Kas smiled and whispered back, 'It is of no matter, Mia, as I was running out of things to say to him myself!'

We both laughed, and I noticed Tray was not his usual self, sitting at the end of the boat looking down into the water. When we usually arrived at a settlement, Tray was always immediately surrounded by pretty young maids, clamouring for his attention. I could understand why, too, as he was young and very handsome, with a mass of long, golden curly hair that fell across his tanned face and blue eyes. He had a very cheeky smile, which was also very attractive. To see him sitting in the boat looking down at the water like that was really unusual, so I shouted over to him, 'What are you doing here, Tray? Have you not got any pretty maids to have fun with?'

Tray turned and smiled at me and replied, 'There is only one pretty maid worth talking to in this place, my sweet, and that is you!'

I laughed at his comment and replied, 'I am sure that is not the case. There are many beautiful maids here, do they not fall for your charms?'

Tray walked over to me, and leaned over the rail of the jetty and replied quietly, 'That is true, very true. There are some really lovely maids here but ...' he looked around to see if anyone was listening to us and continued, 'they are all watched by their families, and you only need to look at one of them to be attacked by a hoard of their brothers and relatives!'

I nodded and replied, 'Yes, they do have some very strict rules here. Borg cannot even sleep in my hut while I am here, either.'

Tray smiled at me and replied, winking as he did, 'That might not be such a bad thing, as he is not your brother really, and you are beginning to look pretty fine these days, you know.'

I looked at him and smiled, as he was laying on his charm, and replied, 'Your sweet words don't work with me Tray! I have seen you go from maid to maid at every settlement we have been to with the same words!'

Tray laughed heartily and replied, 'You are far too clever, my sweet, for one so young!'

We noticed something happening on the beach opposite us, and realised it must be the preparations for Brigit's binding that evening.

'Will you have a special place in the ceremony the evening, Mia?' Tray asked.

I shook my head and replied, 'No. In fact, I am not allowed to attend, as I do not have thirteen full summers yet.'

'Oh, are you very upset, not to be able to see our good maid Brigit be bound?'

I thought that he would not call her "our good maid", if he knew what she had been saying about Kas behind his back. But I just shook my head, and said that I would actually prefer not to be there, as her man had to humiliate her in front of the tribe, and that I did not want to see.

He nodded and replied, 'Quite right too! You are far too young yet to see such worldly things!'

I did not want to say anything more about it, so I sat at the end of the boat and watched the men and women prepare the binding platform. I started to think about my feelings for Sten, when he had kissed me. I was glad that I was not old enough to be bound, or I might have said yes to him. Then I would have to live my life eating scraps from his table, I thought.

I was lost in those thoughts when Borg tapped me on the shoulder and asked, 'How goes it with my lovely Mia today then?'

I smiled at him, and saw from the corner of my eyes Tray wink at me, as he walked along the jetty.

'It goes well enough,' I replied. 'Look, you can see the platform for the binding ceremony being prepared from here.'

He leaned over and watched with me for some time, and then said, 'It looks like we will be leaving Brigit here after all.'

'Hopefully,' I said.

He looked at me quizzically, asking, 'What do you mean, hopefully? Surely Dennak has not changed his mind. I am sure Brigit would not, as he is just perfect for her, and he even has his own hut.'

'Yes, but will she want to be eating scraps off his table, and be pulled along with a cord around her neck for the next summer or more?'

He looked at me intently and asked, 'What on earth are you talking about? What scraps, and what cord?'

I turned and replied, 'What? Has no one told you about the normal binding ceremony in this tribe? By the look on your face, I will take that as no. Well, it all starts at full moon, with a feast on the platform; Dennak and Brigit are King and Queen for the feast. Then the platform is cleared, and Dennak eats from the table; Brigit has to eat the scraps he throws to her on the floor. Oh, and then he has to tie a cord around her neck, with the other end tied onto his belt, and push her into the water three times from that platform.'

I pointed to the platform and continued, 'After which they are to go to his hut, and they are bound. But from then on she must always eat the food he gives her on the floor, like a dog! And sometimes wear the collar around her neck for maybe a year or more. It seems that before you are bound here the men treat their maids like princesses, but once they are bound they become their slaves!'

Borg was looking a little guilty for being glad to have finally got rid of Brigit, for he would not like to see any woman treated in that way. He thought for a moment, then asked, 'Does she know all of this?'

I looked up at him and nodded, feeling a little guilty myself for taking such pleasure in telling Borg about poor Brigit's predicament.

After a while he said, 'Maybe we should persuade her to come with us, and not be bound to Dennak? That is no life for any woman. That is how you treat a dog. I would not like to let her think she has no choice but to stay here.'

I knew how much he disliked Brigit, and wanted her to leave the boat. I nodded and replied, 'Oh Borg, I do love you, you know!'

He hugged me tightly and replied, 'I know, sweetie.'

I pulled away in mock annoyance and said, 'You have to spoil everything, do you not! I told you not to call me sweetie!'

He laughed, and we left the boat and walked back to the hall for it was time for midday food, and with nothing but dried fruit for first food I was always hungry by then. The hall was full of chatter as the people talked about Dennak and his new maid. I think they were a little surprised that she had agreed to be bound to him, so soon after meeting him. But they did not know that Brigit would have done anything not to have to travel with us again.

I sat next to Sannis, and was just about full of clay-baked pork when Sten came in and sat next to me. His mere presence so close to me made my heart race, and I wondered what magic those people worked to make their young men so desirable. I tried to distract myself by looking at some of the older men in the room, and saw how wrinkled and old they all looked. Maybe their beauty faded fast in the hot sun of that land. But those thoughts were not helping the growing desire within me, to want to kiss him again, as he sat so close to me. I felt his hand touch mine on the bench, and delighted in the contact.

I was just about to say something to him when Effy and Borg suddenly appeared from behind me, and almost in unison they said that Brigit needed me. I got up, and caught Sten's eyes looking at me, and was half pulled and half dragged out of the room. As soon as we were out of the door, Effy and Borg scowled at me.

I looked back and said, 'What? We did not do anything!'

Borg looked at me sternly and said, 'And how long would that have lasted? Mia, I could see how close you were sitting next to him. We are going to have to watch you all the time now, for talk of this binding ceremony is all that people can think of.'

I meekly followed them, wishing that I could have stayed next to Sten just a little bit longer. But I knew they were right, although that did not stop my desire for his attention having a mind of its own.

As I entered the room, the women stopped what they were doing and looked at me. They stood like a wall, blotting Brigit from view. Then they moved apart and I saw her. She looked really beautiful in her yellow dress, and with the yellow flowers in her hair and around her waist and neck. She looked so very happy too, and at that moment, all the annoyance she had made me feel with her tales about Kas were gone. I really wished her well in her new life, and said, 'Brigit, you look beautiful!'

She beamed at me, and gestured for the women to leave us.

'I feel beautiful, for the first time in my life. I want to thank you Mia, for taking me away from my lake and bringing me to this one. I know sometimes I might not have been the best of friends to you, but I have never meant you any real harm, and I will always be grateful for this chance of a new life.

'I keep thinking of the dream I had that you were in, in that grey world. It was so real! Are you sure it was only a dream, and we were not in some dark land with Laguz and Inja again?'

I could see she was still very disturbed by it, and I replied, 'Of course you were dreaming! How could there really be such a place?'

I felt ashamed then for laughing at her, and joking with Borg, for she was just a very insecure person.

'I do hope you will be very happy with Dennak. How are you feeling about the ceremony?' I asked.

She looked a little nervous and replied, 'I am actually looking forward to it really, but I am not sure how I am going to cope with the cord around my neck. I just hope he does not keep it on me for long. As for eating food that he gives me from the floor that would be no less than I was used to at home.'

I thought about the way her mother had treated her, and could imagine that she was given the scraps of food no one wanted. I leaned forward, and taking care not to crush the flowers she wore, kissed her gently on the cheek.

She was a little taken aback by that, and looked at me a little curiously and said, 'Thank you Mia, for all you have done for me. I really do not deserve your affection. That night on the boat, when I had that horrid dream, I was thinking such bad thoughts about you too. I really hated you for your beauty, and your personality and your kindness. I am truly sorry.'

We hugged again, and said we would not speak of such things any more, and I left her to her binding preparations.

The rest of the day went quickly, with endless streams of women coming in and out of the hut with words of wisdom, but mostly giggles about the forthcoming ceremony. Very soon it was time for Brigit to be led to the feast to be bound. Effy had prepared my bathing boat early that night, so as soon as Brigit and the women had left, it was almost ready for me to get into. I soaked in that wonderful herb scented water and relaxed. I heard various cheers and claps from the lakeshore, but I could not have thought of a place I would rather be. After I had bathed I went to bed, and slept peacefully until the morning.

23. Sten's Shame

When I left my hut at first light, the settlement was unusually quiet. I think there had been a lot of drinking to celebrate the binding the previous night. I wanted to find someone who could tell me how it all went, so I walked into the cooking hut and found Effy's mother, cutting string again. I asked her about the ceremony, and she replied, 'It was a good ceremony, and your friend Brigit is a fine young maid. They will be in Dennak's hut now, and I doubt they will come out for a few days yet you know.'

She winked and smiled at me. I smiled back, a little embarrassed by what she meant.

I then saw Uin passing and asked him, 'Uin, how long do you think we will be staying here now?'

He looked at me curiously and asked, 'Why, Mia, are you not happy here?'

'No, it is not that. I just wondered what plans Kemit has made.'

'You had best ask him that, sweetness. I would wait until after midday food though, as he had a lot to drink last night and will probably be asleep for a while yet.'

'All right,' I said, 'I will look for him later.'

I decided to walk onto the shore and see where the ceremony had taken place. It looked as though no one had been back there since the night before. I could see there was a lot of trampled earth, where the crowds must have waited for Brigit to be pushed off the platform. I was just thinking about what it would be like to become a woman when I passed Dennak's hut, and thought of Brigit in there with him. I walked quickly past.

By the time it was midday food I was ravenous again. And after I had eaten, I asked Kemit if I could speak to him in private for a moment, and we walked along the platform and got into the boat.

'Well, Mia, what is it?' he asked. 'I am glad Brigit has found a man, as I do not think she had any wish to travel with us again. Are you feeling lonely now that she is bound?'

'No, not at all. I have Effy to talk to, and she is very good company. I was just wondering when you planned to leave, that is all.'

He looked at me seriously and replied, 'Are you just asking out of curiosity, and nothing else?'

'Yes,' I said. 'I was just wondering what your plans were.'

'I plan to travel inland with some of the crew and Borg, to collect some of the silver stone that is found in the mountains near here first. For it is good to trade, with the peoples of the southern shore of the Inland Sea. Do not worry about us though, as we will be going with some of Sannis's men too, and his son, Sten.'

'Oh. Sannis is not going with you then?'

'He was going to come, but Borg particularly asked if Sten could accompany us. As you know, he and his father must never leave the lake together, so Sannis will stay here. He thought it would do Sten good to go as well, as he has too much time on his hands apparently. Sannis says he has too strong an eye for the maids than is good for him.'

'Oh,' I said, trying to sound uninterested. 'Does he have his eye on any maid in particular?'

'No. From what Sannis says he does not care what they look like, as long as they are maids. It is already planned that he is to be bound to a maid from one of the settlements on the western coast. In fact, when we leave here after my trip to the mountains, he will be travelling with us to this maid's home, to bring her back here with him.'

'Will they not bring her here to be bound?'

'I think they have a different ceremony in her tribe, and it is usually the maid's home settlement where the binding ceremony is performed, if it is possible. Did you want anything else, sweetness? For if you do not, I think I will take to my bed for another hour, as I am still tired from last night's drinking.'

I smiled and he went to the fur pile in the middle of the boat, and was asleep in seconds. I sat there looking at him, feeling stupid to have thought Sten's feelings for me were somehow special. As Kemit had said, any maid would do, until he is bound. I smiled though at Borg's plan for getting Sten out of the settlement until we leave.

The following moon, while they were away from the settlement, was wonderful. Not that I did not miss them, I did, but the routine I had each day was so very relaxing. Especially after the turmoil my life had been in since I left Dogger. I did not realise how much I needed some rest and relaxation. Each day, after I had eaten, I walked with Effy to the shore of the lake and made necklaces of flowers, or collected stones, or just talked about the land and the neighbouring settlements. We would sometimes ask for the kitchen women to give us some food to take down to the shore with us, so we could sit on the edge of the lake in the cooler air to eat it. I started to learn to float in the water, and even to move about in it too. In the north you did not go into the water at any time, apart from mid-summer, or you could die from the cold. But here, you could stay in the water for hours and not suffer any harm, other than having wrinkled fingers and toes for a while. Effy could not understand how anyone could get to my age and not be able to float and move about freely in the water, so she took it upon herself to teach me.

The evenings were spent eating with Sannis in the hall, and having wonderful conversations with him about his country, and the countries that he had travelled to in his youth. Each night I would enter my hut, and the hot water was ready for me to bathe in. Each day was very much the same, and I grew to be very good friends with Effy.

Brigit, however, was very distant from me now. For the first six suns she spent day and night in her hut with Dennak, and I wondered what they could be doing for all of that time. When she eventually did start to walk about the settlement, she would walk behind Dennak with the cord around her neck and her head held low. If he was away on a hunt, she spent most of her time chatting to the other settlement women. It was good she had made so many friends, and I was very happy for her. As for my feelings for Sten, they dwindled with every day he was away, until after half a moon I could not understand how I had been so stupid as to have been taken in by him.

So it was over a moon later when a man came into the settlement, saying he had seen Kemit and the crew returning across the plain. Effy and I were on the beach, and we ran with the rest of the people to the trees I had gone to with Sten, to watch them walk back across the plain towards us. Everyone was excited at their return, for a lot of the settlement men had gone too, and their women had missed them. I saw Borg first and decided not to wait another minute, but run out onto the plain to meet him. The people around me looked at me as if I were mad, for it was the tradition to wait under the shade of the trees for the hunters to reach them first. However, as soon as they saw me breaking the tradition, they all did the same. So much so, that Kemit and the crew stopped walking to watch us all running towards them! I reached Borg first and flung myself into his arms, and hugged him tightly. His skin was very brown from the sun, and he laughed at my enthusiastic greeting.

I then ran to Kemit and did the same to him, and he shouted over the crowd to Borg, 'It looks like she has missed us, do you not think?'

'You could say that!' Borg replied, laughing.

So it was a happy group that walked back to the settlement across the plain, until Kemit saw Sannis waiting under the trees. I noticed that his mood changed.

'What is the matter?' I asked.

He looked at me grimly and replied, 'I have to speak to Sannis alone. Stay here Mia, with Borg and the crew.'

Kemit strode over to Sannis, who was looking decidedly worried by then. I had noticed, as had he, that Sten was not amongst the returning men. I whispered to Borg, 'Where is Sten?'

Borg pulled me to one side, so we were out of earshot of the others, and replied, 'You had a very close escape from that young man, Mia. He has shamed his father, and I do not quite know what Sannis will do about it. All I hope is that he does not blame Kemit for it.'

I looked at him and asked, 'What happened? And where is he?'

'Not now,' Borg whispered back. 'I will tell you later.'

I saw Kemit then put his hand on Sannis's shoulder, and speak to him intently. The mood of the crowd changed too, as the fury on Sannis's face became evident. No one spoke, we all just looked at Sannis in silence as he talked to Kemit a little way ahead of us. Then Sannis said angrily to the man that was their guide, 'Kib! Come with me!'

The tall man behind us left his frightened woman and walked over to Sannis, and followed him as he strode back towards his hall.

Kemit came over to me and said, 'I think it best if you go back to your hut now. This is tribal trouble, and we must leave them to sort it out between themselves.'

'What has happened?' I asked then. 'Where is Sten?'

'Borg will tell you. I must go and talk to the crew in the boat.'

Borg and I walked quickly to my hut and asked Effy if she would leave us alone. Once she was gone I asked, 'What on earth has Sten done?'

'He was caught with the daughter of a mountain chief, who was giving us hospitality for the night!'

'No!' I said. 'He was supposed to be bound to the daughter of a chief on the western coast soon, too!'

'Yes, I know, he told me about it on our journey to the mountains. He might have looked handsome Mia, but his heart was ugly. He just looked on maids as if they were animals, waiting for him to pay attention to them! I hate to think he actually kissed you. Kemit must never know.'

I nodded, feeling even more stupid to have thought he actually cared about me.

'What happened when he was caught? And when was it?'

Borg told me that it was only a few suns ago, for they were almost home, but Kib thought that they should stay the night at a mountain settlement, for they had a heavy load to carry across the plains. They were all eating a fine roasted venison with the chief, who is apparently a good, kind man, when one of his men came running in with the news that Sten had been caught in one of the stores with his daughter. The chief asked for them both to be brought in and it was clear that he had made advances towards her, for her clothes were covered with mud. She had a bruise on her face too, as though he had struck her. When they brought Sten in it took two strong men to hold him. He was furious, and his face had been scratched in many places by the maid defending herself. It was clear to all that she had not wanted his advances.

Then Borg said the words that really struck home to me, 'Maybe she had let him kiss her, but then he wanted more, as it was evident from the state they were both in that she had tried to stop him. The chief ordered his daughter to be covered and taken to another hut, and then he looked at Sten and said in a very calm voice, "Is this the way you repay my hospitality? You violate my daughter? I know your father, and I know he would want me to punish you for this. Take him away and beat him."'

I looked at Borg with wide eyes and asked, 'What did Sten say then?'

Borg shook his head and said, 'He told the chief that if he had him beaten, his father would send his warriors in and kill them all. But the chief took no notice of him and they took him out. After a few minutes the chief followed his men to watch the beating. We all just sat in the hall, not knowing what to do for the best. Kib said that Sannis would have ordered the beating himself, if the chief had not. So, after a while the chief came back in, and said that although he did not want Sten for a son, he would have to be bound to his daughter that night, and stay with her in the mountains.

'The next day we left Sten tied to a post in one of the huts, with the chief's daughter sitting tearfully next to him. You should have seen the look of desperation on his face, Mia. It was really pitiful! You had a very close escape with that one, Mia, and no mistake. For if he had made advances to you like that, Kemit would have had no hesitation in killing him instantly, Sannis or not!'

I looked at Borg and then looked away, and he left the room and went to the boat. Effy came in then and said sombrely, 'I cannot believe the news. Sten has certainly sealed his fate now! You were very lucky, my lady, that he did not spend more time with you alone.'

I nodded and asked, 'What will Sannis do now?'

'Well, he will have to send word to the chief on the coast that Sten cannot now be bound to his daughter. He will offer Mais, his second son, instead.' Then she smiled and continued, 'They will be happier with the second son anyway. Sten will no longer be the heir now, and I should imagine the Shaman is casting him from the tribe as we speak.'

'What does that mean?'

'When a father disowns a son here, there is a casting out ceremony that the Shaman performs, to disinherit the son from his father and to banish him from the tribal lands.'

'Oh, so if Mais marries the daughter of the coastal tribe, he will eventually become chief, and so it will be the same honour for their daughter?'

'No, not the same, better. For Mais is a good boy, and will make a better chief for our settlement than Sten ever would.'

I did not want to go for midday food in Sannis's hall that day, as I would not know what to say, so I went to the boat. Kemit and the men were busy stowing some heavy looking bags in the boat when I got there. Borg came over to me when he saw me and said, 'I think we had better all eat on the boat for the moment. The men have some lines over the side, and if you could help with the fire we will be eating fresh fish before long.'

I nodded to him and got on with my job of building up the embers of the fire to cook our food. The fish the men caught were strange to look at, but after they were cooked they tasted as good as any other fish.

After we had eaten, Kemit called the crew to one end of the boat and said, 'Well, I think it is time to move on men. We have had a good stay here with our friend Sannis, but he has troubles of his own to sort out now, and we would only get in the way. We had a good trip into the mountains, and have our trade bags full. So, I think it is time we went and did some trading, do you not think!'

The crew mumbled in agreement, as none of them thought it appropriate, under the circumstances, to cheer. After a while, one of Sannis's men came onto the boat and asked if Kemit and I would follow him. We walked after him, and I wondered what he wanted me for. As we walked into his hall, it was empty for once apart from Sannis and his son, Mais.

He gestured for us to come over and said gently, 'I am sorry you are here to witness my shame, Lady Mia.'

I nodded, not knowing quite what to say, and he continued, 'Kemit, good friend, I am sorry also for your embarrassment with my friend the chief of the Serra settlement.'

Kemit replied softly, 'Think nothing of it. I only I wish I could have stopped it from happening.'

Sannis shook his head and replied, 'There was no way it could have been stopped, for he would have shamed me before long anyway. I knew he let his passion for maids control him. Would that he could have waited for his bound woman though. Still, what is done, is done. I know you are thinking of leaving, and would ask of you a favour.'

'Anything, you just have to just ask,' Kemit replied.

'I have sent word to the tribe of Sten's future woman, to tell them he is no longer my son, and I am sending Mais to be bound to his daughter instead. I would be grateful if you could take him with you, and leave him there for his binding.'

'Of course, dear friend, it will be an honour to take this fine young man to his woman.'

Mais blushed, and his father patted him on the back and said, 'He is a little timid and pale compared to the other, but he has a good heart, and that is worth more than good looks any day. He will be a good chief here too, when I have gone.'

'You have many summers ahead of you, so stop talking of when you are gone, you old rogue!'

'Aye, you are right in that,' Sannis said, and laughed. 'When will you go, my friend?'

'I think we will leave in two suns, as the men need some rest from the trip inland.'

I looked at Kemit, and thought that I would really be ready to go by then. The heat in the valley seemed to get hotter with every passing sun, and even swimming in the lake did not cool me for long. So we left Sannis with his son, and I went back to my hut.

Effy was waiting for me as usual, and I said, 'Effy, we are leaving in two suns, so if you wish to spend more time with your family before we go, I will understand.'

She looked at me with an expression that was a mix of excitement and shock, as she had not thought we would be leaving quite so soon.

'I would like to go and tell my mother and sisters, if that is all right,' she eventually replied.

'Yes, of course it is! Go and spend as long as you want. I can look after myself, you know.'

She smiled, and ran out of the hut to tell her news to her family, and I felt guilty then that I was the cause of her leaving them. Not long after Effy had gone, Borg came in and sat next to me.

'Well, that was quite a change around. Who would have thought Sten would have been banished to some poor hill settlement.'

I looked at the glee in his eyes and replied, 'You could not have planned it better yourself, could you?'

He said blankly back, trying to look offended, 'I do not know what you mean.'

Then I said, 'All right, I admit it. I was stupid to fall for such a boy. You have to agree though, he was very handsome!'

'I suppose so, in an Iberi sort of way. But look at them when they reach thirty summers, they look like wrinkled old men, like Brigit's man. By the way, have you seen her much while we have been away?'

'No, not at all. She is truly part of this tribe now, and she seems very happy,' I replied.

'Good, for I would have probably thrown her overboard on the next trip, if she had annoyed me again.'

I laughed, and without another word he went back to the boat to help the crew sort out the stores for our journey. As Borg left, I told him to make sure he got some of those wrinkled fruits to take with us, as they were really good.

The next few days were spent thinking of what we wanted to take, and what we did not, from the various gifts we had acquired during our long stay at the lake. Effy was rarely with me, and kept apologising for being with her family most of the time, which I did tell her I understood. I told her that the night before we left I would like to take a very long bath in the bathing boat, for I had really got used to them. I also knew I would sorely miss my nightly soak, when we were on the boat.

When the day came to leave, the whole tribe was on the platform to say farewell to us. Brigit kept hugging me in floods of tears, as Dennak stood proudly behind her with the cord in his hand. Sannis gave us such a lot of the delicious dried fruit that I thought I might actually get tired of eating it on the journey!

So, with Mais waving farewell to his father from the end of the boat, the crew slowly paddled across the lake, away from what had really started to seem like home to me. Effy stood next to Mais, and she too waved and waved, until the jetty was just a distant speck on the horizon.

24. THE TUNNEL TO MORGA'S HAVEN

As we started to enter the river, I asked Mais if he had been to the settlement of his future woman before.

'Yes, not more than two summers ago. It is a fine place, and they are good people. I used to play with Bellina when I was a boy. Sten and I would tease her all the time.'

His face saddened when he mentioned his brother's name, for it was obvious he loved him dearly. I continued talking to him, to take his mind off Sten.

'What is their settlement like?' I asked.

Mais's expression lightened then, and he replied, 'It is very dramatic! There are very few landing places on that part of the coast, as there are sheer cliffs all the way to the far south, for the most part. This place, Morga's Haven, is built on the steep slopes of a little bay that was cut into the cliffs by the sea long ago. You actually have to take the boat through a tunnel in the cliffs at low tide to get to it at all. When I was a boy I used to love to visit that place, as it was very exciting to paddle through the rock tunnel. With the torches on the boat you can see the sparkle of crystals on the rocky roof. Unfortunately the roof is too high to touch them, but they really look beautiful.'

I knew then what Effy had meant about him being a good young man. His delight in such a thing showed he was not like the normal men of our world. Or maybe most men like the sparkle of crystals, but they are just too manly to say so. I wondered if that was true. I fingered the crystal around my neck, and it must have looked like I was not interested in what Mais was saying so I said quickly, 'Sorry, I was just thinking of my own crystal.'

'Yes, I noticed it. It is very beautiful, and the cord too is very fine,' he said.

'I am going to like this tunnel, I think. Go on, tell me what is at the other end of it?'

'Well, after you come out again into the daylight you are blinded by the brightness of the sun, and when you adjust your eyes, you are confronted by a perfectly round bay. This is surrounded by silver sand, and the settlement is set across the steep slope on the eastern shore. There is very little land to gather food from, but there are many lemon trees growing wild on the rocky slopes, and some fig trees, and olives too. The people live mostly on fish, and they make very fine bone harpoons from the seals that they catch, which they use to trade.'

I realised that there was so much to know about these people, and wondered what lemons and seals were. Mais saw my face and asked, 'Have you not seen seals before?'

'I do not know,' I replied. 'What do they look like?'

'They are big creatures that live in the sea. Sometimes you see them sitting on rocks, and talking to each other.'

I thought for a moment, and then knew what he meant.

'Yes, I have seen those creatures in the north, but we have never caught them to eat on my island. They are very quick at swimming away, and you have to avoid falling in the northern sea or you could die of the cold.'

'I cannot imagine the sea being so cold that just being in it could kill you!' Mais said.

I smiled to think that at least I knew something about a land he that did not know, and said, 'Oh yes, for there are always pieces of ice floating in it, even in the summer months.'

Mais raised his eyebrows and said, 'Really? I do not think I would like it in the north then!'

We both laughed, and I thought that I didn't think he would like it either.

We looked at the wide river ahead of us, and the dense shrubby forest that lined the shore, and I wondered why people were not living there. I asked Effy about it.

'Do you know who lives in those forests?'

She looked at me, and suddenly looked very pale.

'Are you all right,' I asked. 'You do not look well?'

She smiled and replied, 'I have not been on a boat very much in my life, other than just off the shore on the lake. I am also a little afraid of this river, for as a child we were always told that dangerous people lived in those forests!'

I looked at Mais and asked, 'Do you know about the people that live on this part of the river, for Effy says they are very dangerous.'

He smiled and said, 'They might be dangerous to young maids, but they are a cowardly people really. Our elders would tell our young maids about those people, to stop them from wandering on the far shore of the lake, near the river mouth. In my grandfather's day, some maids went there for a walk, and the forest people captured them and took them back to their settlement. When my grandfather and his warriors went to search for them, they found the maids tied up in one of their huts. Thinking they were going to have to fight to get them back, they charged into the settlement holding their spears ready to attack. But when the men saw them, they ran away into the forest.

'When they asked the maids what had happened, they said that the men had captured them and tied them up. The maids told the warriors that the men thought that they were very beautiful, and that they wanted to keep them to be their bound women. Apparently the men thought that the women in their tribe were very ugly. So my grandfather said that maids should never go near those parts, just in case they were captured again. I think they must be a very sad sort of people, who just hide in the forest when there is trouble, and do not even like the looks of their own women!'

He and Effy both laughed, and she became much more relaxed about our river journey after that. Especially when I told her what fine warriors the crew were. I saw two crewmen that were nearest to me listening to what I said, and they smiled at my description of them.

We put the stone weights in the middle of the river that night, and two men kept watch while we slept. At first light they were paddling again, and we started going with the flow of the river as it pulled us towards the sea. We made good time, and before long we could see the steep cliffs ahead that bordered the entrance to the Great Western Sea.

I pointed to them and said to Effy, 'Look, we are nearly at the end of the river. Just past those steep cliffs is the Great Western Sea!'

She shot me a fearful glance and I said, 'It is just like a really big lake, and Kemit is the best trader in all the seas and has been here many times before.'

Kemit told the men to stop paddling then, and they put the weights in the river and some of the men put lines over the side of the boat. I went up to Kemit and asked if Effy and I could do anything to help, and he told me that when the fish was cooked we could give it out to the crew. Effy had not seen fires on boats before, and she marvelled that it did not burn the boat.

After we had eaten Kemit spoke to the crew, 'You might as well rest for a while now. We have to wait for a high tide to enter the sea, as you know. So enjoy your rest while you can, there are fierce currents on this part of the coast and there will be no let up until we wait to enter the tunnel.'

The men nodded. Borg came over to me and said, 'I have been talking to the crew that know these waters, and they say it might be best if you and Effy tie yourselves to the hooks for the first part, until we get over the surf at least. Mais, have you paddled much before?'

Mais nodded, and Borg said they would need every man they had for that stretch of water. Mais followed Borg as he took him along the boat to find him a place to paddle. Also to a place where Kemit could keep an eye on him, for he did not want to lose Sannis's last heir overboard while taking him to his woman.

I turned to the wide-eyed Effy then and said, 'Do not worry. I have been in many seas where you have to be tied down. It is so that you will not be washed overboard if a wave hits us.'

Her eyes widened even more then, and I could see I was not making her feel any better, so I called over to Uin and said, 'Uin, could you tell Effy that just because we are tied down, it does not mean we are going to sink the boat!'

Uin laughed and replied, 'I am not surprised you are frightened Effy, with Mia trying to make you feel better! Mia has been in some really wild seas and rivers with us, but I am afraid she is not saying the right things to put your mind at ease at all! Come with me and I will take you to Kemit. He will tell you exactly what is going to happen.'

She smiled and went ahead with Uin. Borg came over to me and said, 'I think she was more worried after you spoke to her than before!'

'What do you mean?' I replied. 'I was just explaining what was going to happen.'

Borg leaned over to me and whispered, 'Yes, but did you have to mention sinking the boat?'

I smiled, and shaking my head replied, 'Well, maybe not. Oh dear…'

'Do not worry, Kemit and Uin will put her mind at her ease,' Borg replied, 'but I suggest you keep your mouth shut next time you want to stop her being frightened!'

I scowled at him and he laughed. Then we both smiled, and I suddenly felt alive again, at the prospect of a new adventure.

Effy came back, looking much happier having spoken to Kemit, and not long after that we were under way again. Effy and I tied each other to the side of the boat, and I held her hand as we raced between the cliffs on either side of the river mouth. Suddenly we were confronted with the surf of the western sea ahead of us. I was frightened myself to see such huge surf, and from the river mouth it almost looked as if the sea was higher than the river water itself.

The men started to paddle, and instantly I was transported in my mind to the surf of Dogger, the night I left the island. The surf seemed to continue for an age, too. Wave after wave we cut through at the river mouth, and then suddenly we were in the calmer waters of the sea. I think we all let out a sigh of relief at that moment. The crew paddled on for the rest of the day, and I found it hard to imagine any settlement appearing along that coastline. There seemed to be an endless line of sheer cliffs, as the men paddled past them. We did not stop much for food either; Kemit said we had to get on, as that coast was also known for sudden storms.

Effy and I would walk up and down the crew, giving them pieces of dried fruit and fish, and water. By the evening of the next day Kemit asked the men to stop paddling, and he came over to Mais and asked, 'Mais, the tunnel is best at low tide, is it not?'

Mais looked at Kemit and nodded.

'I can see by the look of those rocks that it will be low tide at first light. What do you think?'

Mais looked at the rocks then replied, 'I would say so, and you will see the full height of the shell beds clearly by then, too.'

Kemit looked at me and noticed that I looked a little worried, and asked me, 'What is the matter? Do you doubt my judgement suddenly, sweetness?'

'No,' I whispered, 'I was just wondering why you asked Mais about the tides, if you have been here before?'

Kemit smiled and whispered in my ear, 'It always helps to have some local knowledge to confirm what you were thinking, does it not?'

'Of course,' I said, and he winked at me when the others were not looking. I realised he had asked Mais to make him feel more important before we arrived at the settlement.

All through that moonlit night I wondered where this tunnel was, as the cliff line ahead looked unbroken. The crew started to paddle again, quite slowly, as the light of the new day dawned, when suddenly Kemit shouted, 'Uin's paddles only!'

The men on the opposite side of the boat to Uin stopped paddling, but Uin's row paddled furiously, and even though I had seen them do it before, I still marvelled as the boat slowly turned into the direction we had come from. Then suddenly I saw it! There, behind the line of the cliffs, was the tunnel! If you had not known where it was, you would have paddled right past it.

Kemit then said, 'I want both sides paddling now, but only every other man!'

Every second man stopped paddling, and we slowly moved towards the black hole in the cliffs. The way the men did exactly what Kemit told them to do showed how much they all relied on each other. I found myself smiling with pride, that they were my family, and that they were the best crew in all the seas, as Uin had said so many times.

Just before we went into the tunnel Kemit had torches lit at both ends of the boat, and slowly we entered the darkness.

The most startling thing about the tunnel was not the darkness, but the silence. Soon after entering, the sound of the sea had gone completely. All we could hear was the slipping of the paddles into the still water, and the echo of drips somewhere deep inside the blackness of the sea cave.

No one spoke, for when they did, the echo of their voices in the blackness made them stop again. Mais touched me on the shoulder, which made me jump as we moved though the eerie passage. I could see his smiling face reflected in the torchlight, and saw him pointing to something on the roof. Then I saw them, thousands and thousands of sparkling crystals, all catching the light of the torches. I gasped at the sight, and touched Borg on his arm and pointed up too. He followed my gaze, and I could see by the expression on his face that he was as transfixed by the beauty of it, as much as I was.

I decided to lay some furs on the floor of the boat, so that I could lie on them to look up at the roof, as I was getting a pain in my neck with looking up all the time. Borg, who was not one of the men paddling, lay down next to me and we watched the magical roof slowly drift by. It was as if we were watching a mantle of stars in the night sky. But they were far more beautiful than stars. Every so often the light would catch a particular part of the roof, and rainbows of light would cascade down around us. I held Borg's hand tightly, and I knew that it was one of the most magical moments I had had in my entire life. It was so beautiful as the endless waves of colour and light flowed past us, as we moved through the blackness, that I somehow never wanted it to end. I felt I wanted to hold on to each moment and make it last. I could tell by the silence of the crew that the beauty of that dark place overwhelmed them as well. I wondered if there were lots of caves like that, under our feet as we walked on the earth above, and marvelled at the hidden magical world that maybe no one knew existed. I also thought of the other realms that most people did even not know about, that I seemed to belong to as well. I felt that the Dark Realm could not touch this place, for there was a hidden light in this darkness.

Then, long before I wanted it to end, there was a mutter at the front of the boat and Kemit said quietly, 'All paddles now!'

Borg jumped up and started to paddle, and I could see a speck of light quickly racing towards us. The light grew and grew, and then I could see a bright blue stretch of water ahead of us. Suddenly we were in daylight again, bright blinding daylight, as the sun had come up while we were in the tunnel. It was so bright, that for a few moments it was actually painful to see. But when my eyes adjusted to the light, I saw the settlement, just as Mais had described it, clinging like rows of shellfish to the steep slopes that surrounded the bay.

I asked Mais if there was any other way to get to that place, other than through the sea tunnel, and he said that there was not. Then I asked, 'How on earth did these people find this place? For no one would go through a tunnel that long, unless they knew that the bay was on the other side, surely?'

Mais smiled and said, 'I do not know exactly, but there is a legend that the people here tell their children. A man and his family were wandering the cliff tops, looking for a place to camp, when the man caught sight of the bay. It is said that he had been climbing the cliffs looking for bird eggs, and after he had seen the bay, he spent many summers trying to find a way to get to it. He became so obsessed with finding it, that his woman and son left him to go with a tribe that was passing by one day. But he would not give up his search for a way down to the bay. He decided that it could only be reached by the sea, so he travelled south. He made a basket boat, and spent almost all the rest of his life searching the cliffs for a way in to the bay. Eventually he found the tunnel, and followed it, as we just did, until he arrived at this heavenly place. He made himself a home, and after a season left it to find a woman to share it with. Which he did, and many generations later, you have the settlement that you see before you.'

I smiled at Mais, and told him I liked the story, and that I was sure it must be true, for it would certainly take some determination to discover such a place. As we paddled across the bright blue water I could see groups of people running about on the shore, jumping up and down.

Mais laughed and said, 'They do not get many visitors here, and they are always happy when anyone arrives. Look at how they are dancing up and down on the beach!'

I looked to where he was pointing, and laughed with him, for they certainly did seem to be a happy lot.

Kemit suddenly hailed a man standing on the jetty, saying, 'Morga! How goes it with you?'

'Better for seeing you, old friend!' the man shouted back.

Kemit laughed, and as we approached the jetty we could see it was full of people, leaning over the rails, looking at us and pointing happily at everything on the boat. Kemit jumped onto the jetty and hugged the man that had shouted to him. How wonderful it must be for Kemit, I thought, to have so many friends in so many distant lands, and all so glad to see him again, too!

As soon as the crew had tied up the boat we were all jostled along the jetty to a big open area that had tables filled with food under cloth-covered roofs. We all sat down, and Mais, Kemit, Borg and I sat with Morga, the chief, and who looked to be his wife and four daughters. We were certainly expected, and I wondered how Sannis's message boat could have got there so soon.

I asked Kemit this while they were bringing something for us to drink, and he answered, 'The boat Sannis sent was very small, with only four men paddling. A small boat can hug the cliffs and does not have to go out into the surf, as ours does. If we had travelled the way they had, we would have wrecked our boat on the rocks, as we sail very low in the water at the moment. The people here received the message about Sten a few suns ago, and knew it would take us this long to arrive. Morga is a really nice man, but unfortunately his woman has only given him daughters. He needs to find a son to be bound to one of his daughters who will want to stay here, and be the chief when he has gone.'

I looked at Mais, happily talking to one of the maids, and said, 'Mais will not do that, will he?'

'No, as he is now Sannis's heir. He will have to take his woman back to Sannis's land. Morga will find one though, I am sure, for his daughters are very beautiful and his settlement is quite unique!'

'It certainly is in an amazing place,' I agreed. 'I do not think I will ever forget that journey through the tunnel. It was so very beautiful.'

Kemit smiled at me and said, 'Such dark places under the earth usually are, sweetness. Come, let me introduce you to my friend.'

Kemit stood up as Morga came back with the drink and said, 'May I introduce you, good friend, to Mia, heir to the throne of the Icin of the North.'

I looked at Morga as Kemit said the word Icin, and saw a faint shadow cross his smile which really worried me. But he replied, smiling, 'I am honoured to have such a visitor. I hope you and your travellers will be staying for the binding?'

I looked at Kemit, who shrugged his shoulders and replied, 'We would be delighted. I am sure the crew would be too!'

The men thumped their tables in approval, and started to eat. I whispered to Kemit, telling him what I had seen when the word Icin was mentioned, and he looked puzzled and asked, 'Are you sure? I would not have thought Morga would have had any contact with the Icin. Do not worry, I am sure we are safe here. I will ask him what he knows later.'

I could see from Kemit's expression that he was a little taken aback by what I thought I saw, and I hoped I had been mistaken.

The food laid out in front of us was a delightful mixture of different types of fish, cooked in different ways. There was a stew, which tasted delicious, and had big, flat leaves in it that seemed to have given it flavour; but if you tasted the leaves on their own they tasted bitter. I asked Mais what they were, and he said they were the leaves of the lemon trees that grew on the cliffs above us.

The drink we were brought was also from the same tree. It had been sweetened with honey, and was wonderful to drink in the heat of the day. Even though we had some sort of shade from the cloths above us, the sun was fierce, and there was no wind in the bay for the cliffs surrounded it so completely. We had a good meal, and Effy seemed to make friends with the daughter who was to marry Mais. I wondered, as I watched her, if she would like to stay there rather than travel on with us. I asked Kemit what he thought, and he said we would have to wait and see what Effy wanted. And, of course, Morga would have to agree.

After we had eaten we were shown to some huts halfway up the slope, so we that could rest after our journey. I did not think I wanted to rest, but by the time we had walked up the steep slope to the huts in the searing heat I was exhausted, and could think of nothing better than to sleep for a while in the shade. Effy and I were shown into a small hut, and the crew were given one right next to it. That made me feel a lot better, as I liked to be close to Borg. Borg and the crew were tired too, so we all slept for the next few hours. I noticed however that Kemit was not with us, and I wondered where he was.

I slept fitfully, and dreamed of Laguz and Inja, looking into a pool of water and talking about me. Laguz was saying, 'We must help the Icin to find her, not for them, but for us. For she has great power in her that she does not know about yet. We will turn her, and we will not be stopped then by any, not even Zundel's high priests!'

Then Inja said, 'I will clip the wings of that owl, and those accursed swans, that Iona keeps sending to help her. My black beauties will see to that, will you not!'

I looked around the cave that they were standing in, and every ledge, every space, had a black bird perched on it, silently listening to them. When I looked at the pool they were peering into I gasped, as I saw my own face in it. I was in the log boat, and we were approaching an island in a very blue sea. Borg was there, and he was very sad, as were the faces of the crew.

I was wondering what it could mean, when Laguz spoke again, 'As long as she never reaches Mallata, we can control her. If she ever enters the temple of the womb, we will probably never be able to turn her. For then she will remember all that she is, and all that she can be...'

I heard someone drop something outside the hut, and woke up. I lay on my furs for some time, trying to remember all the details of the dream. Where was Mallata, and why was everyone so sad? And what did they mean, I would remember all that I am, and all that I can be? I meant to ask Kemit if there was such a place as Mallata, but as soon as I was really awake I had forgotten the name, and the dream almost completely.

As I lay there, I could see that the sun was taking colour from the light streaming in through our open doorway. When I went outside to look, Borg was already standing there looking down at the bay. The far side of the bay was already quite dark, and the sun was gone from sight behind the sea cliffs. The huts on the eastern side of the bay kept the sun the longest, and as we stood there we watched the shadows move quickly across the huts and up the cliffs, until it was almost dark. The sky however, was like a round disc of colour above us, as the sun gave colour to the wispy clouds that passed over us. It was as if we were in a settlement in a completely separate world, cut off by the cliffs and with only one entrance. As I thought about that, the beauty of the place suddenly changed, in my mind, into a beautiful trap.

I looked at Borg, and he noticed my expression and asked, 'What is it?'

'I do not know, but I am suddenly worried about the Icin again, and how there is only one way out of this place.'

He put his arm around me and replied, 'Do not worry, we are a long way from the Icin's reach here.'

Then I told him what I had seen, when Kemit mentioned the Icin to Morga, and how Kemit was going to ask him about it. I told Borg how I could see that Kemit had looked a little worried too.

Borg looked at me and said, 'Come, let us go and find Kemit, and ask him what he has found out. Or we will just sit here in this beautiful place, worrying about things that probably are only in our minds!'

I smiled at him, and held his hand as we walked carefully down the steep paths through the settlement towards the shore. It was obvious which hall was the chief's, as it was the biggest, and it was right next to a stream that flowed down from a waterfall on the cliffs above. The stream had been trained to follow a channel lined with stones, so that it passed through the chief's hall and made the air cooler.

We went into the hall and found Kemit sitting on his own on some furs. He gestured for us to come in and said gravely, 'I am afraid I have some disturbing news to tell you. You were right, Mia, when you said you noticed something in Morga's face when I mentioned the Icin. A Galli trader heading for the Straits was here not more than a moon ago. They told Morga of a great reward for news of an Icin heiress that was missing, and travelling in these waters. Apparently the Icin did visit Mount Land, not more than a sun after we left. So take heed of your dreams, Mia, next time, for they are wise ones!'

As he said that, I tried to grasp back from my mind the dream I knew I had just had. I knew it was important, but I also knew it was gone from me completely. I simply nodded and asked, 'Did they suspect that Gimble had helped us?'

Kemit shook his head and replied, 'Apparently not, as he put on such a convincing show. They did not stop there more than a few hours before they went to the south shore and Galli Land. Iona has enough power to protect her people, and they are all safe, so this trader said. We were right not to go up one of the Galli Rivers though, for the Icin put two boats at the end of them and sent scouts up river to see if we were there. Then they realised they had lost us. They told all the Galli traders that they could take as much gold stone as they could carry on one boat, if they found you and brought you back to Icin Land. This worries me, Mia, for that is a lot of trade wealth they are offering, and I have no love for the Galli traders as they would sell their own family for less.'

Borg then said, 'Should we leave now?'

'No, I think we are safe enough for a while, as all the Galli traders will be away from here now, and will not be coming back until near winter time. We will have to be careful not to tell anyone who Mia is though, until we are well into the Inland Sea. I think it might be best to keep it to ourselves even then, at least for a while. Most Galli traders only go to the Straits and back, so when we are through, I am sure we will be all right. The Galli have a southern coast that is in the Inland Sea too, so let us hope they have not told those tribes about the reward. Somehow, I doubt they would, for the northern Galli tribes are greedy and would not want to share any reward with them.'

'I think it might be best if Effy did stay here though. She behaves too much as if she is your slave, which I know she is, but it will draw attention to you as we travel. It is best that you become my daughter again, helping to feed the crew. No one would imagine an Icin heiress would do that kind of work.'

I nodded, knowing that it would probably be best for Effy to stay there too. At that point Morga came in, and we asked him if Effy could stay. He thought for a moment, and then asked why she was not bound. I felt it best to tell him the truth, as word of her could reach him from Sannis.

After I told him her tale, he shook his head sadly and said, 'What is it about that tribe of Sannis'? They are good people, but when it comes to maids and boys they are totally out of control!'

He laughed, as did we all, for he was so very right about them. He continued, 'We do not have such rules here, as we are a more cautious people when it comes to love. I am very sad to hear poor Effy's tale, she should not have to suffer for one small mistake made when she was just a child. If she wishes it, I would be glad to give her my name, and she can eventually be bound to one of my young men, when she is ready. I have so many daughters, and as I am losing one to Mais, I might as well replace her, as my good wife will give me no more!'

I knew Effy would be delighted with the news, and Morga urged me, 'Go, little heiress, go and get her. Then I can meet my new daughter!'

I ran out of the hall with Borg, happy to get the thought of the Icin out of my mind, for a while at least. We raced up the hill, which was an easier task in the cool air of the evening, and saw Effy sitting outside, waiting for us.

'Effy! We bring good news!' I shouted to her from the steps.

She looked down at us, bewildered, as we lay on the grass trying to get our breath back. 'What news?' she eventually asked.

'How would you like to be the chief's new daughter, with all the status that that brings, and eventually choose a young man of your own, when you want one?'

She looked at me as if I had gone mad, and said, 'What are you talking about? I am your slave, and I am disgraced. No chief would want me for a servant, let alone his daughter, when he knew my story.'

She looked down, and I could see she was starting to cry.

'No, do not cry. I told Morga your story.'

She looked at me then with a mixture of shock and horror, and I continued, 'It is all right! He said you should not have to pay for one mistake you made as a child. Really, he wishes to adopt you, as he is losing a daughter to Mais, and he seems to like having daughters!'

I could see she was starting to believe me, but then she said, 'But I am your slave, for the rest of my life.'

'Then I give you back to yourself. You are, from this moment on, free!'

She leapt over Borg to me and hugged me, and laughed, and cried, and it was some time before we could get her to stop. I told her that her new father would like to meet her, and we walked down the hill again hand in hand.

When we entered Morga's hall, he had brought all of his daughters and his woman there, ready to meet Effy. I almost had to drag her across the room, she was so frightened. But when she saw the smiling faces in front of her, she relaxed her grip on my hand, which I was glad of as she was starting to hurt me. Morga's wife put her arms out to Effy, and she hesitantly walked over to her and into them.

The woman was obviously delighted to have gained another daughter, just as she was about to lose her eldest. Morga patted Effy on the head and said to us, 'I think she will do. Do you not think so, Arwa?'

'She certainly will, Morga!'

They all started to cry a little then, even the daughters, at their parents' obvious delight in having gained a new daughter. Borg looked at me and raised his eyebrows, and I did the same. It was quite amazing, the generosity these people had for a complete stranger. It was a happy night we spent in the hall, with Effy sitting between her new sisters, and Arwa fussing over her. Mais looked happy too, sitting next to Morga's eldest daughter. She did not look too sad either, at not being bound to Sten.

The following day was the binding ceremony, and I could not imagine what these people would do to a poor maid on her binding day. But I was ready for anything! The feast was served in the same place as the day before, and a hut on the edge of the area had been covered with flowers gathered from the cliffs, so that it looked more like a flower mound than a hut! Mais and his new maid held hands in front of the hut, and walked over to a special table that was set right in the middle of the open space. They ate their food, and I was waiting for the ceremony to start when they both came over to Morga's table.

Morga took some string, made from the bark of the lemon tree, and bound their joined hands together. After that, he threw lots of flower petals over them, and they walked along the tables so that everyone else could do the same. I noticed bowls placed on the tables, filled with petals waiting to be thrown. Main and his new woman then bowed together to the crowd, and went into the hut covered with flowers, shutting the door. The crowd cheered, and carried on eating.

I looked at Kemit and asked, 'Is that it, then?'

He laughed at my amazement and replied, 'Yes, they are now bound together. They have to keep their hands bound until the next setting sun, and then they are bound for life!'

I looked at him and smiling, replied, 'I think I like that ceremony!'

He patted me on the shoulder and laughed, telling Morga what I had just said, who laughed too.

As I started to walk up the slope that night, to go to sleep, Kemit called me over from the doorway of Morga's hall. As I turned to him he said, 'I need to speak to you for a minute, Mia. Come, let us walk to the jetty. I have been thinking about what Morga said, about the Galli trader, and I think we should leave at first light.'

I looked up at him and nodded, saying, 'Yes, I think so too, for when I realised that the tunnel was the only way in or out here, I felt trapped.'

'Do not worry, we will be all right. I am just being cautious, that is all. We do need to do something to you though, before you go to your bed.'

I looked up at him, wondering what on earth he could mean. He smiled and said, 'Do not worry. I just think we need to change your looks a little, as that hair of yours is very noticeable. Arwa told me that maids in this settlement like to make their hair very black sometimes, by adding a mixture of soot from the fire, and herbs and olive oil. Follow me, and we will ask Arwa if she can make your hair black too.'

I thought that was a very good idea, as I knew how different my hair was from other people's. I would also have felt happier saying I was Kemit's daughter, if I had black hair, as he had. We walked to a hut just behind the main hall to find Arwa waiting for us, with her daughters and Effy. They gestured for me to come in, and Kemit left me there saying, 'We leave at first light, so sleep well, sweetness.'

I nodded and went inside. Effy led me to a bowl of hot water and started to wet my hair, and before I had time to think about it, Arwa poured a black sticky mass from another bowl over it. She rubbed it in, and then I had to sit by the fire for a while to let it dry a little. The daughters spent most of their time giggling at me, which made me feel a little uncomfortable, as I did not know what I looked like. Arwa then washed the black mess off my hair, over and over again, until I thought my hair would fall out. She then put a cloth on it to dry; I looked down at my hair, as I sat by the fire, to find it was as black as the night sky. It was as if I was looking at someone else's hair! They were all very pleased with the result, and Effy said, 'You look completely different, my lady! I doubt that even I would be able to recognise you in a crowd.'

I smiled at her, and told her we were leaving the next day. She went over and asked Arwa something, who nodded, and when she came back she said, 'I will stay with you this last night, my lady, rather than in my new home. For I would not want you to have to sleep alone.'

I smiled at her, as I was not really looking forward to sleeping alone in the hut after the dream I had had there earlier. So we walked together out of the hut, waving our farewells to Effy's new family. As we walked, Effy told me all about her new sisters, and how nice they were. She also said how wonderful it was to leave the burden of shame that she had been carrying for the last few summers, behind her. I was really happy for her, but felt a little nervous about our next journey, especially as there were probably lots of traders looking for me, in order to get the Icin reward.

I did not sleep well that night either, but at least I did not dream, and was glad when I heard the crew collecting their things together in the next hut and heading for the boat. It was not quite first light, and when Borg came in to get me he did not notice my hair. Effy walked down to the jetty with us, and as the sky started to lighten Borg glanced back at me, nearly tripping over on the steep pathway.

'What? By all the gods! Mia? It is you, Mia, is it not? What devilry is this?'

I smiled and replied, 'Hey, calm down, it is still me. Kemit had Arwa colour my hair, so that I will be thought of as his daughter and not be recognised.'

Borg stood a little way from me then and said, 'Well, it certainly works! For I was not quite sure if it was you or not! You could certainly pass for Kemit's daughter anywhere now. How long will it last?'

'Arwa said it will last for half a moon, if I do not get it wet too much.'

I got the very same reaction from the crew as they saw me walking towards the jetty. Kemit finally said to them, 'Yes, it is Mia. She has had her hair made black, so she will not be recognised. May I introduce you all to my daughter, Mia, travelling with us to taste adventure before she is bound back in Scan Land!'

The men bowed and cheered at me in their funny, jokey way. Then we said our farewells to Morga and his family, and to Effy, as the crew pushed the boat away from the jetty.

We paddled towards the tunnel mouth just as it became fully light, and the shadows on the cliffs above us deepened. I looked back at the small figures waving on the jetty, and wondered if I would ever see that wonderful place again. One thing was certain though, I was sure I would never forget it.

25. ON THE EDGE OF THE INLAND SEA

Borg was paddling as we entered the tunnel, so I lay on my furs alone at the end of the boat, and waited as the men lit the torches before we entered the cave. It was just as magnificent as it had been the first time, cascade after cascade of rainbows reflected in the light of the torches. I looked at the sides of the caves more that time, and saw bright green rock that also glowed in the torchlight. There were many side caves, I noticed, and I wondered what marvels they might hold, secret in the blackness. The tunnel journey seemed to be much quicker that time, and I felt a deep sadness when I started to hear the roar of the Western Sea in the distance.

All the men were paddling then, and suddenly we were in daylight again, being buffeted about by the waves as we turned the corner and saw the sea ahead of us. It was wild! It must have been stormy the night before, for there were huge waves out there, and Borg came over to me and tied me down securely, and with a brief smile went back to his paddle.

After the tranquillity of the tunnel, and Morga's world, it seemed suddenly terrifying! We did not seem to move very much either, as each time the crew paddled hard to pull us away from the cliffs, a huge wave would push us back. Yet each time, we were not pushed back quite as far, so overall we made very slow progress. After about an hour we were free of the cliffs, and moving southward, fast through the water.

The next few days were spent far out at sea, so that we could only just make out the coastline in the far distance. On the morning of the third day, Kemit came over to me and said, 'We are going to rest for a few days on a beach I know near here. It is not close to any settlement, just in case any Galli traders are about.'

I smiled, and he patted me on the shoulder, for he knew I was as weary of that journey as I am sure the men were. They all looked exhausted, for they had been paddling hard for days with very little sleep. I marvelled at Kemit's knowledge of the sea too – how could he know where we were, so far out of sight of land? I supposed that was one of the things that made a good trader, knowing just where you were at any one time.

The land approached us quickly as there was an ingoing tide, and the waves were doing a lot of the work for us. The sun was just coming up when I saw the beach ahead of us. It looked very like the beach near my home on Dogger, with endless stretches of sand cliffs as far as the eye could see. We beached the boat and I jumped out with Borg, glad to be on solid ground again, although for a few minutes the land still seemed to be moving. Borg laughed at me as I tried to walk in a straight line, but just staggered.

Then he said, 'You have to find your land legs, Mia!'

I looked at him as I fell onto the soft dry sand and asked, 'Land Legs?'

'Yes,' he replied. 'After you have been at sea for a long time, it can take a while for your feet to be able to walk steadily.'

I sat on the sand, hands on hips, and asked, 'Oh, and how do you know about that then?'

'Actually, Kas just told me!' he said, and laughed as he ran away from me up into the dunes.

I caught up with him before long, and we stood together on the top. 'This so like the Dogger cliffs, is it not?' I asked.

'It certainly is,' he answered.

We were both lost in our own thoughts about Dogger, as we sat down on the top of a grassy platform and looked at the crew starting to make a fire on the beach. Then I broke the silence and asked, 'What do you think the Inland Sea will be like?'

Borg paused for a minute, then replied, 'I do not know Mia, I really have no idea. One thing is certain though,'

'What?' I asked.

'We will have even more adventures when we get there!'

Leaving me with those words, he jumped over the cliff and rolled down the steep sandy slope towards the men on the beach. I ran after him to help with the fire.

It was good to be sleeping on solid ground again, as I lay under my furs by the fire on the beach. I drifted off to sleep, and dreamed such dreams that night! I dreamed, at first, that I was diving into a pool lit by torches. I can only imagine it was in a cave of some sort, because there was a kind of echo, the kind that you only get in caves when you splash water. I also felt very, very old, too. Then I dreamed that I was standing within some flames, but they were not hot flames, and as I looked through them I felt such darkness, and nothingness, and then desperation. The feelings were so intense that I woke up, only to see the snoring crew sleeping all around me by the fire.

I decided to sit up then, because I wanted to rid myself of the terrible feeling of desperation that I had felt during my dream. I picked up a dry stick and threw it into the embers of the fire to make it flare. Just as I did that, I heard a voice behind me, and I turned to see Kemit's smiling face. He asked me in a soft voice, 'Can you not sleep, sweetness?'

I nodded at him and he said, 'You were having some sort of bad dream just then, as you cried out a few times before you woke.'

I looked at him keenly and asked, 'What did I say?'

'I don't know. I could only make out a word or two. One was Zundel, or something like that. Do not worry about it though, we all have bad dreams now and then. Come and sit next to me for a while.'

I pulled my furs around my shoulders and sat with Kemit. We sat together for a long time before we spoke again, and then Kemit said, 'If ever you are worried about anything, I hope you feel you can always tell me about it, sweetness.'

I looked at him and smiled, wishing I could tell him about the little Golden Goddess that I had taken to that far away hill, but I knew that I could not. I knew that was part of my other life, a life that was filled with darkness as well as light. In that world, Laguz and Iona lived on opposite sides of the void to the world that the crew and Borg knew. I snuggled up to Kemit, and drifted off to sleep again. That time it was a dreamless sleep, and I woke to the smell of first food being cooked.

Some of the crew were already packing the furs into the boat. There was nothing for me to do, so I decided to run up to the top of the sand cliffs again. As I sat on that windswept spot, I thought about how Kemit and the crew had become more like my true family, much more than my Dogger Island relatives had ever been. Maybe, I thought, the people you are born with are just your temporary family, only there for your childhood, and that you find your real family during your life. And if you still had a bond with your birth family in adulthood, it should be looked upon as a bonus, but should never be expected.

As I watched the crew preparing to leave, I thought of all the places I had been since I last sat on my sand cliffs on Dogger; of all the people I had met, good and bad. I thought of Brigit, living in that hot valley by the lake; and Sten, trapped in that mountain settlement for the rest of his days. I wondered, too, about some faint memory I had, about an island in a bright blue sea. Then I thought of Gimble, and Iona sitting on her stone seat, and somehow I felt she was also thinking of me. I then thought about the other realm that I had seen, and the knowledge that somehow the darkness within it made the light from Iona seem so much brighter.

Suddenly a feeling of peace came over me as I thought about Iona, and the Golden Goddess figurine that I had left on that distant hill. I tried to imagine my future self, who was going to find it again, thousands of winters from then. The thought that I would have a life so far in the future somehow did not surprise me. I looked down at the crystal, hung on the golden cord, and watched it faintly glow. I knew then, that whatever adventures the Inland Sea had in store for me, Iona and the image of the Golden Goddess figurine would somehow always be with me.

Printed in Great Britain
by Amazon

68527818R00174